BEFORE I GO

BEFORE I GO

A MARIA KALLIO MYSTERY

LEENA LEHTOLAINEN

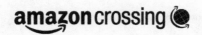

Previously published as by *Ennen lähtöä* by Tammi in Finland in 2000. Translated from Finnish by Owen Witesman. First published in English by AmazonCrossing in 2017.

Published by AmazonCrossing, Seattle

www.apub.com

Amazon, the Amazon logo, and AmazonCrossing are trademarks of Amazon.com, Inc., or its affiliates.

ISBN-13: 9781477822999
ISBN-10: 1477822992

Cover design by Cyanotype Book Architects

Printed in the United States of America

CAST OF CHARACTERS

THE COPS

Maria Kallio .... Commander, Espoo Violent Crime Unit
Kaartamo .... Deputy chief of police
Jyrki Taskinen .... Director, Espoo Criminal Division
Ilkka Laine .... Commander, Organized Crime Unit
Pekka Koivu .... VCU detective, Wang's boyfriend
Lähde .... VCU detective
Ville Puupponen .... VCU detective
Petri Puustjärvi .... VCU detective
Pertti Ström .... VCU detective (deceased)
Anu Wang .... VCU detective, Koivu's girlfriend
Eija Hirvonen .... VCU administrative assistant
Mikko Mela .... VCU trainee
Hakala .... Agent, National Bureau of Investigation
Jukka Muukkonen .... Agent, National Bureau of Investigation
Jukka Airaksinen .... Patrol officer
Haikala .... Patrol officer
Makkonen .... Patrol officer
Liisa Rasilainen .... Patrol officer
Mira Saastamoinen .... Patrol officer
Yliaho .... Patrol officer
Hakulinen .... Forensic technician
Himanen .... Assistant medical examiner
Dr. Kervinen .... Medical examiner

THE POLITICIANS

Aulikki Heinonen .... City Council chairwoman
Eila Honkavuori .... City Planning Commissioner

Petri Ilveskivi .... City Planning Commissioner
Reijo Rahnasto ..... City Planning Commission chair, city councilman
Johanna Rasi .... Espoo Green Party chairwoman

THE CROOKS

Hannu Jarkola .... Salo gang member
Õnnepalu .... Prison inmate, Salo gang member
Pirinen .... Skinhead, Väinölä crony
Niko Salo .... Prison inmate, drug kingpin
Marko Seppälä .... Thief, fence
Mikke Sjöberg .... Prison inmate
Jani Väinölä .... Skinhead

SUPPORTING CAST

Antti Sarkela .... Maria's husband
Iida Sarkela .... Maria's daughter
Einstein .... Maria and Antti's cat
Ari Aho .... Prosecutor
Turo Honkavuori .... Eila Honkavuori's husband
Jukka Jensen .... Lauri Jensen's partner
Kirsti Jensen .... Eva Jensen's partner
Lauri Jensen .... Architect
Eva Jensen .... Psychiatrist
Kim Kajanus .... Eriikka Rahnasto's boyfriend, Petri Ilveskivi's lover
Laura Laevuo .... Author
Tommi Laitinen .... Petri Ilveskivi's partner
Eriikka Rahnasto .... Reijo Rahnasto's daughter
Katri Reponen .... Prosecutor
Joel Sammalkorpi .... Reijo Rahnasto's defense attorney
Suvi Seppälä .... Marko Seppälä's wife

1

The first blow came as a surprise. Petri hadn't noticed the figure standing to the side of the path. He was late for his meeting, and he was preoccupied with an argument he had just had. The blow knocked Petri off his bike and cracked his helmet, but it didn't knock him out. Then a metal pipe struck him in the face and broke his nose.

Petri wasn't one to give up easily. Though he was short and slender, he was more agile than his leather-clad opponent. A sharp kick to the shins threw his attacker off balance but only resulted in making the bludgeoning more violent. Petri tried to get to his feet.

Then the attacker pulled out a knife. Petri had only made it to his knees by the time the blade came at him. He screamed as it sank into his left shoulder. For a moment the visor of the attacker's motorcycle helmet was level with his own face, and Petri saw his own terror reflected in it. Then the attacker pulled the knife from his flesh and stabbed him again.

The last sound Petri heard was the triumphant song of a chaffinch in the nearby woods. By the time the motorcycle's engine started up, he had already lost consciousness.

2

No matter how hard I tried to stop them, tears ran down my cheeks. I had never learned to dice an onion without crying. When I heard my phone trill, I fumbled blindly for it.

"This is Maria Kallio."

"Hi, it's Koivu."

"Hey! Wait just a sec. I need to dry my eyes." I set down the phone, turned off the stove, took the frying pan off the burner, and blew my nose thoroughly.

"Were you watching *The Bold and the Beautiful?*" Koivu asked when I picked up the phone again.

"No, just chopping onions, you twit. I'm making a smoked-salmon sauce."

"Well, you're going to have to leave the cooking to Antti. We've got an aggravated assault in Latokaski—no info on the perp. The victim is in surgery, and there isn't much hope that he'll survive. Anu and Puustjärvi are combing the area, and they need backup."

"Got it. Go ahead and call in Patrol and try to get ahold of Lähde. Where are you?"

"At the station. I'll be heading to the hospital soon."

"Jorvi Hospital? I'll be there within the hour."

I hung up the phone, turned the burner back on, and switched on another one. Best to get the pasta cooking. The sauce wouldn't simmer as long as it was supposed to, but that couldn't be helped. I hadn't had time for lunch, and the four miles I'd run after work had sapped the last of my blood sugar. Without some food, I was going to be useless.

I threw some minced garlic in the pan along with the onions and cooked them in a rich extra-virgin olive oil until translucent. The zucchini and cold-smoked salmon were ready in a matter of minutes. I wasn't a master chef by any means, but my pasta sauces were decent. After dumping the pasta in the pot, I tossed the salad and added some crème fraîche, pink pepper, and a splash of white wine to the sauce. Then I went to call my family to dinner. Antti was in the yard pruning an apple tree that had barely survived the winter, and our daughter, Iida, was building a castle for her dolls out of rocks and mud, which she had also managed to get all over her face.

"Time to eat!" I yelled. By the time Antti got Iida cleaned up, the pasta would be done. Einstein, our cat, slipped inside. He'd smelled the salmon and knew he would get whatever Iida dropped.

"Do you want some wine?" Antti asked as I tied on Iida's bib.

"No. Koivu called. I have to go in to work."

"Too bad. It's really nice out. I thought we could go for a walk," Antti said as he poured himself a generous glass of wine.

"I shouldn't be long. I have a meeting in the morning, so Koivu probably just wants to make sure he has all his ducks in a row," I said, then continued in a whisper, "It's an aggravated assault." Though Iida was only two and a half, I tried to avoid talking about work in front of her. Even on TV the only shows we let her watch were *Teletubbies* and *Tiny Two*.

After hurriedly eating, I put on a more professional shirt and checked to make sure my ponytail wasn't crooked. My official Saab looked ridiculously shiny and new in the driveway of our run-down rental. The road was rutted from wintertime wear and tear, and the freeway construction had transformed what had been the view of fields and trees. On the side of one of the front-end loaders at the construction site, someone had spray-painted "tree killers" in big red letters. Oddly enough, damaging a machine could get someone a stiffer sentence than hurting a person.

Jorvi Hospital was quiet, but every now and then there would be a flurry of activity, and then a siren would start as an ambulance took off. Koivu was waiting for me in the lobby. He was six foot two and built like a hockey defenseman. His brown eyes were tired, but his expression brightened when he saw me.

"Howdy, boss! Ilveskivi is in surgery. His prognosis isn't good. Serious spine and lung injuries, and one of the stab wounds perforated his pericardium. His heart stopped in the ambulance, but they managed to revive him. Besides the knife, a blunt instrument was used, maybe a metal pipe."

"So we have the victim's identity?"

"Petri Olavi Ilveskivi, born April 1962. He's a furniture designer, and he's also on the City Council."

"That's why the name is familiar. He's openly gay too, if I remember right."

Koivu nodded. "No criminal record himself, but some skinheads attacked him and his boyfriend just before the last elections."

I vaguely remembered the incident, but I had been on maternity leave at the time. Ilveskivi and his partner had had their arms around each other on a bus late one night, which apparently irritated a gang of skinheads so much that they got off at the same stop and beat both men.

"This is going to be a big case," Koivu said. "Forensics is on the scene, and Anu and Puustjärvi are interviewing the jogger who found him. Lähde and Mela are canvassing houses around the area until nine. The place is a little out of the way, and a whole pack of elephants went through the crime scene before we got it cordoned off. The paramedics thought reviving him was more important than preserving evidence."

"Was Ilveskivi robbed?"

"His wallet with cash and cards was still in his jacket pocket. There was also a briefcase by his bicycle."

"Strange. Did that earlier attack result in any convictions?"

"All of them got fines, and the leader of the group was already on parole so he ended up finishing his sentence in the slammer. He's been out for a little over a year. I've already asked Patrol to bring him in first thing tomorrow. Eija is pulling together everything she can find on Ilveskivi."

"At Christmas there was an article in *Z Magazine* about how Ilveskivi and his partner were celebrating the holidays."

"How do you remember things like that?" Koivu asked.

"Occupational hazard," I said with a laugh. Having a good memory for names had served me well in all sorts of investigations, and I tried to keep it up.

Koivu's phone rang.

"Koivu." Pause. "Oh, hi."

Based on Koivu's tone of voice, I could tell the caller was Senior Officer Anu Wang, our unit's other female detective and Koivu's girlfriend.

"Motorcycle? Harley or roadster? . . . OK . . . Ask them to come to the station tomorrow to look at pictures . . . At Jorvi with Maria."

Koivu hung up the phone. "Anu and Puustjärvi found a dog walker who claims to have been surprised by a motorcycle speeding on the walking path a little after five. No motor vehicles are allowed, and she tried to get the license plate number, but apparently something was smeared over it." He paused. "Let's find the nurse who called about Ilveskivi."

We set off for the surgical ward. The waiting room there was empty except for a heavyset man hunched over in the corner with his face buried in his hands.

"I'm guessing that's Tommi Laitinen. I'll go talk to him. Come back here once you've spoken with the staff," I said, and then walked over to the man sitting in the corner. He was wearing light-khaki trousers and a dark-blue corduroy jacket. His brown loafers were carefully polished, and his sandy-brown hair was thinning on top.

"Tommi Laitinen? Detective Maria Kallio, Espoo Police. Are you up for answering a few questions?"

A few seconds passed.

"Not now," Laitinen finally said without moving his hands from his face.

I sat down across from him. I had done this before. Conducting an interview under the circumstances would have been cruel, but I knew that Laitinen might need someone he could talk to.

"Do you want me to call a friend or a relative?" I asked, but Laitinen didn't seem to hear me. So we just sat, Laitinen with his head between his hands, me thinking about the story from *Z*.

I recalled that Ilveskivi and Laitinen had been together for fifteen years and engaged for the past ten. The couple dreamed of having a child. Laitinen, who was around forty years old, was a kindergarten teacher.

In the magazine photo, he had looked like exactly the kind of jolly rogue kids love, but now all I saw was his thinning hair. His hands were broad, and the onyx stone on his engagement ring didn't look out of proportion despite being quite large. The round eyeglasses sitting on the bench must have been his.

We sat in silence for five minutes. Then the door opened, and Koivu marched in with two men in surgical gowns. When I met Koivu's eyes, his face was set and he shook his head.

"Mr. Laitinen," the older of the doctors said once they reached us. "I'm sorry to have to inform you that your . . . that Petri Ilveskivi passed away on the operating table. Please accept our condolences."

Laitinen sat quietly for a long time. When he finally lifted his head, his eyes were full of anger.

"I'm not leaving until I see Petri!" Laitinen grabbed his glasses, stood up, and started walking toward the door Koivu and the doctors had just come through. Instinctively I took his arm. He was short, not even five foot seven, but he was strong. I couldn't hold him myself, and Koivu came to help.

"Wait. Let them get him cleaned up."

"Do you think I don't know that Petri was beaten to death? I want to see what they did to him so I can do the same thing to those pieces of shit!"

I felt Laitinen shaking, and tears rolled down his cheeks. Even though he was completely hysterical, I couldn't help asking, "Who do you mean 'those pieces of shit'?"

"The fucking skinheads! They've just been waiting for a chance to get to him."

"Have they threatened him again?"

"We were getting anonymous phone calls until last fall when we switched to an unlisted number," Laitinen said, now calmer.

"The police are looking for them right now. We'll get them," I said, trying to comfort him. Laitinen had stopped shaking, and Koivu and I both let go of him.

"I can take you home," I said. The hospital staff had done their job. Now it was our turn.

"I just can't believe he's dead. If I could only see him . . ."

I looked at the doctor, who nodded. "Yes, you can go see your friend."

I felt the shaking start again, and then Laitinen bellowed, "Petri was my husband!"

I followed Laitinen. I had seen enough bodies in my life to not have to worry about having a big reaction. I wasn't afraid of the dead, just the living and what we are capable of doing to one another.

Laitinen rushed into the recovery room where the body had been taken. When he saw the figure lying on the gurney, he stopped and closed his eyes for a moment. A nurse pulled the sheet aside, revealing only the swollen, blood-smeared face. He stared on mutely, trembling as he wept. After a few seconds, he walked over to the gurney and gently touched Ilveskivi's cheek.

"He's still warm," Laitinen whispered and pulled his hand away. If this had been a body at a crime scene, I would have asked him not to touch it, but that was pointless now. During the autopsy, the medical examiner would look for any evidence of the attacker, but finding any would be a matter of chance. I would have liked to check Ilveskivi's hand, to see if anyone had looked at his nails yet, but this wasn't the time for that.

"Are you ready?" I asked Laitinen, who gave a whimper. Suddenly he took my arm, and we walked back to Koivu in the waiting room.

"The doctor went to his next surgery. I'll get a statement from him tomorrow," Koivu said.

"We can take you home or to a friend's house," I offered again.

"Home," Laitinen said faintly.

We walked out together into a cool spring evening that smelled of budding birch trees. I opened the passenger-side door for Laitinen, and Koivu crawled into the backseat.

The house was only a few blocks from the site of the attack, a small residential area the Violent Crime Unit rarely had reason to visit. Single-story row houses sat on exposed bedrock, surrounded by well-kept trees and shrubs. The copper plate on the door read "Ilveskivi and Laitinen."

Tommi Laitinen didn't seem surprised when we followed him inside. The house was dark, but he didn't turn on any lights. When Koivu starting looking for a switch, I shook my head. We walked through the entryway into a large living room. Laitinen sat on the couch, which was a soft burgundy leather, and Koivu chose a matching easy chair. I remained standing next to a narrow bookcase.

"We'd prefer not to leave you alone. Who could we call to come keep you company?"

Laitinen sat motionless, staring at the floor. The light outside was a gossamer blue. This was a time for reverie, but the atmosphere in the room was bereft of hope.

I repeated my question.

"I don't want anyone but Petri," Laitinen said, then burst into tears.

On the coffee table was a half-finished glass of juice and the latest *Donald Duck* comic book. The walls were painted a pale lemon yellow, and through a doorway I could see that the kitchen cupboards were the color of dandelions. The dark steel appliances and severe gray of the floor were a carefully studied contrast to the brightness of the yellows. The kitchen table and chairs were steel, as was the paper-towel rack. I was surprised to see a pet turtle glaring at me from under a chair.

I went into the kitchen and got a paper napkin and a glass of water, which I brought out and set on the coffee table in front of Laitinen. Then I sat down next to him on the couch and asked who his best friend was. The only response I received was a shake of his head.

"Or Petri's best friend," I continued, unperturbed, even though Koivu was shuffling his feet, looking as though he wanted to leave. This aggravated assault had turned into a homicide, and the first twenty-four hours were likely to be crucial in solving it. Koivu would want to get back to the station to compile all the information we had so far.

The sound of a telephone ringing cut through the silence, and when Laitinen made no move to answer, I grabbed it.

"Ilveskivi and Laitinen residence, Maria Kallio speaking."

"Hello. This is Eila Honkavuori," a confused-sounding female voice said. "Is Petri at home?"

"Unfortunately he isn't available now."

"I was just worried that something might have happened to him, since he didn't come to the committee meeting. Is Tommi there?"

"Just a moment. Let me see if he can come to the phone."

The phone was the same model as mine, so I quickly found the mute button and pressed it.

"It's Eila Honkavuori for you."

I received another shake of the head. Honkavuori had mentioned a committee meeting, so she must have been one of Petri's political colleagues. If she wasn't very close to Petri, I could give her the bad news over the phone. But I hesitated, since I didn't really know anything about her.

"I'm sorry, but Tommi isn't available either. Can I give him a message?"

"Who are you?" Honkavuori asked dubiously. "What's going on there? Why wasn't Petri at the meeting?"

Suddenly Laitinen put out his hand. I handed the phone to him, and he took a deep breath.

"This is Tommi. Petri is dead. Someone beat him to death on his way to the meeting."

Even though Laitinen was holding the phone close to his ear, I could still hear the cry from the other end, and then the agitated tone of voice that followed.

"I would give anything to be lying," Laitinen said. "We don't know yet, but probably those skinheads . . . Yes, you can come over. The police were hoping someone could be here anyway. What about Turo?" Laitinen asked just as the line went dead and an empty beeping began to echo in the room.

"Eila will be here as soon as she can get a cab. You can leave." Laitinen hung up the phone, then tore off a piece of the paper towel and used it to dry his eyes. Then he gingerly felt around in his jacket pocket and pulled out his glasses. One earpiece was bent, and he straightened it with fingers that seemed accustomed to tinkering.

"Is Ms. Honkavuori coming from far away?"

"No, just a few miles."

Laitinen stood up and walked out of the living room, apparently headed for the bathroom. While he was gone, I glanced at the books on the shelves: mostly art and architecture. One shelf had a number of gay classics, including Armistead Maupin, E. M. Forster, Pentti Holappa, and Uuno Kailas. The painting above the couch depicted a young man standing with an erect penis. Would I be accused of sexual harassment if I hung something like that on my office wall?

Hearing Laitinen banging around in the entryway, I glanced over to see what he was doing. He was shoving coats and shoes into a black trash bag. *What a strange time to be packing winter clothes for storage,* I thought before I realized that he must be putting Petri Ilveskivi's things into the bag. I went into the entryway.

"Shouldn't you think this over first? You might regret it later if you throw everything away," I said to him.

"I can't stand to look at his things," Laitinen replied, but he stopped what he was doing.

I took the trash bag out of his hand and put it aside. The entryway was almost entirely dark now, but I didn't turn on the light. Maybe Laitinen wanted the darkness to soften the outlines of the world, to somehow conceal the fact that Petri was never coming home. In the silence I heard the rumbling of a stomach, and it wasn't mine. Koivu's phone rang, and he had a terse conversation. Apparently Lähde and Mela had discovered something new.

We stood in the entryway for another few minutes, and then there was the sound of a car pulling up outside. It stopped and then left again, and footsteps on the front walk were followed by the ring of the doorbell. Laitinen opened the door. When he and the woman standing outside saw each other, they burst into tears and fell into each other's arms. I retreated to the living room.

"Mela called. We already have three more drivers who saw the motorcycle. Tomorrow is going to be a busy day," Koivu said with a sigh. "We can leave now, right?"

"Yes. Let's just say good-bye."

Eila Honkavuori was one of the most imposing women I'd ever seen. She was tall, almost six feet, and weighed a good two hundred pounds. Black curly hair cascaded down her back, and jewelry sparkled at her neck, ears, and wrists. Her floral-print batik dress had a particularly feminine flow. Her beautiful round face was swollen from crying, and her long eyelashes were wet.

I introduced myself and Koivu and gave them my contact information. Then we shook hands with both of them and left. The spring night now smelled intensely of fresh earth, and birds sang, each competing for the world's attention.

"You handle the delegating assignments in the morning meeting, OK? I have a joint drug task-force negotiation in Pasila. Keep looking for witnesses and send someone to Ilveskivi's work. We'll probably have to hold a press conference in the afternoon," I said as I dropped Koivu off in the parking lot at the station. "I should be out of my meeting in Pasila by noon, so I'll call then to see where we are."

I don't usually believe in premonitions, but when a black cat nearly ran under my car on the way home, it rattled me. Luckily I was able to brake in time, and luckily no one was behind me. Still, I needed a big cup of chamomile tea and a couple of chapters of a Kinky Friedman book I had borrowed from Puupponen before I could fall asleep.

3

I woke up to Iida padding into our room. The morning sun shone directly onto her bed—we would have to get a blackout curtain or resign ourselves to these early-morning wake-up calls. Iida crawled over Antti to get between us and started playing with my hair. She had done that ever since she was a baby, tugging on tangles in my usually tousled red curls.

In the fall Antti had started working for a pollution-monitoring project at the Meteorological Institute. That meant we needed to find somewhere for Iida to be. We had been lucky to find a woman named Helvi who ran a small day care out of her home. She was a sensible person with a good sense of humor, and when I picked up Iida we would frequently get caught up in conversations about how to save the world.

We ate an unhurried breakfast. The licorice-black winter mornings when no one felt like getting out of bed and one mitten was always missing seemed like distant memories. I chose a light-gray pantsuit and then set about doing my hair and makeup more carefully than usual. I needed to look competent for my meeting. Once again I would be the only woman present.

Iida wanted to put on lipstick too, and managed to spill the contents of my earring box on the floor. I counted to ten three times to stop myself from yelling. My patience had never been great, so living with

a child had taken some getting used to. But we were able to make it to
the day care without a catastrophe.

"Antti's going to pick her up. This is going to be a long day for me,"
I said to Helvi with a sigh.

"The bicycle murder? I read about it in the paper."

"That's the one," I replied. Over the course of the winter, Helvi
had learned not to ask about the cases I was working, and fortunately
she wasn't one of those people who liked hearing about the details of
violent crimes.

After kissing Iida good-bye, I set off toward Pasila, where the
Helsinki-Espoo-Vantaa joint drug-crime prevention task force meeting was being held. There were also a few other violent-crime detectives
involved, since most of the violent crimes in the metro area involved
drugs.

As I drove past the bay, I admired the meringue surface of the Baltic
Sea. The ice was already so thin that you could almost make out the
movement of the waves beneath it. It wouldn't be long before it was
gone entirely. The winter had been long and the snow deep, and spring
had seemed to come out of nowhere during Easter week. Suddenly it
was fifty degrees out and the snow drifts were shrinking before our very
eyes. Skylarks cried in the fields, and both my cat, Einstein, and I waited
for the first wagtails. On Good Friday I had found the first coltsfoot
on a sunny shoulder of the road. Then spring stalled for a while. It had
taken until now, a week before May Day, for summer's arrival to start
looking like a possibility again.

As I was parking in the Pasila police station lot, my cell phone rang.
I didn't recognize the number, but the caller's name was familiar when
she introduced herself. Johanna Rasi was the chair of the Green Party
in Espoo. She asked how the investigation into Petri Ilveskivi's murder
was going. I didn't have any comment to offer and used my meeting as
a pretense for wriggling out of the conversation.

The police station smelled the same as it had when I worked there one summer years ago. The damage from the explosion a few years back had been repaired. The floor was freshly polished, and I nearly slipped as I walked in my heels toward the conference room.

We agreed on a tougher strategy, which included stepped-up prisoner monitoring. Getting drugs on the inside was ridiculously easy, which chafed the police and the prison administration. Everyone suspected that there were officers acting as couriers—unfortunately that was the only reasonable explanation.

In the fall I had nailed a drug kingpin in Espoo. He had tried to send a mule who had cheated him to the bottom of a pond. A police patrol found the man unconscious and took him to the hospital. After coming to, he requested a police guard. Eventually we convinced him to talk. The result had been a whole slew of convictions. After receiving his sentence, Salo, the drug lord, had promised to kill me and the prosecutor. That had meant installing an expensive alarm system at our house.

Salo would be locked up for eight years, but he had connections. That was why I was extra cautious. I chose my jogging routes more carefully than before and had moved Antti's and my bed to avoid a clear line of sight from outside for any would-be shooter. Death threats had become routine for our narcotics detectives. Few of them thought of themselves as heroes, and they kept doing their jobs despite the danger.

In typical Espoo fashion, the sergeant from Narcotics and I drove back to our station separately, each in our own cars. My office was on the fourth floor. The windows faced south, toward the Turku Highway, and in the summer it was hot and noisy.

I removed my jacket and wiped off my lipstick. Aulikki Heinonen, the City Council chairwoman, had left a call-back request. I was just sitting down and reaching for the phone when it rang.

"Kallio," I said, expecting to hear Koivu's baritone.

"Is this the detective lieutenant?" asked a male voice.

"Yes, this is Detective Lieutenant Maria Kallio."

"Hello. This is Reijo Rahnasto. I'm a member of the City Council. Are you the one investigating the Petri Ilveskivi murder?"

"Yes," I replied, not bothering to correct the term "murder" with "homicide." Although the perpetrator's use of a knife and another weapon certainly pointed to premeditation. Who had notified Rahnasto about the case when the identity of the victim hadn't even been made public yet?

"Shocking affair. Have you caught who did it yet?" Reijo Rahnasto had a deep voice, at once dry and throaty, as if he had a bad cough.

"Do you have something that might assist in our investigation?" I asked. I didn't have time to waste shooting the breeze with every random person who happened to be curious. How had Rahnasto convinced the switchboard to connect his call to me in the first place?

"I'm the chairman of the City Planning Commission. Petri Ilveskivi was on the way to our meeting last night when he was attacked."

Even though I followed local politics relatively closely, I could never remember all of the City Council members' names and faces. Rahnasto's name sounded only vaguely familiar.

"Do you have any idea who could be responsible for such a brutal act?" Rahnasto continued.

"Our investigation is ongoing. We'll be holding a press conference at two o'clock this afternoon. Unfortunately that's all I can say at this point," I said.

"Both as a member of the City Council and as an ordinary citizen, I truly hope the police are able to solve this case quickly!" Rahnasto said bombastically.

Just then there was a knock at the door, and Koivu came in.

"We'll do our best," I said in as friendly a tone as I could manage and then hung up without waiting for a reply. The chief of police had pointed out my lack of finesse in terms of public relations on numerous occasions—hopefully Rahnasto wasn't one of his good-old-boy pals.

Koivu collapsed in a chair, and I could see that he hadn't slept. When I first met him, he was twenty-four and resembled a tame bear cub. As the years had accumulated, he had gone from cute to handsome. Laugh lines suited him.

"What's new?"

"Here's the important stuff." Koivu plunked down a stack of interview reports. He knew I would rather read printed versions than look at a computer screen.

"Give me a summary."

Koivu stretched, and his blue collared shirt tightened across his chest.

"We have three motorcycle sightings, but they're all contradictory. One witness said that the bike's chain clicked like a Kawasaki he used to own. Another one was certain it was a Harley, and the last one kept calling it a moped but describing a motorcycle. The rider was wearing a black leather jacket and pants, and a black helmet and boots, which suggest a motorcycle, not something smaller. According to one witness, the rider was small and slim, but the other two say medium size. No one was sure about the gender, because women have broad shoulders in motorcycle leathers too. The visor was down on the helmet, so they couldn't make out any facial features. The only thing we know about the license plate is that it either started with an *A* or an *H*. Like the dog walker said, apparently something was smeared over it."

I considered how accurately a random eyewitness could estimate the size of a motorcycle rider with thick clothing, a helmet, and the crouched riding position distorting the visual.

"So it looks like an individual perp, not a gang?"

"So far, yes. All the evidence points that way. But we still pulled in the guys who attacked Ilveskivi a few years ago. Two of the three were easy to find. One had an alibi, and the other said he was at home asleep. I didn't bother holding him. Pirinen is his name, and he's as tall as I am and weighs about two forty. The witness who said the rider had a small build seemed really sharp."

"And the third skinhead?"

"Jani Väinölä? Still looking. He wasn't home at eight this morning when Patrol went by his place. They didn't go in, since they don't have an arrest warrant. They're camped out in front of his building now."

"Good. Have you notified the next of kin?"

"Ilveskivi's parents live here in Espoo, and his sister's in West Pasila. Anu and the police chaplain went to see them. Apparently no one ever told them that Ilveskivi lived with a man."

In the interview I'd read in *Z*, Ilveskivi and Laitinen had talked about how proud they were to have been together so long and said they wanted to get married. Perhaps Ilveskivi's parents hadn't wanted a son-in-law.

"The medical examiner thinks there was a metal pipe used in the attack in addition to the knife. You'd think someone would notice somebody running around with something like that. I'll probably ask for witnesses during the press conference. We could put a notice on *Police TV* too," I said half to myself. "When is the autopsy?"

"Tomorrow morning," Koivu replied dryly. One of the benefits of being unit commander was that I didn't have to go to autopsies anymore. I could send whatever sergeant was heading up the investigation. Koivu didn't like autopsies any more than I did, but someone had to do the job.

Sometimes we wondered together why we had gone into policing, especially murder investigations, which constantly tested our faith in the basic goodness of humanity. In this case, having a clear motive for Ilveskivi's attack would have made things easier, even if it was just the skinheads' grudge. The creepiest thought was that some random passerby in a drugged-out haze had beaten him to death. That happened all too frequently.

"If this was just a random attack, what could have set off his attacker? Could he have recognized Ilveskivi?"

"Maybe Ilveskivi was trying to hit on—" Koivu began, but I cut him off.

"Don't start with that nonsense about gay men humping anything that moves! And how would a guy on a bicycle hit on somebody riding a motorcycle?"

"Maybe the dude on the motorcycle stopped and asked for a light." Koivu was grinning now, well aware that what he was saying was ridiculous. To his credit, he did his best to be open-minded, but the testosterone-saturated environment of a police station was a prime breeding ground for homophobia.

"But if the attack was premeditated, how did the guy on the motorcycle know that Ilveskivi would be riding that particular route at that particular time? Ilveskivi was on his way to the city building for a City Planning Commission meeting at six o'clock, which was public knowledge. But what about his bicycle route?"

Koivu spread his hands. I said he should probably ask Tommi Laitinen. Maybe Ilveskivi rode his bike to meetings all the time and everyone knew it.

"That Eila Honkavuori lady is still with Laitinen. She answered the phone when I called. Will you have some time after the press conference? Let's see what comes in from the field by then."

"Sure. Antti promised to get Iida from day care. Do you have time to eat? I have to get some food in me, or I'm never going to be able to handle the reporters."

Koivu had already eaten, so we talked a little more about how to divvy up tasks. Dutifully I placed a call to the chair of the City Council, but she was in a meeting, so I left for lunch with a clear conscience. The cafeteria downstairs, which was decorated with artificial plants, was packed. I had the soup of the day. I was in luck because Jyrki Taskinen, the head of the Criminal Division and my predecessor in

Violent Crime, was sitting alone at a corner table. I had expected to see him at the meeting in Pasila, but he hadn't shown up. In front of him sat a half-eaten ham sandwich, and he looked distracted as he stirred his cup of coffee.

"Hi, Jyrki. You couldn't make the meeting?"

"Uh, no. I had to go help Silja. She got in an accident this morning."

"Oh no! Is she alright?"

"She's complaining about her neck. She must have strained it in the impact. Another car came through a yield sign and T-boned her. Thank goodness they weren't going very fast. Silja's Škoda just has some body damage. So all that's lost is money, and the other driver has to pay the bill. It was a kid who just got his license."

Taskinen's daughter was a top figure skater who spent most of her time training in Canada. Fortunately her taking fifth place in the world championships and bronze in the European championships had attracted new sponsors, so Taskinen didn't have to pay for all her training by himself anymore. There were rumors that Silja was dating the current men's figure-skating world champion, and Taskinen had complained about their insane phone bills.

"How is the Ilveskivi investigation going? If you need more resources, we could probably move a couple of guys from Robbery."

"Could you?" I asked, pleasantly surprised, even though unsolved homicides were always at the top of the priority list.

"I listened in on Koivu's briefing this morning, and the case seems pretty wide open. Has anything changed?"

"Nope. We have the press coming in at two, and we're going to ask the public for help."

"Did Ilveskivi have any drug connections?" Taskinen asked suddenly, and I realized that that idea hadn't even crossed my mind. Nothing at the Ilveskivi-Laitinen home had indicated drug use, but you never could tell these days.

"We don't have anything back from the lab yet."

"This is going to be a high-profile case. The mayor talked to the chief first thing this morning."

"How did he know? We haven't announced the victim's identity."

"Word gets around."

"So it seems. I've had calls from the head of the Espoo Greens, the chair of the City Council, and another city counselor who seemed to think he's a big deal. The press are probably going to rip me apart," I said gloomily. Ilveskivi's sexual orientation was going to be a juicy nugget for the media; people were always more interested in homicides that could be connected to sex somehow.

"You'll do fine," Taskinen said and placed his hand on mine for a moment before he stood up. "You can have as many people as you need."

Taskinen's smile was warm, and it was easy to return. As a unit commander, Taskinen had been my dream boss, and he was handling his new position leading the Criminal Division just as well. The first time we met, I worried that he might lack a sense of humor, but soon I realized he was just a very direct person who demanded a lot of himself and others, and also he knew how to say what he wanted and what he didn't want. When there wasn't any snow, Taskinen ran fifty miles a week. He was fit and well groomed, if not particularly handsome. There had always been a spark between us, enough so that other people noticed. When I was promoted to unit commander, one colleague accused me of sleeping my way to the top. In reality we had never even kissed.

On my way out, I grabbed copies of the tabloids to see if Ilveskivi's killing had made it to press. The pictures were big, but there were only two columns of text. In the hallway I ran into Lähde and Mela. They had spent the whole morning canvassing the area around the crime scene, hoping to turn up more sightings of the motorcycle, but they hadn't found anything.

"People don't pay much attention to road signs these days, so probably no one would notice if you drove a semi down a walking path,"

Lähde muttered. He was the oldest officer in our unit, fifty-five and overweight enough that he could sweat outside in the dead of the winter. Since our former colleague Pertti Ström had died, he had put on even more weight. The two had been as close as men like them could be. Mela was Lähde's diametric opposite, a twenty-two-year-old athlete who was completing his field training in our unit.

"And you're heading to interview Ilveskivi's coworkers now, right?"

"Yeah. What did he do again? Something with interior design? 'Yes, ma'am, this yellow sofa cover will look absolutely fabulous with the rose shade of those drapes,'" Mela said, mimicking a stereotypical gay lisp. Lähde elbowed him in the side, not so much to shut him up as to warn him. I let it pass, even though I didn't like my subordinates mocking the victim of a crime or making homophobic jokes. But Mela was still a baby, and I had other things to take care of at the moment.

The press briefing went as well as it could. Someone had leaked Ilveskivi's identity to a crime reporter at one of the tabloids, giving him time to do some background research.

"Ilveskivi was openly gay. He even seemed proud of his homosexuality. Did his sexual orientation have anything to do with his murder?"

"So far we don't have any evidence of that."

"No? Ilveskivi's partner was forced to change jobs a few years ago when the parents of the children at his school discovered he was gay."

I hadn't heard about that. Apparently Tommi Laitinen's current employer knew that homosexuality and pedophilia were unrelated. I changed the subject to our request for tips from the public. I knew we would get a lot of them, and I also knew that only a small percentage would lead anywhere. The camera shutters clicked, and I tried not to blink at the flashes. I didn't want my picture in the paper, but I couldn't stop it. Tomorrow my mother would call and complain that I still hadn't learned to do my hair properly.

When I finally escaped the press conference, my blouse was damp with sweat. I went back to my office to freshen up. On the door I found a note from Koivu: *Come see me. Forensics found the metal pipe.*

Koivu was clicking at his computer attentively. I still wasn't used to the reading glasses he recently had been forced to buy. Wang had chosen 1970s-style aviator frames reminiscent of the hard-boiled heroes of the first American TV police procedurals.

"So they found the pipe?" I said at the door and then made for Puupponen's chair. On the way I managed to bump the edge of the desk and send a pile of papers cascading to the floor. As I picked them up, I noticed that they were photocopies from a Finnish language textbook meant for high school students. Why would Puupponen be reading something like that? Was he trying to improve his case notes?

"In the forest about thirty feet from the scene of the crime, they found a two-foot-long plumbing pipe with dried blood on it. It's already on its way to the lab. There were motorcycle tracks too, and apparently they got pretty good molds of the tire tread. Then there was a cigarette butt, fresh-seeming, and that's going to the lab too. It isn't necessarily from the same person, but we have to test everything."

"Great! Maybe we're getting somewhere. Taskinen promised more bodies from Robbery, even though this isn't a theft."

"Maybe it was, and Ilveskivi resisted more than the perp expected. We haven't showed the briefcase to Tommi Laitinen yet. Maybe something's missing."

"True," I said just before my cell phone rang.

"Hi, this is Liisa Rasilainen from Patrol. Jani Väinölä is in his apartment. He just answered the phone. He hung up when he realized it was the police, though. We're going to need an arrest warrant."

"I authorize patrol number five-two-five to arrest Jani Juhani Väinölä on suspicion of complicity in a homicide," I rattled off, fulfilling the formality. "Take it easy, and call for backup if you need it. Koivu and I will be there soon." I motioned to Koivu and then went to grab my jacket from my office. After a moment of thought, I decided to also take my sidearm.

"You itching to make an arrest?" Koivu asked in the elevator.

"I've been sitting around in meetings too much. I need some action. Väinölä may be a murderer, so shouldn't we go at him with everything we've got? Did you bring your revolver?"

"No," Koivu said in confusion. "Are you carrying a gun all the time now?"

I shook my head, and then we got in the car and Koivu started driving. There weren't many public housing developments in Espoo, and they were cleaner and more upscale than average for the country. Espoo was Finland's fastest-growing city, and it actively worked to attract highly educated, high-earning residents. People without education or jobs couldn't be forced to move away, but there was no desire for more of them. That was why the powers that be wanted to build condominiums instead of rental apartments.

In the older parts of this particular housing project, the trees had grown large and their branches were covered with buds just about to burst into greenery. A group of children spilled out of a school, and a kid about eleven years old pulled a cigarette out of his pocket as soon as he left the school grounds. Of course someone should have intervened, but we were in a hurry. Two patrols were outside the apartment building, and the situation seemed calm.

"Väinölä still won't come out of his apartment?"

"He seems to know his rights a bit too well," Rasilainen said. "He yelled through the door that he isn't going anywhere without an arrest warrant."

Liisa Rasilainen was one of Espoo's most experienced female cops. We had just celebrated her fiftieth birthday in the fall. She was about six inches taller than me, slender but well muscled. Her short, thick dark hair was developing wide silver streaks. She looked like she might have been born in her navy-blue police jumpsuit. When she was younger she had tried to become a motorcycle cop and even made it through the motorcycle lifting test that everyone thought was impossible for a woman to pass, but after the psychological testing they claimed she wasn't tough enough for the job. Rasilainen thought that it was simply a matter of her test having been evaluated by men wanting to protect their last bastion of machismo.

"I'm guessing there's something in Väinölä's apartment that he doesn't want us to see, like drugs or an illegal weapon," Rasilainen said. "Shall we go up again?"

"And get a search warrant just to be bitches about it?" I asked with a grin.

"Not a bad idea," Rasilainen replied, returning the smirk. We went upstairs where Rasilainen's partner, Jukka Airaksinen, was waiting with the building superintendent. They had called for him to bring the keys as soon as I issued the arrest warrant, but hopefully we wouldn't need them.

I rang the doorbell a few times and then lifted the mail slot.

"Väinölä, open up. We have a warrant for your arrest. You've been implicated in a homicide. If you don't open the door, we're coming in anyway."

About a minute passed before we heard reluctant steps shuffling on the other side of the door, and then it opened slowly, just as far as the chain would allow.

"Show me your badge," Väinölä demanded, his voice artificially deep. That was when I started to lose my temper.

"Stop screwing around. This isn't Hollywood. Come out now with your hands up!"

Slowly Väinölä complied, and Rasilainen cuffed him. From the way he moved, this clearly wasn't his first time.

Väinölä was relatively short, but he was broad enough to make me think his weight-lifting diet might include more than food. His shoulders barely fit through the door, and a sleeveless black shirt showed off impressive biceps. A swastika adorned one arm, and the other sported a tattoo of the Finnish flag. Another large swastika was tattooed on the back of his shaved head.

"Are all pigs fucking chicks now?" he asked, ignoring Airaksinen and Koivu standing in the background.

"No," Rasilainen replied. "But these chicks are going to take good care of you like a woman should. I'll just go grab your jacket. Wouldn't want you catching cold."

"The fuck you will. Where's your goddamn search warrant?" Väinölä screamed, and Koivu and Airaksinen grabbed him while Rasilainen and I went on our little jacket expedition.

True, we couldn't conduct a search, but getting a suspect's jacket was a perfectly good excuse to have a glance inside. We stepped into the entryway, which offered a view into the rest of the apartment.

Väinölä's studio apartment looked like a veritable Nazi shrine. I wondered what Finnish heroes like Marshal Mannerheim and General Ehrnrooth would have thought about occupying the same altar as Adolf Hitler. One poster invited all the Somalis to go back to Somalia, and another encouraged Swedish-speaking fags to get the hell out too. The most amusing one was a "Niggers are Stealing Our Women" poster that showed a towhead Finnish boy trying to pull the ample-breasted girl we all knew from our breakfast cereal boxes away from a kinky-haired black man. Did Väinölä need constant reminders of who he hated so he could keep on hating, instead of realizing that the rest of the world didn't share his opinions?

From a hanger, Rasilainen grabbed a green bomber jacket, which also had a Finnish flag sewn to it.

"Suspicion of incitement of racial hatred. That should be enough to get a search warrant," I muttered to Rasilainen as we locked up the apartment and prepared to catch up with our colleagues and Väinölä.

"Come on, Kallio. Having a swastika tattooed on your head isn't a crime," she said.

"Well, no, but it sure looks pretty damn stupid. Oh, that reminds me, have you thought about playing soccer?"

"Yeah, let's do it!"

At Rasilainen's birthday party we had hatched the idea of putting together a female team at the station. Apparently Rasilainen had played in a boy's league when she was younger too, but irregular work hours had made her give it up. I promised to schedule some field time.

Väinölä was sitting in the back of a patrol car. He glared at us as we walked by.

"Take him to Interrogation Room 4," I told Airaksinen.

"Listen to this, Kallio," Koivu said when I got to the car. "I think that dude just gave himself up. He said he knew we thought he had murdered Ilveskivi. If he isn't mixed up in this somehow, how would he know that Ilveskivi is dead? We only released the name an hour ago."

4

Koivu and I held a quick meeting before we went to Interrogation Room 4. I was going to play the bitchy bad cop, and Koivu was going to be the chummy good cop. In reality he had harbored a special animus for skinheads ever since one of them had stolen his girlfriend a few years ago.

"If we interrogate Väinölä about this murder charge, he's going to lie through his teeth," Koivu said darkly.

"Yes, he will. But we can't help what the basis for the arrest warrant was."

Interrogation Room 4 was a windowless box with a desk lamp perfect for blinding the person being questioned while leaving the interrogator's face in shadow. Väinölä sprawled in his chair, looking like he owned the whole police station. Koivu sat down behind the computer and opened a new interview record. Väinölä, Jani Juhani, born April 13, 1976. Profession: unemployed. Criminal record included suspended sentence for assault, then prison time for a combination of assault, robbery, and concealing stolen property. No previous drug charges.

"According to Sergeant Koivu, you already know the crime you're suspected of," I began.

"For that fucking fag's murder! Duh! I didn't do it, even though that dick-sucker deserved it."

"How did you know that it was Petri Ilveskivi who was killed when the victim's identity was released only minutes before your arrest?"

"Don't you pigs listen to the fucking radio? It was on the Radiomafia three o'clock news. And besides, I called Piri and he said you pigs asked him about it too."

Koivu cast me a suspicious glance. Of course he hadn't told Pirinen whose killing the police were investigating.

"Do you own a motorcycle?"

"Look at your fucking computer," Väinölä said.

"A loser like him wouldn't have money for a bike," I whispered to Koivu just loud enough for Väinölä to hear. Väinölä had been through plenty of interrogations in his life and knew how the game was played. We had to be careful to avoid him filing a complaint. Strange that he hadn't refused to speak and asked for a lawyer. Unfortunately that suggested he was innocent.

I stood up, and Väinölä flinched involuntarily as if he thought I might attack him. That was one mistake I'd never made, though I had felt like it more than once. Instead I walked to the darkest corner of the room, as far away from Väinölä as possible. We would have a search warrant by tomorrow, and for all I cared Väinölä could languish behind bars for the full forty-eight hours the law allowed before we had to file formal charges.

I looked at Väinölä's hands. They were small with short fingers.

His knuckles showed no signs of bruising, but that didn't prove anything. The attacker had probably worn leather gloves. We didn't have to ask Väinölä whether he smoked, because he and his apartment stank of tobacco.

"What were you up to yesterday between five and six?" Koivu asked with impressive composure.

"Yesterday . . . Probably watching *Tiny Two* with the kids while the missus cooked dinner, you stupid fuck. Let me think. I don't wear a watch. Was I at the gym . . . ?"

"What gym?"

"No, I was in the city. Shopping."

"At what stores?"

"I don't remember all of them." Väinölä wiped his shaved head with his hand. He was starting to sweat. Maybe it was just because of the lamp.

"Did you buy anything?" I asked.

"A pack of condoms and a bottle of vodka," Väinölä said.

"Do you have receipts?"

"Who saves receipts?"

"Maybe you should. They could have helped you prove that you were in the city," Koivu said, still sounding friendly, and then continued quizzing Väinölä about his shopping trip. Väinölä sounded convincing enough, but he had had almost a full day to think about what he would say in this interview. Strange that he hadn't asked any of his pals to confirm his alibi.

"The store detective at Stockmann would remember me. The skinny one with the mustache. He followed me from men's socks down to the music department."

That was also possible to check, as was the state liquor store Väinölä claimed to have visited. The swastika on his head was conspicuous enough so that it wouldn't be too hard to find people who, if he was telling the truth, could verify his story.

"Why did you and your friends attack Petri Ilveskivi and Tommi Laitinen three years ago?"

Väinölä turned toward me.

"Can't you read, bitch? Everything is in the case files and court ruling."

"Why are you afraid of seeing two men kissing? Does it make you want to do it too?"

"I should have known only a goddamn lesbian would want to be a cop!" Väinölä shouted, and then he refused to answer any more questions. So we sent him back to his cell.

"He doesn't have a motorcycle. I checked this morning," Koivu said as we were walking back to our unit. "But he could borrow or steal one. I'll have Anu and Puupponen check out his alibi and talk to his friends."

"Väinölä is one line of investigation, but we also have Ilveskivi's circle. Have you talked to Tommi Laitinen today?"

"Just briefly. He was still pretty messed up. We'll have to interview him tomorrow."

"I have some friends in common with Ilveskivi. I'll drop by their place today."

"More work in your free time," Koivu said with a smirk, even though he was just like me. Work had to come before everything else sometimes. But this was an easy opportunity to mix business and pleasure: our mutual friends the Jensens had four children, so I could take Iida along.

I was just getting ready to go home when the phone rang. It was the same tabloid crime reporter from the press conference, wanting confirmation on a tip about an arrest in the Ilveskivi case. Where on earth could he have heard that?

"What if I said that we currently have an individual at the police station who is assisting our investigation?" I said evasively.

"Jani Väinölä? The same man who attacked Ilveskivi and his boyfriend a few years ago?"

"Making any names public at this point could hinder our investigation."

We continued to argue. The reporter was tenacious, but so was I. Finally, apparently I'd put him off enough and he hung up.

On the way home, I stopped at the grocery store, along with what felt like half of Espoo. Fortunately the delicatessen sold premade samosas, which were a handy solution to the dilemma of what to feed the adults. Iida could eat last week's meat loaf that was still in the freezer.

Sometimes planning menus for the family was a nice break from work, but right now I didn't feel like I would be able to remember what we were out of. At least I knew we needed cat food, so I bought ten cans of Einstein's favorite. As he aged he had become fussier and now turned up his nose at leftover liver casserole.

Because of the Ring II beltway construction, driving home was an adventure. The landscape changed almost daily. The coltsfoot, which were doing their best to beautify the torn-up shoulders of the road, made me long for the way things used to be.

After dinner I called the Jensens and asked if we could come by for a visit. They said yes, so I installed Iida's seat on my bike, dressed her warmly, and together we set off. Antti stayed home, even though the Jensens had been his friends originally. Kirsti Jensen had been his officemate at the university. I was closer to her wife, Eva Jensen, who worked as a psychiatrist. The family's youngest, Talvikki, was six months older than Iida, and the girls got along well.

I rang the doorbell on Eva and Kirsti's half of the house, even though the person I really needed to talk to was Lauri Jensen. He was an architect, and I was pretty sure he knew Petri Ilveskivi from his work. All in all, the Jensen family had four parents and four children. Sometimes Antti and I were jealous that it was easier for both couples to go out, since they could take turns watching the kids. When we said that out loud, the Jensens offered to take Iida into the herd whenever we wanted.

Two golden retrievers rushed to greet us, and Iida started cavorting with them. I exchanged news with the women, and Iida slipped off to play with the older children. We were lucky she wasn't usually shy of new things and new people. After a few minutes, Lauri Jensen appeared from the dining room. He looked as though he'd been crying.

"Oh, Maria," he said and came in for a hug, which made the tears start again.

"I'm sure you know what happened," Kirsti said. "One of Lauri's good friends just died."

I blushed. "That was one of my reasons for coming." I felt like I was taking advantage of a friend in a time of grief. "I remembered that you knew Petri Ilveskivi, Lauri. I'm sorry for what happened."

"Are you in charge of the investigation?" Lauri asked as he dried his eyes.

"Yes. Would you feel up to talking about it?"

"All night if it would help. Is it true that Petri was beaten to death?"

I told them everything that had been covered in the press conference. They didn't ask any questions, since they knew that I had to maintain confidentiality. Then Eva went to tamp down the commotion coming from the children's room, and Kirsti went to make tea. I stayed alone with Lauri.

"I mostly got to know Petri at work, even though we ran into each other at LGBTI Rights Finland. Petri was active in the gay-rights movement, and he was a member of the LGBTI Rights board for years, but then local politics took over. At one point Petri worked in our architecture firm, but then he moved over to furniture design. He specialized in couches, and he designed pieces for Asko and Skanno. He was really talented, but he never wanted to tie himself to one single thing. He was always doing a lot of freelance work, contracts for interior-design magazines and stuff like that. Petri designed that couch you're sitting on right now. Nice, isn't it?"

Lauri continued, explaining that he and Petri had met about once a month and exchanged e-mails almost daily. Lately he had thought that Petri seemed restless, but he didn't know why.

"Maybe he was working too much. He had to earn a living, and then were the elections. And the City Planning Commission is swamped right now because of all the new construction in the city. But I think there was something else too. Petri was depressed because there wasn't any headway being made on adoption rights. Petri and Tommi really wanted a child. They even asked Eva and Kirsti if one of them would make them a baby, but . . ."

"We both want to live with the children we have," Kirsti said from the door. "And we can't just keep expanding this little commune. Petri was angry at us, and I think Tommi was even more upset." Kirsti sighed. "But I've already done all the birthing I'm going to do. I'm over forty, and I don't think I could handle another pregnancy."

Even though I should have been thinking of Petri Ilveskivi's baby worries instead of my own, this stung. I had turned thirty-five recently, and Iida was two and a half now. If we wanted any siblings for her, we would need to get to work. But I just didn't know if that's what I wanted.

"Petri and Tommi were looking for a woman who would be willing to share custody. And we do know people who've done that. But so far they hadn't found anyone, and now . . ." Lauri wiped another tear from his cheek.

"Was Petri a predictable person? Did he follow the same routines?"

"Yes. He thought a freelancer needed to be systematic about everything if he was going to stay employed. He joked that because he worked in an arts-related profession and was also gay that everyone assumed he was reckless, even though in reality he was incredibly meticulous. Tommi is the same, and their place is so clean I can barely stand being there."

"They couldn't handle it here with all this chaos," Kirsti interjected.

"Did Petri always travel the same routes? Was he generally punctual?"

"He was always early. And he repeated the same patterns to a fault. Every morning he ate the same breakfast: coffee, bread, juice, and yogurt. Once we stayed together at a hotel in Turku that didn't serve yogurt for breakfast. Petri had to go to the store to buy some." A smile momentarily lit up Lauri's brown eyes.

"He would have been a good dad. Little kids love routine," Kirsti said with a laugh.

Eva returned and reported that the children had started a beauty salon. Apparently Iida was getting a princess makeover. Then Eva went to finish making the tea Kirsti had started.

"Petri was the quintessential devoted father type, and he happened to love men," Lauri continued. "He and Tommi were very happy. A child was the only thing missing. And the child didn't have to be their own. They were starting to get desperate, beginning to hatch crazy plans."

"Such as?"

"Such as finding some junkie girl who was pregnant and wouldn't be able to take care of her baby. Petri said he was afraid sometimes that Tommi would go and start a relationship with a woman under false pretenses just to get a kid."

"Wow. Interesting. So who is Eila Honkavuori?"

"Eila is Petri's friend. She's on the City Planning Commission too. I've only met her at parties. She's quite a phenomenon."

"I could totally fall for her if I wasn't happily married and if Eila wasn't straight," Kirsti said. "Kind of a Mother Earth type."

We moved to the table for tea, and Lauri continued his reminiscing. Eva seemed strangely quiet, mostly focusing on monitoring the children and serving them their bedtime snack. As I rode home with Iida dozing off behind me, I thought about everything I had heard. Lauri thought that Ilveskivi would have fought back furiously if attacked, and so the attacker's leathers would likely show signs of a struggle. I had requested the search warrant for Jani Väinölä's apartment and would probably have it by morning.

I realized that I wanted to be there for the search and also to question Tommi Laitinen myself. Even though I was ambitious and enjoyed my position as unit commander, I was most in my element in the field and conducting interrogations. I didn't want to admit to myself how important my work was to me, how much I wanted to be good at it. In those occasional moments of clarity, I could admit to myself that I was a police officer first, then a mother, and a wife last of all, but then the shame would hit, and I'd push the thought out of my mind.

In the morning I took Iida to day care before eight and then stopped for coffee on the sixth floor, where the police leadership met to share news. I asked the lieutenant over in Narcotics whether Jani Väinölä was ever suspected of connections to the drug trade. According to him, Väinölä had been under occasional surveillance, but they'd never found anything.

"The City Council chairwoman sends her regards," Assistant Chief of Police Kaartamo said. "She hopes that Councilman Ilveskivi's killer will be caught soon."

"We're trying," I replied. "In the meantime, tell your politician friends to authorize some hiring."

I awaited the tabloids with terror. Hopefully some former beauty queen would announce a divorce or say she'd been born again and push the Ilveskivi case out of the headlines. Thankfully, the morning paper had taken a relatively restrained approach to reporting Ilveskivi's death.

Our morning briefing in the Violent Crime Unit was mostly routine, since most of the other cases we were working were routine. I reviewed the main lines of investigation for the Ilveskivi case and made assignments. The meeting was wrapping up when our trainee, Mikko Mela, decided to open his mouth.

"What if this was revenge? Maybe Ilveskivi had AIDS and gave it to someone."

Lähde and Puupponen guffawed. I only sighed. Mela was an enthusiastic kid who hadn't learned yet when to keep his mouth shut.

"Any diseases will turn up in the autopsy," I replied. Revenge was a common motive for assault, even though Mela's theory seemed absurd.

Koivu was headed for the autopsy. His eyebrows went up a bit when I said I would be accompanying Wang and Puustjärvi on the search of

Väinölä's apartment. The Forensics team would be ready at ten. I was just rushing down to my car when my phone rang.

"Hello, this is Reijo Rahnasto." I recognized the dry, low-pitched voice. "How is the Petri Ilveskivi murder investigation going?"

Irritation rose in my throat. What made Rahnasto think he had a right to ask about the investigation?

"We're making progress."

"The newspaper said that the police are looking for information about a motorcycle rider."

"Yes. Do you have information about that?" I asked.

"No, but . . . so you don't know who was on the motorcycle?"

"Excuse me, but I have to go. Thank you for your call," I said coolly. Rahnasto just had time to tell me to call if anything new came up before I hung up.

We looked like winter soldiers in our white protective suits. Narcotics had sent one of their dogs along with the Forensics team. His name was Jerry, and he caught a scent right at the door. His ears perked up, and he made for the bathroom. The handler, Kettunen, and two men from Narcotics followed behind the dog, and they took up all the room in the small bathroom, so I was happy not to go in. Instead I stepped into the studio apartment's only real room to examine the neo-Nazi posters covering the walls.

"You take the kitchen. Puustjärvi and I will take this side and the bathroom once Jerry and Kettunen let us in," I said to Wang.

Such a small space was easy to search. The kitchenette had the standard furnishings: refrigerator, cooktop, battered laminate cabinets, small table, and two chairs. Väinölä's bed was in an alcove, along with a couch and a bookcase holding a few books, video cassettes, and other random junk, plus a TV and VCR. In one corner were a couple of cardboard boxes.

As an old punk I felt a strong distaste for neo-Nazism, but I tried to view the posters with a professional eye. Väinölä was no different from some of the people sitting in Parliament or trying to get there, although they tended to express their xenophobia less explicitly. But at the moment I wasn't interested in racist material; I was looking for confirmation that Väinölä still held a grudge against Ilveskivi.

Kettunen and the Narcotics team were banging around in the bathroom. Based on the noise, I figured that they were trying to remove some tiles. Puustjärvi went through the clothes closet. Wang searched for knives and would collect any possible murder weapons she found. Although Väinölä probably would have had the sense to get rid of the knife.

I started browsing the books on the bookshelf. Hitler's *Mein Kampf* appeared to be unread. However, the *Commando* comic books about World War II were full of dog-eared pages, even though in the end the Finns drove the Nazis out of Lapland. The video shelf was full of hardcore porn and war movies. Väinölä's apartment seemed almost too faithful to the role he was playing.

Something fell in the bathroom, and I heard Jerry's tail banging against the toilet. Kettunen whistled, and Jerry appeared in the living room with a ball in his mouth. He thought he was looking for his toy, not drugs. Kettunen poked his head out of the bathroom, smiling big with a foil packet wrapped in plastic in his hand.

"Based on Jerry's reaction, this is something more than Väinölä's parents' wedding rings." Kettunen took the packet to the kitchenette, set it on the table, and opened it with tweezers. Inside were hundreds of small white tablets. Ecstasy.

"Well, would you look at that! Väinölä seems to have a new line of work. And what do we have in this one?" Kettunen undid a smaller foil packet, which contained a brown, mealy lump about two inches thick. "Heroin. For smoking. Väinölä isn't quite the Boy Scout we thought he was."

"Not by a long shot," Puustjärvi added, holding up a Colt .45. "I found this wrapped in a rag inside a pillow. I'm guessing he doesn't have a permit."

"No," I said.

"You questioned Väinölä, Kallio. Did he have any needle tracks?" Kettunen asked.

"I didn't notice any, but the tattoos could have hidden them. Maybe he just takes Ecstasy. You should take a look, though, since you have a better eye."

After I'd finished with the books, I started rummaging through the cardboard boxes. The first one was full of random junk, so I dumped it out on the dirty gray rug. In the jumble I noticed a familiar-looking copy of *Z Magazine*, the one that had the interview with Petri Ilveskivi and Tommi Laitinen. The magazine fell open to that very article when I picked it up. There were smudges on the pages, as though they had been flipped through several times.

Petri Ilveskivi also appeared in other clippings from the box. Väinölä had collected his election flyers and reports from the local paper on meetings of the City Council and Planning Commission. In addition to Ilveskivi, Väinölä also seemed interested in articles about his own misadventures. There were three versions of a brief report on his conviction. The collection also included clippings of his ideological brothers' achievements all around the country.

Some of the papers were racist Nazi-inspired leaflets, including English and German ones. Apparently Väinölä needed those to strengthen his faith as well. I took everything that indicated homophobic tendencies.

Wang had finished searching the kitchen. Väinölä's bread knife and paring knife would go with us to the station, although neither was a likely murder weapon.

"Could there be something behind those posters?" Wang asked and then began systematically taking them down. General Ehrnrooth, Marshal Mannerheim, and the black man making off with the Finnish girl came off the wall easily, but Hitler's corner got ripped. Wang's

expression didn't waver, but I was sure she had torn that poster on purpose. There was nothing under the posters except dirty walls.

The second cardboard box was full of more random junk, including combs, an unmatched sock, a half-used package of condoms, and a
photo album. On the first page was a baptismal picture from 1976. A
very thin girl with long hair in a diagonally cut skirt and a tight blouse
held a bald baby who was crying as an irritated-looking priest sprinkled
water over his head. On the next page there were two more pictures of
the same baby, then a few elementary school class photos with a minia-
ture Jani Väinölä hidden in the crowd. The final class picture was from
the seventh grade. After that the album was empty.

Kettunen and Jerry were finished searching the bathroom and had
moved on to the rest of the apartment. When they'd gone around the
small space a couple times without Jerry finding anything, Kettunen
said he was going to take the dog out to the car to rest and then they
would take one more pass. I looked out the window at a small super-
market across the street. Outside, a circle of men were passing a beer
bottle around. No one seemed to be intoxicated or underage, so the
police didn't have any authority to intervene. Within a few hours they
would be drunk enough that someone would have to pick them up for
the drunk tank.

We didn't find any motorcycle leathers, and the leather jacket we
had taken with us before had already been sent to Forensics. Even
though the drug stash we had discovered would let us keep Väinölä
behind bars for a while, I was disappointed in the results of the search.
Of course it was interesting that Väinölä had been keeping tabs on
Ilveskivi, but a few newspaper clippings didn't make him a murderer.
In the cupboard was a half-empty bottle of booze, which could easily
be the one he had claimed he was buying when Ilveskivi was attacked.
There were no receipts in the trash or in the plastic liquor-store shopping bag under the sink.

Väinölä's apartment revealed a life of poverty, neglect, and loneliness. I took another look in the bathroom, which the Narcotics team had turned over quite thoroughly. I wasn't a clean freak by any means, but the mildewed grout and thick layer of grime on the toilet made me feel sick to my stomach. Väinölä did at least own a toothbrush, although the bristles were thoroughly splayed. There was no sign of a washing machine. Maybe the building had a laundry room.

Väinölä had removed one of the bathroom tiles and scratched out a hole about four inches across and twice as many deep. The work was clumsy enough to make me think that this was Väinölä's first time hiding drugs. He also hadn't had the sense to flush the goods, even though he should have known we'd be conducting a search.

Maybe he was more afraid of his supplier than he was of the police.

We didn't have to clean up after ourselves, but Wang shoved the posters out of the middle of the floor with her foot, somehow managing to get the Blu-Tack on the Hitler poster stuck to her shoe and ripping the poster in half.

"Do you want some matches?" Puustjärvi asked dryly, but Wang shook her head and didn't even crack a smile. She had come to our unit three years earlier, just as I was going on maternity leave. She was the first Vietnamese-born police officer to graduate from our police academy. She had moved to Finland as a small child, and as an adult, despite her parents' objections, she had changed her first name to make it sound more Finnish. But even with the name change, Anu Wang couldn't escape the banal racism of the Finnish people, which revealed itself not only in some of our clients but also certain coworkers.

I told Kettunen that Narcotics should handle Väinölä's processing from here on out. We would only question the neo-Nazi if something new came to light, but of course Narcotics would need to keep an ear out for anything related to the Ilveskivi attack. Maybe Väinölä was involved indirectly somehow. The brown heroin was serious stuff that could take even an experienced user by surprise. Over the course of the spring, I had investigated four junkie deaths. They had all been overdoses.

Koivu had made it back to the station after the autopsy. He, Wang, and I gathered in my office. Koivu looked pale and tense, and he seemed disappointed when I told him the search had been unilluminating in terms of the Ilveskivi killing.

"Did the autopsy shed any light?" I asked, sipping my coffee with its triple dose of creamer and three sugar cubes. On some mornings I remembered to make myself a salad and a sandwich for lunch, but this morning hadn't been one of them.

"It mostly just confirmed what we already knew. Ilveskivi was in great shape. He didn't have any injuries other than a scar on his forearm from that assault three years ago. He didn't smoke and his liver looked good, so we can assume he didn't drink much. The actual cause of death was cardiac arrest caused by the perforated pericardium."

"So no support for Mela's AIDS theory?" Wang asked.

"No, although the full test results aren't in yet. The hospital checked his blood type and did alcohol and blood testing before he went into surgery. Nothing." Koivu wiped sugar crystals from his mouth. He had stopped for donuts on the way back. Koivu loved pizza and donuts, which may have been why he was looking even stouter since the past winter.

"Based on Ilveskivi's injuries, it seems likely that the attacker hit him with the metal pipe first, apparently trying to do the job without touching the victim. For some reason he pulled out the knife next, and as we all know, stabbing someone requires getting up close and personal. There were black leather flakes under Ilveskivi's fingernails. He was wearing biking gloves, but they didn't completely protect his knuckles. He obviously hit his attacker."

"So the original purpose may not have been to kill him," I said. "Maybe it was just some druggie who was looking for someone to rob and saw the briefcase on the back of Ilveskivi's bike. Maybe he lost his cool when his victim resisted. What about prints on the bicycle?"

"Forensics found a couple of prints besides Ilveskivi's, but nothing with a match in the database. Same thing with the briefcase and helmet, although there was only one set besides Ilveskivi's on the helmet."

"Probably Tommi Laitinen's. We'll need to get his for comparison."

Koivu's cell phone beeped, and he pulled it out to read a text message. His expression brightened momentarily, and he wrote something down. Then he entered a reply: *OK*.

"That was from the lab. They've identified the tire type from the motorcycle tracks at the crime scene. Only the center of the pattern is visible, but apparently the tire is a . . . wait . . . Metzeler ME 99. Either 120 or 130 centimeters."

"Is that common?" I asked, since I knew embarrassingly little about motorcycles. Koivu didn't know either.

My own phone rang, and the duty officer at the reception desk in the lobby said that I had a visitor who was demanding to see me immediately. When I asked the name, the answer was a shock:

"Tommi Laitinen. He says he has some extremely important information about a murder investigation, and he refuses to talk to anyone but you."

5

I threw Koivu and Wang out of my office. They both looked a bit confused, but they knew me well enough not to object.

Tommi Laitinen looked haggard. A dark-brown wool jacket hung from his shoulders, and the light-brown shirt underneath hadn't been ironed. His brown shoes, the same ones that had been so shiny in the hospital hallway, were scuffed, and he had two days' worth of stubble.

"Hello," I said. Laitinen avoided my outstretched hand, so I motioned to the couch. "Please, sit. Would you like coffee or tea?"

Laitinen shook his head and sat down heavily. He stared at his hands for what seemed like minutes before saying anything.

"I wanted to talk to a female detective because women are usually more open to things, even if they are police officers. The police were anything but pleasant three years ago when Petri and I were attacked. The detective wouldn't even shake our hands. He seemed to think that homosexuality is contagious, and the other officer wasn't any better. They made it clear that they might not be able to restrain their fists either if they saw two men kissing."

The detective in question had been my deceased colleague, Pertti Ström, who had been well known for his prejudice. Lähde had been the lead detective on the case. Ilveskivi and Laitinen had lost at the game of detective roulette, even though the case had been solved and convictions made.

"Lauri Jensen said that you're a friend," Laitinen continued. "So you don't have anything against people like us?"

"No, not in the slightest," I said, somewhat irked. Lähde and Ström had succeeded in tarnishing the reputation of our entire profession.

"I have to ask: Did my husband fight back?" Laitinen asked.

"Yes, he tried to defend himself," I replied. If Laitinen was the murderer, he would know that anyway.

Laitinen gave a pained groan and then spent the next minute or two staring at his stubby hands with the curly blond hair growing on the backs. Finally he started speaking again.

"Petri is . . . was . . . quite hot tempered. He didn't approve of violence, but he had a mouth on him. He never hit anyone, but if someone hit him and he got mad, then . . ." Laitinen shook his head and a smile flitted across his face.

"Did anyone ever attack him other than that time three years ago?"

"Well, once. At Café Escale. It was stupid. Petri had drunk a couple more cocktails than normal, and he started mouthing off to this guy who was trying to cut in line at the bar. Then this guy flicked ash from his cigarette into Petri's empty glass, and Petri pitched a total fit. Both of them got thrown out, and it was all I could do to get Petri into a taxi without another confrontation."

I nodded. The person who wouldn't defend himself when attacked was rare. Even though Jesus had taught the importance of turning the other cheek, that doctrine didn't work very well in practice. Maybe nowadays Jesus would tell people to run away.

"I'm telling you this because Petri and I had a terrible argument before he left for his meeting," Laitinen said. "He left in a rage, and I'm afraid that . . ."

Laitinen paused and again stared at his hands, which had started to shake as if he were cold. He was a professional caregiver, a kindergarten teacher, but did he know how to care for himself? In my experience, people who cared for others professionally tended to neglect themselves.

They knew how to give others good advice, but they didn't always know how to follow it.

Laitinen started to speak again, quickly now as if wanting to get rid of the words he was saying.

"Petri hadn't asked my permission before settling things with Eila. Of course that made me furious. Of course I yelled and said all those things that I shouldn't have said."

"Settling what?"

It was like Tommi Laitinen hadn't heard my question.

"What if Petri was angry and rode his bike at someone on purpose? Then it would be all my fault!"

"There's no indication of something like that," I said reassuringly. I was having a hard time imagining a scenario in which Ilveskivi started the fight. I was curious to hear why the couple had been arguing, but I wasn't going to ask again. Laitinen could tell me when he was ready. Every detail was important in a homicide investigation, and you had to gather all the information you could. Only through experience could you learn to tell the difference between the wheat and the chaff.

"Do you have any acquaintances with motorcycles?" I asked, and after mulling it over for a moment, Laitinen listed a few names, none of who were close friends. He couldn't think of a reason why any of them would attack Petri. Still, I took down the names, and I would check to see if any of their motorcycles could take a Metzeler ME 99 tire and whether any of them had a criminal record.

"Did Petri usually ride his bike to work and to meetings?"

"Whenever there wasn't snow. It's a matter of principle and a good way to keep in shape. We don't even have a car, and bikes are usually faster than the bus."

"I've noticed. Did he always take the same route to get downtown?"

"Yes, he usually went the same way, since that way has the least traffic. Sometimes he would come back through Central Park, but that adds a bit of time."

So it wasn't at all improbable that someone who knew Ilveskivi's routine could have been waiting for him by that path. Were we going to find someone with a motive from his political activities or at his work? Wang and Puustjärvi were going to Petri's office in the afternoon to interview his colleagues and figure out what projects he had in the works.

My stomach grumbled. It was already past one. Soon my hands would start shaking too; I could no longer handle low blood sugar as well as I did when I was younger. The coffee, which was half milk and sugar, would help for the next hour or so. I decided to drop the formalities and use his first name. Hopefully that would make us feel like we were on the same side.

"Excuse me, Tommi, I'm going to get a cup of coffee," I said. "Can I get you anything?"

"If there's any juice. Or maybe tea," he said.

Mela was slouched in a chair in the break room reading a tabloid.

"Hi, boss," he said, straightening up slightly. "Have you seen the papers?"

"I haven't had time." I grabbed the one he was holding. "Oh God, do I really look like that?" I said involuntarily. I really would have preferred Mela not to have heard that.

In the newspaper photograph, I practically had shopping bags under my eyes, and my bangs had gone completely frizzy on the way from the women's restroom to the press conference. On the bright side, the crime reporter was a pro, and so all the facts were right, although of course Ilveskivi's sexual orientation received inordinate attention and was suggested as a motive for his murder. The most offensive thing, though, was that the article mentioned that Tommi Laitinen, who was described as Ilveskivi's "live-in boyfriend," worked in a kindergarten. This wasn't the first time I had considered the fragility of the privacy of victims and their loved ones. Grief often drove people to talk to the media, and later they usually regretted it. Homicides always shattered the lives of those left behind, and there was no point picking at those wounds in the press. Of course there were always those who enjoyed their fifteen minutes of fame, but I didn't think Tommi Laitinen was one of them.

"Where is Lähde?" I asked as I returned the tabloid. I didn't feel any kind of connection with Mela, even though I was one of the people who was responsible for familiarizing him with the duties of Violent Crime.

"Smoking. After that we're going to Helsinki to see if anyone remembers Väinölä from Tuesday afternoon."

"Good. Anything new?"

Mela shook his head and went back to the newspaper, and I remembered that Tommi Laitinen was waiting in my office.

I poured a cup of coffee from the pot, filled another cup with hot water, and grabbed a tea bag, sugar, a small carton of milk, and some napkins. Laitinen probably needed the blood-sugar boost even more than I did. He was still sitting on the couch staring straight ahead when I walked into my office. Through the window a small piece of hazy blue sky with a couple of lazy, tattered clouds was visible.

Laitinen dunked his tea bag, looking distracted. I sipped my coffee, which had obviously been sitting in the pot for a couple of hours, and then added a little more milk. I hadn't drunk milk in years except with coffee, and the strong taste of the creamy, sugary brew suddenly brought to mind my summers as a child on my Uncle Pena's farm, Grandma's sweet cardamom *pulla* baked with fresh milk from the cow, and the scent of hay just cut and drying in the field. Just a few days ago I had been searching for Iida's birth certificate in a drawer when a picture of my grandmother at my age happened to fall out of a file. Her work-worn face had shocked me. She looked so much older than she should have, with her hair back in a severe bun and her tired, catlike eyes that had the same expression as mine after a hard day of work. By the time the picture was taken, Grandma had given birth to eight children and buried two, and a ninth was kicking inside of her. I had been seven when my grandmother died and didn't remember much about her other than the taste of her pulla and the way she stooped.

Laitinen took the tea bag from his cup and then looked around the room, obviously at a loss about where to put it. I moved the trash can over to him. He tossed it in and put the cup to his lips, then grimaced as if it were whiskey burning his throat instead of a standard Lipton tea. The color of the liquid did bear a strong resemblance to Jameson.

"Do you have any idea what really happened? Have you arrested those skinheads?"

"We've questioned all of them, but so far we haven't found any evidence of their involvement with Petri's killing."

I didn't bother telling him about Jani Väinölä's arrest, since it was none of his business. Laitinen put a lump of sugar in his tea and then stirred it so vigorously that a few drops splashed on his trousers, but he didn't seem to notice.

"You have to find the killer! Tell me what I can do. I'll to do anything, even risk my own life, if it means catching Petri's murderer!" Laitinen said with a frightening glint in his eye. For the first time during our conversation, he looked straight at me.

"Don't do anything! You are not a detective. Virtually every homicide in Finland gets solved. We know what we're doing. The best way to help is to tell me everything you can think of, anything that could possibly have a connection to Petri's death. Start with your fight. What was it about?"

Tommi stared at his teacup as if he hadn't heard my question, and I let him arrange his thoughts in peace. I wanted to know everything about Petri Ilveskivi. Knowing a victim well had brought results before, even when the objective evidence had run out. A few times during my career, a victim or one of the subjects of an investigation had been a previous acquaintance of mine, which was always tricky. In this case, however, I wasn't going to have to put personal feelings on the line.

"Do you have any children?" Laitinen suddenly asked.

"My daughter, Iida, will be three in August."

"Did you have her when you wanted to?"

"Yes, actually," I said, laughing. I didn't share the story of the failed IUD and my surprise pregnancy. Now I couldn't imagine not having Iida.

"So you can't understand what it feels like to not be able to have a child. We knew it was irrational, but Petri and I always hoped that the adoption laws would change. But that hasn't happened. So we were looking for . . . for a woman willing to be a surrogate, but we couldn't find anyone. But Petri still could have asked me before talking to Eila! Turo, Eila's husband, is sterile, so . . . Petri and Eila . . . They're such good friends . . ."

"So Petri asked Eila to be your child's mother?"

"Yes, without asking me first! He told me about it just before he left for that Planning Commission meeting. Eila was supposed to come over afterward to work out the details. Petri only gave me that much time to think about it. I can't understand how he could have been such an idiot!"

Laitinen's fist thudded against the table so hard it knocked his teacup over and onto the floor. Neither of us bothered to pick it up. I remembered what the Jensens had told me about the couple's desperate desire to have a child. The law only allowed adoption for married couples and unmarried people who lived alone, which meant that Ilveskivi and Laitinen couldn't adopt, even though they had been together for ten years. One of them would have had to move out so that either of them could have the right to adopt.

"So I gather you didn't think it was a good idea," I said.

"I like Eila a lot. But there is more to it than that. We wanted a child of our own. And I couldn't imagine Turo agreeing to that. Not having any children must be hard on their marriage too. That wasn't what I was worried about, though. The real problem was that Petri had made all these plans with Eila without mentioning any of it to me. That was what we were fighting about. My last words before Petri left were 'Go to hell.'"

Tommi Laitinen seemed like your average, forthright Finnish man, someone it would be easy to like. But killers were usually close to their victims. What if Laitinen had gone after Ilveskivi and the motorcyclist being there was just a coincidence? Maybe the story about the fight was a way to avoid having to admit something to himself.

"Now all I want is to be able to take back what I said and tell Petri how much I love him," Tommi said and then began to cry.

I didn't know what to say. I was tired of grieving people. The situation didn't demand anything of me—no one expected me to be a priest or a therapist, but I couldn't stand not being able to help. Finally I handed Laitinen a napkin I had brought with the cups.

"I don't have anything else to tell you," he said after calming down slightly. "I just wanted the police to know Petri's mental state when he left home. I was up all last night. It felt like someone had slashed my wrists and left me lying there, all my blood draining out, leaving nothing but an empty shell. When I turned on the lights, I was surprised the sheets weren't covered in blood."

Laitinen blew his nose again. Red veins crisscrossed the whites of his eyes.

"The only hope I have left is that Petri's killer will be brought to justice."

He stood up, swaying like a drunk. I didn't want to keep him any longer, but I still had one question to ask.

"Had Eila Honkavuori already talked to her husband about the baby?"

"I don't know. What would that matter now?"

I didn't have an answer for that. I told Laitinen that I intended to ask the phone company for records of all their recent incoming and outgoing calls. One of my junior officers could go through all the numbers.

Maybe that would lead us to some sort of solution. I offered to arrange a ride home for Laitinen, but he said he'd prefer to take the bus.

After he left, I went downstairs to buy a sandwich. I called Koivu to ask whether he had assigned anyone to interview Eila Honkavuori, but all I got was his voice mail. Back at my desk, I tried to wrap my mind around the big picture, but instead it kept wandering back to Petri Ilveskivi and my grandmother. Neither of them had the opportunity to choose whether they had children with their partner or not. Birth control hadn't existed in my grandparents' Northern Karelian mining town in the 1930s, and Grandma would have considered it a sin anyway. I had a memory of a radio gospel hour and Grandma's delicate soprano joining in with a hymn.

Whereas I had the complete freedom to choose whether I had more children. Not that that made the decision any easier.

When I found a moment, I looked up Eila Honkavuori in our database. She was a couple of years older than me, and her husband, Turo Honkavuori, was forty-five. The couple owned a Nissan Primera sedan, which was five years old. Neither had a criminal record.

Next I went online to look for minutes from the Espoo City Council meetings. I discovered that Petri Ilveskivi had been one of the more vocal council members. He had been particularly interested in city planning. He had advanced a couple of initiatives about environmental issues and one about reducing day-care overcrowding. I found a link to his homepage and read some old blog posts about adoption rights for same-sex couples, environmental policy, and local politics. He supported the development of regional centers, telecommuting, and organic farming, as did many members of his party. Ilveskivi was a native of Espoo and had serious reservations about half of Finland moving to the Helsinki metro area and the construction that such population growth would cause. His website was professional, but it didn't tell me anything I didn't already know. Just then my door buzzer rang and in walked Kettunen from Narcotics.

"Do you think you'll need to question Jani Väinölä again?"

"Why? Are you letting him go?"

"Have to. Not enough reason to hold him. He says he doesn't know anything about the drugs hidden in his bathroom. No one believes him, but what can we do?"

"Hold him for the full forty-eight hours. My boys are checking his alibi for the Ilveskivi attack right now," I said. "We're going to have to question him again either way."

"Got it. We still do have until tomorrow afternoon. Väinölä is one slippery bastard," Kettunen said with a despondent sigh. "His friends are probably running for the Salo gang, but we haven't nailed them for anything yet."

Kettunen had been working Narcotics for fifteen years. He hated drugs and the people who sold them with all his heart, and everyone knew why. Kettunen's older brother had died of a heroin overdose in the early seventies. That was when the fourteen-year-old Kettunen decided to become a cop and catch every drug dealer in Finland. During our last department Christmas party, he had told me that nowadays he felt like he was trying to fix a broken leg with a Band-Aid.

After Kettunen left I called Koivu again. This time he picked up, and he was delighted when I offered to take over Eila Honkavuori's preliminary interview.

Honkavuori worked in the department of Civil Engineering and Community Development at the Helsinki University of Technology. I called there and reached her easily. She promised to come to the police station at three thirty.

Before the meeting with Eila Honkavuori, I handled a few outstanding items, including scheduling time on a soccer field for our women's team practice. I was really looking forward to bounding down the field and sending an opponent flying with a perfect slide tackle.

When I met Eila Honkavuori in the lobby, I was astonished at her posture and how she unashamedly embraced being big. I'd noticed how many ample women swathed themselves in boring tents and were constantly pulling in their stomachs, but Eila Honkavuori seemed to enjoy her body. She wore a low-cut crimson blouse, high heels, and flashy earrings. Even though I was curvy and well muscled, I felt small and drab next to her, until I was brought to by the frightened expression in her violet eyes. I asked her to sit on the couch where Tommi Laitinen had been a scant hour earlier. A hint of rose-scented perfume spread throughout the room.

"I understand that you and Petri Ilveskivi were close. How long had you known him?"

"A long time. We were in the same class in middle school and high school. We were both in drama club. After our college-entrance exams, we didn't see each other again until several years later, when I was serving my first term on the City Council and Petri came to a discussion about city planning. We immediately hit it off again. Since the last election we've been on the same committee together. Even though we're from different parties, we see most things in the same way."

Despite the tremor in Honkavuori's voice, it was low and warm. I would have liked to hear it when she was happy.

"Do you have any idea who might have wanted to attack Petri?"

Honkavuori vigorously shook her head, sending black curls whipping across her forehead.

"Petri could have a sharp tongue, but no one would want to hurt him for that—at least not physically. Some of the male politicians have had a hard time with him being openly gay. But political backstabbing is to be expected, especially if someone stands out from the crowd."

I nodded. The atmosphere around the city bureaucracy in Espoo had been extremely tense for the past few years as different administrative cultures clashed with increasing frequency. It was common knowledge that the mayor and several of his deputies were in open conflict.

Many of the leading officials felt that the city should be run like a business, while others argued that a city existed for its residents, not the companies that filled the coffers. Because of his politics, people had accused Petri Ilveskivi of being a socialist and a tree hugger, and several leading politicians had freely expressed their disdain for him.

"Who specifically did he irritate?" I asked. Honkavuori's face twisted in anger.

"I don't think it's fair for you to blame Petri for someone attacking him! No matter who was irritated by him, that's no excuse for murder!"

"I agree. I am not blaming Petri Ilveskivi for his death. I just want to find whoever is responsible. How did your husband feel about your friendship with Petri Ilveskivi?"

Honkavuori's eyes went wide. "Feel? Why should he have felt anything about Petri any more than any of my other friends? You don't really mean to suggest he was jealous, do you? Petri was one hundred percent gay!"

I didn't feel like getting into an argument over whether anyone was one hundred percent gay or not, so I just got to the point.

"Did your husband know about your intention to have a child with Petri Ilveskivi?"

The violet eyes opened even wider.

"No! How do you know about that?"

"Tommi Laitinen told me."

"And you assumed that my husband was angry about it and so killed Petri! Life isn't that simple, sister. If that's your best theory, I should leave right now." Honkavuori stood up.

"The police have to consider every alternative," I shot back, annoyed that I had managed to raise Honkavuori's hackles so quickly. I didn't want to get lumped together with idiots like Ström and Lähde.

"Our not being able to have a baby has nothing to do with Petri's death, and I don't want to talk about it anymore!" Honkavuori huffed, her hand already on the door handle. "Are you sure this was even a personal attack on Petri? The newspapers are constantly full of stories about people being beaten and stabbed for no reason at all. You must know better than me how common that is."

I didn't bother answering, even though I was thinking it increasingly likely that Ilveskivi had indeed been attacked without cause. Obviously my promotion had killed my ability to get people to talk. Even Lähde would have a done better job.

"If you asked me here just to accuse my husband, I'm leaving. Good luck with your investigation," Honkavuori said and opened the door.

"Now wait just a minute," I said, without any attempt to keep the exhaustion from my voice. "Even if this was a random attack, any information we can get about Petri Ilveskivi is helpful. How many people knew his bicycle route?"

"When Petri didn't show up at the meeting, the chairman said that he must have had a tire failure and laughed. He thought he was so funny. Anyway, the whole commission knew that Petri had been biking to our meetings since Easter. I imagine his neighbors knew too. I know how my neighbors get around anyway." Honkavuori closed the door. "As I said, I'm prepared to talk about Petri all night if it helps." She sat back down on the couch and crossed her ankles as daintily as a ballerina. I had never learned to sit well in a skirt, and slim suit skirts and short skirts always caused me problems. I decided to practice the same position at home.

I asked Honkavuori to describe Petri Ilveskivi, and after talking for a while she started to open up. She told of an energetic, gifted friend who had stood out from the crowd in school from people who were just interested in sports and listening to the Hurriganes. According to Honkavuori, everyone but Ilveskivi himself had sensed his sexual orientation.

"Petri's father never learned to accept his homosexuality and always talked about Tommi as his 'friend.' He was more of a traditionalist—he was born in 1926 and fought in the war. In February Petri and his dad went to see that new movie about the Karelian campaign, and he said it was the only time he had seen his father cry. Petri's dad has had heart trouble for a while, and he probably doesn't have much time left. I sent him flowers, but I haven't been able to talk to him yet."

Honkavuori paused before continuing.

"I hadn't had time to talk to Turo about the baby. About this new development anyway. We've considered artificial insemination and adoption, although our time is running out, especially for adoption. Turo is forty-five, and no one really wants to give someone that old a baby. I was still thinking about Petri's idea, and I wasn't sure what to make of it. I didn't really know what 'it' was yet. I didn't see any point in telling Turo."

"What did Ilveskivi suggest in terms of custody?"

Eila Honkavuori shrugged. "A child born in wedlock always belongs to the husband. I don't know what would have happened if Turo denied paternity and Petri had acknowledged it. And I don't really feel like talking about it right now."

Fortunately Antti had promised to pick up Iida, because Honkavuori's reminiscing went on until almost five thirty. Although her memories brought Ilveskivi into better focus, they weren't much use for our investigation.

Once she left, I found Puustjärvi in the break room. He had completed the profile I'd requested of everyone who had recently committed a random assault. The profile fit Jani Väinölä perfectly: male aged eighteen to thirty, unemployed, loner, alcohol or drug problems, and previous convictions for violent offenses. Many of them had been marginalized since birth, and society didn't seem interested in figuring out how to help them live harmoniously with the rest of the world or even themselves. Puustjärvi had assembled a list of people we could start questioning if we weren't making any progress finding Ilveskivi's killer. Even though the whole unit had been working overtime, it had been nearly two days since the crime, and the more time that passed, the worse for the investigation.

"Does anyone on your list own a motorcycle that could use a Metzeler ME 99 tire? If so, let's talk to them first. Do we know yet whether it was a 120-millimeter or 130-millimeter tire?"

"No. The ground was soft, and the edges of the track were indistinct. Luckily newer motorcycles tend to have wider tires. This is either an old beater or someone's expensive restoration project."

"Ah. The eyewitness statements were contradictory. Do we know if it was a Harley or what?"

Puustjärvi shook his head and rubbed his eyes.

"How many comp hours have you not taken?"

"Thirty."

"Well, add these to the pile."

"Yeah. Tiina has the night shift, and the kids are going to have to be home alone again. They call every half hour, and at least I can answer when I'm at the computer," Puustjärvi said ruefully. His wife worked at the cheese counter at one of the larger local supermarkets. Of course the customers liked the store being open until nine, but Puustjärvi's ten- and eleven-year-old children didn't like being home at night without their parents. But at the rate he was racking up overtime, Puustjärvi was going to be able to spend all the time he wanted at home with his kids playing Go.

Then, to top it all off, Lähde called and said that a salesperson at the liquor store and the store detective at Stockmann recognized Jani Väinölä. The store detective remembered following Väinölä on Tuesday around five thirty, so there was no way he could have been in Espoo killing Petri Ilveskivi.

6

The spring evening glowed an inviting blue, so we went out for a bike ride to Central Park. Iida shouted at the dogs jogging by, and I laughed for the first time all day.

"You aren't going to make it out to Inkoo this weekend to work on the boat, are you?" Antti said when we stopped on the side of the path to hunt for liverwort.

"No. You should go without me," I said. I didn't even bother recording my overtime since I would never be able to take enough time off to make up for it. Koivu had at least a week of banked time too, which he was trying to add to his summer vacation. Going to Inkoo would have been a nice break. We had been planning to clean Antti's parents' sailboat, whose upkeep had increasingly fallen to Antti's sister's family and us in recent years. I would have liked to watch the ice recede and listen to the migrating birds, but instead I would be sitting at the police station. Just thinking about working through the weekend made me tired.

I felt like I was always exhausted nowadays. Even when I slept, it was a fragmented sleep full of terrible nightmares. Although a year and a half had passed since Ström's death, at least once a week I still had visions of his brains splattered across his painfully tidy living room amid the smell of blood and gunpowder. I still wondered whether I could have done anything to prevent his suicide. Listening to Tommi

Laitinen reminisce had reminded me of Ström. Ström, whom I had mostly detested while he was alive but now missed.

That fall a year and a half ago, I had returned from maternity leave to take over as unit commander for the Espoo Police Violent Crime Unit. That time had been the most trying of my life. Ström's suicide had been one in a whole series of things that made me want to avoid thinking too much. That first winter as unit commander I had worked harder than I had my entire life, and the second year wasn't bringing much relief, although I was becoming more confident in my decisions. Leaving work behind during my free time had become increasingly difficult. Even when I was jogging, an activity that used to help quiet my mind, I now tended to think about open cases. I could only find relief when we were sailing or I was playing with Iida.

Iida's rubber boots squelched in the damp forest meadow where tiny green leaves were already pushing through the brown of the previous year's vegetation. The brightness of the purple liverwort flowers was surreal against the gray of the forest. I let Iida pick a few. The rest of the flowers we left to delight the others who took the trouble to slog off the trail.

Iida decided that a fallen tree was a horse and its branches were reins. Antti and I watched her riding practice, and sometimes I could almost see the bay pony my daughter was imagining. I sat down on a stump to watch. Antti sat on the ground in front of me and rested his head in my lap.

"The first edition seems to be a success. What would a sequel look like?"

"You feel like trying again?" I asked gently, trying to temper my anxiety over not being ready to make this decision. Would I later regret it if Iida remained an only child?

That night I read Iida a Pettson and Findus story, *The Fox Hunt*, and laughed for the second time that day. Usually Antti was the melancholy one in the family, the one who spent evenings staring at the wall with a glass of red wine in his hand. This spring I had joined him more often, although my glass usually had whiskey instead of wine. Now I settled for chamomile tea, because first thing Friday morning I was going to have to go back to the drawing board on the Ilveskivi case.

Even though I went to bed at eleven, I couldn't sleep. I didn't want to wake my husband, who snored softly beside me. I looked at his sharp profile, his black eyebrows, his Roman nose, his lips slightly twitching in some dream rhythm. Snuggling in as close as I could, I'd just started to relax when Tommi Laitinen popped into my mind. He probably couldn't sleep either. That thought kept me awake until almost three.

In the morning I blessed the chamomile tea bag that I had accidentally left on the counter. Iida seemed confused as she regarded me drinking my morning coffee with a tea bag pressed against one eye. Antti looked worried when I told him that I hadn't slept and made me promise to wake him next time.

"I feel terrible leaving you alone here. At least go to a movie with somebody if that would cheer you up," Antti said and then mussed my hair with a kiss.

"Well, we'll see. Maybe I can come out tomorrow night," I said. "Maybe this morning there will be good news about the Ilveskivi case."

My hopes were quickly dashed, because it turned out that half of the leads we were following had gone nowhere. We'd already determined that Jani Väinölä was innocent, and we didn't have any other serious suspects. The police sketch artist had put together a picture of the motorcyclist based on the eyewitness reports, but it was exceptionally vague.

"When will the DNA analysis of that cigarette butt from the crime scene come back?" I asked Koivu.

"They promised it by Tuesday. Three different hair types showed up on Ilveskivi's coat too, and we sent them in for DNA testing. It'll be expensive, but there isn't any choice."

"You're right. Has anything new come out of the interviews with the person who found the body or any of the other witnesses who showed up before the paramedics?"

Puupponen shook his head.

"The person who found him was able to give a detailed description of Ilveskivi's position, though, and we have a drawing. We'll compare that to the ME's statement."

The only line of investigation that showed even the slightest promise came from Puustjärvi's discovery that six of the repeat offenders on his list had motorcycles, and all but one were Harley-Davidsons. I asked him and Lehtovuori to figure out where they had been Tuesday evening.

Puupponen hung back in the break room after the meeting, shooting the breeze about the upcoming hockey world championships, which I didn't have the energy to be interested in. Only when the last person poured their coffee and left did he turn to me with feigned nonchalance.

"Hey, Kallio, is it true that a man's butt is the first thing a woman looks at? And having a 'tight butt' is a good thing, right?"

"Who said you have a tight butt? Not that there's anything wrong with your butt," I said playfully. Puupponen turned almost as red as his hair, and the freckles on his narrow cheeks nearly disappeared in the flush. I realized that if one of my male bosses made a similar comment to me, I would be offended.

For a second I thought with horror that I had been tricked into committing sexual harassment. But Puupponen persisted.

"I'm not talking about my ass. But is it true that women—"

"That's probably just as much a cliché as saying that men always look at a woman's tits first."

"So what do you look at first?" Puupponen asked, his face still red.

"Hmm . . . well, facial expressions probably. Why do you ask?"

"Well it's just . . . I was thinking of this one woman. About whether she could think, 'Wow, that guy sure has a great butt.'"

I stared at Puupponen with amused confusion. What was going on here?

"Yes, of course. Any woman might think that about a man. And yes, if you heard someone say that, she could easily have meant you."

"We're not talking about me!" Puupponen snapped and rushed out of the room, his face looking like a strawberry. I stared after him. Puupponen had an average build, slim, without anything particularly special about it one way or the other. His freckled face was pleasant in a boyish sort of way, and his broad grin always made it seem like he was about to make a joke. Was Puupponen worried about his success with the ladies, or was something else bothering him?

I forgot about Puuponen's freak-out as soon as I got back to my desk and saw the Petri Ilveskivi autopsy report. Blood from the knife wounds definitely would have splattered on the assailant. It wouldn't be obvious on black riding leathers, but someone should have at least seen something. Half an hour later my phone rang, and it was Puupponen on the line, calling to beg me not to mention our "butt conversation," as he called it. He said he would explain later.

This left me even more confused, but I promised to keep my mouth shut. Because Puupponen was one of the quickest wits in the building and enjoyed his reputation as a comedian, other people were constantly looking for ways to one-up his wisecracks. Of course I would keep quiet.

For once I had time to sit down for lunch with Taskinen. Going somewhere outside the police station so we could talk in peace would have been nice, but the half hour we had wasn't enough for that. You couldn't talk about anything terribly personal in the cafeteria, so we settled for going over open cases and discussing his daughter Silja's whiplash.

"Next week is that Safe City 2000 seminar," Taskinen said by way of reminder. "It would be good if the Ilveskivi case was solved before then."

"Yes, that certainly would be a great way to put on a good face for the mayor's office. I just had to go and promise to be a speaker! I was planning to focus more on things no one likes to talk about, like domestic violence, even though I know the audience is just going to want to hear about how upstanding citizens can survive among drug dealers and Satanists."

Taskinen snorted. He said that because of Silja's accident, he felt like talking about declining standards in traffic safety, but it was no surprise that the organizers wanted him to talk about preventing drug crime and improving security for businesses instead.

"You could discuss how the city is segregated when it comes to security issues. The rich folks on the shoreline have the money to buy security systems for their mansions and Mercedes, but there are other neighborhoods where an old lady doesn't feel safe going to the ATM to withdraw her tiny pension because she's afraid of drug dealers."

"And of course you think protecting that old lady's pension is more important than protecting yachts in Westend," Taskinen said, his smile growing even warmer. "It's nice that you still have a bit of punk spirit left in you. Recently you've been sounding awfully cynical. I've been worried about you."

Meeting Taskinen's gaze was difficult, because I was also worried about how so little could bring me joy these days. As if to reassure both him and myself, I continued to joke about the city government. Taskinen's wife, Terttu, was a day-care administrator, and he couldn't help letting slip the occasional bitter comment about attempts to privatize municipal day-care centers and to guilt trip unemployed parents who kept their kids in day care in case a job came up on short notice.

Taskinen rarely joined in my criticism of the powers that be or my schemes to save the world, but today we both let loose and laughed loudly enough for Laine from Organized Crime to peer around one of the potted plants, his eyebrows raised.

"What is it that my esteemed colleagues find so amusing? Is it the terrorist attack on the Ring II construction site? Was that your husband's doing?" he asked, his tone meant to convey that he was only half joking.

Some environmentalists had spray-painted "tree killers" on one of the front-end loaders. The scene of the crime was less than half a mile from our house. Of course Antti didn't have anything to do with it, but Laine still held a grudge, ever since seeing Antti at an anticar demonstration. He was certain my husband was an eco-terrorist, and whenever he got the chance he ribbed me about it. Even though he always couched it as a joke, real indignation smoldered underneath. For the time being, I had managed to rise above.

Laine came over and sat down at our table without asking. Taskinen immediately adopted a serious expression and started talking more decorously. I ate the rest of my veggie lasagna and left to work on my files.

Puustjärvi knocked on my office door at one o'clock, and from his expression I knew that something had changed.

"Hey, Kallio, something strange just happened," he said excitedly. "I called this one guy from my list, Marko Seppälä. A kid answered, about seven years old or so, and said that his dad hasn't been around for a few days. Apparently he came home all bloody on Tuesday and then left again, and his motorcycle is gone too. When I asked how he knew that it was Tuesday, the kid said because Tuesday is when *Tiny Two* is on, and also *Country Mouse and City Mouse Adventures*, which his stupid sister likes to watch."

"That's right. Iida watches that too. What did the kid's mother say?"

"She wasn't home."

"OK, tell me about Seppälä."

Puustjärvi handed me a rap sheet. Marko Tapani Seppälä was born in 1971 and was first convicted for a series of car break-ins at seventeen.

At eighteen he had already graduated to armed robbery, which led to a couple of years in the Kerava Youth Detention Facility. During the early nineties, Seppälä did regular short stints inside for various assaults and property crimes. As an adult, he had given up cars so that he could focus on fencing stolen goods. He didn't have any drug convictions, but I noted that he'd been in the same prison at the same time as Jani Väinölä and the drug kingpin Niko Salo, and that one of the other fences he worked with had been a mule for Salo.

"This guy's spent more time in jail than at home. At what point did he manage to get married and have three kids?" I asked, trying to hide my disgust and doing a poor job of it. Seppälä did fit our profile. But could he also be Jani Väinölä's friend? And what if Väinölä sent Seppälä to attack Petri Ilveskivi?

"Seppälä has a Kawasaki GPz750, and one of the witnesses swore that the chain on the bike he saw clicked like his own old Kawasaki does. And he seemed like the most reliable of the witnesses. Anyway, the kid who answered Seppälä's phone said his mom would be home at three. Should we go have a chat with her?"

"Yes, but first we need to question Väinölä," I said as I dialed the number for Holding.

"This is Kallio from the VCU. Do you still have Väinölä?"

"I don't know. He might be gone already. Kettunen came and signed him out two minutes ago.

"Goddamn it!" I shouted and sprang out of my chair. "Puustjärvi, come on! We need to catch Väinölä!"

Puustjärvi was slower, and I was already on the stairs before he'd left my office. The holding cells were in the basement, and Violent Crime was on the fourth floor. Charging down to the lobby, I almost ran right into the department mascot, a giant stuffed octopus. I missed it by inches.

Jani Väinölä was nowhere to be seen. I ran to the front desk.

"Have you seen a guy in a bomber jacket with a swastika tattoo on his head?"

"He just left. Maybe a minute ago. Lit his cigarette before he was out just to give us the finger," said the duty officer, who I knew had quit smoking recently.

Rushing outside, I looked past the parking lot and saw Väinölä out there, a few hundred yards away. I could feel the ground through the thin soles of my flats as I ran out to catch up with him.

"So you think I'm so sexy that you just have to run after me?" Väinölä said, sneering unpleasantly as I stopped, panting, in front of him. I could see that Puustjärvi was coming, but he didn't bother running. The sunshine was suddenly as hot as though it were July, and I wasn't cold, even though I was only wearing a thin shirt.

"No. I came to ask you to return to the station."

"Why? They just let me go. There are witnesses who confirmed that I wasn't anywhere near that fag when he got stuck."

"We still have some questions for you."

Väinölä looked down at me. In the shoes I was wearing, I was barely five foot three, and although Väinölä was only four inches taller than me, he was still milking the height difference for all it was worth. He lit another cigarette and blew the smoke in my face. Väinölä played the tough guy role so perfectly that it almost amused me.

"Are you going to arrest me again, baby?"

"I will if necessary. I want to have a little chat with you about your circle of friends."

Puustjärvi finally reached us. A bead of sweat ran down his nose, and he pulled a blue checked handkerchief from his pants pocket and wiped it away.

"Do the narcs think I'm going to rat out one of my buddies? Yeah, right."

"I'm not interested in that. Tell me about Marko Seppälä."

I couldn't interpret the expression that flashed across Väinölä's face. Was it only relief?

"Who? I don't know anyone by that name." Väinölä started walking again, taking quick, short steps, his thick thighs rubbing against each other. Keeping up with him was not a problem.

"Oh, so you don't remember. Let me remind you then: you spent six months with him in Sörnäinen Prison."

"That's a big place. I didn't know everyone."

"Even though you were in the same cell block?" I said. I was just taking a guess, since I had no idea where either of them had been housed.

"Is he sort of a thin guy with a face like a rat and a stupid long mullet? Sells stolen bikes and other chickenshit stuff like that? Yeah, I know about him, but I don't know him. I don't hang around with clowns like that," Väinölä said.

I considered what he'd said for a moment. Whether Väinölä was telling the truth or not was irrelevant, because the most important thing at this stage was to catch Marko Seppälä.

"If any fond memories of Seppälä come back to you, give me a call. You can reach me at the police station," I said, as if I were flirting, and then turned back the way I had come. Puustjärvi took ten seconds before he realized that he should follow me.

"What was that?" he asked indignantly after he'd caught up to me at the front door of the station.

"A test. I wanted to see how Väinölä would react. We have a travel ban on him, so if he goes anywhere we can bring him back in. Will you go with Lehtovuori to question Seppälä's wife?"

"Yeah, I can go, but Lehtovuori went to the dentist and won't be back this afternoon. He's getting a wisdom tooth taken out, and he's been wound up about it all day. He can look at other people's blood no problem, but he can't stand his own."

I laughed. "You men!" I said and then heard myself say, "I'll go with you. My paperwork can wait. At three, you said?"

Puustjärvi nodded, but a bewildered expression had appeared on his face. Hopefully he didn't think I was coming to spy on him.

"This could be our breakthrough. At least it sounds promising."

"How much should we trust the word of a first grader?" Puustjärvi asked, already backtracking, but I dug in my heels.

Before we left we looked deeper into Marko Seppälä's background. During his last stint in prison, Seppälä had asked to be moved away from the drug offenders. Apparently he had had trouble either with drugs or with drug dealers. Seppälä had married after his first child was born. He was nineteen at the time, and his wife, Suvi, was seventeen. Now they had three children, nine-year-old Janita, seven-year-old Tony, the one whom Puustjärvi had spoken with on the phone, and three-year-old Diana. I asked the Organized Crime and Recidivism unit for their tracking info on Seppälä. I didn't know what profession he claimed on his tax forms, but he had acquired significant skill as a smash-and-grab artist. The armed robbery had involved emptying the cash register at a convenience store while threatening the clerk with a knife. His take had been eight hundred marks and three packs of cigarettes. Four years later he attacked a random passerby because the man didn't have a cigarette to lend him. Seppälä could have assaulted Petri Ilveskivi for some equally absurd reason.

We set off at quarter to three. We took my department car, which was unmarked. Puustjärvi couldn't bear sitting in a silent car, so he started turning the radio dial. To my surprise he landed on Maija Vilkkumaa's "Fairyland Tango." I had expected a middle-aged Go player to prefer something a little more restrained, but I was happy to be mistaken.

The Seppäläs lived in a row house on the western outskirts of the city. Once again I was startled by the two faces of my city: the ugliest city center in Finland had grown up in the middle of farm country, and to this day a quick peek beyond the prefab concrete buildings revealed nearly virgin forests. The days of this contrast were numbered, though, as every remaining patch of green in the city was going to be paved in the next few years. Real estate prices had jumped like a pole vaulter. Nowadays someone would pay a cool million for our little house and acre of ground. The lot was zoned for more construction, so the siblings who had inherited it might be tempted to sell. Of course they would offer us the right of first refusal, but we weren't sure we would accept it, since the area had changed so much recently.

"It's unit J 62. There's the visitors' spot."

I parked in the narrow stall and tried to squeeze out of the car without catching my clothes on the bushes. Children played on the asphalt parking lot among the cars, and a handsome red cat lounged on the front stoop, enjoying the warmest day of spring so far. I greeted it like an old friend, which made the cat squint and stretch as Puustjärvi looked on in amusement.

The Seppäläs' door had a wrought-iron nameplate with the names of all the family members. Maybe it was from the Sörnäinen Prison metal shop. Maybe Marko was a stand-up father who used his time in prison to make useful home furnishings. I rang the doorbell, and a slight girl with long hair answered. She wore a pink Spice Girls shirt that was too small for her, and in the background I could hear the sound of guns firing, apparently coming from the TV.

"Hi. Is your mom or dad home?"

"No." The girl shook her head, sending her six silly pigtails swinging back and forth. "Mommy will be here soon. We're not allowed to let people in."

"That's a good rule. We can wait outside," I said and sat down on the front step to take in the sunshine. After the darkness and snow of the winter, the warmth felt like a luxury, and I drank in the light like medicine. Puustjärvi remained standing, looking morose. After a while, though, he started picking dried leaves off the honeysuckle vine that climbed along the wall.

We waited perhaps ten minutes before a bright-yellow Datsun Cherry appeared in the parking lot. A wave of nostalgia washed over me: our band's bassist's older brother used to have the same car. I had spent more than a few rainy nights on the main drag in our small town with a beer bottle in my hand, listening to the Hurriganes and trying in vain to get the boys to change it to the Clash or Eppu Normaali.

A woman got out of the Datsun and hauled two Eurospar plastic shopping bags from the backseat. She was thin in the way of women who live on coffee, cigarettes, and microwave pizza. Her dark-blue jeans were tight, and she wore heavy black eyeliner. Her short, yellow-blond hair showed a quarter inch of dark roots. As she walked toward the door, she glanced at us in irritation.

"What do you want?"

"I'm Lieutenant Maria Kallio and this is Senior Officer Petri Puustjärvi from the Espoo Police. How are you?" I said, extending my hand. Suvi Seppälä didn't take it.

"The police? Have those fucking social workers been spying on us again? It isn't my fault that I couldn't find after-school care. I was waitlisted for this class and got in at the last second! And Marko is usually home. He might be inside right now." Suvi Seppälä dropped her bags on the ground, sending a package of frozen French fries tumbling out. "Goddamn it!" she said, then pulled a pack of cigarettes out of her fringed leather jacket and lit up.

"And they yell at me about this too. I can't even smoke in my own home, and the neighbors bitch about smoke coming in their windows if I smoke outside. You tell those hags that the employment office forced me to take this class or else they'd cut off our benefits. They can find us an after-school program or leave us alone!"

Suvi Seppälä voice was piercing and apparently loud enough to hear inside, because the door opened and the delighted face of a little boy appeared.

"Mommy! I was the best at long jump out of the whole class!"

"Wow!" When Suvi Seppälä smiled at her son, her entire demeanor changed. There was no hint of that hard edge.

"Come inside and look around if you want. Our kids are fine." Suvi stubbed out her cigarette and threw it in a nearly full one-liter glass bottle on the porch. With a sigh she picked up her shopping bags and headed inside.

When we stepped in after her, we found a familiar-looking jumble of shoes in the entryway. Now the sounds of a car chase were coming from the living room. We followed Suvi into the cramped kitchen, where she started putting away the groceries. In front of us she set out the frozen French fries, a carton of 2 percent milk, and a pack of bologna, as if to show us that the children were being fed regularly.

"Our business has nothing to do with your family situation. We're looking for your husband, Marko Seppälä. When might he be home?"

"Marko?" A cup of yogurt trembled in her hand. "Marko is on a trip."

"When will he be back?"

"I don't know."

"How can we get ahold of him? On his cell phone?"

"He's riding his motorcycle and can't answer when he's on the road," Suvi said, the defensive tone in her voice again. Her head turned toward a cupboard, so I couldn't see her expression. We hadn't been able to find a mobile phone number for Marko Seppälä in any of our directories, so I asked Suvi for it.

"What do you want with Marko?" she asked and slammed the cupboard door.

"His phone number," I replied just as unpleasantly. "Where is he traveling and when did he leave?"

"He has business in Kotka, and he left on Tuesday night," Suvi muttered. "Janita and Tony, have you had your snack? Good. I have to go pick up Diana from day care now. You should have seen how I had to fight to get her a spot when the order came to go to this leather sewing class. There may be a day-care law on the books, but do you think this city follows it? There are people who break laws but never get sent to prison like my husband does. No one will hire him because he's been arrested so many times. You try raising three kids on the basic daily allowance!" Suvi turned on the range hood fan, lit another cigarette, and blew it into the updraft. Her nose wrinkled in pleasure as she drew the smoke into her lungs. Her silver Kalevala Jewelry snake ring looked enormous on her left ring finger, which was barely thicker than a cigarillo.

"Does Marko have friends in Kotka or is he staying in a hotel?"

"I don't know. I have to leave now to pick up Diana. She's been at day care since seven. This damn class starts at eight, and it's all the way across town." Suvi Seppälä stood up and walked toward Puustjärvi, who was standing in the door.

"You'll be better off answering our questions now so that you don't have to come down to the police station," I said firmly. I had no interest in arresting a mother of three who obviously had a hard enough time just getting through the day, but this was a murder investigation.

"To the police station? I haven't done anything wrong!"

"We can arrest you for obstructing an investigation. I doubt the day-care center is going to close in the next few minutes. Answer my questions, and then you can go pick up your daughter."

Suvi knew that if I arrested her and Marko was AWOL, Child Protective Services would take away the children, and of course she didn't want that. She ripped part of an advertisement out of a magazine laying on the table, grabbed a pen from the refrigerator door, and wrote a phone number on it.

"There. Marko's friend. He runs a flea market in Kotka. He told me that he hadn't seen Marko when I called yesterday. If he's with another woman, I'm going to kill the fucking bastard!"

I tried to quickly add all this up. Suvi obviously didn't know where Marko was, but she also didn't want us to know how concerned she was.

"So he left Tuesday night," Puustjärvi said. "Did you notice anything out of the ordinary about him?"

"No."

"Come on in here, Tony!" Puustjärvi said into the living room, but the little boy was glued to the screen. So Puustjärvi and I went into the living room, with Suvi trailing after.

"What do you want with Tony? He's only a child! Leave him alone!"

"Tony, do you remember talking on the phone with me earlier today? You said your dad came home Tuesday night with blood all over him," Puustjärvi managed to say before Suvi rushed at him.

"You can't question my child without my permission! I could sue you!" she yelled and pushed Puustjärvi away from Tony. She paused, then said quietly, "Marko did have some blood on him. He got hit in the forehead by a rock bouncing off a dirt road. It freaked the kids out, but he was fine."

"Doesn't he wear a helmet?" I asked.

"The visor was up or something. He bandaged himself up and then left again that night. He said he had to take something to Kotka. Some antique dealer whose name I don't remember asked him to deliver something. And yeah, it's all cash under the table, so sic the tax man on us too! Leave your number, and I'll tell Marko to call you when I hear from him. That's all I can do. Now I'm going to go get Diana, and I'd appreciate it if you left."

Puustjärvi and I left our business cards next to the home phone. Once she got us out the door, Suvi took off at a jog.

After watching her for a few seconds, I glanced at their little square of lawn, which hadn't weathered the winter terribly well. Dirt showed through in patches, and there were depressions that looked like tire tracks.

"Looks like Seppälä keeps his bike on the lawn, since the family Datsun takes up the parking spot. We don't have enough evidence for a search warrant, so we can't take plaster casts of these tracks, but we could try to draw them. Maybe the tread is the same as the one from the crime scene. Aren't you pretty good at drawing? Give it a try, but be fast. Suvi will be back soon."

Puustjärvi did his best to measure the width of the track and accurately sketch it in his notebook. When we drove past the neighborhood day care, Suvi Seppälä was pushing an energetic little girl in a stroller. I thought of Iida and Antti, who were probably already on their way to Inkoo, and suddenly I missed them terribly.

7

At the station, Puustjärvi and I compared his sketch to the tire track mold we had from Forensics.

"What, you didn't take a hair from her jacket or steal a comb for a DNA sample?" Koivu asked with a grin.

"This is when we need that DNA registry. Too bad Seppälä hasn't ever committed a crime that would have warranted taking a sample. How does it look, Puustjärvi?" I asked. With his magnifying glasses on, Puustjärvi looked like the caricature of a detective.

"I think it's possible that the tire type is the same, but there are lots of similar ones," Puustjärvi replied. "But at least this doesn't rule him out."

Koivu called the junk dealer whose number Suvi had given us. The man claimed he hadn't seen Seppälä in weeks.

"I was thinking we could call the station in Kotka and ask them to pick up Seppälä," I said. "They could also check with other fences in the area to see if someone has any information about him."

I was on the phone with my counterpart in Kotka for a long time, and I found myself slipping back into my North Karelian accent. The previous summer, Iida had spent a week with my parents and her cousins and had come home speaking fluent Savo-Karelian, albeit with the vocabulary of a two-year-old. Antti, who had lived in Espoo or Helsinki all his life, had been astounded.

Around seven, just as I was considering a well-earned departure, Koivu appeared at the door.

"Do you have a minute? Want to grab a beer?"

"Now? I've got my bike, but maybe I could have just one. Is Anu coming too?"

Koivu shook his head. I hadn't been alone with him in ages. Apparently he wanted to talk about something other than work.

"If I leave my car here, will you give me a lift?" Koivu asked in the hallway. "You don't think we'll be out past the time that the thirty-five stops running?"

"No, we won't be out late. I'm still planning on coming in to work tomorrow. I have to get that presentation for next week ready."

"Being a lieutenant sure is busy," Koivu said and then started trying to convince me to ride on the rear rack so that he could pedal the mile to the bar.

"I certainly will not! That would look great in the tabloids. 'Police officer seduces boss, breaks traffic laws.' Take the bus if you aren't up for walking. I'll see you there!"

Even though I was on a busy street the whole way, the five minutes of biking perked me right up. Coltsfoot brightened the ditch banks, and it was still so warm that I would have been fine in only a shirt. The sun shone high in the sky with the promise that it would linger longer and longer each day. Blackbirds called from the tops of the birch trees whenever the noise of traffic subsided, and dust billowed under the tires of the cars, many still with their winter studs.

Koivu waved from a bus window, and I waved back while barely managing to dodge a man who had decided to go rollerblading in honor of spring. I was thirsty by the time I got to the restaurant, and a large Kilkenny sounded fantastic. Koivu was already camped out in a booth with a beer stein in front of him.

"Did you have something you wanted to talk about?" I asked after we had made it halfway through our beers.

"Yeah." Koivu was suddenly uneasy. "Anu and I have been talk-ing . . . about maybe moving in together. Or at least I've been talking about it for a long time, and she just agreed. Yesterday she said we could start looking for an apartment."

"That's great!" I said sincerely. I wasn't terribly surprised.

"There's just one 'but.' Anu's parents. They want us to get married first."

I laughed. "Then I can be the best man!"

Koivu was not amused.

"I just never thought I'd get married. At least not after Anita . . . What's the point of making solemn vows when a person's mind can change so easily? And I hate all that church stuff."

"You don't have to get married in a church. Isn't Anu Buddhist anyway?"

"Her parents are. Anu belongs to the Lutheran church. That was another part of her teenage rebellion. She wants a traditional Finnish church wedding with the veil and everything."

"You'll look delicious in tails," I said, trying to lighten the mood, but Koivu sulkily downed the rest of his glass.

Then he went to get another. He was most of the way through that one too, before he spoke again.

"It just bugs me. Why do we need permission from some church or judge? Isn't it enough to just live together?"

Five years ago I had contemplated these very same questions. Antti had been much more eager to put a legal stamp on our relationship than I was. To me, marriage had seemed hopelessly bourgeois, but I didn't regret my decision.

"Couldn't you just move in together and then get married later when it feels right?"

"Anu's parents don't approve of couples living together outside of marriage. What I don't understand is why she suddenly feels the need to please them. She's a grown woman! And it worries me a little that she's twenty-six and still lives with her parents. The only time she's ever lived alone was at the police academy, and that was in the dorms."

"Of course you're nervous. You'd be stupid if you weren't. But if we're comparing Anu to Anita . . . remember that you're the one who followed her to Joensuu. And there's no question you've raised your standards since then," I said, taking on a maternal tone.

Koivu was like a little brother to me, and right now our age difference felt like much more than four years. I liked our sister-brother relationship, but it came with some problems—even though I was now the unit commander, sometimes he still expected me to be some sort of compassionate mother figure who was going to look the other way when he screwed up. When I didn't, I was an uptight bitch, but when my predecessor, Jyrki Taskinen, had done the same thing, he was just being a hard-nosed professional.

"I heard about a two-bedroom apartment in Leppävaara, right next to the park. Eija Hirvonen's brother's family is upgrading, and the landlord would love to rent to another police family. Since we're so reliable."

Now Koivu cracked a grin.

"Tell Anu how you feel. Being honest with each other is key if you're starting a life together. There will be plenty of things you'll have to keep your mouth shut about, but this isn't one of them," I said, remembering my own pain one and a half years earlier, when I'd send Mikke Sjöberg to prison. Crying over another man on your husband's shoulder wasn't a nice thing to do.

I didn't feel like another beer, so I moved on to water. An empty house and intoxication were a bad combination. And besides, I was on my bike. I helped Koivu through the worst of his anxiety, and we hugged for a long time before parting. I pedaled home as fast as my thighs could stand, took a cold shower, and then ate three sandwiches. Sleep came surprisingly easily.

Saturday morning I was peeved. I could have gone to Inkoo with my family, since the investigation was treading water. If Marko Seppälä appeared, I would be able to get back from Inkoo in plenty of time. So I dressed for riding and biked to the police station to make sure nothing new had come up. The trip to the cabin in Inkoo was only twenty-five miles, which I could ride in a couple of hours without hurrying, especially since the wind was in my favor. But instead I left the station and headed for the Ilveskivi crime scene.

The fields were still brown, but the newly turned earth smelled of spring. I rode slowly on the rutted dirt road, which had blades of grass poking out of it here and there. The sun had lured children outside to try out their new bikes, and a hardy runner passed, his upper body bare and pink. The elderberry bushes were awash in a violet plumage of buds, and a few wood anemones had already appeared on a sunny slope. Spring was here again, but just as we noticed Mother Earth putting on her delicate dappled coat of spring, it would all be gone. Soon the exuberant spinach green of early summer would overwhelm any nuance.

Deeper in the forest was still brown, and the most-shaded depressions still held snow. A pheasant crowed in the middle of the path before lazily flapping out of the way of my bike.

I recognized the place from the pictures. The hill was short but steep, and I was forced to slow to a pace that would have made me easy to attack. Still, the attacker had taken a huge risk.

Had Petri Ilveskivi been on his guard or had the attack come as a surprise? And had the attacker meant to kill? What if Petri had something with him other than the briefcase, something that Marko Seppälä had considered worth stealing? Maybe he had just been acting on a whim. Seppälä had stopped in the forest to smoke a cigarette and saw Petri Ilveskivi carrying something on his bicycle. A laptop?

Tommi Laitinen hadn't mentioned anything like that being missing. I left my bike on the side of the path and walked into the forest. The ants in their hill still slept, but the skylarks were already constructing their nests, their cries audible from the edge of the fields. Otherwise it was quiet. Then a sudden rustling came from behind and startled me.

Instantly Salo's gang came to mind: following me into the deserted forest would have been so easy.

But it was just an off-leash Irish terrier coming to make friends. Relieved, I petted it and didn't bother to remind the apologetic owner that dogs were supposed to be on leash inside city limits.

I biked back home through Central Park. As I got out of the shower, I stepped on one of Iida's glittery play earrings. She had received a princess jewelry set with a tiara from my sister Helena and loved prancing around in her baubles, even though the clip-on earrings pinched. I had barely managed to restrain myself when Iida claimed that it wasn't a problem because the earrings looked so nice. It was frightening that already a two-and-a-half-year-old girl thought she had to suffer for beauty.

Of course, I reminded myself, I had dressed up in lace petticoats and my friend's mother's wedding dress when I was a girl too, and what was wrong with that? Would I be so worried if I had a son who worshipped Formula 1 drivers? What kind of female role model did I hope to be for Iida?

Recently I had found myself staring at that picture of my grandmother, the thirty-five-year-old with the face of an old woman and eyes just like my own. Why did I keep remembering her? Why did I fight memories of my mother, who was alive but seemed distant even when she was present? Sometimes when my mother talked and cooed to Iida, I could make out the same tone I had heard when I was that age. As a child, I had admired my mother's old, carefully preserved schoolbooks, which had dozens of detailed drawings of princesses on their pages. I had never seen my mother draw, but after seeing those books I'd started begging her to draw paper-doll princesses. I tried to draw ones just as nice, but the curls always got tangled and the complicated beadwork of the dresses turned into a mess. But Mother didn't have time to draw, since she was busy with my little sisters. Then I realized that a knight in armor was much easier to draw, so I changed to playing with male paper dolls.

A few years later, when I had moved from paper dolls to soccer and saved up to buy my first electric guitar, my mother suddenly had time to draw princesses for my sisters. I despised those paper dolls, but I only tore into them with my words. Later, when my sisters fell in love with *Charlie's Angels*, they asked my father to make wooden guns for them to play with. I was the only one who detested their American trading cards, and I proclaimed that the Angles didn't have any real power—they just did what some faceless man told them to do. When I made it into the police academy, my sisters played me the opening monologue "Once upon a time, there were three little girls who went to the police academy . . ." and claimed that they weren't jealous, even though I was the only one of us who got a real gun.

Why had I always tried to differentiate myself from my mother and sisters? We were similar in many ways: my mother had her own career, and both of my grandmothers had worked just as hard as any man their entire lives. My sister Eeva was the first woman in the family to achieve a financial position that allowed her to stay home until her children were all in school. So who was the woman I didn't want to be? How would I feel if Iida wanted to be as different from me as she possibly could?

The buzzing of my cell phone saved me from these uncomfortable thoughts, and I ran to answer it. Usually a call on that phone meant work. Maybe Marko Seppälä had turned up.

"Hello, my name is Kim Kajanus. I apologize for calling outside of business hours, but I wanted to talk about the Petri Ilveskivi murder. I understand that you're in charge of the investigation. Would it be possible to meet?"

The man's voice was young and clear, and there was a refined Espoo Swedish lilt to his Finnish.

"Do you have information about Ilveskivi's death?"

"No, not really . . . but I have a lot of information about Petri."

"Were you his friend?"

I heard an embarrassed swallow before Kajanus continued.

"I got your number from Eva Jensen. She's my therapist. She suggested that I talk to you. Petri and I . . ."

The pause lasted ten seconds.

"We were in a relationship, and now I'm afraid that Tommi . . ." Kajanus must have heard my surprised intake of breath, because he continued quickly.

"No one knew about it, or at least I didn't think they did. Now I'm not so sure."

My thoughts took off like an Olympic sprinter running the two-hundred-meter. Petri Ilveskivi was supposed to be the model of marital fidelity. But then I remembered Eva Jensen's reserve on the night after Ilveskivi's death. She had known about Kajanus, but of course she couldn't reveal confidential information, even to help a homicide investigation.

"Would you be willing to meet at the Espoo police station in one hour?"

Another sandwich replaced the bean-and-nut salad I had been planning, and I had to slow my pace as I biked back to the station so I wouldn't end up drenched in sweat. I ran a background check on Kim Kajanus. Age twenty-eight, resident of Espoo, professional photographer, unmarried, no criminal record. I felt like calling Eva Jensen, but I could only interview her if Kajanus turned out to be Ilveskivi's killer and we needed a statement from his therapist.

I would talk to Kajanus alone first—I should be able to find someone in the building to act as a witness for a formal interrogation if that became necessary. The duty officer downstairs called me five minutes before the arranged time. I ran down the stairs.

In the lobby I found an attractive man of about five foot nine inches with a graceful build and long limbs. Wavy auburn hair fell to his neck. His gray-brown eyes were large with long lashes, his mouth expressive. His nose was narrow and aquiline like my husband's, but where Antti's face had a vaguely eastern look, Kajanus was more reminiscent of a Polish count. He would have looked very attractive in a lace collar. His handshake was firm, but his polite smile did not extend to his eyes.

I took Kajanus to my office, and instead of the couch he chose an armchair, crossing his legs in their brown jeans and trying to look relaxed but failing to conceal his agitation.

"Is there any news?"

"We have a couple of promising leads. But any help is welcome."

"Yes, of course. At first I just didn't know what to do. It was such a shock to read in the paper Wednesday morning that Petri was dead. Eriikka was sitting on the other side of the table, so I just had to keep it in. This is still . . . hard to believe."

"My condolences. And it's good that you decided to come to the police. You said on the phone that you and Petri Ilveskivi were in a relationship. How long had it been going on?"

"Eva said that I would regret it for the rest of my life if Petri's killer got away. I know you're Eva's friend, so you must understand . . ."

My job wasn't to understand—my job was to solve the crime. Still it felt wise to let Kajanus take this at his own pace.

"It's hard to start, since I've never talked to anyone but Eva about Petri. I started therapy because of him. I never imagined anything like this could happen to me. Or . . . I don't know."

Kajanus sighed heavily and closed his eyes. "I'm sorry that I'm being so confusing. I should probably start from the beginning. My whole life I've thought I was only interested in women. I've had a few serious relationships, and I've been with my girlfriend, Eriikka, for a couple of years now. We don't live together, although there's been talk of that. Guys have hit on me every now and then, and that didn't bother me, but I wasn't interested in any of them. I'm a magazine photographer, and in this line of work you run into all kinds of people. Like Petri."

Kajanus shifted in his chair and brushed a stray lock of hair off his cheek. After a moment he continued his story.

In early January, Kim Kajanus had started shooting the spring edition of *Gloria Home*, and three of Petri's sofa designs had been subjects. Petri had participated in the shoots, and he and Kajanus hit it off. At one point he asked Kajanus for a ride home.

"I agreed, even though it was out of my way. When Petri was getting out of the car, I felt like saying, 'hey, don't go yet' or 'let's get coffee sometime.' I didn't understand why I felt like saying that. Then the idiot I had given the negatives to managed to spill acid on one of the rolls, which turned out to be the one with all the pictures of one of the couches. So we had to set up a new session in a huge rush, and I didn't know whether I really wanted to see him again or not. I was afraid of what I felt. Petri had told me he lived with Tommi, and he had a ring and everything. And then I was in the heat of the shoot and found myself flirting . . . with a man."

Kajanus shook his head and gave a sad, crooked smile.

"It didn't make any sense, and I had no idea what I was doing. I finished taking the pictures and then suggested that we go out for tea at a nearby café on the waterfront.

"We did, and we talked and talked, and finally Tommi called Petri and asked what on earth was taking him so long. When Petri walked away from the café, I realized that I didn't want to lose touch with him. I ran after him and said that I wanted to meet again. 'Why?' Petri asked, since I had mentioned Eriikka so many times. I didn't know the answer, and we agreed to just e-mail. But in e-mails it's easier to say things that you would never be able to say in person. Finally I invited him over. I've never been so nervous about a date before. And Petri was too. He said he hadn't been with anyone else since he and Tommi got engaged. But we couldn't keep away from each other."

Kim Kajanus spoke to me as if I were a therapist rather than a cop, but I didn't interrupt. I had thought I had a clear picture of Petri Ilveskivi, but Kajanus was shaking the kaleidoscope so thoroughly that some time would need to pass before the new shape came into focus.

"So we ended up in bed. I tried to explain it away as simple curiosity, that I just wanted to see what it would be like to be with a man before I finally committed to Eriikka. But it wasn't that. I didn't know who I was anymore. Petri and I decided not to tell anyone. He made it clear at the beginning that he had no intention of endangering his relationship with Tommi. And I had enough to deal with, now that I had fallen for a man. I decided I needed a therapist, and I found Eva on the LGBTI Rights website. I guess I was afraid that a regular psychiatrist would think I was sick," Kajanus said, laughing nervously.

A simple story began to take shape in my mind: Kim Kajanus had never admitted to himself that he felt attracted to men, and so his relationship with Petri Ilveskivi forced him to face the part of himself he'd rather leave buried. The only way to destroy it was to kill his lover. I had heard of things like that happening before.

"It was completely insane. But I didn't love Eriikka any less, and Petri was in the same situation. I guess things were pretty hard for him and Tommi sometimes, since they wanted to have a kid so bad. Maybe for Petri I was some sort of escape from that. I don't know. I've been going over and over this all spring. I don't know, and now I never will."

"So you didn't tell your girlfriend about Petri?"

"No, I didn't."

"Are you sure she doesn't know?"

"Eva asked that too. I don't think Eriikka would have ignored it if she had found out. Everything is so clear-cut and straightforward for her, and she probably would have torn me limb from limb and then left me. And how could she know? Petri always met me at my place when Eriikka was at work—she's a flight attendant—plus a couple of times at a hotel in Turku over a weekend. Petri had clients in Turku, so Tommi didn't suspect anything. And I deleted all of his e-mails, even though I didn't want to."

"What is Eriikka's last name? Does she have a key to your apartment?"

"Rahnasto. She does, but she doesn't come and go as she pleases. She always lets me know ahead of time."

I nodded, even though I knew that affairs weren't as easy to conceal as Kajanus seemed to believe. Eriikka Rahnasto might have observant friends in Turku, or a sloppy hotel clerk might have given Tommi Laitinen the phone number to Petri's room and he may have discovered that his husband wasn't alone.

"Where were you last Tuesday between five and six o'clock?" This question seemed to surprise Kajanus. I saw anger flash in his eyes, but he controlled himself.

"I imagine you have to ask that. I was in Helsinki doing PR portraits for a new author whose book is coming out this fall. That went from five to about seven. The lady was so shy that it took a while to get her to relax enough to smile. You can check."

After pulling out his calendar, Kajanus took a sticky note from my desk and wrote a woman's name and phone number on it.

"After the shoot, I met Eriikka at a restaurant in downtown Helsinki. We're regulars there, so they'll remember us." Kajanus returned his large black leather calendar to the side pocket of his shoulder bag, then asked quietly, "Do you know when Petri's funeral will be?"

"The medical examiner hasn't released the body yet."

"Why am I even asking? Petri taught me more about myself than anyone, and I can't even go to his funeral!" Kajanus said dramatically.

"Why not? You knew each other through work," I said, once again meddling in business that wasn't even remotely mine.

"I'm a terrible actor," Kajanus said angrily. That was exactly the sort of line a criminal with a few days to plan ahead would feed the police.

"Was Petri afraid of anyone? Had anyone threatened him?"

"He told me about the time those skinheads attacked him, and some people had threatened him on the street after he came out against the new amusement park and the loan guarantees the city wanted to give for that ice arena, but he said that was just a normal part of local politics. He told me that Tommi wasn't very interested in politics, that he spent his days taking care of children and his evenings cooking. I can just imagine him bustling around in the kitchen with his apron on!" Kajanus snorted, and then closed his eyes and clenched his jaw.

"I don't know who would have wanted to kill him, other than Tommi if he had found out about me. But then he probably would have done it at home. But no—this way he's more likely to get away with it . . ."

"Have you ever met Tommi Laitinen?"

"In passing, in the cheese aisle at the grocery store. It was a crazy situation. Eriikka and I were buying a gift for a party a friend of ours was throwing, and suddenly I heard Petri's voice. We just said hi and didn't even introduce our partners. In the checkout line, I couldn't help sneaking glances and neither could Petri."

"What did the two of you plan to do? You said that Petri wasn't going to leave Tommi. Are you sure?"

"Yes," Kajanus said without the slightest hesitation. "And Eriikka and I . . . we've been talking about getting an apartment together for a while now, but Eriikka wants to live near the airport and I want out of Espoo. I've put the brakes on that a little, though, since first I need to figure out if there are other men in the world I could love like Petri or if he was just an anomaly in my safe, normal, heterosexual life."

Kajanus leaned back in his chair, and the spring afternoon sun flooding through the window tinted his auburn hair copper. The color was almost certainly natural, unlike my own faded bottle red, to which I seemed unable to discover an alternative. The room was warm, and beads of sweat glistened on Kajanus's forehead. Before long I'd have to start keeping the blinds closed.

"What did you want from Petri Ilveskivi?"

"I don't know. I was living one day at a time. I guess now I don't have to worry about it!" Kajanus stood up suddenly, walked to the bookshelf, and stared at a dreary row of binders. His eyes didn't seem to register what they saw. "That's all I have to say. I just want to help find Petri's murderer."

"Do you know where Eriikka was last Tuesday between five and six o'clock?"

Kim turned abruptly, and his voice rose to a shout.

"What does Eriikka have to do with this? She had the day off. But Eriikka . . . no woman would do something like that."

I didn't agree in the slightest, since someone physically weaker would be the one to use a knife. After calming him down, I escorted Kim Kajanus down to the door of the police station, where I ran into my colleague Liisa Rasilainen. We chatted for a while about soccer as I watched Kajanus leave. He had a black hybrid bike with a fat frame.

"The first game is scheduled for the first week of May," I told Rasilainen. "Kettunen from Narcotics already asked when the men's team can play us."

"Man sweat. Yuck," said Rasilainen. She didn't usually advertise being a lesbian, but over the winter we had started trading crude anti-chauvinist banter when no one else was around to hear. I asked her whether she ever sang karaoke at Café Escale, which had been Petri Ilveskivi's regular hangout.

"That's my secret life!" she exclaimed. "Karaoke princess of Escale. You want to come?"

"Do they ever play any punk rock?"

"I think we could probably find you something on the playlist. Tell me if you ever want to go, seriously."

I laughed. "Sounds tempting," I said and then returned to my office. My next task was to run a background check on Eriikka Rahnasto. She didn't have a criminal record, but according to the database, her father's name was Reijo. Was that the same city councilman who had called me? He hadn't been following his daughter's boyfriend, had he?

I grinned at the thought. We weren't in Italy after all. Then my grin froze, because the vehicle registry database turned up an interesting hit.

Eriikka Rahnasto owned a motorcycle, a Harley-Davidson 883 Sportster DLX. I checked Puustjärvi's list of motorcycles that could use a Metzeler ME 99 tire, and Eriikka's bike was on the list.

No wonder Kim Kajanus was worried.

8

On Sunday I rode the bus to Inkoo, where Antti picked me up. The sea was still frozen, the waves rocking their icy shell slowly but purposefully, waiting for rain to make it brittle enough for the next south wind to break it up. Iida threw rocks off the dock onto the ice on the shore, which boomed and crackled strangely as the rocks skittered across its surface. Finally a rock the size of Iida's head penetrated the ice with a loud plop, and water droplets sprayed out, glittering in the sun.

On Monday I returned to the office for our usual morning meeting, which turned out to be as fraught as usual. The warm April weekend had drawn people out, and the residents of the city seemed to have acted as rationally as calves set loose in a pasture for the first time. There was a fight at a beach that ended with three people needing patching up, and then there was another one in town. Robbery had transferred a purse snatching to us because the two skateboarding assailants had tripped an eighty-two-year-old woman as they were making their getaway, resulting in a broken hip.

"Puupponen, you go with Virtanen from Robbery to interview the victim. Gerda Grönberg. How's your Swedish? Grönberg's Finnish isn't great."

"I know a phrase or two," Puupponen said, "although I might offend her if I use them. But I guess I can ask *vad hande sen*, and maybe Virtanen will understand the answers."

Our police district included several neighborhoods and small towns with majority Swedish-speaking populations, but we'd long had a shortage of officers who spoke the country's official second language. We were used to having to use Russian, Somalian, and Arabic interpreters, but everyone was supposed to know Swedish.

"Puustjärvi and Lehtovuori, you handle the beach fight, and Mela and Lähde, you'll take the other one. Koivu and Wang will stay on the Ilveskivi case, and everyone else, you'll help them when you can. Wang, will you check Kim Kajanus's alibi with this author, Laura Laevuo? Let me know what she says. Koivu, do you have any ideas about how to approach Eriikka Rahnasto?"

On Saturday night I'd called Koivu and told him about Kim Kajanus's visit. Koivu had been just as frustrated as me: the case branched off every which way, and every branch seemed like a dead end.

"We could say that we're interviewing all potential Metzeler ME 99 tire users," Wang suggested.

"Will that work? Well, it's worth a try. You two go find her. Then report back to me. It's probably time to start going through Pete's list of motorbike owners too. And the APB is still out for Seppälä as well."

The day went well, with subordinates dropping in every so often to ask my advice. Wang left a message on Laura Laevuo's machine and fretted about not being able to reach her. At noon Koivu called, irritated that Eriikka Rahnasto was on a flight to Los Angeles and wouldn't be back until Wednesday afternoon. I told him to ask Finnair about Rahnasto's schedule the previous Tuesday. Ten minutes later he called back to report that Rahnasto had indeed been off the day of Petri Ilveskivi's killing. He and Wang intended to look for Rahnasto's motorcycle in the airport parking garage.

"Does Eriikka Rahnasto ride her Harley to work?" I asked in surprise.

"So her neighbor claims. We're going to go check so we don't have to meet her on Wednesday unnecessarily," Koivu said, sounding tired.

"Even though motorbikes can use different tires, and changing them isn't a big deal. Plenty of places will do it while you wait."

"Tell me some more good news," I said sarcastically and then went back to putting together my presentation for the safety seminar on Wednesday. I wasn't the slightest bit interested anymore, but I couldn't cancel after having promised to speak. I was too conscientious, at least when it came to work. After finishing the presentation, I decided to get out of the building for some fresh air. No one had been able to make time to interview Tommi Laitinen again, so maybe I could do it myself. Koivu and Wang were leaving the airport to talk to a cop up north in Hyvinkää who claimed to have seen Marko Seppälä the previous night.

I arranged to meet Laitinen when he got off work at three. A faint green had appeared on the trees, and the aronia bushes already had thumbnail-size blackish-green leaves. Friday was May Day Eve, which every cop in the country hoped would turn out rainy. I hadn't been out on the town for May Day since I was in college, and if I did end up going out, I'd just spend the night nursing drunk teenagers and breaking up fights. Fortunately, this year we had been invited to the Jensens'. Except that if Lauri had also invited Tommi Laitinen to the party, I would have to stay home. Mixing my work with my private life would only cause problems.

When I got out of my car in the parking lot of Laitinen's kindergarten, I saw a man with light-brown hair and a deep tan jogging down a nearby walking path. For a split second, I thought he was Mikke Sjöberg and my heart skipped a beat. Then the moment passed, and I knew that Mikke was far away, in prison. Once the man was gone, I turned and leaned my head on the car. I had to calm down.

Then it hit again, this uncontrollable, paralyzing pain. A year and a half had passed since I had arrested Mikke for killing his brother. Now he was serving seven years in prison, which for a first offender would mean only three and a half. There wasn't any sense in grieving over a man who had only briefly crossed my path, but I did. I tried to be cynical and laugh at myself, but it didn't work. Recovering from Johnny, my first love, had taken almost twenty years. Now that was passed. The momentary pain of our reunion a few years ago had faded, and all that was left was a warm friendship. We talked on the phone now and then, and we saw each other when I was home visiting my parents. Johnny put me in a good mood.

I didn't want to mourn Mikke for the next fifteen years. That would be pointless. I was a sensible adult, not some twenty-year-old police-academy cadet who was going to fall for the first charming blackguard who happened along. With Mikke I had acted like a professional and done the only thing I could.

I loved Antti, and I was happy with him. Of course the initial infatuation had passed, and in August it would be seven years since we'd started dating. As far as I could tell there was no seven-year itch on the horizon, so we were doing well. Still, there were memories that could hurt so damn much that they sent me running to the nearest whiskey bottle.

Earlier in the year I had given a presentation about the homicides the unit had solved during my time as unit commander. I spoke about Juha Merivaara's murder and Mikke Sjöberg's conviction with cool professionalism and answered questions as if I were talking about the weather. Koivu saw right through me. After the presentation he took me outside and dressed me down.

"Don't be an idiot! You were just doing your job when you sent Mikke Sjöberg to prison. End of story! There isn't anything to feel bad about."

Because Koivu was so ruthlessly realistic about the case, I almost always talked to him when the grief hit. He knocked me back into reality. I had deserved the bruises that fall had inflicted.

Now I kicked myself in the mental shin and headed for the kindergarten. A squirrel scampered up the trunk of an enormous spruce tree, and then a pack of children streamed out the doors to the playground.

"Atte, come play cops and robbers! I'm going to arrest you!" yelled a little guy, who had big eyes and was about five years old, to a larger boy with a round head.

"Whose mom are you?" asked a nicely dressed little girl.

"Iida's."

"Is she in our class?"

I answered no just as the tiny cop ran smack into me and instinctively wrapped his arms around me to reduce the impact.

"Oops. I think you caught the wrong robber," I said with a smile, which he returned sweetly before running off. The little boys kicked up a terrible clamor. Would Iida do that too if she had a partner in crime?

I watched the children's antics for a few minutes. In that time the kid with the big eyes had captured his friend twice, using a jump rope as handcuffs. Then Tommi Laitinen appeared in the doorway, and all forty little voices happily yelled "bye" as we exited through the gate.

"Should I take you home or should we go to the police station?" I asked. Tommi still looked exhausted, and his jacket hung limply from stooped shoulders.

"Home. Although it isn't a home anymore."

Laitinen sat down in the passenger seat, the harsh sunlight revealing his pinched cheeks and the wrinkles under his eyes.

"How can you stand to work right now?"

"Luckily there's one place where I'm still needed. Anyway, there isn't any money for substitutes, and if someone is gone, it isn't just the other staff who suffer. The children need us. Our enrollment levels are completely illegal."

"But you still enjoy it there?"

"I love being with children. Yes, I know why you're asking. Of course you would have found out about how I had to leave The Little Lamb."

"Why didn't you take them to court when they fired you?"

"I wasn't fired; I was pressured to resign. Little Lamb Kindergarten is a private Christian school, and for some of the children's parents, my sexuality was simply too much. I didn't have the energy to start making trouble. I had enough of the church condemning me when I was young, even though I tried to be a good Christian. I was lucky that I was able to get a new job so quickly."

We drove past a field being taken over by nearly identical two-story houses. On the sidewalk I saw Silly String scattered around. Apparently the children had already begun their May Day celebrations.

Laitinen's house smelled of loneliness. The turtle was nestled on a boot in the entryway. Was it able to miss its master like a dog or cat would?

The living room looked the same as it had on my first visit, but on closer inspection I could see dust on the bookshelves and smudges on the surface of the table. I flung myself down on the red couch, which felt heavenly. Could I afford one of these on my salary?

"What have you discovered?" Laitinen asked and leaned back in his red easy chair, which made his Adam's apple and the veins in his neck momentarily tense.

"Does the name Marko Seppälä mean anything to you? Here, take a look at this."

I took Seppälä's mug shot out of my bag and set it on the table. Laitinen looked at it greedily, but gradually the expression faded.

"I've never seen him or heard of him before. Is he a suspect?"

"We have an arrest warrant out for him for Petri's killing, but we also have other leads. Think hard. Seppälä is a small-time crook. He has three children. He rides a motorcycle or drives a Datsun Cherry."

Laitinen wasn't looking at the picture anymore, though, just leaning back with his eyes closed.

Had he sensed that Petri Ilveskivi had been seeing someone? And if he didn't, would he want to know?

I thought of Antti. Would I want to know if Antti had another woman?

Of course I would.

My cell phone rang, and I asked Laitinen to excuse me while I went into the hall to answer it.

"Hi, it's Koivu. We found Eriikka Rahnasto's motorbike. Just a little seventy-thousand-mark toy. Pink saddlebags and everything. The tread pattern and tire width match. What now?"

"Meet her at the airport on Wednesday. We'll talk more in the morning."

"We're still going to hit Hyvinkää to check on that Seppälä tip."

"OK, call me after. I really hope we find him," I said half to myself. We'd issued the APB for Seppälä late enough that he already could have slipped over the border. We hadn't seen his name on any passenger lists, but he could have bought fake papers. Maybe he had driven up to Lapland and crossed into Sweden or Norway. I had asked Patrol to send a car by the Seppälä house a couple of times a day to see whether he had come home, but so far there hadn't been any sign of him.

I returned to the living room, and Tommi Laitinen opened his eyes.

"I don't know if I'm just imagining things," he said slowly, "but have you spoken to Turo Honkavuori? He called me yesterday. At first I thought he was just expressing his condolences, but then he started complaining about Eila and Petri's baby plan. He claimed Eila hadn't told him until last weekend, but I got the feeling he was lying."

I added interviewing Turo Honkavuori to the constantly growing list of tasks to delegate. Laitinen offered to bring me something to drink. A moment later the sounds of a juicer started coming from the kitchen, and then Laitinen returned with two glasses of bright-yellow liquid. It was grapefruit mixed with orange, and it had a fresh, bitter taste.

"I don't really know Turo. They were here once for dinner and for Petri's birthday party in February, but Turo didn't seem to like us much. He always looked away when Petri and I showed any affection."

"Why do you suspect he was lying?"

"Because he kept pressing me to tell him whether I knew about the plan and what I thought about it. When I said that I thought it was a bad idea and had fought with Petri about it, he almost sounded pleased. I don't know."

That was what Kim Kajanus had said too. And so I asked Tommi Laitinen to recount the past month's events one more time.

"Sometimes Petri seemed upset. A couple of times I saw him going through some papers and muttering to himself about wishing he knew what to do. But when I asked him about it, he wouldn't answer. I thought it must be something political. The Planning Commission has been working on the new master plan for South Espoo, and they've been under a lot of pressure. Ask Eila's or Petri's party colleagues. They'll be able to tell you about it."

"Alright, I will. For now, I've brought these phone logs with me. Would you mind taking a look at them?" I asked.

At first Laitinen looked confused, but then he started going through all of the calls that had been made to or from their home and mobile phones. Ilveskivi didn't have a separate work phone, just his personal cell. Laitinen didn't recognize some of the names and numbers, like Kim Kajanus's, as well as a few that Detective Lehtovuori had already determined were Petri's clients.

"There isn't anything strange here. Eila calls here every day, and these calls are from Järvinen, another Green member of the Planning Commission. These are from Rahnasto, the chairman. This is Petri's mother's number."

I knew all of this already, but I had hoped that something might jump out at Laitinen. But nothing did.

"The body will be released tomorrow," I said when I couldn't think of anything else.

"Yes, to Petri's parents. They're the legal next of kin."

"Even though you're the one listed on all of Petri's medical records? Is there some sort of disagreement between you and Petri's parents about the funeral arrangements?"

"Petri's father still only talks to me when he absolutely has to. And Petri didn't leave any instructions for his funeral. I really have no idea what kind of a funeral this is going to be. Petri probably would have wanted me and his friends to carry the casket, but his dad is rounding up relatives who didn't mean anything to Petri. Maybe his 'friends'"— Tommi added a derisive emphasis to the word—"will hold our own celebration of his life."

"You did make out wills, though, right? The house is in both your names."

"Yes."

Puustjärvi and Lehtovuori had interviewed Petri Ilveskivi's parents and his sister's family, but all they found were grief and bitterness. For years the father hadn't had much contact with his son, and the mother had shut out of her consciousness everything about her son's life other than his work and political activities. The sister had liked her brother, but her husband hadn't wanted Ilveskivi to be in too close of contact with their sons. Lehtovuori's report made it obvious that neither the interviewees nor the interviewers were comfortable talking about Petri Ilveskivi's sexual orientation. I felt like rushing over to the parliament building right that very instant and protesting for marriage equality. Then I smiled at myself. Taskinen was right. The old fighter in me was reawakening. In a strange way, it felt comforting.

Tommi Laitinen glanced at my smile in confusion. Since it didn't look like I was going to get anything new out of him without telling him about Kim Kajanus, I decided it'd be best to leave.

At the station I read through the reports of the interviews with Petri Ilveskivi's coworkers and the other Green Party members on the City Planning Commission. There wasn't anything noteworthy in them. Marko Seppälä seemed to be our only lead. So I decided to head home.

At the front door, I ran into Koivu, who looked irritated.

"What happened with that Seppälä sighting?"

Koivu sighed. "Dead end. A patrol cop in Hyvinkää thought he'd seen Seppälä in a bar on Saturday, but then he started backpedaling. We went to the bar and showed Seppälä's picture around, but nobody recognized him. We got nothing from Kotka either. One coat-check attendant who's done time for fencing stolen goods said that he knows Seppälä but hasn't seen him in a couple of months. Harry Houdini would be jealous of the disappearing act this guy pulled."

"We'll have to go back and question the wife again tomorrow. And then we'll see what Eriikka Rahnasto has to say on Wednesday when she gets back from LA. At least Patrol caught those skateboard bandits when they tried the same stunt again. Where's Anu?"

"At home changing. We're going to look at that apartment tonight."

"So things are moving forward?"

"Eh, we're just going to look." Koivu shrugged as if it was no big deal, but he couldn't fool me. After giving him a friendly slap on the back, he left and I unlocked my front door and went inside.

Dinner was macaroni and ground-beef casserole à la Maria from the back of the freezer. Iida wanted to squirt the ketchup on her plate herself, which resulted in ketchup all over the tablecloth and her previously clean pants. I somehow managed not to lose my temper. What did it matter after all? Spring had sprung, the sun was warm even in the evening, and I was going to a movie with a friend.

A Long, Hot Summer was Finland's answer to *The Blues Brothers*, and since the misadventures of its teenage protagonists were set sixty miles from my hometown, this was going to be a serious trip down memory lane. To get myself in the right frame of mind, I put punk rocker Pelle

Miljoona's greatest hits on the turntable and cracked open a beer. Then I pulled on my most faded jeans and an old white men's shirt. Tennis shoes, my leather jacket from school, and an unfashionable amount of eyeliner finished off the look. Much to Iida's delight, I started getting into the groove, even managing to do a few pogo hops to the beat, but "Violence and a Drug Problem" put a stop to it, since it reminded me of work, with its story of neglected children spiraling into street life.

Leena was waiting in the lobby of the theater, dressed like the middle-aged lawyer that she was. I, on the other hand, bounced along in my sneakers as if there weren't any gray in my hair. We had known each other since law school. She had been more into ABBA than punk rock, but she was just as familiar as I was with all the three-chord bands from our youth and their big dreams of breaking into the Helsinki club scene. Those days were so long ago that we could laugh about it now, and we probably made more noise than the fifteen-year-olds in the audience. By the end of the movie I was weeping and laughing at the same time from the pure joy of recognizing my own life on the big screen.

"Now we just need somebody's older brother to sneak us some wine coolers or hard cider," I said to Leena as we were weaving our way through the teenage crowd toward the exit. "Let's go to Corona. Nobody will care that you're overdressed there."

When they didn't have any of the cheap drinks I wanted, I settled for beer, which I had drunk plenty of as a teenager too.

"That was good. Now when my kids ask what it was like when I was young, I can show them that movie." Her son was ten, and Leena had already been forced to talk with him about drugs and pedophiles.

"But we can't tell them everything we did, the drinking and the sex, can we?" I asked, almost shocked. "I mean, I've smoked a few joints in my day, but drugs are going to be absolutely off limits for Iida. Is that hypocritical?"

"No more hypocritical than demanding more power for the police to prevent crime and then getting upset when the police slaps you with a speeding ticket for going forty in a twenty-five-mile-per-hour school zone. That happened just last week by Juho's school. Some important CEO type had just written a letter to the editor about security for business property and the need to increase police authority. But when he got pulled over, somehow speed limits didn't apply to him."

"The losers think they're outside the law and the leaders think they're above it. But we're here to forget about work. I'm going for another. You want anything?"

We moved on to chortling about the mishaps of everyday life, and the medicine of laughter made me breathe easier and drink slower. Neither of us had a quiet laugh, and I noticed people staring at us with as much interest as disapproval. This wasn't the first time I had noticed that laughing women drew attention, that we evoked attraction and fear. Maybe we were occupying a space that people didn't think belonged to us, or that they couldn't believe we could laugh and have fun without a man around to tell the jokes.

After two pints it was time to head home. Two men were kissing passionately in front of Con Hombres. That took my thoughts back to the Ilveskivi case, but I pushed it out of my mind by recalling the movie I had just seen. During the time period it depicted, the most any girl could hope for was to play roadie, so I really had been an exception with my bass guitar. Thank goodness Iida wouldn't be a freak if she wanted to play in a band, whether an all-girl one or one with boys. No one would think anything of either.

I walked to the nearest bus stop. The sky was cloudy and the temperature was noticeably colder than it had been the previous two days, and since it was eleven, the sun was down. I had left my bike at another bus stop between this one and home, because public transit wouldn't get me all the way there this late. At the bus stop, a Somali boy of about fifteen was waiting. We both jumped when two people suddenly emerged from the little park across the street. I recognized the small, burly bald man from his gait, and the bigger one seemed familiar. Then the light hit their faces: Jani Väinölä and his pal Pirinen.

I stepped back into the darkness because I didn't want to interact with Väinölä. Ignoring the honks of a taxi, the men crossed the road and then stopped to dig into their pockets. A well-dressed middle-aged man walked up to the stop, giving the skinheads a wide berth. Pirinen was already lighting a cigarette when Väinölä said, "What the fuck are we doing smoking our own cigarettes when that licorice kid probably has some?"

Väinölä moved over to the Somali boy, and even though Väinölä was shorter, he had at least sixty pounds on the boy. When Pirinen also approached, the boy seemed to shrink even further.

"Hey, blackie. Give us a smoke. Or don't you understand fucking Finnish?"

The well-dressed man smoothly slid away, back into the night—he had no intention of getting involved. Civilians had the right to make that choice, but I was a police officer.

"Leave the kid alone," I said and stepped out into the light. Just then there was a flash of steel as the boy flipped open a butterfly knife.

"Fuck off," he hissed. No one noticed me until I shoved my way between the men.

"Väinölä, leave the kid alone!"

"What the hell, bi . . ." Väinölä began as he turned to me, and then his expression changed from hostility to amusement.

"Oh, it's you, Detective. Night off, eh? Or are you under cover? Infiltrating hippie punk gangs?"

"Give me the knife," I said to the Somali boy. "I'm a cop."

The boy looked confused. He was obviously having a hard time believing me. But finally he handed me the knife.

"And you two beat it!" I said to Pirinen and Väinölä.

"This is a fucking free country. We can stand at whatever bus stop we want. And we didn't do nothing. Asking for a smoke isn't a crime. He's the one who pulled the knife."

"Leave now unless you want to spend the night in jail," I said as I reached for my phone. I couldn't do anything to two men by myself, but the place was public enough that they wouldn't dare attack a police officer.

"Detective, I'm getting a little sick of you fucking with my business," Väinölä said menacingly. The spit landed two inches from the tips of my shoes. "Come on, Pirinen. Let's go get a beer."

"Where are you going?" I said, turning to the boy, who clearly would have liked to get away from me too, but didn't dare leave my protection.

"Home."

"Where?" I asked quickly. My own bus would be arriving any second, but I didn't want to leave the boy alone.

"Kivenlahti."

"When does the bus come?"

"Eighteen after."

"My bus is coming now! Come on. We'll go to the Tapiola transfer station. You can switch there."

The boy glanced at me, clearly suspicious, but he followed. Once aboard, I took a seat next to him on the bench reserved for senior citizens.

"What's your name?"

"Abdi." The boy stared at his shoes.

"I'm Maria. Why did you pull out that knife? You know that carrying something like that in a public place is a crime."

"They would have beat me up."

I didn't have much to say to that. Abdi would just buy a new knife tomorrow to replace the one I'd taken. Most of the Somali refugee kids only traveled in large groups, because they weren't safe if they were alone and in the wrong area.

We sat in silence for a few stops, and then I dug a card out of my wallet.

"I'm the boss of the Violent Crime Unit in the Espoo Police. If those two or anyone like them threatens you, call me instead of pulling a knife. Nobody ever wins a knife fight."

Abdi didn't answer, but he took my card before getting off at the transfer station. Not until that moment did I realize that Väinölä and Pirinen might be coming on the next bus and would see Abdi at the station. I probably should have paid for a taxi.

My trek home from the bus stop was a solitary one. Only a few cars drove by, and Abdi's knife weighed heavily in my pocket. I hadn't told him that I always carry a knife too. I had only had to use it once.

The night smelled of the memory of the sun and opening leaves. I couldn't help but flinch at the sound of the wind in the old trees that lined the road. My sleep was restless again, and I had a dream about skinheads and punks squaring off in a knife fight. Abdi and Petri Ilveskivi were there too.

9

The next morning I asked the duty officer if anyone had been attacked during the night. I was relieved when the answer was in the negative. I took Abdi's knife to the confiscated property locker, where it would stay until some indefinite point in the future. In the morning meeting, I again thought of Jani Väinölä, who was unlikely to be a free man for long. Väinölä was one of those people who needed enemies to know who he was. There seemed to be more people like that every day. Racists, anticommunists, EU opponents. Some friends had tried to convince Antti to run in the local elections, and we had spent a hilarious night coming up with ridiculous campaign slogans about opposing plastic bags and motorsports. Ultimately he decided not to run. I had been relieved because I already caught enough flack at work about Antti belonging to the Nature Conservancy, and the boys in Organized Crime always managed to stay surprisingly up to date on my husband's life. One of these days I was going to bribe somebody in IT to hack into the Organized Crime and State Intelligence databases to see what they were saying about my husband.

Except for the Ilveskivi case, everything was moving along nicely for the unit. Mela was pleased with himself because he had quickly solved the fight he had been investigating, and he imagined it was because of his brilliant police work. The case had been extremely simple, and Mela's partner, Lähde, had known the parties from a previous incident.

But I let the boy gloat, because in policing, success was never in excessive supply.

"I'm still trying to get in touch with Laura Laevuo," Wang said when I asked about how the Ilveskivi investigation was proceeding. It took me a few seconds before I remembered that Laevuo was the writer Kim Kajanus had said he was photographing at the time of Ilveskivi's attack.

"The DNA results from Ilveskivi's body should be in this afternoon," Koivu said. He sounded tired. "Maybe they'll tell us something."

I wondered how I could put some fight back in my unit when I was short on it myself. Just as the group was dispersing, my phone rang.

"This is Kallio," I responded, slipping into the hall away from the clinking of coffee cups and Lähde's heavy sighs.

"Hello, this is Suvi Seppälä. Have you caught up with Marko yet?"

"No, why?"

"Shit. Goddamn it." Suvi's voice cracked, and I heard a sob on the other end of the line. "Something isn't right. The neighbors said the cops have been coming by all the time to see if Marko is home."

"You still haven't heard from him?"

"No! And . . . he would kill me if he knew I was talking to the cops, but . . . he's never been gone this long before, at least not without telling me. And I lied: he isn't in Kotka."

"Are you at school now?"

"I'm on a smoke break. But I can leave if I need to."

"Can you come to the police station? Ask for me downstairs."

"I'll be right there," Suvi said and hung up the phone.

I noticed that my hands were shaking with excitement, and I rushed to Koivu's office to tell him about Suvi's call. We decided that three of us would question her: Koivu, Wang, and I. Suvi must have pushed her Datsun to its limits, because within fifteen minutes she was sitting in my office.

"So you want to change your story about what happened last Tuesday?" I said amiably.

"I know I don't have to testify against my husband." Suvi's sharp jaw rose defiantly, but fear shone in her heavily made-up eyes.

"That's correct, but the truth might help him. What happened Tuesday night?"

Suvi squirmed in her chair, her skinny limbs twisting in acrobatic positions. I gave her time, since she had volunteered to come.

"Of course you won't let me smoke, right?" she said.

"Go ahead. Koivu, will you go grab a cup from the break room to be used as an ashtray? Would you like some coffee?"

"No," Suvi said, and lit up. Koivu rolled his eyes as he left the room. I didn't like tobacco smoke, but sometimes you had to compromise a little to get what you wanted. Hopefully the smoke alarm in my office wasn't overly sensitive.

"I'm sure Marko is in some kind of deep shit," Suvi said after taking a few deep drags. Wang opened a window, and the noise of the Turku Highway came in. The exhaust fumes didn't improve the air much.

"He was on a high all weekend, drinking beer and bragging about how our life was about to change, that he had a big job coming up. I just kept quiet, because he's always dreaming about a job that will let us move to Majorca and never have to see rain or sleet again. He wants so badly for us to have the same things other people do. To buy new clothes for the kids instead of always going to the flea market . . . He said that if he could just get some capital, he could set up a motorcycle shop on Majorca. One of his friends went there and complained that there weren't enough good repair shops. Although I don't know how he was going to run the shop, since he's all thumbs. He's lucky if he can pound a nail into a wall! I had to weld the Datsun's tailpipe myself, since Marko couldn't figure out how."

Suvi sniffed, and a tear blackened by her eyeliner rolled down the side of her nose. "I knew there was never going to be a big job. Marko is a little like my mom, always dreaming of hitting the jackpot. Mom is always telling the kids she's going to buy them a nice TV and movies and a computer and all the games they could want when she wins the lottery."

"I've never heard of anyone whose big job came through," I said almost sympathetically. "Marko didn't happen to tell you what kind of a job it was, did he?"

"I don't usually ask. I've made him swear he wouldn't get mixed up in drugs. I don't want our children having anything to do with that crap. He has a reputation that he can be trusted with money, and I thought he might have some courier job. Maybe somebody killed him for that."

"Tell us what happened Tuesday. Was that when Marko was supposed to do this big job?"

"Yeah." Suvi twisted in her chair again, and I marveled at how she could move so easily in such tight jeans. "Like I said, he'd been talking about it all weekend, and he even took us to McDonald's and everything, since there was going to be money for once, and he bought the kids a video."

"Did Marko get an advance for the job?"

"No!" Suvi said intensely. "We . . . we have some savings." She lit another cigarette, and I saw a vein in her gaunt neck pulsate. She was lying. So where was the money Marko had been paid? If we could get our hands on a bill, we might be able to trace it by its serial numbers.

"I came home from school on Tuesday at the normal time and was surprised to find the kids home alone. Marko usually watches them. They said Dad had said he was going somewhere important that morning and that he would be home after six. When he finally did come home, he was beaten and bloody and frantic. He told me not to ask why and said everything would be fine, if he could just get ahold of someone. But he couldn't. Whoever it was wouldn't answer the phone. He left again at nine."

"You said Marko had blood on him. What was he wearing?" Koivu asked.

"Motorcycle gear."

"Which means?"

"Helmet, black leather jacket and pants, boots. Why do you ask? What's going on here? What do you think Marko did?"

"We must have forgotten to mention," I said, genuinely confused. "Last Tuesday a man named Petri Ilveskivi was beaten to death. A person riding a motorcycle and wearing black leathers was spotted at the scene."

"Oh, yeah, the fag," Suvi said. "Why would Marko do something like that? He didn't care about fags just so long as they weren't trying to get in his ass."

Then the cigarette stopped halfway to her mouth.

"Oh, fuck, are you telling me he took a hit job? He always said he was going to show everybody he wasn't just a small-time punk, but—"

"Where are Marko's leathers now?" Koivu asked, interrupting Suvi's raving. Suvi had started to cry again, and she shook her head.

"Murder . . . oh my God! That would be eight years at least! I'm done talking. You can't make me talk, and if you harass my kids, I'll send Social Services after you. It can't be good for my kids to have cops interrogating them . . ."

I stood up, grabbed a packet of tissues off a shelf, and handed it to Suvi. She blew her nose long and hard, leaving streaks of mascara on the tissue.

"So you got the impression that something went wrong with Marko's job?" I asked, ignoring Suvi's threat not to speak. Apparently the threat wasn't serious, because Suvi nodded and then blew her nose again.

"He'd really screwed up. He wouldn't tell me who he was meeting or where he was going, and he hasn't called in a week. He's never gone this long without calling. Even when he was in prison he called every other day. And none of his friends know where he is. I've talked to all of them."

"We have an APB out on Marko. We'll find him. You said he had blood on him when he came home. Was he injured?"

"There were scrapes on his face, and he was limping on his left leg. His ankle was swollen. Someone must have kicked him really hard to have gotten through his boots."

"So the blood wasn't his own?"

"His scrapes weren't that deep. Oh God, if he stabbed that fag . . ." Suvi lit another cigarette.

"Did he leave wearing the same clothes?"

"Yes. He always wears them when he's riding. He didn't even change his shirt."

"Did he clean up at all?" I asked hopefully. Maybe they still had a bloody towel somewhere in the house. But no, Suvi claimed that she hadn't found anything like that: if Marko used a towel when he cleaned his face, he had taken it with him.

Who would have paid Marko Seppälä to attack Ilveskivi? Could it have been Jani Väinölä? Had the heroin hidden in Väinölä's bathroom been meant to get money to pay Seppälä? Was Väinölä hiding Seppälä or had he gotten rid of him?

"Did you receive any phone calls from someone you didn't recognize before all this happened?"

"No! I don't know who Marko talked to when I was at school. Why didn't that idiot tell me? I never would have let him kill anyone!"

I tried to drag more information out of Suvi, but apparently she'd decided that Marko had attacked Ilveskivi and that was that.

"We'll file a missing-person report along with the APB."

Wang had recorded the conversation on the computer. If we didn't find any signs of Seppälä by Friday, we would put his picture in the paper and on TV. We would also need to shake Europol's tree—Marko Seppälä could have covered a lot of ground in a week.

Suvi Seppälä stood but hesitated at the door. Her nose was red, and she blew it again before opening the door. I decided now was the time to take the risk.

"Oh, and Suvi? If it turns out that Marko did receive an advance and didn't tell you about it, so it would be a surprise, and if you happen to find some bills, could you bring one in to us? I'm going to get a search warrant, which we'll probably execute tomorrow. You have a right to be present, and I can notify you before we come."

"I have to be at school. I'm going to be in enough trouble over this as it is."

"You can come when you're done. Four o'clock?"

Suvi nodded and then disappeared, the door banging behind her. For a moment it was quiet, and then my colleagues exploded.

"Goddamn it, Maria!" Koivu bellowed.

"You warned her!" Wang said in shock.

"Maybe. I don't know. Seppälä wouldn't have taken a job like this without an advance. Hopefully he left a little for his family."

"How do you know she isn't in on the plot?" Koivu asked angrily.

"A lifetime of experience," I said with a laugh. "Of course I can't be sure. You go search the house tomorrow. Bring back a toothbrush or something that might have Marko's DNA. All these tests are expensive, but it can't be helped. Didn't the lab promise the DNA results from the crime scene by today? Koivu, can you check if they're in? And Wang, you get in touch with Europol."

After my subordinates had left, I considered whether I had acted correctly with Suvi Seppälä. I probably should have pressed her harder. She was no angel, even though her criminal record was clean. I submitted the paperwork for the search warrant. Koivu stuck his head through the door and said the DNA results would be ready by afternoon. Wang popped in too.

"Laura Laevuo called. She confirmed that Kim Kajanus was with her when Ilveskivi was attacked. Her boyfriend can back her up, since he was with her for moral support. Laevuo said she hates cameras."

I had recently reinstated our unit's case partner system, because it seemed to work better than anything else we'd tried over the years. Wang and Koivu had been working together since before they'd started dating. They rarely showed their feelings publicly, so I didn't have any problem pairing them up. But what if they moved in together? We would have to talk about it, since I didn't think it would be good for their relationship if they were together all the time. On the other hand, Koivu and Wang were a good team. I usually assigned them to rapes and domestic violence cases because most rape victims preferred to talk to a female detective, and in domestic violence cases, the presence of a female cop usually helped calm down the wife and children. However, there were also people who were uncomfortable with Wang but more because of her ethnic background than her sex. She was still the only immigrant cop in the country. We were used to white Finns wearing police uniforms. In Finland we had the same clothing brands and furniture stores as everywhere else in the world because we didn't harbor any prejudices about the free movement of goods. Only of people.

I would have to talk to Wang and Koivu. Maybe Puustjärvi's calm, methodical personality would be a good fit for Wang. He preferred to keep quiet and let other people ask the questions. Puupponen and Koivu could be troublemakers at times, but they were basically good guys. Wang and I had trained most of the chauvinism out of Koivu.

After putting some last-minute final touches on my presentation, I went to the weight room for the one hour of PT a week my contract allowed. I kept my workout clothes in the closet in my office. At first the smell of sweat that clung to them was unpleasant, but the police station's basement weight room smelled just the same. I left my phone on, since Koivu would be calling about the DNA results any minute.

I spent fifteen minutes on a stationary bike to warm up, even though riding indoors had always struck me as ridiculous. If only there were a radio or a TV to turn on to keep my mind off of work. Instead, the weight room was quiet. A couple of guys from Patrol had been there doing their cooldown stretching when I arrived, but they were gone now. I moved on to leg press, loading something close to my body weight and then getting down to work. During the second set I remembered that I didn't have a clean shirt ready for the seminar the next day. I would have to do laundry that night.

I wasn't training systematically, and after working my legs I switched to abs. The punching bag was calling to me too, but I didn't have my gloves with me, and despite my requests, the only loaners were in men's sizes. So I did bench presses instead. I had to settle for small weights because I didn't have a spotter.

Then the door banged, and a short man entered—Ilkka Laine, the unit commander from Organized Crime. He was wearing the latest style of fitness attire. I looked down at my faded tights and holey Ramones T-shirt. Good running shoes and a proper bike helmet were about the only fitness equipment I was ever willing to spend money on.

"Hi, Kallio. Do I have the pleasure of being alone with you in here?" Laine feigned a flirty smile and started warming up.

"The underlings are working while the bosses are sweating in the gym," I answered lightly. Laine was in impeccable good shape, with muscles that showed he worked out regularly. His tight shirt revealed washboard abs, and his short black hair was spiked like a professional model.

"Not much weight on that bar. Are you afraid of bulking up? Those biceps are so big that I'd think you were doing 'roids if I didn't know what your job was," Laine said and moved behind me. "Women do tend to sag pretty quickly if they stop working out. What's your body fat percentage?"

"I haven't measured it." I banged the bar down on the rack. Suddenly exercising wasn't so fun.

"Let's put a little more on. I can spot you. Eighty kilos good?"

I hate people interfering with my workouts unless I've asked them for help. A few reps at eighty kilograms was about my limit, but I didn't bother saying so. I let him spot me and lifted the bar with ease.

"I hear you decided not to arrest a refugee who was waving a knife around yesterday," Laine said suddenly as I was pushing the bar up the second time.

"What do you mean?" I said, panting and dropping the bar to my chest a little too quickly.

"My neighbor was at the same bus stop. He told me that a short chick in a leather jacket showed up, claiming she was a cop. Based on the description, it couldn't have been anyone but you."

Laine kept a careful eye on my reps as they slowed, his face wearing simultaneous expressions of amusement and concentration.

"Are you sure that wasn't misconduct? Did you at least take the knife away from the nigger?"

I wasn't sure I was going to be able to rack the bar anymore. My pecs and shoulders were burning, full of lactic acid. If Laine decided not to spot me now after all . . .

Somehow I found the strength to rack the bar, every muscle in my arms shaking.

"Of course I took the knife away," I said, standing up a little too quickly. "Didn't this neighbor of yours inform you that two skinheads started it? And he slunk away, even though it was two grown men against a child."

I picked up my towel and dried my face.

"Do you really expect a civilian to intervene in a fight? Wouldn't that just make it worse?"

"It depends on the situation. I don't like the idea of children being threatened and adults just walking away. How would your neighbor have felt if someone got stabbed to death and he hadn't even tried to stop it?"

"Well, you certainly jumped in fast enough," Laine said mockingly and then grabbed a rope and started jumping. To my relief the door opened and a trainee from Patrol walked in. I spent a little more time on my abs, then my back and glutes. Laine, who didn't seem to have broken a sweat jumping rope, moved to the kickboxing bag. He obviously had some skill, his jabs and kicks quick and strong. I heard the puffs of air from the bag as each shoe or glove impacted it. When I started stretching out, I noticed Laine looking at me instead of the bag.

Sometimes when I was boxing I imagined the bag was someone I was angry at, and I could see blood and hear bones cracking. The target of my aggression had never been present, though.

Why did Laine wish that punching bag was me? I forced myself to take my time, and I exchanged a few words with the woman from the passport office when she came in. Then I left and took a quick shower. Today was my turn to pick up Iida, so I couldn't stay later than four thirty. Helvi, who operated the day-care center out of her home, started work at six fifteen when the first child arrived. The hourly wage for a private childcare worker like her wasn't great. Public day-care employees had strict instructions to call Child Protective Services if parents didn't show up on time, but private facilities were usually flexible. Once, when Antti was away on business, I had been forced to call Helvi and tell her that I wouldn't be able to make it before six, and then when the day got even longer, my mother-in-law had had to bail us out.

Koivu hadn't left me any information about the DNA test results, and I couldn't find them on the computer either. I knocked on his and Puupponen's office door, but only the latter was around, engrossed in something on his computer screen.

"Hey, have you seen Koivu?"

Puupponen jumped, and his face turned red. Was he looking at porn?

"He went with Wang to check on a stolen motorcycle in Helsinki. It might belong to the Ilveskivi killer," Puupponen replied, quickly clicking the mouse. He clearly wanted to close something before I saw what he had been looking at. Because I was not only curious but mischievous, I walked behind him, but he had managed to close the window in time.

"You caught the skateboard muggers, right? How is Mrs. Grönberg doing?"

"She got out of the hospital today. At most it's going to be a simple assault. Virtanen had a good tip on the perps, and Robbery is questioning them," Puupponen replied. "Have you ever heard of a drink called a 'bloody idiot'?"

"No. What is it?"

"Fernet Branca, tomato juice, and garlic."

"Ugh! When did you start drinking stuff like that?"

"I didn't . . . I was just thinking. A few nights ago me and the guys were trying to come up with the worst possible drinks," Puupponen replied. "So you don't think anyone has thought of that before?"

"It would take a pretty perverse imagination," I said dryly, and Puupponen smiled in satisfaction.

"I'll make you one when we catch that Seppälä guy," he said. "Doesn't all the evidence point to him?"

"Almost all of it," I said.

Because there was no sign of Koivu, I headed home. Spring's progress seemed to have stalled. The delicate stage where all the greenery was just emerging seemed to be going on for weeks. Buds were opening slowly, and the leaves were only growing half a millimeter a day. The wood anemone just kept coming, even though in most springs they were done blooming by Mother's Day. I didn't have anything against a long spring, just so long as it was followed by a real summer, not six months of generic Finnish rain and sleet and fifty-degree days and nights. Back when I was a kid, there had been one May Day that I had swum in a lake that still had ice chunks in it. I'd made fun of my older cousin because he didn't dare get in the water.

When I got to Iida's day care, the children were playing in the yard Helvi shared with her neighbors. One little guy in denim overalls sat in the middle of the sandbox, beating the ground happily with his shovel and yelling "bap, bap, baa!" which, in my experience, could mean almost anything. Iida's go-to word had been "kaa," and last Christmas she had explained that Santa Claus brought "bobettis." I was sad when she gave up her own words and started speaking the same language as the rest of us.

I spent a minute watching Iida play. She chatted with the wooden play horse and stroked its rope mane. Then she climbed on its back and took off at a gallop that I thought would separate the horse from its concrete base. Finally she noticed me and emergency braking ensued. Her face filled with joy and she rushed into my arms.

"Iida took a long nap today, like maybe she's coming down with something. The Sormunen children have both been sick," Helvi said.

Antti was going to be away all of Thursday and Friday on an important EU-funded research seminar. If Iida got sick, I would have to ask my mother-in-law for help. *If we had two children, the situation would be twice as difficult,* I thought as I prepared one of my classic dinners that evening, creamy carrot-cheese soup. Iida slurped down almost as much of it as Antti and I did. Just as I was considering a third bowl, Koivu called.

"The stolen motorcycle was a blind alley. It didn't have Metzelers, and the wheel size was wrong anyway. Did you get my message that the DNA on the cigarette butt and the hair on Ilveskivi's clothes was the same?"

10

The Safe City 2000 seminar was held at the Espoo Cultural Center.

I would never have predicted that nearly all of the auditorium's eight hundred seats would be full, and I had a moment of terror as I looked out over the audience in their dark suits and freshly shined shoes. Apparently almost all of them had come in their own cars, because Taskinen and I had to leave our car in the garage at a nearby shopping center. Luckily we had come early.

Koivu and Wang had gone with Forensics to the Seppälä house to execute the search warrant, which had been moved to the morning for scheduling reasons. Suvi hadn't been pleased about not being there, but Koivu was still muttering as he left about my intentional slip, which had given Suvi plenty of time to hide anything that might implicate Marko Seppälä. Koivu usually didn't criticize my methods, but in this instance he probably had good reason.

"Text me when you're done. I have to be at this damn seminar until lunch," I'd said to Koivu. I would have preferred to be at the search, but there was no way. Back when I was in the field, I never could have guessed just how much talking and schmoozing was required of a unit commander. I tried to get motivated by telling myself that words mattered, but when I looked out at the crowded auditorium, I wasn't so sure. These people were more interested in the security of commercial property than preventing street violence, and it was likely that most of them had never taken public transportation.

We had been instructed to go to the front of the auditorium to the places reserved for the speakers. Eila Honkavuori's black coiffure and purple velvet dress were visible a few rows back. She flinched when she saw me and didn't return my smile. I took my seat just as the mayor began his welcome speech.

The last time I had been in this auditorium was to hear the Tapiola Sinfonietta with Jorma Hynninen as Topi in Sallinen's *The Red Line*. As the mayor spoke, I remembered Hynninen's baritone. In the opera, Topi, a tenant farmer, worries that the pen required for marking his ballot during the first-ever election in Finland won't stay in his hand, deformed by hard labor as it is. Nowadays there were still people like Topi who doubted that there was any point dragging themselves to the voting booth, who had hands made useless by unemployment or fingers exhausted by twelve-hour days. And they had much more data than Topi did about what influence their vote had—which was exactly none.

The people sitting in this auditorium clapping sedately were sure to vote. For themselves or for the party that best represented their personal interests. The ideological fervor that drove people to participate in that first free election in Finland was in short supply these days. We still had plenty of small ideas like Jani Väinölä's neo-Nazism, but nothing as big as the original Green movement.

After the mayor, the traffic-planning manager spoke, and then it was Taskinen's turn. I admired his presentation style, through which he exuded the expertise and assertiveness that people expected from the police. His listeners seemed to agree about the importance of preventing drug crime, but in reality, these same decision makers were cutting funding for addiction treatment, and it wasn't like local businesses would step up to sponsor the rehab programs. Even though breaking the grip of addiction was hellishly difficult, every junkie who recovered saved society money because of all the crimes they didn't commit. That was something that the people who took their red pens to the budget rarely remembered. They thought it was more important to pass out free Viagra.

Taskinen also touched on security for commercial property, but his cynicism occasionally revealed itself as he ruminated on the sorts of background checks businesses should run on their job applicants. People had once doubted Taskinen's chances for advancing to the position he now held as head of the Criminal Division because of his membership to the Finland–Soviet Union Friendship Society in the seventies.

The only official police uniform that I had ever felt at home in had been the blue coveralls field officers wore. Taskinen looked good in his dress uniform, but mine was half drenched in sweat before I even got to the podium. I wanted my speech and the lunch to follow to be over as soon as possible. To me, the Seppälä search and Eriikka Rahnasto's interview were much more interesting.

My legs trembled as I stepped up to the podium. From the stage the audience looked very uniform. The men were well dressed and clean shaven, and the fifth of the audience that were women were all wearing suits, except for Eila Honkavuori and a couple of other outliers.

Given its population, Espoo was a peaceful city. I talked about the street violence the city did have, its causes and how to prevent it, and then about domestic violence. That made some of the audience stir restlessly: maybe they were getting hungry, or maybe the subject struck too close to home.

"Of course none of us wants to be a victim of crime, and in most cases the wisest course of action is to step away from a fight and call in the professionals. However, in one case I would make an exception. If a child is the target of violence, adults must intervene whether the perpetrators are other children or adults."

I related my experience from two nights before, just giving the facts, without commentary. When I ended, I stared at the audience for fifteen seconds like a stern schoolmistress before they realized that it was time to clap. Just as I was leaving the stage, a hand rose in the third row.

"May I ask a question?" I recognized the voice from the phone. It belonged to the chairman of the City Planning Commission, Reijo Rahnasto.

"I imagine we have time for one," the deputy major in charge of organizing the seminar said from the front row.

"Last week an elected official was beaten to death while he was on his way to a city meeting. How is the investigation going?"

Rahnasto didn't bother to introduce himself, apparently assuming that everyone knew who he was. He seemed younger than I had imagined from his voice, maybe forty, slim but broad-shouldered, with a strangely unremarkable face.

"The investigation is ongoing," I said. "As soon as there's anything new to report, you can be sure we'll hold a press conference. Any other questions?"

I saw Eila Honkavuori cover her face, and the man sitting next to her wrapped an arm around her. Rahnasto looked shocked. Maybe I had misjudged him. Maybe he hadn't called me to pressure me. Maybe he was simply mourning the death of a colleague and wanted the killer found. I didn't want to reveal the DNA results yet because we still didn't know the sex of the individual who had left hair on Ilveskivi's clothes and dropped the cigarette butt. I had asked the crime lab to continue testing, even though it cost more. I had hoped I could eliminate Eriikka Rahnasto from our list of suspects based on the DNA results, but unfortunately that hadn't happened yet.

No one else wanted to ask a question. Everyone seemed to be in a hurry to get to the buffet being served in the lobby. The throng was dense. Taskinen and I were happy to hang back and wait our turn, even though my stomach was complaining louder than the five-year-olds at Iida's day care.

"You did well," Taskinen whispered in my ear as he pulled me by the arm closer to the wall and himself. I pulled out my cell phone, but there weren't any messages from Koivu. Worst-case scenario, that meant the search hadn't turned up anything.

The crowd drove Eila Honkavuori over to us. The same man who had comforted her in the auditorium was holding her hand. They radiated togetherness. Turo Honkavuori had dark hair, a mustache, and black-rimmed glasses. He appeared delicate next to his buxom wife. In his corduroy trousers and dark-blue Marimekko striped shirt, he was one of the few men present who wasn't wearing a suit.

A man I didn't recognize came to talk to Taskinen, and Eila Honkavuori suddenly pulled her husband over to me.

"Thank you for your speech," Eila said and forced a smile. "I'm glad to hear you're making progress solving Petri's murder. He should have been here, not lying in the morgue."

I nodded. Turo Honkavuori and I introduced ourselves and shook hands. He smiled too, but only out of politeness. His handshake was brief and firm.

"Tommi said you were asking him again about them wanting to have a baby," Eila said. "Hopefully the investigation will be over soon so you won't have to keep harassing people who are still in mourning!"

I looked at her in surprise because when we last met, she had claimed that Turo hadn't known about her and Ilveskivi's plan to have a child together.

"Eila told me a couple of days ago," Turo Honkavuori rushed to explain. "We don't keep secrets from each other." He wrapped his arm around his wife's shoulders and looked at her adoringly.

"This isn't the right place for it, but I'd still like to talk to you about Petri's death," I said to Eila. "One of my detectives will be in touch later in the week."

Taskinen turned back to us. The food line had shortened, so we went to eat. Could I question Eila Honkavuori myself? I wanted to know two things. First, whether Petri had told her about Kim Kajanus. After all, Eila had been Petri's best friend. The second question would be easier to ask: If Seppälä had been paid to attack Petri Ilveskivi, who could be responsible for funding it?

The buffet table had lines on both sides, and Eila Honkavuori ended up across from me. I'd noticed that usually larger people, especially women, limited what they ate in public, as if they didn't have the right to indulge in the offerings like skinny people did. But Eila Honkavuori piled her plate just as high as I did. The fish was especially tempting.

"This definitely beats cafeteria food," I said to Taskinen, whose plate was mostly pasta salad.

"I've got a twenty-five K on my training plan for today. Have to carb up," he replied.

Taskinen had begun preparing for the Helsinki City Marathon as soon as the snow melted. He had joked about needing some kind of goal in his personal life now that he had advanced as far as he could in his career. Taskinen had already run a good twenty marathons and tried to lure me into it too, but I didn't have the nerve to commit. I could squeeze in a couple of hours of jogging every week, but that wasn't enough preparation for a marathon. During the summer when it was light at night I could go running, but somewhere at the back of my mind I was still afraid of empty paths where it would be easy for someone to surprise me and where no one would be around to help.

We found an empty table near a window. Outside, ducks swam in the pond, which was surrounded by grass that was tentatively greening. Wineglasses clinked all around us, but we drank mineral water. I was just about to ask Taskinen his opinion about Koivu and Wang being partners after they moved in together when I felt a tap on my shoulder. I dropped my knife in surprise.

"I'm sorry. I didn't mean to startle you," said a scratchy voice, and Reijo Rahnasto stepped into view. "Would you like me to get you a new knife?"

"Thank you, but I'll manage."

"Would you mind if I joined you? I'm Reijo Rahnasto, here representing the City Planning Commission and City Council. Thank you both for your speeches."

Rahnasto's handshake was firm and a touch too long.

"This business about Petri is horrible. I'm sorry I pressed you about it back there, but I'm just so upset about the whole thing. I'm glad to hear the investigation is progressing."

"Did you know Ilveskivi well?"

"Well, I've been on the City Council and the Planning Commission with him for almost an entire election cycle now. Hard not to get to know someone when you work together that much. Petri had a lot of enthusiasm and took our work seriously. Of course we had different opinions about some things. Petri didn't always understand the principles of contemporary urban planning, but our disagreements were only about ideas."

According to Eila Honkavuori, Rahnasto had once told some off-color jokes when Petri was late for their meeting. Maybe Rahnasto was one of those people who told bigoted jokes and then thought that anyone who didn't laugh was just uptight. Because of course they never meant anything by it.

"You called me a few days ago. Have you thought of anything since then that might help us find Petri Ilveskivi's killer?" I asked directly, since Rahnasto didn't seem to be here for small talk.

Rahnasto's brow furrowed. The wrinkles didn't make his face any older or more expressive. They were just furrows and then they were gone, like he was considering what my reaction would be before he said, "Maybe it had something to do with his sexual deviance."

Rahnasto's smile was cautious and not at all lewd. I tried not to show my irritation.

"What do you mean? As I understood it, Ilveskivi was in a healthy relationship."

"That's certainly what he wanted everyone to believe, but he was a man just like anyone." Rahnasto looked to Taskinen for support but failed to draw him into his "boys will be boys" argument.

On a whim, I asked, "Is Eriikka Rahnasto related to you?"

"Yes, she's my daughter from my first marriage. Why do you ask?"

"I just happened to run across her name. Your names are so unique that they stuck in my head," I said evasively. Eriikka was twenty-five, so Reijo Rahnasto had to be about ten years older than he appeared. The idea that Rahnasto had killed Ilveskivi on behalf of his daughter seemed like a stretch. That was more likely in a Verdi opera than in real life. Eriikka Rahnasto's plane would be landing in a couple of hours—I would need to make sure Koivu and Wang would be there to meet her. Or had the Seppälä search turned up something so definitive that we didn't need to question Eriikka Rahnasto anymore?

Why was I trying to protect Tommi Laitinen, Kim Kajanus, and Eriikka Rahnasto from the truth? When I was younger I would have wanted to know everything, because I believed that keeping secrets only deepened wounds. Now things were different, though. I never would have wanted Antti to find out, for example, how much I had liked Mikke Sjöberg.

The mayor came to exchange a few obligatory words with me and Taskinen, and Reijo Rahnasto took the opportunity to excuse himself. We all recited the lines that a mayor and police leadership are supposed to say to each other. Then we headed back to do what the people paid us for.

Summer dresses and graduation caps had started to appear in shop windows. As we walked to the parking garage to retrieve the car, my phone beeped. Koivu's text message said that the results of the search confirmed our suspicions about Marko Seppälä.

"So you think Seppälä killed Petri Ilveskivi?" Taskinen asked.

"Everything points that way, but we don't have a motive yet. We can't figure out if they even knew each other. But unless we find Seppälä, there isn't anything more we can do except wait for the DNA results."

"Things are going better for your unit than for Narcotics or Robbery. They only have time for their biggest cases right now. I wish we could get that Väinölä guy behind bars too, but apparently he's too small time for us to waste a bed on. Your unit will have to handle the Ilveskivi case on its own because after the wave of car break-ins last weekend, Robbery has their hands full, and then we have May Day next weekend." Taskinen sighed.

"May Day keeps us busy too, and if it turns out to be as cold as it looks like it's going to, people will stay home to fight. We'll have to see on Monday morning what the situation is. How is Silja's ankle doing?"

"She got the brace off yesterday, but she still needs to watch her jumps. Next week she's off to Canada again. We'll miss her, even though we're used to her being gone so much. But Silja seems to miss her Canadian boyfriend more than—whoa!"

Taskinen barely dodged the Volvo that had changed lanes without warning, its driver apparently forgetting to activate the turn signal. We were in Taskinen's work car, an unmarked Saab. Out of habit I took down the license plate number. Traffic Enforcement could check to see if the driver had any priors.

When I got back to my office, I found that Koivu had left a report about the search on my desk. It had been quick, and Marko Seppälä's toothbrush and some hairs from one of his shirts were on the way to the crime lab. No drugs had been found, but when they broke open Seppälä's locked toolbox, they discovered a couple of expensive-looking diamond rings and a necklace, all of which Koivu confiscated. A quick call had confirmed that they were likely jewelry stolen during a home robbery that had taken place in March.

Koivu had also confiscated some rifle bullets and a knife from the toolbox. The knife didn't have any obvious bloodstains, but it was on the way to the lab too. The team also collected a couple of unwashed shirts to give to the search dogs later if necessary. Seppälä's little black book was waiting in the evidence room. Even though Suvi had said that she had called all of her husband's friends, we would need to do the same.

In the report I also found a few photocopies. The first was of a photograph of Seppälä in his riding leathers, and then there was one with him working on his bike with a bald friend, who, despite the poor quality of the copy, was easy to recognize as Hannu Jarkola, one of the skinheads who had attacked Ilveskivi.

Here was the link between Seppälä and Väinölä! We hadn't really grilled Jarkola, so now would be the time.

Under the copies, there was a plastic bag with an envelope addressed to me, but the handwriting wasn't Koivu's. The script was small and angular, and "lieutenant" was misspelled. Koivu had put a yellow sticky note on the bag: "Wear gloves when you open this. Maybe it's what you were hoping for."

I took a pair of disposable gloves out of my drawer and opened the plastic bag. Then I thought for a second and called in our unit administrative assistant, Eija Hirvonen, to witness me opening the envelope. Eija looked surprised, but she didn't say anything. She had been at the station for twenty years, and although she was only in her forties, she acted like a kind of godmother to everyone who had been around a shorter time than she had.

Carefully I opened the envelope. Inside was a perfectly normal one-hundred-mark bill. Turning on my desk lamp, I examined the bill under the light. It looked genuine.

In the envelope there was also a note scribbled hastily on the back of a receipt: *Marko gave this to me for grocery money if it's any help. Suvi.*

I leaned back in my chair. Apparently sometimes it payed to bend the rules. I asked Eija to make a copy of the note and the serial number on the bill and then send the bill in for fingerprint analysis.

"I know you've already got too much on your plate, but could you go through the database to see if this matches up with a serial number from any recent bank robbery?"

Eija said she would handle it.

Even though all the evidence pointed to Seppälä, I couldn't dismiss the other possibilities. What if Reijo Rahnasto had borrowed his daughter's motorcycle? I looked up Rahnasto's information on the computer. He had been born in 1948 and he'd gone to engineering school, specializing in construction engineering. He had divorced Eriikka's mother in '86 and his second wife two years ago. Eriikka was his only child. Her plane was just now landing at the airport.

Puustjärvi came to ask for my advice on how to finish up an assault investigation and how to approach the prosecutor. After we'd spent half an hour considering the best way to proceed and poring over the laws on pretrial investigations, Koivu called.

"We've got a nice little situation here at the airport. Eriikka Rahnasto is refusing to come down to the police station. She's never heard of Petri Ilveskivi and doesn't see why she has to come in for questioning," Koivu said. "Will you issue an arrest warrant?"

"Let's take it easy. Where is Rahnasto now?"

"With Anu in the ladies' room," Koivu replied.

Koivu and Wang had arrived at the airport just before the connection from New York arrived. The airport personnel had directed them to the gate. Eriikka Rahnasto had been easy to identify from her name badge, and Koivu had introduced himself. To his surprise, Rahnasto was instantly indignant.

"I was starting to worry our message didn't go through because no one replied!" she'd said. "The troublemaker is with the steward and copilot on the plane. We didn't dare let him out of the handcuffs. And it looks like you have backup coming!"

When Koivu turned, he saw airport security approaching. Apparently eight hours without a cigarette had been too much for the passenger, and even though the flight attendants had offered him nicotine gum, he had declined their help and chosen to down a few beers instead. He'd been handcuffed after hitting Rahnasto because she'd refused to serve him any more alcohol.

Koivu and Wang had let Rahnasto explain the situation to the airport police and then pulled her aside. Eriikka Rahnasto was exhausted from the unusually difficult flight. Apparently her training had gotten her through her run-in with the drunk passenger, but the idea of being questioned by the police after all that was just too much.

"Ask permission to take plaster casts of her motorcycle tires and say that we'll get back to her tomorrow," I said to Koivu. "Then look into how much money she and her father, Reijo Rahnasto, both make. I'm going to put Puustjärvi and Puupponen on Väinölä again because we just discovered that he has friends in common with Seppälä."

Since I had dealt with Suvi Seppälä and survived my presentation, I decided to go home a little early. For once I had time in the grocery store to choose the best tomatoes and then consider whether to buy chives or basil. Marko Seppälä's DNA results wouldn't be in until after May Day. Acting quickly was often crucial in policing, and it also fit my impatient nature, but sometimes you also had to know when to let things be.

At home in the yard, Iida and I admired the first crocuses. Every spring they tenaciously pushed up through the dead grass. We helped them along a little and then went inside to make dinner. Iida wanted to help. She was thrilled to get to rip the basil leaves into the salad bowl.

As the chicken casserole was cooking in the oven, I lay on the bed with Iida and read to her from a picture book. Einstein showed up to listen too, jumping up next to me on the pillow. I would have liked to lie there between daughter and cat forever, but hunger forced me out of bed.

"Let's go to Villa Elfvik to watch the ornithologists," Antti suggested after dinner. "I heard that tonight there should be some good migrations. Let's at least go to smell the spring air and see the ice on the bay breaking up."

"What are the snacks going to be?" Iida asked hopefully. She had already learned that the high point of any nature excursion was the snack break. In the cupboard we found chocolate cookies and my secret *salmiakki* salty licorice stash. My emergency supply at work was completely out, so I would have to stop by the candy shop soon.

The weather was bright and cold, so I put Iida in her winter overalls. Winter cress bloomed on the shoulders of the road like hundreds of four-petal suns. At Villa Elfvik we traded our sneakers for rubber boots, and Antti pulled the binoculars out of his backpack.

"Have to blend in," he said.

"I've never noticed you caring about that before. Look, Iida, that's the building where Daddy and I got married," I said, pointing at the Jugend-style villa. Five and a half years had passed since our wedding, and the time had gone frighteningly fast. Only during maternity leave had the days seemed to stretch like chewing gum, but when I was at work they sped past, sometimes leaving me wondering what day of the week it was.

"When can I go there?" Iida asked, staring in wonder at the horse statue in the yard. "Do you ride a horsey there?"

"Where?" I asked and lifted her onto the back of the statue, since that was why it was there.

"When we go get married."

Antti explained patiently what being married meant while I enjoyed the quiet of the villa grounds and the smells of the wetlands. Memories of our wedding made me like this place even more. It was one of the city's oases, even though the combined noise of the two nearby highways did detract from the effect.

Birds and ornithologists flocked along the shoreline. I looked in interest at the latest trends in cameras, spotting scopes, and outdoor clothing. Antti tried to teach Iida how to look at the world through the binoculars while I focused on the spectrum of greens and browns, the feathered violet tassels of the knapweed and the ruddy willow branches that you never notice in the summer because of all the leaves. I liked the rainbow of colors in a leafless willow stand, almost as fantastic as the colors of autumn.

Suddenly from the southern sky came an excited honking, and I learned what Antti's bird-crazy coworker had meant by good migrations. There were at least fifty geese, all organized in a perfect wedge with a smaller wedge on one side. Last fall I had waved to the departing geese with Iida and practically begged the wagtails to stay. The geese were already back, and we wouldn't have to wait long after May Day for the wagtails to be fanning their tails and teasing Einstein. The bird-watchers pointed their scopes at the skein of geese, but I waved and Iida joined in with a serious look on her face.

We circled the cane grass to the north until we came to a peaceful meadow with patches of blue-and-white anemones on the shore. A fascinating collection of dwellings surrounded the meadow: little huts built from branches and grass, apparently left over from the previous summer's play. Iida was so enchanted by the little huts that she demanded to inspect each one and then eat her snack in the one that seemed most fun.

"Let's hide in that one back there while Iida's busy with her chocolate cookies," Antti whispered as he pulled me into his arms. We slipped into the stick hideaway to make out, giggling like teenagers who had snuck away from a school field trip. Just as I was getting to Antti's zipper, Iida realized that her parents had disappeared, and that was the end of that. Iida's face was so sticky that we had to wash it in the frigid seawater. All the cookies had tasted just right.

As if to make up for interrupting us, Iida fell asleep in her bike seat and didn't even wake up while I undressed her for bed. The chocolate cookies would have to do as her bedtime snack, but the adults would indulge in each other. Before falling asleep, I wondered if making love would feel different if the goal was to create a new child.

11

The next morning the sky was spitting sleet, and even though a cop should have been happy about the turn in the weather just before a major drinking holiday, I grumbled all the way to the station. Koivu was uncharacteristically irritable in the morning meeting, stating that we should drop all our other lines of inquiry on the Ilveskivi case unless the DNA test results ruled out Marko Seppälä. So far the serial number on the bill hadn't turned up anything. Maybe Suvi had just given us part of her change from the corner store or maybe the advance Seppälä received was legally earned money. How much did it cost to have somebody taken out? A few thousand marks would have been enough for Seppälä if there was a promise of more once the job was done.

But had someone really paid Seppälä to kill Ilveskivi? Had the Rahnastos wanted to take revenge on Ilveskivi for seducing Kim? Both the father and the daughter had the money. Reijo Rahnasto was the CEO and majority shareholder in a company that made security systems. The company's market value was tens of millions of marks. Eriikka had earned a degree in tourism before landing a job as a flight attendant. She hadn't taken out any student loans and had bought herself an apartment with money inherited from an aunt. Eija Hirvonen had an astonishing ability to get her hands on theoretically secret information. I was afraid White Collar Crime would notice her talents and steal her away from us.

My answering machine said I had four new messages, and I was just deleting them when the phone rang. I barely managed to say my name before an angry male voice launched into me.

"Why the hell are you harassing Eriikka? What have you told her?"

"Good morning, Kim," I replied dryly. "We aren't harassing Eriikka. We're simply conducting a routine investigation of everyone who owns a motorcycle with Metzeler ME 99 tires. You didn't mention that Eriikka owns a motorbike."

"I didn't think it mattered. Eriikka didn't even know about me and Petri! You aren't going to tell her that . . ."

"Maybe that won't be necessary, if you cooperate more fully. Does Eriikka smoke?"

"Sometimes, when she's partying or maybe if she's nervous. A flight attendant can't have a nicotine addiction."

"I would think not. Now, take it easy, Kim. Our only goal is to eliminate Eriikka from our list of potential suspects. If she can explain to our satisfaction what she was doing when Ilveskivi was killed, we won't bother her anymore. I believe Sergeant Koivu has an appointment scheduled with her today."

"Eriikka said she was meeting with a detective at eleven, so she's probably on her way there. Someone already came and took a cast of her motorcycle tire. It wasn't even eight yet! Why do you even suspect Eriikka? I saw her the same night Petri died. She had a couple of days off, and we spent them together. She wasn't acting like someone who had just stabbed a person to death. I don't understand this. I told you private information to help with Petri's murder investigation, and now you're going to screw up my entire life!" Kim Kajanus said, then hung up. Cell phones weren't as dramatic as landlines because you couldn't slam the receiver down the same way you could with an old-fashioned phone. I considered calling back, but just then Koivu entered my office without knocking.

"Eriikka Rahnasto will be here in fifteen minutes. Do you want to sit in?"

"I think you and Wang can handle it without me."

"A third party would be useful," Koivu said, and I realized that the investigation wasn't the only thing responsible for his bad mood.

"You guys having a tiff?"

"It's the marriage thing again. I don't understand why it's so important."

"But you're still moving in together?"

"The apartment is good, but Anu's principles are getting in the way." Koivu spread his arms, looking miserable. He then blushed. "You wouldn't talk to her, would you?"

"To Anu? Uh, no. And besides, I'm the wrong person to talk about not getting married, since my marriage is so happy." I still felt a pleasant pain in my abductors from last night, and I knew there were bite marks on my right shoulder.

"This week," Koivu said huffily and then apologized immediately. I agreed to help with Eriikka Rahnasto's interrogation only because I was curious. Koivu had reserved Interrogation Room 2. As I walked there, I realized I needed to get moving on assigning them new partners.

Wang escorted Rahnasto into the interrogation room. Eriikka resembled her father, but what was forgettable and expressionless about his face created a pleasing symmetry in hers. Her gray-blue eyes were set just the right distance apart, her nose was delicate, and her cheekbones were high. Those she must have inherited from her mother. Her cotton pantsuit was at once casual and stylish. Apparently Eriikka had come by some other mode of transportation than her motorcycle. Her straight blond hair was fastened at her neck. When she heard my rank, her carefully plucked eyebrows went up.

Eriikka Rahnasto gave her personal information politely but impatiently. Koivu explained the situation to her again and told her that she was being interviewed as a witness, not as a suspect.

"I've never heard of Petri Ilveskivi," Eriikka said, and nothing we knew contradicted that.

"Are you sure? He was a highly visible local politician and served on a committee with your father."

"I've never been interested in politics. I probably developed an allergy to it, since my dad was never home because of it. I don't even know what committees he's sitting on these days."

Eriikka Rahnasto lived in Helsinki and therefore would have no reason to follow Espoo politics. I had lived a couple of blocks from her apartment at one time, and every now and then a certain nostalgia for the place bubbled to the surface. And even I didn't know the name of the chairman of the Espoo City Council right now, let alone all the other members.

"I would have thought that in a country like Finland, the police wouldn't drag people in for questioning just because they own a certain kind of motorcycle tire," Rahnasto continued. Her voice was low and carefully trained, with the simultaneously warm and impersonal tone of a flight attendant. "Couldn't we have handled this over the phone?"

"You would have had to come in to sign the interview record anyway," Wang replied calmly. "Tell us, what were you doing last week on Tuesday, the twenty-second of April?"

Eriikka Rahnasto looked from Wang to Koivu to me, and then bent down to get her calendar out of her purse.

"Last Tuesday . . . in the morning I flew in from London. I'd spent all Monday flying back and forth between there and Helsinki. Wait a second . . . I don't have anything on my calendar. But I probably slept in, did my laundry, went to the gym. Stuff like that. In the evening I met my boyfriend, Kim Kajanus. We had a dinner date at seven. Someone at the restaurant might remember us. We go there pretty often. Kim even had an exhibition there once. He's a photographer. We had dinner and then went to Kim's apartment, and I was there for the next couple of days. Is that sufficient?"

"So you don't have anyone who can confirm where you were between five and six?" Wang asked.

"I don't even remember what I was doing then! When I'm at work, everything is planned to the minute, so on my days off I hardly ever look at the clock. Maybe I was at aerobics. Maybe I was riding my motorcycle . . . which of course is exactly what you want to hear. This is absurd. Why would I have beaten someone I don't even know?"

"Just think back," Wang said calmly. "We have time. Do you keep a diary?"

Eriikka Rahnasto shrugged.

"Why would I? I really don't remember. I can think about it, though, and maybe my boyfriend will have some idea what I was doing. Or . . . wait."

Eriikka flipped back in her calendar, then forward, and nodded to herself.

"I must have been at the gym on that Tuesday from four to five thirty. I try to go to a class at least three times a week, and I didn't have time on Sunday or Monday, so I must have gone on Tuesday. I can't swear to that, but maybe someone there will remember seeing me."

"Are your visits recorded anywhere?"

"I have a monthly pass to the Adlon just off the square near my apartment. That's all I can tell you, though. I don't particularly like the idea of you going to my gym and making everyone think I'm suspected of murdering someone, but I can't stop you either. My father told me to get a lawyer, but why would I need one?"

"You probably don't. Thank you for your cooperation. Please call if you happen to remember anything more specific about that Tuesday. Our forensic team says the imprint of your tires is good, so we won't need to do that again. That should be enough to eliminate your motorcycle," Wang said and then escorted Eriikka Rahnasto back to the lobby.

Koivu sighed. "Poor girl," he said as we walked back to our offices. "Should we have told her?"

"It isn't any of our business. Could you come to my office for a minute? I'll go put a note on Wang's door, because I need to see her too."

Koivu went to get coffee for himself and Wang, while I stuck to water.

"Pretty strange situation," Wang said as she walked in. Koivu was sprawled on the couch, but she took one of the armchairs instead of sitting next to him. "I almost hoped that the tire prints and DNA would knock Eriikka Rahnasto off our list."

"She isn't the first woman with a boyfriend who cheated on her," I said lightly because I wanted to move on to discussing the unit-partner situation.

"Do you think it's somehow more acceptable to cheat on a girlfriend with another man than with another woman?" Koivu asked acerbically.

"No, but if Kajanus is bi—"

"He can't help it, is that it?" Koivu said, interrupting me. "Sometimes it feels like you have this idea that gays and lesbians are somehow better people than us heteros, as if there was something special about being a minority—"

"There isn't anything special about it. I think we all know that by now," Wang said, interrupting in turn. "At least Kajanus's and Rahnasto's alibis seem to match up. Should we go to her gym and the restaurant to check?"

"Let's wait for the lab results," I said. "I'm still betting on Seppälä, but that wasn't what I wanted to talk to you two about. I have a question for you: Do you feel like it's a good idea to keep working as partners after you've moved in together?"

Wang stood up angrily.

"Who says we're moving in together?"

"I was under the impression that you'd looked at an apartment," I responded patiently, even though I was feeling like I had had just about enough of this situation. Usually Koivu and Wang were the kinds of coworkers who gave me strength rather than sapping it. If I didn't have people like that around me, this line of work would be impossible.

Koivu didn't look at me or Wang, instead focusing on cleaning his glasses with a paper tissue that seemed to be doing more smearing than polishing. Wang looked me in the eye and said, "You probably know that Pekka and I disagree about moving in together without getting married."

"I don't want to get involved, other than to say that if you're going to live together, you shouldn't also work together. Even if your relationship hasn't interfered with your work up to this point . . ."

"Oh, hasn't it?" Koivu said. "That interview just now went to shit because we were both just thinking how we would feel in the same situation. We slept maybe an hour last night because we were up rehashing this. You can bet your ass it's affecting our work!" Koivu closed his eyes, and he really did look like he could fall asleep right there on the couch. Wang pursed her lips and looked at me as if to say we should just ignore him because he was being an idiot.

"We'll stick to the way things are for now, but think about it. If you decide to move in together, maybe we could pair Wang with Puustjärvi and Koivu with Puupponen. Or would it be better the other way around? Puupponen has been here almost eight years, but Puustjärvi hasn't been here much longer than you, Wang."

"I'd go crazy if I had to listen to Puupponen's corny jokes all day long," Wang said. "Let's go, Pekka."

"Kallio, have you thought about getting a wiretap warrant for Seppälä's phone?" Koivu muttered, his eyes still closed. "Sooner or later he's going to call his wife."

"Let's wait for the test results. If the Huovinen case file is ready for the prosecutor, go home and get some sleep. Both of you have at least twenty hours of overtime already, and next week we're going to have the joys of May Day to deal with."

Wang and Koivu left me to wonder whether I was running a couples' therapy clinic or a violent crime unit, and whether I was any good at leading anything at all. The police academy had requested a preliminary evaluation of Mela's field training, which I would have to write up with Lähde. The light on my answering machine was blinking insistently, so I pressed the button to listen. The first message was from Kirsti Jensen:

> *Tommi Laitinen isn't coming to our May Day party. He can't stand the idea of being around drunk people, so you can go ahead and come. I tried to call Antti but couldn't reach him. Anyway, see you tomorrow!*

After a beep came the next message.

> *Hello, this is Reijo Rahnasto. I was appalled to hear that you're wasting taxpayer money questioning innocent people like my daughter. Were your assurances that the Ilveskivi investigation is proceeding just a lie? I'd like an explanation for this double-dealing. Call me.*

The he rattled off his work number. After another beep I heard Rahnasto's voice again:

> *This is Reijo Rahnasto again. I expect to hear from you as soon as possible.*

I sneered at the answering machine. Luckily the final message was calmer:

> *Hi, it's Jyrki. I know you're in an interview. What's the deal with questioning Rahnasto's daughter? I just got an angry call from Rahnasto complaining that you weren't returning his calls. Call me before you call him.*

There was a knock at my door, and for a second I was sure it was Rahnasto, come to skin me alive. I must have looked relieved when Eija Hirvonen walked in. She was bringing the new DNA results that had just been faxed over.

"I think you were waiting for these," Eija said, misinterpreting my expression.

"Yes. Would you please get in touch with the switchboard and ask them not to connect any calls to me for the next hour? I'm going to have a meeting with myself."

Eija laughed and disappeared into the hallway. The DNA report was the usual indecipherable laboratory jargon, but at least one thing was clear: the cells under Ilveskivi's fingernails had both X and Y chromosomes. So the attacker had been a man. We would have wait for Monday to get Seppälä's DNA results.

Taskinen's office was on the top floor. I didn't bother to check that he was in before jogging up the stairs and ringing his buzzer. The green light illuminated immediately, and I was glad to find him alone in his office.

"Thanks for coming," he said tiredly. "The chairman of the City Planning Commission called me half an hour ago to complain about you. He was totally pissed off. Why did you question his daughter?"

"Rahnasto definitely doesn't want to hear the real reason." Then I sat down and told Taskinen about Kim Kajanus and his affair with Ilveskivi. Taskinen seemed to become more and more uneasy as I spoke, and he ran his slender fingers through his graying blond hair.

"So the DNA test eliminated Eriikka Rahnasto?" asked Taskinen.

"Exactly, assuming that the skin cells under Ilveskivi's fingernails were from the attack and not some passionate sexual encounter," I said.

"And what if Rahnasto knew about the relationship between Ilveskivi and his potential son-in-law, even though his daughter didn't? That would explain his interest in the case."

"Too melodramatic."

"I didn't mean that he attacked Ilveskivi or ordered the attack, but what if he knew?" Taskinen asked.

"I don't see why that would matter to us. I'll call him and tell him how many motorcycles we've looked into, but before that I need some food. Would it be too much pampering for you to go to lunch with me two days in a row?" I asked.

"Far too much. Shall we go now?"

The spicy veggie casserole and a little flirtation perked me right up, so when I got back to my office, I had the energy to dial Rahnasto's number. His assistant answered; Rahnasto was still at lunch. I got his cell number, but his phone was off. So I resorted to the second most common form of communication in Finland after text messaging—leaving a voice mail.

At two I had a meeting with a district prosecutor, having promised to give statements on two restraining-order cases. Katri Reponen had been my tutor in law school, and I was delighted when she had moved over to the Espoo circuit court prosecutor's office. The meeting went long, since we kept taking detours. Working with friends wasn't without its problems, but with Katri I didn't have any conflicts of interest or differences of opinion.

Since she had come to Espoo, violent crime sentences had stiffened. And she was especially intense about rapes and domestic violence cases. Some male colleagues claimed that Katri's law books were missing the entire concept of "mild rape," but I thought she was more right than the majority of Parliament.

My phone rang just as we were finishing, and I steeled myself to hear Reijo Rahnasto's scratchy voice. But the caller was Eriikka Rahnasto.

"I tried to reach the other detectives, but neither of them were around. I just wanted to say that I really was at aerobics last Tuesday. The instructor remembers me being there. And now I'm handing the phone to my boyfriend. He can tell you I was with him for the rest of the night."

The phone crackled a bit, and then an agitated voice said, "Hello, this is Kim Kajanus. I'm Eriikka's boyfriend. Eriikka was with me at dinner on the night you're asking about. And we have other witnesses."

"Thank you. That clears things up. We won't need to bother your girlfriend anymore," I said seriously, hoping that Kim understood what I was saying. I wanted to laugh, or at least kick a chair, but work was work.

The plaster-cast analysis came back the next day. It erased Eriikka Rahnasto from our list of suspects once and for all, because her motorcycle tires were ten millimeters too wide. Based on the patterns, the forensic technicians had been able to determine that the Metzeler ME 99 tire in question was the 120-millimeter model. So now we had exactly one name on our list. Since I had forgotten to ask Katri about it, I spent some time reviewing the relevant laws on wiretapping. I hoped that the holiday would drive Seppälä back to his family. Too bad we hadn't been able to spare anyone to surveil their house 24/7. And Patrol definitely wasn't going to have any extra hands over May Day.

Koivu and Wang went to question Hannu Jarkola, who was already drunk by ten a.m. in honor of the holiday and managed to act stupider than he usually did. Yes, he was friends with Marko Seppälä and Jani Väinölä, but he didn't have a clue whether the two knew each other.

We considered whether we should bring him in to dry out, but thankfully Koivu was in a more relaxed mood than he had been yesterday. Ultimately Koivu decided to let him be. "We can visit him again on Monday if we need to. By then he'll be hung over and might talk just to get rid of us."

The temperature had fallen overnight to almost freezing, and the sleet was only coming down more as I left work. I drove to the liquor store to buy champagne. I had thought the worst rush would be around five and that by now people would be at home getting dressed for their parties, but I was wrong. The checkout lines wound down the aisles, and over the whiskey shelf I happened to spot Kim Kajanus's ruddy brown curls. I glanced around to make sure the coast was clear: no sign of Eriikka Rahnasto.

"Hi, Kim!" I said.

He nearly dropped his bottle of cognac when he saw me.

Just then the line started moving, so Kim yelled, "Can you wait outside? I have something to tell you!"

Antti had gone to pick up Iida, so I wasn't in any rush. I waited outside with all the teenagers and winos who usually sat outside no matter the weather. Ten minutes later, Kim came out with his shopping bag clinking cheerily, but his face was downcast.

"Thanks for yesterday," he said. "What did you mean when you said that you wouldn't be bothering Eriikka anymore?"

When I told him, his face relaxed. I guess I hadn't realized how strongly he suspected her.

"Now that you've said that, I'm starting to feel like I might actually be able to celebrate tonight," he said, attempting a smile. "I'm afraid to drink in case I let something slip, and I'm afraid not to drink because I feel so bad sober."

I felt like saying I knew the feeling, but I didn't. Kim's car was in the same parking structure as mine, so we walked together, talking about our plans for the night. Near a bowling alley we ran into Eila Honkavuori. I sensed Kim tense next to me. Apparently he knew that Eila and Petri had been best friends, but Eila only said hello to me. She did glance at Kim curiously, as anyone would who understood something about male beauty.

"Do you know anything about Petri's funeral?" Kim asked as we were climbing the stairs to the top floor.

"His body has been released, and I believe the services are scheduled for next Saturday."

That would be a good deadline for solving the case. All we would need was the DNA to be Seppälä's and for him to confess.

"Maybe I'll have my own funeral for him," Kim said and then feebly wished me a happy May Day. On the way home, a group of kids carrying shopping bags full of beer bottles stumbled down the middle of the road, and the tires of the Saab in front of me squealed as it braked to avoid hitting them. The only response to the ensuing honking were raised middle fingers. Hopefully none of them would end up with hypothermia.

There would be about thirty people at the Jensens' party, partial acquaintances and strangers, adults and children. I affixed an old "Anarchy in the UK" pin onto my white-and-black student cap and wriggled into my old leather miniskirt. Laine from Organized Crime was the lieutenant on duty for the holiday, so I figured I could forget my phone and my cares. I did my makeup completely differently from how I wore it to work, and I mixed myself a stiff anise vodka to get myself in the partying mood. Iida had a new flowery party dress and fairy clips in her dark curls.

We had planned to ride to the Jensens', but Lauri called and offered to pick us up.

"If you can't get a taxi, you can just stay the night," he said cheerfully. We decided to take a risk and left our toothbrushes home.

"I'm going to ask this now and then shut up about it for the rest of the night," Lauri said just before we arrived at the party. "Is there anything new about Petri?"

I said that we were 80 percent sure we knew who the killer was. Lauri had agreed to act as a pallbearer. Petri Ilveskivi's mother had asked Tommi Laitinen to be the head pallbearer and to choose the others. That much Petri's father had been willing to budge.

The Jensens' four children had decorated the porch. The colorful balloons and streamers provided a nice contrast to the gray sleet outside. The porch had been designated as the smoking lounge, and Antti warned me that I was likely to have a man that tasted like cigars in my bed that night. He rarely smoked, but Kirsti Jensen, who was a cigar enthusiast, had succeeded in drawing Antti in.

The children were sent over to Lauri and Jukka's side of the house, where the golden retrievers were playing babysitter. The stereo was blaring music appropriate to the occasion, currently a choir of Young Pioneers praising "Uncle" Lenin. I staked out a spot next to the snack table. A thirty-something guy who looked like a bodybuilder came over to pilfer the pistachios and stopped to talk to me about the current state of Finnish rock music. He was a former semiprofessional musician who had toured some with his band in the late eighties and worked for a record company without much success.

Even though I had decided to get only mildly drunk, my punch glass always seemed empty. Juuso, the musician, stuck to my side, even though he must have noticed my ring and surely realized that Antti was my husband. We succeeded in getting into a heated argument over Popeda, who some called the Finnish Rolling Stones. Juuso claimed he had never met an adult woman who liked the band in question.

"You must hang out with the wrong women," I said with a laugh.

"Apparently my friends are too highbrow. By the way, what do you do for work?" Juuso said, sitting down casually on the arm of my chair. His aftershave smelled of bergamot and leather.

"I'm a cop."

"For real?" My conversation partner was visibly shocked. "What kind of cop?"

"A detective lieutenant. Head of the Espoo Violent Crime Unit."

Juuso looked at me for a few seconds, and then a smile formed on his angular face. "You almost had me there. What do you really do?"

"I'm not kidding. Ask the Jensens."

Juuso stood up and placed himself before me as if to challenge.

"So you're a police big shot. Do you enjoy putting men in hand-cuffs or something?"

"I don't really get a chance to do that much these days," I replied, but without the flirtatious tone I had been using. When Juuso started prying about what cases I was working on, I was done. The last thing I wanted to do was talk about work. Fortunately, just at that moment I heard Iida crying in the kids' room and was able to slip away.

Iida wasn't in any danger. Her disagreement with Kerkko Jensen had only been momentary. Juri, who was nine, was playing teacher to the smaller children, and Iida was diligently studying her letters. Another guest was nursing in Kanerva Jensen's room, and a melancholy feeling came over me as I listened to the gentle suckling sounds and caught a whiff of mother's milk.

"Here you are. I was starting to think you'd run off with that musician," Antti said and then wrapped his arms around me from behind.

"I don't want to run off with anyone."

"Not even with me downstairs to the sauna? There's a lock on the door." Antti laughed, and there was more in his eyes than his buzz. We stumbled down the stairs, locked the sauna door behind us, and went at it. I remembered the time in school when a boy named Kristian and I had blocked the door to the student union's club room with chairs, and our contract law adjunct professor had tried in vain to get in to retrieve his wallet. Taking off Antti's shirt, I inspected the valley between his chest muscles, the trail of hair leading down from his belly button, and the rise of his back that led to his buttocks. My nipples hardened, waiting to be touched, as my mouth moved over Antti's skin, eventually taking in his flushed penis. Finally I pushed Antti to the floor and got on top of him, then watched the changing expressions on my beloved's face, the twisting of his mouth and the fluttering of his eyelids, his obliviousness to the existence of anything else in the world.

Giggling, we rejoined the party, and Eva cast us an amused glance. Apparently she had noticed our absence. But after a second her attention turned—it was time to pop the champagne. Drinking it washed the taste of Antti from my lips, but I knew I could taste him again any time I wanted.

We spent almost no time together the rest of the night, but the memory of making love hovered between us the whole time. We didn't even need to touch each other. Knowing was enough. The sleet had finally let up by the time the party started to wind down, and we took a taxi home around midnight, drunk on wine, good company, and each other.

On the Sunday after May Day, we went on an outing to Central Park. The weather was warmer again, and a darting fly buzzed along the sunny hillside while the first stiffly moving ants plodded along the border of their hill. The grass was still a bit wild, but it had dried out enough that we could sit without having to worry about getting wet.

Lilies of the valley rose from the ground in tight brown rolls, a small green tip protruding from the end of each. They stood on the south-facing hillside like a company of tiny brave soldiers. One more week and their tightly wrapped leaves would start to unfurl. The swordlike leaves would relax and reveal the slumbering, fragrant strings of bells inside. Antti and I picked some leaves and tickled each other with them while Iida watched a lesser spotted woodpecker raising a riot in a nearby dead tree. But she got bored when the overgrown coltsfoot wouldn't bend enough for her to weave a garland. At home in the yard, Einstein was waiting proudly to display an emaciated field mouse he had caught.

On Monday I had no interest in going to work. However, our case list was shorter than I had feared: one beating, one attempted rape, and one fight in a taxi line. Delegating them was no trouble. Lähde and I were filling out Mela's training evaluation paperwork when my phone rang.

"Hi, this is Liisa Rasilainen. Hopefully you've had time to recover from the weekend, because I've got a job for you. Someone just found a body at the dump out on the E18."

12

I ordered Lähde and Mela to come with me to the landfill, since the others were busy with their own cases. Forensics had already left, so we took my car. It was faster than taking one of the Soviet-made Ladas that the department was still issuing from the motor pool. Mela insisted on driving. He was clearly excited by the acceleration of my Saab, which was only a couple of years old, and pushed it into high gear once we got out to the Turku Highway.

Rasilainen's patrol car had been nearby when the call had come in from the dump. The crew whose job it was to spread dirt and form the hillside along the outer slope of the landfill had noticed a foot sticking out of the trash heap. According to Rasilainen, all that was visible was a size-seven boot. Based on the shoe size, it could just as easily belong to a small man or a woman.

"Have you ever seen a corpse?" Lähde asked Mela as we approached the dump.

"Yes, I have," Mela replied and sped up again as though in a hurry to get to the body. "At home a couple of years back a neighbor dude strung himself up. His wife came and got me and my dad to cut him down. Of course we didn't. We called the police and told them to come look at the yo-yo."

"Oh, so you've seen a 'yo-yo,' have you," Lähde said dryly.

"Yep. And when I was in school there was this car crash, and then in the morgue of course," Mela hurried to add.

We announced ourselves at the front gate to the dump, from which we were directed on to the actual landfill. A flock of hundreds of seagulls circled over the burial mound of discarded goods, with sparrows flitting in between. The line of garbage trucks at the gate was stopped, but there was still activity at the composting facility, and bulldozers were working on an expansion area. A couple of patrol cars and the forensics vans were parked higher up on the mound. We drove toward them, passing a sign pointing toward the asbestos-disposal area.

"Landfill gas danger," Mela said as we passed another sign. "No smoking today."

The smell of methane became stronger the higher we climbed. The lower portion of the mound was covered in grass, and the coltsfoot already looked tired next to the bright-yellow winter cress. While Mela parked next to a front-end loader, I searched my investigation kit for a respirator. Even with it on, outside the car the stench was almost over-whelming, and I pulled on a plastic cap to protect my hair. I completed the outfit with plastic booties over my shoes.

Rasilainen waved from behind the forensic team. The crime-scene photographer was hard at work, and Airaksinen was setting out blue police tape around the area. Surrounded by broken chairs, lime-green sheets of insulation, and scraps of tent fabric, a left foot with a heavy boot on it protruded from the trash.

"Is there a whole body, or is this like Hyvinkää again?" Mela asked.

"Looks like more than a foot," Hakulinen from Forensics replied. "Kallio, do you want to have a closer look or should we dig him out? The manager of the dump thinks he's probably been in the trash for a while. The last time the compactor ran through here was just before May Day."

"Yeah, go ahead and start digging," I said and then went in for a closer look, though I didn't really want to. Carefully the forensics team began removing trash from around the foot. First they revealed a slender leg in black leather pants, then hips and the other leg. It was definitely a man's body, but his build was more like a teenager's. The stench grew worse when they dug out the torso. Worms had sucked out the blood, and flies had laid eggs in the gaping chest wound.

"Must have been shot," Lähde said expressionlessly.

The head was covered with a garbage bag. Scraps of black plastic also lay around the legs, so the body may have been covered with two bags that had been ripped by trash or machinery. Hakulinen carefully uncovered the face. It was blackened by decomposition. I asked Mela to get the computer from the car and pull up the lists of missing persons and APBs.

"What do you think, Mela, could this be our guy?" I asked when he came back with the laptop. Trying to hold the computer in one hand while plugging his nose with the other, he looked back and forth between the mugshot and the body lying in the trash. Even though the face was in pretty bad shape, its narrowness, small jaw, and crooked nose were still distinguishable.

"I think we found Marko Seppälä," I said quietly.

Next to me, Mela took a deep breath. All the color had drained from his face. I pulled him off to the side and made him sit down and put his head between his knees. Then I ordered Forensics to call in reinforcements and asked Lähde to get the rest of our unit.

"And the meat wagon, right?" Hakulinen said.

"Yes. I want this body opened up as soon as possible." According to his police record, on his right upper arm Marko Seppälä had a tattoo of a heart with the word "Suvi" in large letters and smaller hearts with their children's names that had been added later. That would be enough to identify him, assuming the decomposition hadn't progressed too far. Unfortunately, because it had been under the trash and partially covered in plastic, the body had stayed warmer than the air outside.

Mela still sat with his head between his knees, and Lähde gave me a wink. Hopefully he wouldn't give Mela too hard a time, because this body was an awful sight for anyone, even someone with experience. I felt sick too. I walked toward the car to make a task list. As I passed Mela, I started to say something but then decided to leave him in peace.

Reinforcements from Forensics arrived within about fifteen minutes, and I ordered them to search the area for a potential murder weapon and any other clues. A recent dismemberment case nearby in Hyvinkää was on everyone's mind, and the jokes flying around were even darker than usual. Koivu and Wang arrived with the ambulance. I tried to schedule an autopsy for the same day at the Institute of Forensic Medicine, because determining Seppälä's time of death was critical.

"I'm glad you came," I said to Koivu, who jumped out of the car but then quickly retreated to look for a respirator. "You two start interviewing the landfill staff, and try to figure out how the body got here. They keep records of every load of garbage, and the area is fenced off, so it wouldn't be that easy to just pull up and dump a body out of a trunk. Mela, you could start going through the security logs and figure out when the loads for this area came in. Ask the office how we get access to those records."

Mela nodded, clearly relieved at the chance to get away from the smell of methane. I would be going to witness the examination of the body and possibly the autopsy as well. If all else failed, dental records could conclusively identify the body. If this really was Marko, Suvi Seppälä would have to perform the official identification, but that could wait until the body had been cleaned up. What time did the Seppälä's older children get out of school? Who could come to support Suvi, and who would go to tell her we had found Marko? I remembered I had promised to pick up Iida from day care, but that wasn't going to happen now. Luckily I reached Antti.

"I'm going to have a few long days here," I said dejectedly, realizing to my horror that I was on the verge of tears. "I've got another homicide on my hands, and I have no idea when I'll be home. We're out of milk and cheese, so you'll need to hit the store too. There's some soup in the freezer."

The mention of soup reminded me of lunch, but the stench of gas quickly drove away any feelings of hunger. I was able to keep my composure while I organized everything, but when I got in the car the anxiety hit. How stupid had it been to think that finding Marko Seppälä would solve the Ilveskivi murder? Now we were just going to have to start the investigation over again with even more complications to deal with. We had all agreed to meet back at the station at four thirty, and Lehtovuori was there consolidating everything he could dig up about Seppälä.

Even though everyone besides Mela knew the routines and could handle their parts, this was going to be rough. As I approached the exit I usually took, the thought occurred to me that I could drive to the station and send Puupponen to identify the body in my stead, but the part of me that was still functioning wouldn't let the weaker me turn the wheel. I turned on the radio for some comfort, and the best I could find was Kauko Röyhkä's "Before I Go." I wished I could be somewhere else too.

When I arrived at the institute, I went to see the forensic pathologist on duty.

"I want to do the identification as soon as possible. This is essential for our investigation. As far as I'm concerned, the actual autopsy can be postponed, but I want at least an examination now so we can be sure the deceased is the person we've been looking for," I said to Dr. Kervinen, who was an old acquaintance. He'd changed aftershaves since I'd seen him last.

"There's already a line. A suspected case of SIDS and an old lady found dead in her home. You'll have to wait your turn."

"I certainly will not. This is only going to take you ten minutes, tops. Is the body already in the cooler?"

"Not yet. We don't have any damn room. There were five suicides over the weekend. Springtime and alcohol seem to make people depressed. Twelve alcohol poisonings are going to funeral parlors this afternoon, which will open up a spot for your boy."

"A visual inspection isn't going to take long," I said and crossed my arms. "We need hair and blood samples to send to the lab ASAP. This victim probably committed a homicide himself, and we may be able to solve that one with these samples."

"So you need me to help your case statistics, is that it?" Kervinen said, but then he realized he wasn't going to get rid of me until he agreed to my request.

"Just wait a sec. I'll see what I can do. Are you going to stay to watch the cutting yourself?"

"Depends on whether this is the person we've been looking for these past two weeks."

"OK, come on. Himanen, will you call the clerk in? Our esteemed colleague here seems to be in a terrible rush. Kallio, put on a suit and we'll go have a look. This may be a little unorthodox, but at least we can see where we are."

After donning a protective suit, I followed Kervinen. The refrigeration corridor had twenty-eight stainless-steel doors and a cement floor that was easy to spray clean when necessary. The body still lay on the stretcher it had been brought in on from the landfill, and the stench made me cringe. Himanen lifted the sheet, and the forensic pathology clerk prepared to record everything that was said.

I forced myself to look at the dead man's face again. The grimace frozen there was the worst I had ever seen, though his jaw already hung limp. There were fly eggs in his eyelashes, but otherwise the face was intact.

A motorcycle jacket covered his neck and shoulders, but there were no gloves on his hands. On his left ring finger was a silver Kalevala

Jewelry snake ring. Suvi Seppälä wore the same one, and she had listed their wedding bands as an identifying mark for her husband.

"Will you take off that ring?" I asked Himanen, who scraped the grime off it into a plastic pouch and then handed the ring to me. Even though the ring was tarnished, I could still make out the inscription: *Suvi and Marko 21.6.1990. Together Forever.*

I asked them to open the sleeve of the leather jacket, which had a zipper running up to the elbow. Himanen unzipped the sleeve and then pulled it up farther to reveal a tattooed heart and four letters around it. The smaller heart added to commemorate Toni's birth was also visible, but Janita and Diana's hearts were obscured by swelling and bruising.

"That's enough for now," I said calmly. "Please send hair and blood samples to the lab and put him on ice. Looks like a single GSW. His name is Marko Seppälä, and you'll find all his information in our file."

"We should be able to get to the autopsy around three. Can you send someone over?"

"I'll try."

Leaving the morgue always gave me the same feeling of relief, but the shadow of death seemed to follow me into the parking lot, and the gentle breeze did little to wash away the stench that clung to my clothes and hair. Leaning against the car, I dialed Koivu's number. He answered after five rings.

"Hi, it's Maria. It is Seppälä. Any idea yet how he ended up in the landfill?"

"No."

"Let's stick with the old plan, then. Four thirty at the station. Puustjärvi and Puupponen can go to the autopsy, which the ME said would be at three. We'll need to keep looking for a bullet, a gun, and Seppälä's motorcycle at or near the dump. I'm going to the station to drum up reinforcements."

"We're going to need them if we want to find the bullet. The dump manager said the killer had bad luck. He didn't know not to leave the body close to the outer slope, since that area gets leveled out and cleaned up more often so the trash doesn't slide off the edge. If the body had been buried closer to the center, it might not have been found for years, if ever."

"But how did the body get to the landfill in the first place? Wouldn't the trash collectors notice if there was a garbage sack that weighed as much as a man? Let's think about that in the meeting."

Low blood sugar was starting to make my hands shake, so I grabbed a slice of shrimp pizza from a nearby takeout joint. At the first stoplight I wolfed it down and wished that I had thought to buy a bottle of water too. At the next light I had a moment of hesitation. I hadn't assigned anyone to deliver the bad news to Suvi Seppälä. Somehow I had the feeling that I should do it myself, but now or later, when Suvi was done with her class? Maybe now would be better so she could have some time before the older children got home from school.

The leather-sewing class was being offered at a nearby vocational school. Earlier, in my days as a sergeant, I had visited the school to pick up students for questioning, but since then the place had changed completely. The old villas on the south side had been bulldozed and replaced by a dense high-rise apartment complex, over which screeched the official Espoo city bird, the construction crane.

I asked the office where I might find Suvi and was directed to the textile shop. The class was made up of a couple dozen women of various ages bent over sewing machines. The purpose was to teach unemployed sewing machine operators specialized leatherworking skills and to encourage them to start their own businesses. Entrepreneurship and self-employment were supposedly the magic ticket to ending structural unemployment. Everything depended on the person herself, and if you were enterprising enough, you could become a millionaire Nokia shareholder or win a trip to the Turkish Riviera on *Wheel of Fortune*, or so the theory went. The course also seemed to be teaching independence, since there was no teacher present.

Suvi sat in the middle of the back row and seemed to be unaware of anything but the thin red piece of leather she was trying to shape into a sleeve. When I walked over to her, she jumped, and the needle skittered across the material's shiny surface.

"Shit!" Suvi said and lifted her foot off the pedal. "What are you doing, sneaking up on a person like that? Wait, is it Marko? Is he . . . is Marko . . . ?"

"Could you come out into the hall?"

Suvi grabbed her bag and coat, not even bothering to turn off her sewing machine. The hallway didn't offer any privacy, but I pulled Suvi away from the doorway to the sewing class before talking.

"Yes, we found Marko. His body was discovered this morning in the city landfill. I'm sorry."

Suvi stood perfectly still for a few seconds. Then suddenly she lunged at me and grabbed my hair.

"Why didn't you catch him in time? Why didn't you do your fucking job! Marko!"

I felt pain in my scalp and the corner of my eye. I grabbed her wrists and squeezed until she released my hair, then twisted her arms behind her back. I held her there until she started whimpering quietly. When I let her go, she slumped down onto the floor and put her head on her knees.

"Quiet in the hall, you're interrupting our class," an older gentleman said from the doorway of the nearest classroom. I waved him away, then collected Suvi's things from the floor. Her purse had fallen open and a pack of cigarettes, a lighter, and a tube of mascara had spilled out. I straightened the fringe on her leather jacket before wrapping it around her shoulders. Sobs wracked her body.

"How?" she finally asked, her voice choked. "Was he killed?"

"We can't say anything for sure yet. There was a wound in his chest that looked like it came from a gunshot. The autopsy is this afternoon."

Suvi stood up quickly.

"I want to get the hell out of here," she said and wiped her nose on the sleeve of her shirt. "I'm going to get my children." Suvi started running down the stairs, and I followed.

"I can take you," I said, because Suvi's eyes were still full of tears and her face was swollen.

"I'm not leaving my car here for someone to steal! I'm fine to drive. The kids get out of school at one."

Suvi's voice was thin and punctuated with sobs. She wrapped her arms around herself as if for comfort, and a black line of mascara ran down her face like the strange mourning symbol of an ancient tribe. I couldn't leave her alone, so I switched on my car's immobilizer and alarm and asked Suvi for the keys to her Datsun. When I got back to the station, I would send someone from Patrol to retrieve my Saab.

In the passenger seat of her car was a beat-up car seat, which Suvi moved to the back. The car stank of cigarettes and oil, and dice and a tree-shaped air freshener hung from the rearview mirror. Before I had my current work car, I had driven a small Fiat, and before that my uncle's Lada junker, but they had been luxury cars compared to this. Finding the correct relationship between ignition and gas pedal in order to start the car took a minute. Suvi dried her face with an unused diaper she had produced from somewhere.

"When did he die?" she asked once we were on the road.

"I can't say for sure. The autopsy will tell us more."

"And you're sure it's Marko?"

When I said I had seen the tattoos, Suvi began to sob again. I had to concentrate on driving because even at such a moderate speed, the Datsun shook so violently that I could imagine it breaking apart at any second.

"You have a bruise on your eye. I think my ring clipped you. I'm sorry," Suvi said. "Are you going to charge me for attacking you?"

"No, of course not. Suvi, is there a relative or friend who could come and be with you and the kids? Or is there a social worker assigned to you that you could ask for help?"

"Don't you dare tell them!" Suvi shouted. "We don't need anyone. We have each other."

"You don't have to do this alone. You have a right to receive support."

"Right, and you really care how I feel!" Suvi screamed and swung in her seat so violently that I thought the car would run off the road from the force of it. "All you cared about was catching Marko and pinning that fag's murder on him!"

As I merged onto the freeway, my phone rang. Taskinen asked where I was. He had heard about the body.

"I'm taking Seppälä's wife home."

"I realize that's important, but it's a more junior officer's work. We need you here. Someone leaked the story to the press, and now I have reporters breathing down my neck. I don't know enough to answer their questions, and neither does the press secretary."

"I'm coming," I said with a sigh. I felt like turning the phone off completely, but I couldn't do that. When I nagged Suvi again about who she could ask to come over and suggested a neighbor or someone from the church, she finally said she would call her brother.

"I know Jari's just going to say Marko got what he deserved, but he does like our children. There's the school. Stop! Let's stay and wait for Janita and Tony. But I won't tell them until we get home. The other kids would make fun of them for being crybabies."

I had been in the third grade when my friend Jaska's dad died. Jaska came to school anyway and cried at his desk while the teacher expressed her condolences. I remember the complete sense of helplessness that hit me as I listened to Jaska cry. I wanted to comfort him, but what could a nine-year-old do? The next day a boy named Esa and I were sent to take flowers from our class to the family. His mother sat in her armchair and offered us juice, treating us like adults. I wanted to comfort her too, but I didn't have the words. Later I heard that she had been confused by the teacher's sending children on such an errand instead of coming herself.

The teacher had been trying to avoid her own emotions.

I offered Suvi my phone so she could call her brother. Suvi delivered the news calmly, like a person who'd suspected the worst and was now just relieved to have had her fears confirmed.

"And what about Marko's parents and the rest of the family? Do you want the police to notify them or would you like to do it yourself?"

"Marko didn't even know who his father was, and his mother drank herself to death just before our wedding. There isn't anyone to tell. He didn't have anyone but us."

Children had started streaming out of the school gates, so I spoke quickly.

"Thank you for the hundred-mark bill. It could really help our investigation. Did Marko say who he got it from?"

"No," Suvi replied and then removed her seat belt as Tony and Janita came out of the schoolyard. Opening the door, she yelled to her children, who seemed surprised to see their mother in the middle of the day.

She flashed a radiant smile. "I got the day off from school," she lied and then helped the kids get buckled in the back. "Let's stop at the day care and pick up Diana too," she said and motioned to me to start the car as royalty might command a chauffeur. The drive was only a few hundred yards. "This nice lady will keep you company." She climbed out of the car but then suddenly stuck her head back in and spoke to me in English as if we were coconspirators. "Say nothing."

"Who are you?" Tony asked as soon as his mother was gone.

"A friend of your mom's."

"No you aren't. You're a cop. You came to our house in a cop car once!" Janita hissed, in the same way her mother did. "There's no point coming to get Daddy. He isn't home."

"I think you're right. I'm just taking you all home."

"Our mom knows how to drive too," Tony said defiantly as Suvi returned with Diana in her arms. She put the girl in the front seat.

"Now we want to be alone," she said to me. "You can leave."

So I got out of the car, even though I didn't know if I was doing the right thing. I stopped Suvi as she was climbing behind the wheel.

"You understand we're going to have to get back to this within the next couple of days. If you think of anything, call me. Here's my card in case you lost the last one." I gazed into Suvi's light-blue eyes, which looked so vulnerable without all the makeup. "I care about what happens to you. Call me at any time if you need someone to talk to."

Suvi muttered something and then got in the car and sped away. I called a taxi and returned to work.

Forensics had some of the photographs ready, and Puustjärvi was hanging them on the wall of the conference room for our meeting. He didn't seem terribly enthusiastic about going to the autopsy, but of course he would go. Taskinen appeared in the conference room too and sighed heavily when I told him everything I knew.

"Is this some sort of underworld score settling or is there a connection to Petri Ilveskivi's killing?" he asked.

"If only I knew. I'm going to have Organized Crime look into all of Seppälä's accomplices and people he knew in prison. With any luck, we'll find some suspects. Anyway, the body has probably been in the landfill for almost two weeks. There weren't any sightings of Seppälä after the night of Ilveskivi's death. As soon as she recovers from the initial shock, I'll have the wife confirm her statement. We also need to get Seppälä's phone records. According to his wife, he came home covered in blood and then tried to call someone. Apparently he seemed pretty desperate."

Before the meeting, I went to my office to check my phone messages. Koivu and Wang came in from the dump. They smelled revolting.

"I have a clean shirt in my office. Do I have time to change before the meeting? I think it would be best for everyone," Wang said, and I wholeheartedly agreed.

The unit met in the conference room, and we started to go over the information we'd collected so far. The landfill was open on weekdays from seven to nine, and everyone who brought in a load had to check in at the gate, sign the log, and note what kind of garbage they were bringing in. During the day most of the traffic was garbage trucks, and in the evening it was mostly private customers. Theoretically, the body could have been brought in with all the other trash, but a garbage-truck driver should have noticed such a heavy bin, and other customers would have noticed someone dumping a body wrapped in black plastic.

"When the dump is closed, there's a guard on patrol," Koivu reported. "Someone could climb over the fence—it's just chain link—and there aren't any alarms or electronic surveillance. A strong man might have been able to lift Seppälä's body over and then climb after it, but no one would take the risk of dragging a body almost half a mile across a guarded area. And then you'd have to pull it all the way up the garbage mound. There could have been more than one person, and maybe they had a wheelbarrow or something, but my guess is the body came in a car. Locks can be picked, and the west gate just has a big padlock on it."

"But wouldn't the guard notice a car?" Lehtovuori asked.

"It's a big area, almost fifty hectares. It would also depend on the weather. In the rain or fog you wouldn't be able to see very far there. We've already talked to one of the night guards, right, Lähde?"

"Yeah, I got in touch with the guy who was working all of last week. He wrote in the log that on last Tuesday night he thought he heard the sound of a car over on the west side of the dump around midnight when he was on his way to the maintenance building for coffee. He went to check but didn't find anything. And there was a lot of fog that night."

"We need to have the gate locks checked for tampering. You handle that right after this meeting," I told Lähde, who nodded.

"The manager thought a driver could make it to the dump without the guard noticing if they drove with the lights off, but only through the west gate."

"Then we need to focus more resources on that area. Koivu, will you call the field team? Are we going to have the guys from Vantaa tonight? Yes? Good. It won't be dark until ten, so we can keep going until then. Mela, did you find anything else in those log books?"

"Not yet. I'll get through the rest tonight, though," Mela replied more sedately than usual. Obviously he wanted to stick to paperwork so he wouldn't have to go back to the dump.

"The lab said the hair DNA test results can be ready on Wednesday, since they don't have to run as many replications when they have a large-enough sample," Hakulinen said. He was a natural-born forensic investigator who loved all the possibilities that new technology was opening up for criminal investigation. But he enjoyed practical investigation more than lab work, which was our good fortune. He had amazingly keen perception at a crime scene.

Puustjärvi called around five thirty to report that the autopsy had confirmed that Seppälä died of a gunshot wound. Probably a pistol. One shot, barely missing the heart. The wound wouldn't have been fatal if he had received medical care immediately. Technically, the cause of death was loss of blood.

According to the medical examiner, Seppälä had been dead for one to two weeks. The warm conditions of the landfill complicated identifying a precise time of death. I had a hard time believing that this was merely a settling of scores. Petri Ilveskivi's and Marko Seppälä's deaths were connected, but how? What or who was the link between these two men?

13

On the way back to the landfill, we picked up my car in Leppävaara. While we were there, Wang suddenly said she wanted to ride with me, and Koivu watched in confusion as we got out and walked over to my car.

"About the partner situation," she said as soon as she had her seat belt fastened. "I thought about it over the weekend, and I think it would be good if I wasn't Pekka's partner anymore. Whatever happens with us, I think that would be best."

"Does Pekka agree?

"Yes, I think so, even though he says he likes working with me better than working with Puupponen or Puustjärvi."

"It's settled, then. As soon as we get these two homicides solved, I'll put the wheels in motion. Do you still have a hard time imagining working with Puupponen?"

Wang gave a wry smile.

"Ville is fine when he stops trying to be funny all the time. Maybe he's different when he's alone with people. At first I think he only liked me because Ström hated me so much, and then it just stuck . . . I'm sure we'd get along, but ask Ville and Pete too."

"Definitely. And what about the moving-in-together issue? How's that going?"

Wang and Koivu were still at loggerheads about marriage. "I think if we're going to move in together, we should do it for real. Like, I can't imagine having a baby out of wedlock. And it kind of offends me that Pekka wants to be free to just leave whenever he wants."

"He did have some bad experiences with past girlfriends. Maybe he's afraid."

"Yes, but that's not my fault. Why should a new relationship have to suffer because of the last one?"

We drove through the gate to the dump. When we left, I had put the emergency flasher on top of the car, which ensured unimpeded passage through the gate. I thought about what Wang had said. My own hesitation to marry Antti had also been because of previous failed relationships. I had been almost certain that I was born to live alone, and my unresolved relationship with Johnny had also loomed somewhere in the background. Koivu's apprehension was easy to understand.

There was still a flurry of activity up on the trash mound. The investigators had found pieces of plastic that could have been from the bags concealing Marko Seppälä. He had died of blood loss, so there had to be a bag full of it somewhere. I tried to imagine how the situation had gone: Seppälä had gone to meet the person who hired him, unaware of the danger. Or had he known he was in danger and had the same knife with him that he had used to pierce Petri Ilveskivi's pericardium? Was that why he'd been shot?

Despite my doubts about finding any fresh tracks after so much time had passed, I had to make my people work until dark. The landfill supervisor had stayed on-site too. He was helpful but got worked up at any suggestion that one of the landfill employees might be involved.

I went home a little before nine. A chaffinch sang in the rowan tree in the yard, presumably the same one that was there every morning and evening. Einstein had decided hunting it was pointless, so he let the bird sing in peace. The next morning as I retrieved the newspaper, a black-and-gray-striped tail fluttered by, followed by another, and a familiar energetic chirping filled the edge of the field. The wagtails had come. The sun was already high in the sky. It painted the sprouting field a deep green, evoking scents of awakening. Spring never ceased to amaze me. Year by year its arrival surprised me, as if I had doubted all winter that I would ever see another.

Inside, my mind returned to work as I dressed and ate a quick breakfast. Antti was shaving in the downstairs bathroom. I kissed his bare neck, which I could barely reach, and left. Antti's meeting wouldn't start until ten, and his mother had promised to fetch Iida from day care in the evening.

In our morning meeting, we learned that the lock on the west gate did have evidence of tampering, most likely jimmied open. The crime lab would tell us more, but I didn't have much hope of them finding fingerprints. The marks on the lock were relatively recent, and although they didn't necessarily connect to Seppälä's death, logic dictated that we direct our investigation to the west gate and surrounding area. A small, rarely used road led to the gate through farms and forests.

"A dog might be helpful for finding blood," Koivu said.

"You're right. Find out how busy the K9 units are. It would be nice to get one out on that road soon."

Lehtovuori had made a list of Seppälä's possible accomplices. I divided the interrogations between my own detectives and a couple of guys from Organized Crime, which didn't have a single woman. Their unit commander, Laine, sat in our meeting too, since he said he was interested in the case.

"Are you absolutely sure Ilveskivi didn't have any drug connections? This stinks of a drug-world hit." I tried to interrupt him, but Laine spoke over me. "What this looks like is that Ilveskivi didn't pay his debts and his dealer hired Seppälä to put the fear of God in him. After things got out of hand, Seppälä was a liability. It took a hell of a cool head to shoot Seppälä and then drag him to that dump. Are all the guards clean?"

"No criminal records."

"Too bad they haven't had drug tests. I think anyone working in security should have to submit to random testing," Laine said. "I'd suggest that someone take Ilveskivi's picture by all the usually shooting galleries and crack houses."

"You're forgetting that the autopsy didn't find any indication of drug use. Seppälä's death might be a drug-revenge killing, but Ilveskivi's death has something else behind it," I said to Laine, who was really starting to get on my nerves. "I'm leading both homicide investigations. If you have any other ideas, I'd be happy to discuss them with you in private. Now, let's get back to the matter at hand."

When I left the conference room, I heard Laine's footsteps behind me.

"You're making a big mistake! Why are you trying to protect Ilveskivi's reputation? We all know how tolerant you are, but that shouldn't get in the way of a criminal investigation. Or do Salo's threats have you so frightened that you aren't willing to get involved in a drug case?"

"Thus far we haven't seen the slightest indication that Petri Ilveskivi had any connections with drug dealers or any other organized crime groups," I said icily and then grabbed Puupponen by the arm as he passed. "Hey, Puupponen. One clarification. Jarkola, the guy who knows Seppälä and Väinölä. He has six months behind him and an ongoing trial for possession of Ecstasy. He might be highly motivated to talk if there's some way it might make the time he's about to spend in prison easier."

"I can think of a few other people who could use some amphetamines right now," Puupponen said with a sigh. "This is such a mess. I'm thinking Marko Seppälä was just a small potato in a big old bowl of mashed crime."

Despite everything that was going on, I burst out laughing. "Oh, Puupponen, have you been reading Kinky Friedman again?"

"Did you like that metaphor?" Puupponen asked enthusiastically.

"I always like your jokes," I replied and slipped into my office. Then I called Tommi Laitinen's work number. After a long wait, he came to the phone. Apparently he had been playing floor hockey with the kids.

"I still have a few more things to talk to you about. What's your day like? Could I drop by your work?"

"No, absolutely not! One of the other teachers is out with the stomach flu, and the Espoo City Incorporated substitute system is crap. I'll be done at three. We can meet then. I'm on my way to visit Petri's parents tonight, since the funeral is on Sunday. Won't this be a nice Mother's Day? I can stop by the police station on my way."

"Please do. Things are starting to look clearer."

After turning on my computer, I dove into the Internet and pulled up the minutes from the City Planning Commission meeting from the night of Petri Ilveskivi's death. Maybe someone wanted to stop him from getting to the meeting. Could Ilveskivi have been the deciding vote on some important decision? But no—the meeting had only considered routine rezoning matters, not anything dramatic. I had heard complaints before that the City Council routinely circumvented the Planning Commission's decisions. They were unlikely to have any real power, although they had seen heated debates about the new general plan for South Espoo and where new residential construction should be concentrated. A few members of the Planning Commission, among them the chairman, thought that building any new rental units was counterproductive, since they only wanted people in Espoo who could afford to own their homes.

I remembered Tommi Laitinen's quip about Espoo City Incorporated and wondered who they would sell stock to. Certainly not me, since I didn't fulfill the home-ownership requirement. The metro-area cities actually designated rental apartments specifically for cops because our pay wasn't enough to allow us to buy homes of our own. Of course no one thought of giving us a raise. That was so unfashionable.

We were even moving to a merit pay system, which meant the bosses would have to evaluate their employees' performances. I still wasn't sure whether the criteria would hang on number of crimes solved, suck-up coefficient, family size, or general prowess.

Eila Honkavuori had been a strong advocate for more affordable housing. What if Turo Honkavuori had wanted to stop his wife from talking to Petri about their plan to make a baby? Turo had brought Eila to comfort Tommi, and apparently Eila had spent the night. Had Turo gone to meet Marko Seppälä during that time and shot him? Turo didn't have a gun license, but that didn't mean much anymore. Anyone could get an illegal firearm if they knew who to ask.

But how would a diffident academic like Honkavuori know anyone like that?

The phone rang. It was one of the tabloid crime-beat reporters looking for more information. She had received a tip about the leathers on the body in the landfill and come to the right conclusion. I promised to hold a press conference sometime during the afternoon, but refused to comment on whether the two homicides we were investigating had any connections.

The whole day went to organizing and negotiating. I was thrilled when the duty officer called at three fifteen to say that Tommi Laitinen was waiting for me. I had been hit by a sudden craving for ice cream, so I suggested to Laitinen that we go downstairs to the cafeteria. All he wanted was some juice. To my great delight, in the bottom of the freezer I found an enormous licorice ice cream cone, which I licked as Laitinen and I sat down to talk. From the beginning I made it clear that this was not an official interview and told him that we had found the body of the man we suspected to be Petri Ilveskivi's killer.

"We haven't ruled out the possibility that this was a robbery. Could Petri have been carrying an unusually large amount of money? Did he ever wear a fanny pack or something else that might be missing?"

"No. I've told you that over and over. Why do you keep coming back to this? Petri wasn't robbed."

"Had he ever used drugs?"

Laitinen squirmed in his chair.

"Yes. Some marijuana when he was younger. Before we met. He took a trip to Amsterdam sometime in the early eighties. Back then it was practically the duty of every young man who was trying to find himself to go to the hottest place on the Dam and get stoned."

"Did you smoke too?"

"No! I've never wanted to go on trips like that. Plus, it wouldn't be smart, considering my line of work."

I showed Laitinen Marko Seppälä's mugshot again and asked if he remembered seeing him before.

He almost smiled. "Not exactly the kind of guy you'd remember. So he's the one who killed Petri, and now he's dead too . . . what the hell is going on?"

According to Laitinen, Ilveskivi had been agitated and distant on the days just before his death. When Laitinen asked about it, Ilveskivi refused to answer.

"He just said whatever it was would be cleared up soon. I've been racking my brain. Yesterday Eila and I went through all of Petri's personal papers, but we didn't find anything. You still have all of his work papers, though, which I'd like to take if I can."

"All in good time. Tommi, listen. Hiding things isn't going to help Petri anymore. The only thing that will help is the truth."

"This is the truth!" Tommi shouted and then buried his face in his hands. I didn't have the heart to torment him anymore.

"I don't dream about it," he said before walking out the door, "but when I'm lying alone at night, I sometimes think about how much it must have hurt Petri. Did he know he was dying? Did he say anything before he died? Who was he thinking of? These are the things I'm going to be wondering about for the rest of my life."

I had seen enough family members of homicide victims to know the in-between space they lived in. The time from a killing to the funeral was like watching the victim cross the river to the underworld, inescapably slipping away. If the perpetrator was known from the beginning, people had to process their desire for revenge. Some people never got over that. Uncertainty cut the deepest, especially in cases where suspicion centered on other loved ones.

My computer, which had been on during my conversation with Laitinen, dinged to alert me of a new e-mail. It was from the lab. Seppälä's hair and blood DNA matched what they had recovered from Ilveskivi's body and the cigarette butt at the crime scene. Another person's blood had also been found on the sleeve of Seppälä's leather jacket, and it belonged to Petri Ilveskivi.

I didn't shout for joy or pump my fist in the air, but I did run after Tommi Laitinen. When I reached the front entrance, I saw him climbing into a taxi outside. I let him go. A message on his answering machine would do for now.

"Did you lose someone again?" asked the officer manning the front desk, the same one who had watched me run after Jani Väinölä.

"Men always seem to be slipping through my fingers," I said jauntily and then jogged back upstairs.

We now knew who Ilveskivi's killer was, although a skilled defense attorney might have been able to come up other explanations. Such as, Seppälä showed up at the crime scene by accident, tried to help, but then got scared and ran away. How would I get Suvi to tell me everything about the night it seemed both Seppälä and Ilveskivi had died?

I called Koivu at the landfill, left a message for Laitinen, and then tried in vain to reach Taskinen. When I was trying to get into the police academy, I thought this job would be fast paced and glamorous and that I would be helping people. But in reality it was mostly endless sitting in cars, talking on the phone, and staring at the computer. I did meet new people, but they were usually either victims or suspects. Sometimes

I was able to help the wrongly accused, but they rarely came around to thank me. Why hadn't I become a midwife? Then I would have been able to help make lives, not clean up after deaths.

I decided to take a trip to the landfill to see how things were going. Mela had set up in the conference room at the main office and created a spreadsheet that cross-referenced everyone who had used the dump with all of Seppälä's and Ilveskivi's known acquaintances. So far this hadn't turned up any commonalities, but Mela hadn't lost his optimism. Lähde had interviewed the garbage-truck driver who'd brought in the first load on the morning after Ilveskivi's death. He had thought a pack of foxes must have been running around the night before, because the top of the pile had obviously been disturbed.

The focus of the search had moved to the road to the west, although some officers continued to root around in the garbage heap. Half an hour earlier, the K9 unit had caught a scent at the edge of the landfill but lost it when the dog ran into a fresh rabbit carcass.

"No one ever comes by here. The nearest houses are kilometers away, and everyone who lives there knows this is a dead end. There are signs that say as much too. The killer could be certain no one would bother him here," Koivu said. "A couple of the Vantaa guys are interviewing the people who live down the road, but who's going to remember what happened two weeks ago? If it's even been two weeks." Koivu shrugged in frustration. He was sporting a five o'clock shadow that was like moss yellowed and dried by the summer sun. I felt an urge to reach out and touch it, to draw strength from that contact, but I didn't because half of the Vantaa Patrol force was standing around watching. Instead, I pulled plastic covers over my shoes.

"When will the dog be ready to search again?" I asked his handler, who was drinking coffee out of a thermos.

"Soon, but we can't demand too much from him. How long are we going to keep at this? Are we sure this guy was killed along this road?"

"No, but keep at it for now," I said, even though I felt like a general giving her final command before issuing a retreat. I didn't think of myself as fighting a war against violence. I didn't understand war very well, and I liked it even less. My grandfather had died for his country, even though he never wanted to be a hero. They were only made heroes after the war. I preferred to try to live without thinking too much about what I was living for. Whenever I attempted to figure that out, I found a new dead end.

The first flashlight beams began glimmering in the forest. The sky had darkened, and gray tatters of cloud approached. I tried to remember how many times it had rained since Seppälä's disappearance, and the result was "too many." Looking for tire tracks would be pointless, and even though there must have been plenty of blood, most of it would have been washed away by now.

The beams began converging into a circle, and excited voices followed:

"There's a motorcycle here! Koivu, come look!"

Koivu and I set off tramping through the thicket with Wang following. Someone had tried to conceal the motorcycle under old logs twenty yards off the road, about five hundred yards from the gate to the landfill. First I checked the license plate. AV 623. I didn't have to check my notes. I knew it by heart. Without a doubt this was Marko Seppälä's motorcycle.

"Great! Keep searching this same area. With luck, we might find the murder weapon too."

We weren't lucky, because the clouds opened up, and when hail the size of my pinky fingernail started pounding my head, I called off the search. The motorcycle, now wrapped in plastic, was dragged to one of the forensic team vans, which could barely turn around on the narrow road.

"Getting that out into the forest would have taken some strength. This isn't a motocross bike, so he couldn't have driven it," Koivu said as we sat safely out of the rain in my car. "Have Puupponen and Puustjärvi caught up with Jarkola? He's strong enough to have been able to carry the bike into the woods and stupid enough to have taken the body to the dump. Why didn't he leave it here in the forest? No one ever comes here."

"Let's go home. We've been at this for ten hours. Meeting tomorrow is at the normal time. Does anyone need a ride?"

No one did, so I drove straight home. The rain and hail softened outlines and muted colors, and so I was forced to take it slow. The lights of downtown Espoo made the city seem beautiful and inviting.

A beat-up-looking van moved into the left lane and sped up to pull even with me. I slowed down to let it pass, but it stayed beside me. Glancing at the tinted windows, I expected to see the muzzle of a rifle or sawed-off shotgun, and for a second I thought the van might try to run me off the road. So I slowed down again, and a heavy truck came up from behind. The van sped up and disappeared, but I spent the whole way home repeating its license plate number in my head. I wrote it down once I stopped. Probably it was just someone who had received a call on his cell phone while he was passing me and got distracted. Salo wasn't going to hire amateurs who would try to make a hit on a cop on a busy freeway, would he?

I spent the rest of the night sorting Iida's clothes to separate out the ones that didn't fit. My mother-in-law had already left, and Iida crawled around in the discards pile, pretending she was a hedgehog. I went downstairs to the cellar to see if any of my sisters' kids' old clothes would work for Iida this spring and summer. Our storage room was in a terrible state, and as I balanced one more box of clothing no one was going to wear anymore on top of the pile, I decided it was about time for some real spring cleaning.

"We probably need to haul a load to the thrift store," I said to Antti, who was sprawled on the couch reading a book. "We have at least five boxes of clothes Iida's outgrown."

"Does that mean we don't need them anymore?" Antti asked, a little disappointed.

"I don't know." Sitting down next to him, I absentmindedly stroked his thigh. "My brain says no, but my body has other ideas. Sometimes my breasts want nothing more than to nurse. They can still feel Iida's mouth on them and the sensation of milk flowing. Sometimes I imagine that someone is kicking inside of me again. Friday I have an appointment to get my birth control prescription renewed. When I'm there, I'll ask her how long we have to dither about this. Or how much time I have. Our responsibilities aren't exactly equal when it comes to this." Standing, I scooped up Iida and took her for her bedtime snack. After she was safely in bed, I lay awake for a while, gazing out the window. A lone magpie dozed in the ash tree in the yard.

In the morning the world smelled fresh and new again. The buds had grown since the previous day. Our first ladies' soccer game was scheduled for this evening, so I packed my gear. Our field time was bad, 5:15 p.m. That cut out anyone who needed to rush home to feed her family, but no other times were available. The best slots were reserved for the men's club teams.

"It's the fifth of May," Antti said as we were leaving. He began to whistle the tune of a rock song by the same name, by Eppu Normaali. When I started the car after dropping Iida at day care, some clever disc jockey was playing the same song on the radio. Of course I sang along.

During our meeting, I started to feel like we were actually making forward progress. Forensics had found a knife in Seppälä's saddlebag and had sent it to the lab. The blade was four centimeters wide, which was a good match for Petri Ilveskivi's wound. The knife seemed clean, but modern testing only required a tiny amount of blood to isolate DNA.

However, we did find a surprise in the phone records. According to them, no calls were made from the Seppäläs residence on the night of Petri Ilveskivi's death, even though Suvi had claimed that Marko had desperately tried to contact someone.

"Did he have a cell phone?" Lähde asked.

"Not as far as I know. We'll have to interview the wife again. Wang, will you try to get ahold of her? Suvi Seppälä may be a key witness. We can be ninety-seven percent certain that Marko Seppälä killed Petri Ilveskivi, but why? Puupponen and Puustjärvi, did you get anything from Seppälä's friends?"

Before either could answer, Mela opened his mouth.

"Come on, the fag was just hitting on him. They're always like that. Once in the bathroom at Stockmann this one perv came right up next to me to show off his dick. I'm lucky he didn't try to shove it in my pants. I felt like punching him in the mouth, but I couldn't because I had already decided to apply to the academy."

"OK, smart guy, so tell us how Ilveskivi managed to hit on somebody while he was riding his bike to the Planning Commission meeting," Puupponen said tersely, then went on. "We interviewed all of Seppälä's accomplices, and according to them, Seppälä had never transported anything harder than marijuana or steroids. But right before he disappeared, he had been bragging about coming into some real money. They said Seppälä had always been a big talker who would say anything to shake off his reputation as just some petty crook. But he wouldn't tell anyone what the job was, likely because he was afraid someone else would try to muscle in on his turf."

"We're still looking for Jarkola. What else do we have?"

Overnight a man had been arrested for driving his wife and children out of their apartment at gunpoint. A neighbor took the family in and called the police. In the cells next to him were the Ronkainens, a couple who had used every tool in their kitchen in their efforts to kill each other. The wife had even tried a cheese plane on her husband's cheek.

"Kallio, are you happy that women are sick of being victims and are giving as good as they get?" Lähde asked, and his chubby cheeks shook with mirthless laughter.

"Why would anyone be happy that women are starting to act as stupid as men? Wang, Lehtovuori, see if you can handle the Ronkainens. Koivu, you can keep things going at the landfill. Lähde, weren't you and Mela almost done at the dump? When you are, process the model father with the pistol and then get back to Seppälä when you're done. We should be able to wrap up the Ilveskivi investigation within a few days. A bottle of vodka to whoever figures out why Seppälä killed Ilveskivi."

"Is that the merit-based pay we've been hearing about?" Puupponen asked, and the meeting disbanded.

Wang tried without success to reach Suvi Seppälä, and I tried a couple of times too, with no luck. Eija Hirvonen and I started putting together the formal preliminary investigation report. Working with such a sharp, energetic administrative assistant was a pleasure. She had gone to vocational school after middle school, and occasionally I got the impression that she was disappointed she hadn't had the chance to go to college. Her job at the police station had come about almost by accident, at the recommendation of her brother, who was a cop. Eija had started out in the passport office, but moved to Robbery a few years ago and then to us. Sometimes, when we were working on an especially brutal crime, she could have strong reactions. Over the winter we had dealt with the gang rape of a fifteen-year-old girl, and Eija had wept as she typed up the final reports.

Around three, the crime lab reported that they had retrieved a few blood cells from the knife in Seppälä's saddlebag. Replicating the DNA would take a week, but I thought it was worth it. When I left for our soccer game, I was in a good mood: things were moving forward, and nothing gave me reason to think we wouldn't be able to solve Seppälä's murder as well if we kept making progress in the forensic investigation. Finding the bullet would be nice, although an experienced weapons specialist could say quite a lot about a bullet and the gun that shot it simply based on the entry and exit wounds.

I changed at work because there weren't dressing rooms or showers at the field. My twenty-year-old cleats still fit. I had bought new ones only two weeks before my sudden decision to stop playing on the boys' team. Otherwise I was wearing normal workout clothes: T-shirt, thick socks, and tights. Wang and Mira Saastamoinen drove with me. At the field we found nearly twenty women, so we would be able to field proper teams. Liisa Rasilainen began leading the warm-up, and we were just getting to leg stretches when a trilling started up at the sideline. It was coming from my gym bag.

"Hi, it's Suvi. You said I could call you anytime. I've been thinking. I think I should tell you everything. Jari took the kids to a movie and McDonald's so I could have time now."

I didn't even give it a second thought.

"Good. We can come there. Yes, I'll bring another officer with me, Anu Wang. We'll see you in half an hour."

Jogging back over to the group, I nodded to Wang to follow me.

"Suvi Seppälä has decided to talk. There's a laptop in the car we can use to take her statement. If we get lucky, we may be able to split that bottle of vodka."

14

We didn't bother changing, even though driving in cleats wasn't ideal. Wang was at least wearing a proper track suit, but my T-shirt had split a seam in the previous wash cycle, which I hadn't noticed this morning in the rush of leaving the house. Warming up had got me sweating a bit, and while we drove it dried into a clammy film.

The grass was growing wild in the Seppälä's tiny front yard, and an aging tricycle looked pathetic next to three brand-new child-size bicycles. Diana still needed training wheels. Tony's BMX bike was every little boy's dream, and Janita's bike was bubblegum pink. Grape hyacinths bloomed in the flower bed under the window.

The door opened before we could ring the bell. Without makeup on Suvi looked young and tired, and the loose men's shirt that hung off her accentuated how slim she was.

I kicked off my muddy cleats at the door. Wang did the same. This time Suvi escorted us into the living room. Wang set up the computer on the coffee table, but then changed her mind and set it on her lap.

The cramped bedrooms were visible from where we sat. One had no room for anything beyond a double bed and a crib, while the other had a bunk bed and the floor was covered in toys.

"I didn't feel up to cleaning," Suvi said defensively. "I'll probably have to before Child Protective Services sends their spies again." She opened the window and lit a cigarette. Wang brought up a personal data form on the computer. Suvi was born in April 1973, so she had been seventeen when Janita was born. Now she was twenty-six, a mother of three, and a widow.

I remembered my grandmother, who had been through a similar situation. Maybe she would have known what to say to Suvi. Maybe she would have done what everyone in her generation did and encouraged Suvi to buck up, comforting her with the knowledge that others had survived what she was going through now. But what could I say?

"Was Marko shot?" Suvi asked after finishing half her cigarette.

"Yes, he was shot."

"Did he die quickly?"

Lying would have been easier, but I told the truth.

"So he suffered. Oh God!" Suvi's face had the translucence of fat-free milk, and her eyes burned with rage. "Of course you think he deserved it because he killed that fag. But Marko wouldn't have agreed to kill anyone. I heard the phone call when he finally reached the guy who hired him. He'd been promised that the fag was a pathetic wimp who just needed a little roughing up. But he wasn't a wimp. He attacked Marko, and Marko had to defend himself."

"So you've known the whole time?"

"Yes. Are you going to send me to fucking prison now too, for being an accessory? Marko never told me about his jobs so I couldn't be accused of anything. He wouldn't have said anything about this either except he had been so scared." Suvi vigorously tamped out her cigarette, leaving only the crushed filter in the Viking Cruises ashtray.

"You said that after Marko got home he was trying to call someone, but there weren't any calls from your phone that night. What is the truth?"

Suvi glared at me.

"Marko thought the cops might be listening in on our phone. He said he didn't dare call but that he'd send a postcard with a false name as soon as he knew how long he would be gone. But no card ever came. He left, and I never heard from him again." Suvi staggered as she walked to the window, and for a moment I was afraid she would fall, but she managed to catch herself. She wiped her eyes with her sleeve. "This is Marko's shirt. I took it out of the hamper. It still smells like him, like the sheets do. I'll never be able to change them again."

"Suvi, where did Marko call from? According to our information, he didn't have a cell phone. Or did he?"

"The person who hired him gave him one. Marko was supposed to use it to tell him when the job was done."

"Who was the client? What did Marko tell you about him?"

"Nothing! I already said that Marko never told me about his jobs. Whoever it was had money, though. They promised Marko seventy thousand marks when the job was done. We were supposed to take the whole family to Euro Disney. Our kids have never been anywhere farther than Tallinn. When Marko got out of prison last time, we took them on a trip. We took the elevator to the top of the Viru Hotel to look at the view. Marko said that one day he was going to be able to give me and the kids everything we wanted."

Suvi wrapped her arms around herself and swallowed. She looked cold but didn't close the window.

"Marko only wanted good things for us. No one would hire him after he got out last time. His parole officer said he should go back to school. But with what money? We already had one kid and another one on the way. Then he got caught working under the table at a construction site, and I had to go on welfare. And now it's all starting again."

Suvi lit another cigarette. Wang carefully recorded everything, and I tried to take Suvi back to the night of Marko's disappearance.

"Try to remember, Suvi. Everything is important. What kind of cell phone was it? Did Marko give you the number? When did he get the phone?"

Based on the new VCR and the bikes out front, Marko had received at least a few thousand in advance. The serial number on the bill hadn't led anywhere, so Marko's client must have earned the money legally.

"It was just a normal gray Nokia. It didn't have any games or anything. Marko kept it in the pocket of his leather jacket, away from where the kids might find it. He got it a couple of days before he disappeared. Maybe it was Sunday."

A charm of finches flitted past the window and then made a black latticework in the sky, which grew and shrank according to its own laws. A gust of wind broke off the tip of Suvi's cigarette, and ash flew in her face, but she didn't seem to notice.

"I'm used to not asking so you all won't lock me up too. The first time Marko went in for a couple of assaults and concealing stolen goods, the cops tried to nail me too. We were living in a little apartment, and Marko kept stolen CD players and car stereos under our bed. But he never told me where they came from. He just told me he was transporting them from one seller to another. He never had a real job, but he promised that he'd never get mixed up with drugs, even though that's where the real money is. Now I wish I had asked more about this job. If I knew who hired him, I could go spit in his face. First he made my children's father a murderer and then killed him. And buried him in the dump like he was trash."

Suvi sniffed and wrapped her flannel shirt tighter around her. "I want a nice casket for him, not the poor-people model, and a burial plot near the sea. We used to sit at the cemetery sometimes when we were first together. We climbed over the wall. For ten years we could go there and be by ourselves, before jerks started going around knocking over gravestones. I want to bury him there. And I can dress him in his favorite clothes, right? His Levis and his Born to be Wild shirt?"

"Of course you can," I said before remembering Marko's partially decomposed corpse. Maybe the mortician would be able to convince Suvi to leave the dressing to him. Anyway, we wouldn't be able to release

Marko's body for a while, since the medical examiner and the lab were busy trying to determine time of death and caliber of the murder weapon. "Did Marko have a gun?"

Suvi shook her head.

"I don't know. I haven't let him bring guns into the house since Tony found one once and thought it was a toy. I came back from the laundry and my son was in here waving a pistol around! He had the safety off and everything. Luckily it wasn't loaded. You think I didn't yell at Marko for that?"

I nodded and smiled cautiously. Wang looked impatient, but I thought we should let Suvi go at her own pace. The chair creaked under me. The thing must have been forty years old. Someone had recently painted the wooden parts of it a light blue and covered the seat with a flowery fabric. The couch had a slipcover made of the same fabric, and the same theme repeated in the curtains. Suvi seemed to be good with her hands.

"Was Marko's client a man or a woman? And why did he or she want Petri Ilveskivi attacked?"

"I think it was a man," Suvi said, obviously thinking. "Marko only talked about one client, and I assumed it was a man. And it must have been, because Marko kept swearing about not being able to get the bastard on the phone!" Suvi's face brightened for a moment, as if determining the gender of the client could bring Marko back. "Of course I thought it was some sort of torpedo job. Like maybe the queer hadn't paid his debts, and whoever he owed was sending a torpedo after him. Marko had never gotten to do torpedo jobs before. He was so proud of himself. He said he was finally going to earn a little respect. That's what he wanted."

Wang and I nodded—that was what everyone wanted. But at the same time I was horrified. Had Laine from Organized Crime been right?

"Marko's client was furious, and Marko was afraid. He knew he had screwed up, but he told me he was going to demand more money because the mark attacked him instead of being an easy target as promised. He was going to ask for a hundred thousand. He was too goddamn greedy! And now we're all paying for it!"

Suvi looked out the window, blinking rapidly, but the tears still came.

I asked who'd connected Marko with the client. Suvi didn't know, but she promised to ask around. Maybe Marko's friends would talk to her, though to police they wouldn't even admit to knowing him.

"How are the children holding up?" I asked, indicating to Wang that she didn't need to get this part down for the record.

"They miss their dad," Suvi said and swallowed her tears. "I can handle my own pain, but when they start asking questions and crying, it's just too much. I want so badly to lie to them. To tell them that Dad will be home if they just wait. Maybe say he's in prison and we can't go visit this time. We missed him when he was gone then too, but he could write and call, and we could visit him sometimes. But not now. He's never coming home."

Suvi stopped trying to hold back the sobs. The tears left red splotches on her pale face, and I thought of a lingonberry in August, when it was only red on one side.

"It's just lucky the queer didn't have any kids," Suvi said after blowing her nose into a handkerchief she had found in her shirt pocket. "Right?"

"No, he didn't have any children. Which of Marko's friends are involved in drugs?"

"At least Tomppa Matveinen and Hannu Jarkola. Hannu and Marko were in the same cell block in prison, and they made moonshine together. Hannu is always ready to help—he's fixed our Datsun before, even got us the parts. He's a nice guy when he isn't hopped up on speed."

"And Jani Väinölä? Was he Marko's friend?"

"Who?"

"Jarkola's friend Jani Väinölä, also a skinhead. He was with Marko in prison too."

"Oh, the crazy one? No. Oh my God . . . Hannu beat up a fag a few years ago! Was this . . . was Marko's target the same one? It couldn't have been Hannu . . ." Suvi hopped off her perch on the windowsill, and a toy forgotten on the floor flew in an angry arc against the wall. "If Hannu had something to do with Marko's killing, I'm going to rip his balls off!"

It took nearly ten minutes to calm Suvi down. I tried to get her to understand that she shouldn't try to solve Marko's murder, that the best way she could help was by discreetly asking the questions we had given her. I appealed to the fact that her children needed her more now than ever. She couldn't take any risks.

"We have an APB out on Hannu Jarkola, so we'll be able to talk to him soon. Remember, Suvi, we're on the same side. We all want Marko's murderer to pay for what he did."

"It's a little hard wrapping my mind around the idea of teaming up with cops. You've always made things hard for us. Although social workers are worse. One even came around after Diana was born to spy on us. She tried to teach me how to boil potatoes, and I told her, 'Listen up, I've been cooking since I was eight, whenever my mom was working nights and my dad was drinking. To this day my brother's favorite food is my home-cooked lasagna. I ain't no helpless leech, even if I do buy a frozen casserole from the store every once in a while.'"

"I do too," I said, smiling, in an attempt to create a connection with Suvi. The sound of a car came from outside, and she ran to the kitchen window.

"Jari and the kids are back. You have to go now. I couldn't tell the kids their dad had been shot. I told them he was in a motorcycle accident. I can protect them that much, can't I?" she asked with panic in her eyes. "Or will they hate me when they learn the truth?"

"You don't have to figure all of this out by yourself. Talking with a therapist might be good for them."

"They aren't crazy, they're just half orphans!" Suvi huffed just as the door opened and the sounds of children filled the entryway.

"Dang, whose cleats are these?" Tony shouted.

"It's good you called us, Suvi. This information has been a lot of help. Call again whenever you need to," I said quickly. Wang closed the computer and stood. For a few moments the entryway was a complete traffic jam, because Suvi's brother was about three times thicker than his sister.

"Do women play soccer too?" Tony asked me dubiously.

"Yes," I said and patted him on the head.

"Dad and me play all the time, but we don't allow girls," Tony said confidently and rushed to hug his mother. Suvi drew all the kids into her arms and tried to distract from the evidence of her tears by asking a question.

"Was the movie fun?"

Wang and I slipped out. We drove a while in silence, and then Wang cautiously asked, "Should we look into the drug theory a little more now?"

"Nothing indicates that Ilveskivi used or dealt drugs," was my cold reply, even though I knew we should at least ask around. "Let's focus on finding Jarkola. Patrol should check his apartment again. Would you be up to questioning him if we can get Koivu to help?"

"Yes, assuming I can get some real clothes on."

But Jarkola wasn't around, so Wang and I both went home. After Iida fell asleep, I decided to make up for my missed soccer practice with a jog. It was a little before ten, and light still lingered, golden rays shining through the tops of the trees, making the buds and emerging greenery of the lindens glow. Familiar dogs with their walkers passed. I usually remembered the animals better than I did the people. A digging machine was still churning up the earth at the construction site, which smelled of freshly poured cement. My glutes were tight from sitting, and I knew I would have to stretch out properly at home. Just as I was having this thought I noticed a car cruising slowly behind me. Since the road was narrow, I moved over to the grass on the ditch bank so it could pass. But the driver didn't seem to want to pass.

I didn't have a bulletproof vest, a helmet, or even a cell phone. The house key in my hoodie was the only thing I had to defend myself, and it wouldn't be any use against a firearm. The dog walkers seemed to have disappeared, and the forest was suddenly silent.

It was all I could do to keep myself from looking back. Then the car pulled up next to me.

"Do you know where Tikaskallio 10 is?" a man asked in broken Finnish. "There are so many new roads here I can't find it."

When I turned I saw a brown face behind the wheel of a yellow-and-red pizza delivery car. I pointed him in the right direction, keeping my guard up the whole time. I would have to start bringing a phone with me when I ran, even though I didn't like the idea. But it was a better alternative than a gun, a bulletproof vest, or helplessness and fear.

Overnight, Helsinki Narcotics had conducted a raid on a restaurant that was selling Ecstasy pills, and they happened to find Hannu Jarkola for us in the process. Our Helsinki colleagues promised that once they were done pumping him for information, they would send him over to us for questioning. Thursday was full of meetings and went by quickly. In the afternoon word came that our search team had found some bloody scraps of leather and fabric about a kilometer from the landfill. I was just about to go home when I heard about the bullet. Using the metal detector had turned out to be worth the effort. The department press officer and I wrote up a brief release announcing that we were close to solving Petri Ilveskivi's homicide, although the motive remained unclear. I still didn't want to call a large press conference, even though

Taskinen and one of the deputy chiefs of police were pressuring me to. I wasn't as satisfied with our results as they were.

After our Friday morning meeting, I went with Koivu and Wang to look at the place where Marko Seppälä had apparently bled out. There wasn't anything special about it. Untouched willow stands, black-and-white birch trees, white wood anemones, and great blue tits enraptured with the spring. What had Seppälä's killer done while his victim bled out? Smoked a cigarette or two? Destroyed the burner phone's SIM card? Or had he left and then come back later in the night to dump the body?

One of the nearby residents remembered seeing a motorcycle sometime before ten on the twenty-second of April. The woman was sure of the date because the next day had been her daughter's birthday, and she had left the sponge cake she was making in the oven.

She had tried to drag the dog outside to do its business quickly so the cake wouldn't burn. The motorcycle had been speeding, and woman and dog had to jump out of the way to avoid being run down.

An aging veteran who lived in another house had been surprised by a van driving back and forth on the road one night before May Day. He couldn't remember the date exactly, just that the van was dark blue and that it had something in a foreign language written on it. The letters were western, though, not Russian. He was sure of that.

Two forest roads, two victims. And two killers.

"How long was Seppälä conscious? Did he know he was dying?" I wondered aloud. "Did he know he was dealing with someone this dangerous? Let's head back. I have a doctor's appointment."

I was seeing my gynecologist at eleven thirty. As I was leaving, I ran into Puustjärvi in the hallway, who said that Jarkola was on his way over for questioning. Puustjärvi and Puupponen would handle the interrogation, as agreed.

My gynecologist's office was easily accessible by bus, but I didn't know if the schedule would work for me coming back, so I took the car.

Even though I supported reducing private driving, I drove an awful lot. As a squirrel made a kamikaze attempt to cross, I noticed that its coat was already almost completely brown. Thankfully, the oncoming driver also had the patience to brake.

Even though the exam should have been routine for a woman who had given birth, every time I found it unpleasant. It didn't help that the doctor was a pleasant woman and that I knew the exam was necessary. My blood pressure was a little high, but not too high to prevent renewing my prescription.

"So what do you think? Is Iida going to be an only child? If you don't want to have any more kids, you should consider sterilization."

"Whose?" I asked, since I knew that for men it was a fairly minor procedure.

"Either one. You have to decide that for yourselves."

That sounded so final that I didn't even want to think about it, so I just took the prescription and headed to a nearby café for a Diet Coke and a mozzarella-tomato sandwich, which I ate in the car. I would have to remember to stop at the pharmacy, although I still had two and a half weeks left of the previous batch.

Puupponen had left a note on my door asking me to come talk to him. So I went and knocked on the door of the office he shared with Koivu. Of course it would have been easier if partners shared offices, but these two had been sharing a space for years now. Koivu wasn't around. Maybe he was meeting with the ballistics experts.

"So how was Jarkola?"

"How do you think? Angry. Wait, I'll pull up the report." Puupponen typed furiously. He complained sometimes about Puustjärvi, who tended to take his time with things. Apparently Puupponen would be halfway across the street before Puustjärvi realized he should start walking. Along with his slightly heavy-set build, Puustjärvi's restrained pace could be an asset in interrogations, making people relax and let their guard down. Puustjärvi could keep an interview going for hours, since playing Go and tying flies had developed his patience. Puupponen, on the other hand, got his best results in fast-paced interrogations that were more like wars of words.

"Pete had to leave. His youngest is sick again. He tried to call you, but your phone was off."

I had turned off my phone during my appointment, because the thought of me crawling off the table with no pants to answer the phone was ridiculous, and I only used my phone while driving if it was an emergency.

"Doesn't he have a couple dozen hours of comp time too? I'm fine with him going. Did you get anything out of Jarkola?"

"Helsinki already knew that the Ecstasy operation was being funded by our common friend, Salo, apparently from behind bars. Jarkola is going to be joining him there, even though he just got out after doing four months. What the hell kind of sense does it make letting these pros out on parole when they just pull new jobs? A guy like Jarkola may never spend more than a couple of months on the outside ever again. Jarkola saw Seppälä a couple of days before the attack on Ilveskivi. Seppälä had been paying a debt, about fifteen hundred marks. He bragged that he was going to throw the May Day party of the century for his friends after the big job he had coming up. He said he was going to be a torpedo."

"Did Seppälä mention any names?"

"He did tell Jarkola that the target was 'a queer you know too.' Then he promised to add a couple of punches on Jarkola's behalf. Jarkola's understanding was that the queer, Ilveskivi, I mean, had been hitting on the wrong piece of meat, and so he needed a lesson. Nothing bad, just a smashed knee or something. Guys who limp don't get as much tail."

"So Jarkola didn't think it had anything to do with drugs?"

"No, but I'm not sure how much we should trust him. He said that Seppälä didn't really seem to know what he was doing. Jarkola was just happy to get his money before Seppälä got himself thrown back in jail."

"Why didn't he tell us anything about this the last time we asked him?" I said bitterly.

"Jarkola isn't a snitch. It's different now that his friend is dead, though. You can be sure he'll do some asking around. Puustjärvi and me took it really easy on him. Jarkola was worried that he wouldn't be able to go to Seppälä's funeral if he was already in prison. It was very moving," Puupponen said dryly. "I almost believed him."

This seemed like an opportune time, so I asked Puupponen what he thought about switching partners. Puupponen didn't have any serious objections, although he complained that Anu Wang didn't always get his jokes. I didn't bother saying there were plenty of other people who didn't either.

As I walked back to my office, I wondered if Reijo Rahnasto had found out about Kajanus's relationship with Ilveskivi after all. But Rahnasto seemed more like the kind of man to punch Ilveskivi in the mouth himself rather than hiring a thug to do it. And Rahnasto wouldn't have had any reason to kill Seppälä.

It wasn't hard guessing whose word would hold sway, the well-known politician and business leader who had never done anything worse than get a speeding ticket or the puny two-bit crook.

I read through the drug test results for Petri Ilveskivi again. Zeros across the board. They hadn't even found any caffeine in his system. Ilveskivi used to sing karaoke at Café Escale. Were there drugs there? I remembered a visit a few years back to Club Bizarre, another LGBT gathering place. Some of the revelers were enjoying more than alcohol and sex, but I was a lawyer then, not a cop, so I didn't intervene. Café Escale was Liisa Rasilainen's usual haunt, so I dialed her number. Liisa was on the road with her partner, Jukka Airaksinen, and clearly didn't want to talk about her private life while he was listening, so she just said she hadn't ever noticed any drugs there. Although plenty of people knew what her job was, so they could have been hiding them.

Kim Kajanus was a photographer and had said himself that he met all kinds of people at work. Did that include drug dealers? Could Kajanus have been taking speed or Ecstasy to enhance his sexual experiences? A lot of teenagers didn't realize until it was too late that MDMA was just as dangerous as other amphetamines.

No matter how hard I tried, I couldn't imagine Petri Ilveskivi dealing drugs. Maybe he smoked a little weed every now and then. But traces of that stayed in your system for weeks, so he couldn't have been a regular user.

Could Marko Seppälä have attacked the wrong person? What if he was supposed to rough up someone else? That sounded too far-fetched. Or maybe someone had tricked Seppälä. In frustration I shoved a stack of paper to the corner of my desk, sending the top layer flying to the floor. The pages were a joint memo from the Finnish Police Federation and the Ministry of the Interior about implementation of the merit-based pay system. I was crawling around on the floor picking them up when the phone rang.

"Hi, it's Eila Honkavuori. I read in the paper that you found out who killed Petri. Congratulations. Why did he do it?"

"That isn't clear yet." After a moment's thought, I asked directly: "Did you ever think that Petri might have been using or dealing drugs?"

"Petri? Not a chance. Why are you still trying to make Petri into some sort of criminal?"

"I'm just looking for a motive. Did Petri ever mention the name Marko Seppälä to you?"

"No. I'm calling because of another man. Tommi and I were going through Petri's papers over the holiday weekend. We found a picture of an attractive young man that neither of us recognized, but I still had this nagging feeling I had seen him somewhere before. I didn't remember where until today. I saw him with you on May Day Eve. Who is he?"

"Kim Kajanus, a photographer, just an acquaintance," I replied quickly.

"Tommi was shocked. Petri wasn't in the habit of collecting pictures of good-looking boys. Do you know if Kajanus knew Petri?"

"I don't know," I lied. "Was there anything special about the City Planning Commission meeting the night of Petri's death?"

"Actually, it was an abnormally boring meeting. Lately we've been having to reassess our old decisions because the City Council keeps overriding them. That happened with the South Espoo master plan and that big superstore controversy. The Commission can be quite critical at times, but the chairman has a lot of power to act on his own. Rahnasto and the head of the City Council are good friends. Sometimes he seems to know things that he won't even tell the people in his party until after a decision is made. There have been some whispers about bribes too. I don't know if it's appropriate for the chairman of the City Planning Commission to make zoning decisions and then, a couple of years later, the businesses that benefited from those decisions buy security systems from his company for their new buildings," Honkavuori said.

"Wait . . . didn't you say that Rahnasto told some off-color jokes when Petri was late for the meeting? Did he seem relieved?"

"He was certainly in a good mood. Petri and Rahnasto didn't like each other. The last thing they squared off about was the plan for Laajalahti Bay. Petri thought Rahnasto and the powers that be were trying to sell the whole city to big business without any thought for people or the environment. And it does feel that way sometimes. When the normal planning process moves too slowly, they find shortcuts. Sometimes they start building even when the planning process isn't finished."

Shivers ran down my spine. This was getting interesting.

"Could Petri have learned something that threatened Rahnasto or someone else on the City Planning Commission? I've read the minutes for that meeting, but I'm not an expert like you. What could Petri have uncovered?"

Eila Honkavuori didn't know, but she promised to look into it. The next Planning Commission meeting was the next week, and she would contact me before then.

"Are you coming to Petri's funeral on Sunday?" she asked just before we ended the call.

"No. I have my own Mother's Day responsibilities," I replied. After the call, I asked our administrative assistant to search for anything having to do with Rahnasto and his company.

Maybe it was real estate money, not drug money, behind Petri Ilveskivi's murder.

15

On Sunday morning I woke up to Iida's excited giggling and a loud rendition of "Happy Birthday to You." It was Mother's Day. At day care Iida had made a card and a clumsily folded paper flower growing out of a brown painted cardboard pot, and I almost cried when she presented it to me. Iida and Antti had picked wood anemones for me too. Images flashed through my mind of my sisters and me secretly baking cookies and cakes for Mother's Day, until we got older and started criticizing the whole motherhood myth.

Sending Mother's Day cards to my own mom and grandmother was much easier now that they were also from Iida. Antti's parents had gone on an orchid-hunting expedition to Estonia, so we didn't have any obligation to visit them. I didn't want to go out to lunch, since Mother's Day lunches were for those mothers who cooked all the family meals.

Petri Ilveskivi's obituary appeared in the morning paper. The timing of the announcement was odd, since the funeral was the same day. As if to say that the funeral was open to the public, but please don't actually come. The poem that accompanied the obituary was outdated and vapid. The text mentioned Petri's mother and father first, then his sister and her family, and Tommi last. A casual reader would never know that Tommi Laitinen was the deceased's partner, not his brother. Why had Laitinen agreed to that?

We spent the day getting our yard ready for summer. Iida collected a pile of dead leaves with her pink plastic rake. I planted a few gladiolus bulbs, which I should have done weeks ago. Right around the time the Ilveskivi case started.

Surveyors had been working across the road in the forest the week before; apparently new building lots were going to be carved out of the woods. Living next to a construction site wasn't a particularly appealing idea, but the idea of moving sounded even worse. We were used to the peace and quiet of our own home, and with rents like they were, we wouldn't have the money for anything better than a two-bedroom apartment. If we wanted to buy a house, it would have to be far outside of the city and not as nice as where we were now. We had put off the decision while we waited for prices to fall. The economy seemed to have a short memory: only ten years had passed since the last bubble, and everyone was making exactly the same mistakes again. Every investor and CEO seemed to believe they were going to win at a game of roulette that could turn into the Russian version at any second.

Einstein lurked under the ash tree, eyes glowing and tail swishing. His aging body tensed and then he lunged toward his prey. This time the mole was faster, and the cat retreated under the house to tend to his mussed fur and his bruised ego. Einstein was clearly entering old age. He spent more time in warm spots, like in the sauna as it cooled or under the reading lamp, and he never played with his toy mice for longer than a couple of minutes. A few times I had found him sleeping at the foot of Iida's bed, even though just a year ago he had always kept his distance from her. But now the spring was clearly affecting him, because fifteen minutes later he was back trying again, and this time he caught the mole. Before retreating to his hideout to eat, he did a lap of honor with the rodent in his mouth.

"Doesn't it hurt the mole to get eaten?" Iida asked, looking worried.

"Yes, I'm sure it hurts," I said and changed the subject. On my day off I didn't want to contemplate the death of a mole, but I couldn't

escape my own thoughts. Petri Ilveskivi's memorial was at the Espoo
Cathedral. A year and a half ago, I had attended Pertti Ström's funeral
there. On the night before the service, I hadn't slept a wink. But fool-
ishly I still thought I could get through it without sedatives.

When Ström's children had gone to lay flowers on the grave, I broke
down completely. I howled like a puppy missing its mother, losing all
self-control and making a frightening scene. I was scheduled to present
the wreath from our unit and read a brief eulogy, but I couldn't even
stand. Taskinen had to handle it for me. At the reception afterward,
Ström's father came to ask whether his son and I had a very close relationship, since Pertti had talked about me so much. That made me lose
it again.

My relationship with Ström had been difficult. Maybe his suicide
would have been easier to bear if I had liked him. I thought of Tommi
Laitinen, whose final words to his beloved had been an invitation to
go to hell. Fate had been listening too closely, and those words had
condemned Tommi to hell on earth.

Lauri Jensen called around seven.

"I thought you'd like to hear about Petri's funeral," he said formally.

"Yes, I would."

The funeral had started awkwardly because apparently the priest
hadn't taken the time to prepare properly and had just rambled on
about a life cut short, the suddenness of death, and the inscrutable
ways of the Almighty. Petri Ilveskivi's parents had been the ones in contact with the church, but apparently they hadn't given any information
beyond Petri's age, profession, and that he didn't have any children.

Before the presentation of the floral arrangements, Petri's nephew
played a melancholy saraband on the cello. Tommi laid his own flowers
down after the immediate family, but he didn't say anything. He just
stood with his face set like stone. At the reception afterward, he sat at
the friends' table, not the family table.

"Jukka and I talked about making a scene. The whole thing was such an appalling pretense, as if Tommi didn't even exist. He did get to carry the casket, but he was just another 'friend of the family' like the other pallbearers. They probably only let him carry it because Petri's father has a heart condition and his brother-in-law has a weak back. I hope someone is keeping Tommi company tonight."

"Was Petri's photographer friend there? Good-looking young guy with red hair."

"Oh, the one who looks like a Russian nobleman?" Lauri asked, and I laughed involuntarily. "Yes, I think he was sitting in one of the wings of the chapel. He spent the whole time staring at the statue of Jesus hanging over the altar, like he was praying. Some of us wondered who he was. Who is he?"

"He's the photographer who did the series on Petri's couches. He was shocked when he heard about the killing and called me to see if he could help with the investigation. I guess a lot of people liked Petri Ilveskivi."

"Yes, they did. I just wished we'd had a different funeral. One that better represented Petri. A bunch of us agreed to go to Escale to sing on Thursday in Petri's honor. We can mourn and be sentimental in our own way."

"Good idea. Was anyone from the city at the funeral?"

"I recognized some of the Green Party people, and some others in fancy suits who I didn't recognize," Lauri replied. He didn't pay attention to politics and had only voted in the local elections because a good friend was a candidate.

I felt desolate for the rest of the evening, even though Iida was adorable, demanding to play hairdresser. My Mother's Day hairdo was five different pony tails, a heap of barrettes, and a piece of streamer left over from May Day. It was wonderful.

"I should go to work like this," I said to Antti, who replied with a kiss. Even that didn't make me feel any better.

In the morning I pressed my most businesslike pinstriped pantsuit, gathered my hair into a low ponytail, and took more care than usual with my makeup. The woman who stared back at me from the mirror was someone who had no intention of apologizing for her ideas. I made it to the police station in good time for the leadership coffee klatch on the top floor. Bright clear blue shone down through the skylights. Summer was almost here.

Another drug raid had happened over the weekend, this time turning up a large cache of weapons along with the illegal pharmaceuticals. I asked Narcotics to check all of the pistols against the bullet that killed Seppälä, although I had no hope of finding our killer that way.

On Friday I had checked Reijo Rahnasto's gun licenses. I was shocked. He was a real collector. He owned more than thirty firearms, from normal hunting rifles to revolvers, semiautomatic pistols, and one rarity, the legendary Suomi KP/-31 submachine gun. Once Koivu got the report back from the ballistics expert, he would compare it to Rahnasto's armory.

"Can't we send the Ilveskivi preliminary investigation to the prosecutor now?" Taskinen asked, and Laine from Organized Crime nodded. "There isn't going to be a prosecution anyway, since the killer is dead."

"I wouldn't close the case yet. Someone paid Seppälä," I said irritably.

"Do you really believe the shit his old lady is shoveling? She's just trying convince herself and her kids that her husband wasn't really a murderer. We've been tracking their family for years. The wife should get the Finlandia Prize for her storytelling. You can bet she was just as mixed up in all the fencing as Marko was. She was just better about covering her tracks so we could never charge her with anything," Laine said, his face a study of disdain.

"You have an amazing talent for interfering with cases that don't have anything to do with your unit," I said and turned my back on

Laine. "Jyrki, let's talk about this after we see what our backlog is like from the weekend. I'll go have a look at that now."

Backlog was right: three assaults, one suicide, one domestic violence incident, and an unusually nasty rape. On Saturday night, a sixteen-year-old boy had attacked his forty-year-old neighbor, knocked her out, and raped her. The woman had remained partially conscious during the rape but couldn't fight back against her larger attacker. The rest of the family, a husband and twin ten-year-old girls, had come in just as the boy was finishing and slamming the woman's head against the floor as he did.

The husband said that if the children hadn't been there, he would have killed the kid on the spot. The boy got away as the man tried to help his wife and call the police.

"We issued the APB immediately," said Lehtovuori, who had been on duty over the weekend.

"Does the boy use drugs?" asked Wang, who knew that the case would be assigned to her.

"Not according to his parents, but when do parents ever know anything? They blame the victim for wearing short skirts and sunbathing in her yard in a bikini. Quit a hot-blooded chick if she's already started tanning this year," Lehtovuori said, but then his expression froze when he saw the way Wang and I were looking at him.

Koivu said that the bullet recovered from behind the landfill was from a .22-caliber pistol. According to our records, Rahnasto owned two, a Hämmerli and a Pardini. I wished we could have a look at them to check whether they had been discharged recently, but we didn't have enough evidence for a search warrant. At this point I didn't want to share my suspicions with anyone but Koivu. After the meeting, I asked him to come to my office. There I told him that Petri Ilveskivi might have found out about a secret land-trade deal, which could have been why Rahnasto wanted to keep him away from the City Planning Commission meeting.

Koivu sat quietly for a couple of minutes and then looked at me long and hard. His blue eyes seemed distant behind his glasses.

"That's quite a theory. What deal could be so important?"

"I don't know, but I'm trying to find out. Eija promised to dig up everything she could on Rahnasto."

"Do you think that those two things together, a possible leak and seducing his daughter's boyfriend, could have pushed Rahnasto over the edge?"

"No. I don't think Rahnasto knew about Petri and Kim." Koivu nodded and then said he had to go. I stayed in my office, wondering whether I was right. Maybe I wasn't the expert judge of human nature I thought I was. Of course everyone would want to protect Petri's memory, Tommi and Eila and even Kim, and they wouldn't freely divulge drug use or other secrets.

And was Eila Honkavuori the right person to investigate a possible zoning scheme? The big political parties, the National Coalition Party and the Social Democrats, usually found common ground in zoning issues. Eila had said she was in the opposition on the Planning Commission, but did that apply to everything? Should I be talking to Petri Ilveskivi's own party members, like his successor on the Planning Commission?

Then I remembered that I was supposed to be leading others' investigations, not going solo.

Time for some salmiakki licorice from my drawer stash. I dove into my paperwork, and I was just getting into a good rhythm between the work and the candy when my door buzzer rang. I pressed the green light and was surprised to find that it was Jyrki Taskinen behind the door rather than one of my subordinates. Quickly I hid the bag of licorice under a pile of papers.

"I came to talk about Seppälä and Ilveskivi like you asked," he said, sitting down on the couch. "Laine shouldn't interfere, but try to tolerate him. He's doing a good job with his unit, and we don't need any in-fighting around here."

"Why can't he let me do my work in peace? You agree with me that we shouldn't cut off the Ilveskivi investigation yet, don't you?" I asked. Taskinen's expression changed to one of embarrassment, and he crossed his legs before replying.

"We may never know Seppälä's motive. Continuing the investigation would be a waste of your unit's resources. Focus on Seppälä's murder instead. Even though it seems impossible right now, with time these kinds of cases usually reveal themselves to be part of other ones. Even a well-organized drug-running operation has someone with loose lips. I don't think we should say anything publicly about Seppälä being hired. Let's just say he killed Ilveskivi by accident during a robbery. We could hint that he took his own life after he realized what he'd done."

I couldn't believe my ears. The world seemed to slip off its rails, becoming distorted like a Dalí painting in which everything was what it looked like but also something else, strange and repulsive.

"The mayor's office wants this investigation closed as soon as possible. Naturally all of our elected officials have been concerned about their personal security after such a shocking incident."

"When did you talk to the mayor?" I asked in a voice that seemed to be coming from somewhere far away.

"He called Assistant Chief Kaartamo this morning. Kaartamo suggested that we have a lunch meeting in his office tomorrow. The police chief would also be there. We can celebrate solving the Ilveskivi case."

"Actually, Iida has a dentist appointment at noon tomorrow," I said quickly. That was true, although Antti had been planning to take her for her checkup. "I'll call off the preliminary investigation if I receive a written order to do so. But the case will stay open, because we're still investigating Seppälä's death. We're not going to bury it with the cold cases."

"Do what you want," Taskinen said with something besides exhaustion in his voice that I couldn't quite interpret. "Think about the lunch, though. Ask Antti to take Iida, or maybe you could change the time."

"The clinic has a two-month waiting list, and Antti is giving a lecture," I said, lying through my teeth. "If you think you have something to celebrate, by all means do so without me."

Taskinen sat for a moment without saying anything and then stood up.

"You'll receive the order to suspend the preliminary investigation as soon as possible. I'll expect your report by Wednesday at the latest."

He slammed the door after him. That meant a lot, coming from him.

I tried to refocus my thoughts. I still had one day left. First I could question Jani Väinölä, or assign someone else to question him, I thought, mentally correcting myself. I'd ask Koivu and Wang to handle it as soon as they finished interviewing the rape victim and her husband.

I went online and brought up all of the City Planning Commission minutes from the past year. The only useful piece of information I could find was that the meeting Petri Ilveskivi never got to ended at nine fifteen. According to Suvi Seppälä, Marko had reached his client at nine thirty and then left immediately. I remembered the neighbor's mentioning the van he'd seen on the back road to the landfill that same night. Rahnasto didn't own a van, but several vehicles were registered to RISS—Rahnasto Industrial Security Systems—including four vans. The company's logo was a patriotic blue and white. The man who had seen the van on the west road to the dump had mentioned white lettering.

Part of me wanted to call Reijo Rahnasto and ask him directly why he hadn't wanted Ilveskivi at that meeting. Of course I didn't do that. Instead I called Tommi Laitinen and asked if I could send someone to collect Ilveskivi's papers from the Planning Commission. Laitinen said he would be home at three fifteen.

"I thought the case was closed, even though no one knows why Seppälä killed Petri," he said.

"No, we haven't closed the preliminary investigation yet. I was hoping you might remember what Petri had been talking about lately in regard to zoning and city planning. Did he ever hint that he had run into something shady?"

"All the time. Important decision are always being made behind closed doors in Espoo. The decisions are already made before they're even brought to the Planning Commission or the City Council. Sometimes I wondered how Petri put up with it. It seemed like he was hitting his head against the same wall over and over again."

"Politics look that way to everyone else too. By the way, how was the funeral?"

Laitinen made a grim sound. I didn't know whether it was a laugh or a growl.

"Just as horrible as I had expected. Strawberry jam in my wounds. I don't usually drink much, but after the funeral I went out and got good and hammered." He grunted again. "Didn't your redheaded detective give you a report on the funeral?"

Redheaded? My thoughts raced—Puupponen hadn't gone to Petri Ilveskivi's funeral. Then I realized that Laitinen meant Kim Kajanus. I didn't feel up to lying anymore.

"We didn't send anyone to the funeral. But one of us will be at your door today before four o'clock. Don't hand over the papers before seeing a badge and receiving a receipt," I instructed, and then realized what I had just said. I wasn't usually paranoid, but Taskinen's strange behavior had put me on guard.

The general development plan for South Espoo had been in the works for years, but it had been delayed because the powers that be couldn't come to a consensus about extending the Metro line. Recently, some of the most obstinate proponents of private driving had cautiously begun to swing their support to the Metro because the major tech companies had announced their support.

Could there be something about the Metro project that someone didn't want the public to know about? Had the mayor told Assistant Chief Kaartamo to end our investigation?

Koivu came to tell me that the teen rapist had been caught, and he and Wang were starting the interrogation immediately. Jani Väinölä, who still wasn't home, would have to wait until the next morning. Mira Saastamoinen from Patrol came by and plunked down two thick folders full of Petri Ilveskivi's Planning Commission documents on my desk. I took them home with me.

When I went to pick up Iida, Helvi was standing in the yard, looking depressed. Iida was the only child left. It wasn't even five yet, so she couldn't be upset that I was late.

"I'm just so furious," she said when I asked what had happened, and she fetched a letter with the Espoo City seal on it—a horseshoe with a crown above. "My contract goes through July. I haven't worried about it, because the city has such a shortage of home day-care providers. But apparently I was an idiot not to. The city still wants to use my services, but they want to outsource them. So I'm supposed to form a company so the city can buy childcare services from me."

"To avoid paying social security costs?"

"Exactly. I don't know the first thing about running a business!"

"Terttu Taskinen, my boss's wife, is a day-care administrator with the city. Call her. I also know a labor law professor who might be able to help. And of course I can call the day-care office myself. If they fire you that would mean all the parents would have to find new a day care for their kids. And none of us wants that."

"Where am I supposed to go? No one wants to hire a fifty-year-old lady," Helvi said, but there was a healthy dash of fighting spirit in her voice now. I gave her the phone numbers I had promised and said I would do what I could.

The situation at home wasn't much more pleasant.

"A real estate agency called," Antti yelled as I was taking off Iida's coat. "The owners want to put our house up for sale. They're offering us the right of first refusal."

Antti's face was pale and dour, and two vertical lines had formed between his eyebrows.

"How much are they asking?" I said as I brushed Iida's dark curls out of her eyes. She scampered off to watch TV. *The Moomins* had just started.

"First they have to do an inspection and have it appraised. They aren't going to find much wrong with it. It needs some paint inside and out, but the lot is big, half a hectare, and according to the zoning there's enough room for a second house. The location is quiet, since we're at the end of the road. The asking price is going to be at least a million and a half. Prices have gone up so much lately. It's crazy."

"What a day. It's like the sky is falling," I said with a sigh and went to grab a beer from the fridge. As luck would have it, we still had some paella in the freezer from the week before, so I put it in the microwave to thaw and went looking for fresh saffron in the spice cupboard. That and a splash of white wine would bring it back to life.

Antti came over and wrapped his arms around me from behind, and we rocked gently to the music playing on the TV while the microwave thawed dinner. The beer disappeared quickly with two people drinking it. Neither of us knew what to say. A million and a half Finnish marks was an enormous sum. We had a couple of hundred thousand in savings after having paid off the last installments of our student loans the year before. Paying off a home loan of more than a million marks wouldn't allow any room for maternity leaves or sabbaticals.

As if by mutual agreement we left the issue to stew and drowned our sorrows with the rest of the white wine over dinner. The buzz built a protective wall between me and my problems, and reinforcing that wall with a glass of whiskey or two would have been easy, but I didn't want to go down that rabbit hole. Instead I played store with Iida—which was currently her favorite game—even though I kept forgetting what I had just bought. After she fell asleep, I read through Petri Ilveskivi's papers. The first thing I learned was that zoning decisions weren't simple. Petri had been interested in the Metro project, apparently giving it guarded support as a member of the Greens, whose positions on the issue had been all over the map.

In addition to the Metro, naturally Petri was interested in the situation in his own neighborhood and in the idea of creating a second central park. Petri supported the growth of dense residential areas that made the preservation of more green space possible.

There were also documents related to the development of Laajalahti Bay. There was intense pressure to expand the Otaniemi technology parks, but there wasn't enough land. Keilaniemi was already full, and I found a draft plan for reclaiming the land between Karhusaari Island and Hanasaari Island. Karhusaari was a nature preserve, so there was no hope of constructing office buildings or luxury apartments there. Espoo was proud of its connection to the sea, but now it seemed that the city was moving toward privatizing public shorelines.

I fell asleep with my clothes on and the papers on my lap, which was what I got for drinking wine that early in the evening. I woke up when Antti shook me, so at least I managed to brush my teeth and put on a nightshirt before crawling under the covers. In the morning I woke up at five. The daylight was so bright that it would have been pointless to try to catch the hem of the Sandman's robe, so at six I got out of bed, drank a glass of juice, and went out for a run.

The sounds of humanity were still faint, just the occasional car braking on the highway. The birds were all the noisier for the quiet, and I had to look twice before I could believe my eyes when I saw a moose on the edge of the forest. It was probably a lost yearling. After noticing me, it stood still and flared its nostrils. Mist hung in the low spots, and the lilies of the valley had unfurled into bundles of swords with flowers concealed by the green outer leaves. Marsh marigolds glowed on the ditch bank.

The others hadn't woken yet by the time I returned. I made coffee and put oatmeal on to boil, and then spent a long time stretching. Einstein wanted to go out exploring. The thermometer had suddenly shot up to nearly sixty degrees.

I arrived at the lobby of the police station at the same time as a bleary-eyed Jani Väinölä, who was being escorted by two officers.

"Where should we take this?" Officer Haikala asked.

"Keep him company for a little while in Interrogation Room 4. My detectives will come have a chat with him after our morning meeting. Give him some coffee to get his brain working."

"What the fuck did I do now?" Väinölä asked me, but he had to make do without a reply. The patrol officers didn't need to know why we had wanted Väinölä picked up. Stories traveled fast enough as it was, rising like steam from the holding cells downstairs all the way to the muckety-mucks' sauna upstairs.

"You want to come with us to the interrogation?" Koivu asked as I was making assignments for the day. "Didn't we already check Väinölä's alibi when we were working Ilveskivi's murder?"

"Only up to six o'clock. Can you and Wang handle it?"

"Yes," Wang said, "but Väinölä won't talk to me. We'll have a better chance if a lieutenant is in the room. It'll make him feel important." She had a point. I promised to come for the beginning of the interrogation, but at eleven I had to leave to take Iida to the dentist. Antti had thought that my sudden eagerness to interrupt my workday was brought on by my chronic bad-mother guilt syndrome, and I didn't bother correcting him. He didn't need to hear about my sudden attack of bad-cop guilt syndrome.

Eija Hirvonen had amassed pages of information about Reijo Rahnasto and RISS Inc. I quickly glanced at the list of shareholders. Eriikka Rahnasto owned 20 percent of the company, and her father owned fifty-five. There were twenty or so smaller shareholders. Revenues had seen strong growth over the past few years. New international information technology companies had been especially eager to buy RISS security services.

Väinölä was helping himself to our coffee and donuts in the interrogation room while Officer Haikala impatiently tapped his fingers on the tabletop. He practically ran out of the room when we showed up. I had printed out a copy of the report from Väinölä's previous interview, and now I started by asking what he had done on the night of April twenty-second after he was finished shopping in the city.

"How the hell am I supposed to remember? That was almost three weeks ago! If I already had my booze and cigarettes, I probably went to find a chick. I think maybe I paid Miia a visit."

"Is Miia your girlfriend?" Koivu asked.

"She isn't a girl or a friend. She's a thirty-year-old chick who likes a good screw sometimes, and she knows she can get one from me," Väinölä proudly declared.

"Name, address, and phone number?" Wang asked and typed in the answers. We then spent a while confirming whether Väinölä really was at Miia's apartment on the night in question. Then I asked about Marko Seppälä. Väinölä admitted knowing him, and that Jarkola had told him about Seppälä's dreams of becoming a torpedo.

"Do you think I hired him? Why would I have hired a fucking incompetent like that? I can take any fag any day. I don't need nobody's help!"

Koivu glanced at me with a look that said he had thought the same thing.

Our questioning led nowhere, but when it was time for me to leave, I asked Koivu to step outside with me for a second and then ordered him to keep pushing Väinölä about Seppälä. Maybe some other team of interrogators would have been better for Väinölä, say Mela and Lähde, who could have at least created a connection with Väinölä by cracking some of their off-color jokes. I hadn't been any help with that.

Iida was over the moon to be going for a drive with mommy in the middle of the day. Her chattering put me in a better mood, because she thought the fire truck that drove by and the cranes at the construction sites were miracles. As she lay in the dentist's chair with her mouth as wide as she could make it, I felt a flash of fear. Iida was so trusting, but soon I would have to smash her naive belief in the goodness of humanity and start warning her about drug needles and strangers who might try to lure her away.

Iida's teeth were in great shape except for a little plaque on her upper back teeth. Again the guilty conscience: I didn't always have the patience to brush carefully. I felt like going home with Iida, to escape into the worlds of Pettson and Findus or Pippy Longstocking, but the time for that wouldn't be until evening. Iida fell asleep in her car seat. I left her on a cot at Helvi's to continue her nap.

I ate quickly and alone in the cafeteria. While I was gone more paperwork had appeared on my desk. One was the order to close the preliminary investigation into Petri Ilveskivi's homicide. Another was less formal, in Taskinen's handwriting: *I gave the order to release Jani Väinölä. We don't have any basis to detain him. I asked Narcotics to investigate Seppälä, so you can let that go for now. JT.*

The disappointment was like a physical pain, as if Taskinen had punched me in the gut. I was useful as the token female moving up the career ladder on the force. But apparently now that I was a unit commander, my bosses thought that I would be content to dance to whatever tune they played.

I had shoved my head through the glass ceiling, but I was caught on my breasts. Now the shards were slicing my sides, and a small voice inside me reminded me that I should have stayed down below. Then I wouldn't have been hurt.

16

I charged on, tasting blood in my mouth. No one was going to catch me, I told myself. I was going to win. But it didn't help. The other team's defender, Sanna Saarniaho, made a perfectly legal tackle, sending me thudding to the ground on my bottom and gaining control of the ball. Saarniaho had been on the women's national youth team a few years before. Losing the ball to her wasn't any big embarrassment, but still it bothered me.

I returned to the game, playing even more fiercely and aggressively than before. The days since closing the preliminary investigation into Petri Ilveskivi's killing had been frustrating. In the morning I had talked with the prosecutor, Ari Aho, and his thinking had been the same as my superiors'. Time to close the investigation completely. If only Katri Reponen had been at the head of the rotation for the next case. Her I could have negotiated with.

"Maria!" Anu Wang yelled to me and then lobbed the ball past midfield. I succeeded in faking out the goalie and launched the ball into the upper-left corner of the net. I screamed in triumph, but in the end my goal didn't matter all that much. Our team lost one to three.

Playing did me good. I was on the sideline toweling off when Liisa Rasilainen walked over.

"Who taught you to kick people in the shins like that?" she asked with a smirk, then took a swig from her sports drink. "I think maybe you forgot you were playing against me and not our bosses."

"I'm sorry. Did I hurt you?"

"No big deal. By the way, I have the day off tomorrow. I was thinking about going to Café Escale for some karaoke in the evening. Want to come?"

I didn't have the day off. Actually, I had another Helsinki-Espoo-Vantaa police coordination meeting in the afternoon, but the thought of karaoke and a few beers sounded nice. If I could leave after Iida fell asleep, I wouldn't be neglecting my maternal duties either.

So I agreed to meet Liisa at nine thirty at the bus station. The next afternoon, I rode home as fast as I could. The weather was warm, and nature seemed to be making up for those long, cold weeks. The birch leaves were already the size of my thumbnail, and dandelions bloomed along the walls of the houses. But as far as my mood was concerned, it could have been November. It was almost as though the sun was taunting me.

Taskinen had been acting as a cushion between me and the higher-ups for the whole time I'd been in Espoo. I didn't know what he really thought about ending the preliminary investigation. And he probably wasn't going to tell my anytime soon why he had decided to do it.

I knew going to a bar in a bad mood wasn't a particularly smart idea, but I didn't feel like being smart. Iida and I splashed around in the shower together, and then I read her a long bedtime story. I didn't take a stiff drink to start warming up for the evening until after she fell asleep.

Antti seemed amused by my enthusiasm for gay karaoke.

"Are you sure Rasilainen isn't into you, inviting you out like this?" he asked teasingly and mussed my hair, which I had just finished lacquering into the style I wanted it.

"Idiot. Of course not. She lives with a flutist, and Marjaana can't stand drunk people singing. Even Liisa only gets to sing in the shower, and she has a great voice." Rasilainen had performed as the lead singer in a band put together for our work Christmas party, and their act was so good they had even gotten Taskinen on his feet.

"And you're going to this karaoke bar to have a good time, not to, say, investigate Petri Ilveskivi?" Antti continued, and I blushed. Of course I hadn't forgotten that Café Escale had been Ilveskivi's regular hangout. Even though I was leaving my work clothes home, I was still a cop no matter where I went.

I dressed in jeans, tennis shoes, and a T-shirt, with a flannel over the top. Let people read whatever messages they wanted to into my outfit. I didn't care. I put on a little mascara, feeling carefree and comfortable. On the one hand, it would have been fun to dress to the nines, but that would have required proper makeup, which I didn't have time for. I intended to ride partway and then jump on the bus.

Liisa was waiting at the station with a drunk who was trying to bum a smoke off her and refused to believe her when she said she didn't smoke. We left him hurling curses after us as we walked the block to the restaurant, where the show was already in full swing. A man in a leather getup that made him look like he'd just climbed off his Harley was singing a sentimental love ballad in a delicate, flat tenor. I wasn't sure whether he was serious.

We grabbed drinks from the bar, me a gin and tonic and Liisa a dry cider. The tables were full, but we managed to insinuate ourselves into a corner spot with two men. Based on their body language, they were not lovers. The slender blond one was eagerly flipping through the playlist and the larger dark-haired one was making fun of his suggestions. Only the best of friends usually endured such abuse. Liisa grabbed the song list from the second one and started reading it to me. I would need another gin before I would be ready to sing. When I walked to the bar, I noticed Lauri Jensen come in through the front door. I tried to shout his name, but it was impossible to be heard over the clamor. Our blond tablemate got up. He sang Mamba's "Don't Leave Me" in such a perfect imitation of Tero Vaara's crooning that everyone was cheering like mad. Even the phrasing was spot on.

The bartender took my order, and I wove my way through the crowd toward Lauri Jensen, who was talking to a serious-looking man in his sixties. For a second Lauri looked surprised to see me, but then he rushed to give me a hug.

"Hi, Maria! I heard you solved Petri's murder. Good work!" Lauri said and slapped me on the shoulder.

"Thanks," I replied glumly, but Lauri misinterpreted my tone.

"I'm sorry. It was stupid of me to talk about your work when you're off."

"Oh, go ahead. I won't sulk." I couldn't tell Lauri anything about how the investigation had been cut short, so I joined in the applause as the song ended.

"Are you alone? You can join me and Mara."

"I'm here with someone from work. Liisa's pressuring me to sing."

"That's why we're here. Do you know what song was Petri's trademark? Kaj Chydenius's 'You, You're the One I Love.' He sang it every time. The progression is difficult with all the half steps, but Petri had a good voice. What are you going to do?"

"I don't have a clue."

The majority of patrons in the bar were male—there were only about ten of us females. That didn't seem to bother anyone, though. At our small table we had no choice but to interact with our tablemates, but fortunately they were pleasant even if they did have sharp tongues. The blond one was just about to complete seminary, and soon we got to the topic of the church's opposition to marriage equality.

"How can you be part of an institution that doesn't accept you as you are?" an overwrought Liisa asked. "I mean, I belong to the church too, but at this point I'm only a nominal Christian. I probably would have given it up entirely if they hadn't allowed female priests."

"The only way to change systems like that is from the inside," the blond man replied. "I believe in God, and I want to be a priest."

Usually I pushed religious questions out of my mind. I had never been able to decide what I believed in, but I also couldn't stand the vague mush of religiosity that people spewed all over the place these days. Priests blessed shopping malls, and people labeled themselves as "Jesus fans" in letters to the editors of religious magazines. Religious conviction seemed to be a possession that every successful person was supposed to own, like a car and the newest model of cell phone. But I didn't have any intention of getting into an argument with a theologian.

Then I saw Kim Kajanus standing in the doorway.

"Who is that?" asked the dark-haired man, who seemed to know all of the bar's regulars. "Looks like a curious hetero."

Kajanus attracted the attention of other customers as well, but he was able to walk to the bar and order a beer in peace. He looked at the walls, not the people, and retreated to stand in the farthest corner of the bar. I glanced at Lauri Jensen, who had clearly recognized Kim. I wanted to scram, but Liisa Rasilainen announced to the table that she was going to sing "Mombasa," and I couldn't not stay and listen. I scanned the playlist, hoping to find something just as tasteless. My gin was disappearing quickly, and I tried to tell myself that I was just thirsty after soccer and biking. Liisa sipped her cider and hummed along with the other singers to get her voice warmed up.

Lauri Jensen stood up from his table, and at first I thought he was going to sing, but then the MC announced that someone named Mika was up next. Instead Lauri came over and crouched next to me.

"Petri's photographer friend is here."

I nodded. The noise was reaching another crescendo because a short fifty-year-old guy was crooning Paula Koivuniemi's "I'm a Woman," and the whole room was singing along.

"I'm going to go talk to him. Little hunk looks lonely," Lauri said with a grin as the song ended.

"Fresh meat," Liisa said. "Nice not to have to trawl for companionship anymore. Sometimes I watch single's shows—you know, like *Ally McBeal*, but I can't see what's supposed to be funny about them. I remember exactly how desperate it all was."

"Lauri is married," I said just as Liisa's turn came up. Her whole demeanor changed when she climbed onstage. She began to sway, and a dangerous glow sparked in her eyes. Liisa was a charismatic woman who wore her few gray strands and laugh lines with style. She sang half an octave lower than normal and flirted shamelessly with the audience as she sang. Imagining what the chauvinist pigs at the station would say wasn't difficult.

"I think I've earned another cider!" Liisa exclaimed as she made her way back to the table, accepting pats on the back and suggestive winks. "Can I get you anything?"

"Sure, one more gin and tonic," I replied as I dug a twenty out my wallet. I turned to see how Kim and Lauri's discussion was going. Lauri seemed to be talking excitedly, and Kim seemed to be focusing his attention on the playlist so he wouldn't have to look at him.

"Well, Maria, have you picked a song?" Liisa asked, setting my drink down with a thud. When I said I hadn't, she and the two men began pressuring me.

"I can't. The table standard is too high," I said, trying to wriggle my way out of it.

"Only until he sings," the theology student said, indicating his friend, who stuck his tongue out like a five-year-old. I flipped through the list of songs and found the disco section at the back. "I Will Survive" seemed like good medicine for my work blues. I could dedicate it to all my bosses. I went to give my slip to the MC and then headed to the toilet. Café Escale didn't have separate men's and women's facilities, but that was nothing new for me. I had gotten used to going with the boys when I was in school, playing on my soccer team, and in my band. I was starting to get tired of being "one of the guys," though.

When I came out of the restroom, Kim Kajanus walked past me to hand his request to the MC. Our eyes met. Looking embarrassed, he said hello and then made for the bar. His all-black clothing accentuated the paleness of his skin and the blazing red of his hair. I wondered where Eriikka Rahnasto was.

Back at our table, the current activity was telling rude jokes about the Minister of the Interior, Kari Häkämies. My turn to sing came all too soon. The shaking hit me as soon as I reached the stage, my legs trembling so violently I was sure it was visible all the way to the door. Why the hell had I agreed to something this stupid? I hadn't sung in public since the last performance of my high school band, Rat Poison. But the opening notes of the song were already eliciting shouts from the crowd.

Of course my voice trembled and went off key occasionally, but I performed with enough bravado to earn enthusiastic applause. At the end I bowed and spread my arms like the finest prima donna. Maybe I should have worn high heels and gold eye shadow after all. Three minutes of stardom was just about right, but then my buzz started to wear off, even though I hadn't realized I was drunk in the first place.

"You sang beautifully," Lauri Jensen said, wrapping his arms around my shoulders from behind. "That redhead is a bit of a toad. He claimed he hadn't really known Petri and only came to the funeral on a whim. Is he even gay?"

"What, you didn't ask?" I said teasingly.

"No. Well, I'm headed home now. I'm ringleader of the family circus tomorrow night, since Jukka will be at work and the women are going to the theater. I won't be able to cope if I'm tired. Say hi to Antti!"

My tablemates had moved on to sharing insane rumors about all the current celebrities, and Liisa and I giggled like two teenagers. Gradually the world began to feel less hopeless. Spring was really here, and I had plenty of gin. We kept up the ruckus until Kim Kajanus was called to the stage. He sang Kaj Chydenius's "Song for a Dead Love" very seriously. He had a dark, slightly rough baritone, and from the rapid movement of his Adam's apple, it was safe to say he was nervous. What kind of ritual was he performing by singing such a dramatic song in Petri's favorite bar?

As he looked out over the crowd, he sang about the thick wine of dreams and endless dark forests. I wanted to laugh and cry at the same time.

After the song ended, Kim slammed the microphone into its stand and pushed his way through the crowd, ignoring the applause and whistling. On a whim, I grabbed my jacket and turned to Liisa.

"Sorry, I have to go. Work. I'll explain on Monday."

My tablemates sent boos after me, but I hurried outside and took off running up the street. I caught Kajanus at the corner.

"Hi, Kim," I said, now out of breath. "How's it going?"

Kajanus looked at me angrily. "What the hell did you tell Lauri? I thought the police had to respect confidentiality." He kept walking, apparently headed for one of the buses waiting at the station.

"All I did was ask him if you were at the funeral. That's all!" I tried hopelessly to keep up with him. Even though I was used to walking with men who were much taller than me, all the gin and the day's physical exertion made my legs feel like lead weights. "You forget that I'm a detective. In homicide investigations we have to ask difficult questions."

"But Petri's murder is already solved! That crook killed him. I read all about it in the paper." Kajanus shoved his hands deep into the pockets of his suede jacket.

"Why did you go to the funeral and then come to Café Escale tonight?"

"The funeral announcement was in the newspaper," Kajanus shouted. "And none of your business!"

"What kind of relationship do you have with Eriikka's father?"

"What does Reijo have to do with this?"

We had arrived at the bus station, and I followed Kajanus to his queue. He said hello to someone and tried to pretend we didn't know each other. The bystanders presumably thought this early middle-aged woman was making a hopeless attempt to hit on a handsome man ten years her junior. I didn't care what they thought. I had things to settle with Kim Kajanus. I marched after him onto the bus and sat next to him without hesitation.

"Did Petri like Reijo Rahnasto? I assume he knew you were dating Rahnasto's daughter."

Kajanus leaned over and shushed me.

"My neighbors are sitting right there! Eriikka knows them. For God's sake, be quiet!"

Even though I had drunk three and a half drinks, I was still able to behave sensibly. I didn't want to complicate Kajanus's life any more than he already had on his own.

"Come to my place!" he whispered unexpectedly. "Eriikka is in Brussels." Turning to his neighbors across the aisle, he said, "This is my cousin from out of town. I thought I'd show her a good time in the city."

Kajanus really seemed to be getting into his role in this melodrama.

"I've never been out to sing karaoke before," I said, matching his artificiality.

Kajanus lived in an imposing three-story apartment building. We wished the neighbors good night at the second floor and continued up the stairs.

The apartment was spacious and refined. The large room was divided by a bar in front of the kitchenette and a movable gray-and-white Japanese screen, behind which Kim apparently hid his bed. The walls were white, decorated with just a few photo enlargements, and the furniture was black leather and chrome. A lot of money had been spent on the audio-visual equipment. Obviously Kim Kajanus was not a poor man. He rubbed his red eyes.

"Damn contact lenses. Cigarette smoke always irritates my eyes. Wait here while I take my lenses out."

Kajanus slipped into the bathroom, and the water ran for a few seconds. When he returned, he was wearing brown-rimmed glasses that made him look older and less delicate.

"So what is this about? What were you doing at Escale? You aren't a lesbian, are you?"

"I'm just like you. Trying to resurrect Petri Ilveskivi in my mind so I can figure out why he was attacked."

"Resurrect," Kajanus said with a sigh. "Yes, I guess that's right. I went to the funeral because I needed confirmation that Petri was really dead. But today . . . Petri said he liked to sing karaoke. He said he thought of me when he sang love songs. Fuck, I'm so pathetic!"

Kajanus collapsed on the couch and covered his face. After a couple of minutes he stood up. "Would you like some coffee?" he asked, calmer now.

"Why not? This might be a long night." I sat down on the same couch Kajanus had just left. It was nice and soft. I kicked off my shoes and folded my legs under me. On the opposite wall was a black-and-white portrait of Eriikka Rahnasto. The stark light and shadow emphasized her high cheekbones and straight nose. Her shoulders were bare, and her blond hair fell over her right ear.

On the other wall was a picture of a sofa. The same red sofa that occupied Petri Ilveskivi and Tommi Laitinen's living room.

Kajanus returned from the kitchen and saw the direction of my gaze.

"Petri's sofa . . . it's a good photo, so I had it printed and framed. You would think looking at it would be painful, since Petri isn't in it. He was standing there to the left, grinning, and the shadow of his left arm fell on the white floor there. Can you see? Every time I look at that picture, I fill in Petri, and his image overwhelms everything else—the couch, the window, the picture itself. I should probably take it down and tell Eriikka I was bored of it."

Kajanus hadn't closed the curtains, and I could make out a few pale stars between the birch branches. Suddenly I was terribly tired, but the scent of espresso wafting in from the kitchen kept me awake.

"I made lattes. You aren't lactose intolerant, are you? Eriikka is," Kajanus said and then disappeared into the kitchenette. A few moments later he came back, pushing a stainless-steel serving cart with two saucer-size latte cups and a few orange-flavored cookies.

"Let's get this over with. Ask me whatever it is you want to ask," Kajanus said, then took a sip of his coffee.

"What did Petri say about Reijo Rahnasto?"

"They seemed to disagree about everything. Petri was shocked when he found out who I was dating. He even asked me if Eriikka was very close with her father."

"Is she?"

For a moment Kajanus didn't answer, instead eating several cookies in a row, as if he were starving. The coffee was strong and hot. The cup didn't have handles, so it warmed my hands nicely as I drank.

"I don't really know. Eriikka doesn't talk a lot about her parents. Her mother lives in Turku. Apparently the divorce was so contentious that her parents couldn't stand to even live in the same city, but that was long before I met her. Reijo has been seeing one of Eriikka's coworkers lately. Why do you ask about him?" Kajanus inquired, and then when he realized, his face flushed with anger. "You don't think that Reijo knew, do you? That he would have . . . no, I'm the one he would have had beaten up if he had found out, not Petri. Never Petri!" Long fingers ran through red hair and then moved, trembling, toward his coffee cup.

"Is he a violent man?"

"He beat Eriikka's mother and his second wife, but that's a secret. Eriikka let it slip once when she had drunk a bit too much, but she's never been willing to talk about it again. Eriikka's mother has, though. She asked me to be better to her daughter than Reijo was to her. God help me!"

"What did Petri say about Rahnasto?" I asked again.

Kajanus stood up and walked to the window. From outside came the squealing of brakes and the blowing of a horn as a freight train rumbled down the railway tracks. I took one of the chocolate cookies, and the orange marmalade filling spurted out on my chin. I took a napkin from the serving cart.

"Petri thought that Reijo was breaking the law by not putting all the initiatives that members suggested on the Planning Commission's agenda. He was relieved when he saw I didn't like Reijo much either. Reijo could go to all the public-speaking seminars in the world, but it would never change his basic ruthlessness. I guess ruthlessness still works in the business world, where you're supposed to only think about your own advantage, but in politics I have this strange idea that you're actually supposed to represent your constituents. Would you like more coffee?"

"Yes, thank you. So I take it you didn't vote for Reijo Rahnasto in the last election?"

Kajanus laughed. He fetched the coffee and milk from the kitchen and refilled our cups. Then he asked why I was still digging into Petri Ilveskivi's death.

"Because I suspect that Reijo Rahnasto hired Marko Seppälä. Why else would he be so interested in the investigation of the murder of someone he detested? You know him. Could he do something like that, hire a thug to beat someone up and then shoot the guy after he bungled the job?"

"Yes," Kajanus replied quietly. "I imagine you know Reijo collects guns."

"Yes, I do."

"Last fall he tried to get me to go moose hunting with him. When I declined, he suggested that I at least come and take pictures. I imagine he wanted to immortalize himself with his rich friends standing around the corpses of the animals they'd killed. Reijo is a skilled hunter. He's shot at least five moose and one bear. I have no doubt he could kill a person if he had reason to."

"The only thing missing is a motive," I said, half to myself. "It has to have something to do with the City Planning Commission meeting or at least something they were dealing with, but what?" I rubbed the coffee cup between my hands, but it was no crystal ball.

"Listen, Kim, do you and Reijo ever get together to take a sauna or anything? Drink half a case of beer and a bottle of cognac and talk man to man?"

"No."

"Too bad.

"But I can try to think of some way to talk to him . . . I could say that I knew Petri. My name is on all the photographs in that magazine article after all. It'd be perfectly natural for me to be interested in the murder of someone I knew through work."

After another fifteen minutes chatting with Kajanus, I ordered a taxi. My bike could wait at the bus station until tomorrow. Being surrounded by the metal shell of a car made me feel safe, even though, as time passed, the effect of Salo's threats was fading. At home I ate a hefty sandwich and fell asleep quickly despite how much coffee I had drunk. Early in the morning I awoke to the sound of a scooter and knew that it must be a little past five. The paperboy's routine was consistent. A little later, I heard the sound of a car idling for a moment before driving on. Sometimes lovebirds used the end of the road as a love nest.

Soon our room was hot, and the sunlight mercilessly assaulted my bleary eyes. I put on sunglasses before venturing outside in my pajamas and slippers. Einstein slipped past me, darting off like a much younger cat toward a wagtail that was mocking him from the birch tree next to the mailbox.

It happened in the blink of an eye. When Einstein bounded past the mailbox, there was a flash. The sound was deafening, but I was able to see a piece of shrapnel hit my cat and throw him in an arch into our ash tree.

17

For a moment I could only stare, and then I started to scream. Iida and Antti rushed to the door. When I saw the look of horror on my daughter's face, I tried my best to calm down.

"Antti, take Iida inside and call the police! Tell them to send the bomb squad."

The mailbox had been completely destroyed, and a tatter of a newspaper advertisement blew past me. Shoes two ninety-five, skateboards one fifty.

There was no sign of Einstein. I called him, but he didn't respond. I didn't dare walk to the tree, because I didn't know how many bombs might be in our yard. I tried to return to the house by exactly the same route I had come. My car was parked by the shed. That was another likely bomb target. Antti was on the phone, giving a confused explanation of what had happened to the emergency operator. I grabbed the handset—this was my department.

"Yes, a bomb. With a pressure timer . . . No human casualties, but it hit my cat . . . No, of course not . . . Good."

Iida was crying, and I stroked her hair as I dialed Koivu's number with my other hand. Antti grabbed the binoculars from the coat rack and scanned the yard, trying to spot Einstein.

"It's Maria. A bomb just went off in our front yard. Einstein might've been hit; I don't know if he made it. You handle the meeting—we're going to be stuck here for a while."

I gave Koivu my instructions as calmly as if I was missing work because Iida was sick. Koivu was a professional, so he didn't waste time on exclamations of shock.

"Salo?"

"Who else? This will go to the NBI for sure."

I picked Iida up and held her in my arms. Some mornings she went out to the mailbox with me, and on the weekends she even fetched the paper herself. She thought it was a big-girl job. What if she had gone out first this morning? Or Antti?

"What will happen now?" Antti asked when I walked into the kitchen, where he was peering out the windows.

"We wait for the bomb squad. Iida, come eat your oatmeal. There's nothing to worry about."

"I can't leave our cat out there to die! I'm going to look for him," Antti said angrily, avoiding my gaze. "We have to get him to the vet."

"No, you aren't! There could be more bombs. We're staying inside. Iida, would you like strawberry jam in your oatmeal?"

I felt as if everything was happening to someone else. Some other person had just walked toward certain death, only to be saved by a cat prematurely setting off the bomb. I fed my daughter her porridge just like I did every morning, drank my coffee, and forced down a hunk of baguette. I would have to get dressed and brush my teeth before my coworkers showed up.

A patrol car arrived first, but it hung back from the edge of the property. The senior officer called my work phone and said that they were closing the road and talking to the neighbors. I put clean clothes on Iida and started a load of laundry while I waited. The rhythmic thumping of the drum was like the soundtrack of normal life, where there was nothing but smooth sheets and safe mornings. I tried to remember the sound of the car I had heard that morning. It had still been dark, maybe around five thirty.

Taskinen called too. He had made it to the station before hearing the news. I could hear the agitation and anxiety in his voice, and he encouraged me to take some vacation time if I needed it.

Along with the bomb squad, the National Bureau of Investigation also sent an agent named Muukkonen. He called me on my work phone, and I could see him through the window talking into his own phone at the edge of the forest. Muukkonen said he was going to Sörnäinen Prison to question Salo as soon as his partner, Agent Hakala, was available. Numerous people had witnessed Salo making death threats against me. After receiving his conviction, Salo had threatened to kill me, the prosecutor, and the Narcotics detective who put him away. He had no shortage of underlings. In my mind I made a quick list of them, even though I couldn't interrogate them myself. I had shifted from investigator to victim.

Through the curtains I watched the bomb squad's slow-motion dance in our yard. Metal detectors groped about like inchworms seeking a new destination, and a bomb-sniffing dog executed its search pattern, simultaneously confident and wary. It was announced that the way from the door to the mailbox seemed clear, after which I asked the squad leader to check the way to the ash tree. I didn't dare hold out hope that Einstein was still alive. His cat dish sat on the kitchen floor with scraps left over from the night before.

Leaving it there was an effort, which reminded me of Tommi Laitinen, who had started cleaning out their coat rack the very night that Petri had died. A call came in that Einstein was lying under the tree, and that he was partially conscious.

Antti immediately went looking for the cat crate and some towels.

"Where are you going?"

"I'm getting Einstein and taking him to the animal hospital.

"Let me call a taxi!"

Antti had been pale and taciturn the whole time, and I had noticed him avoiding me. Einstein was his cat and had been for years before we'd started dating.

"Follow the bomb squad's instructions. I'll ask the taxi to come to the neighbor's house. Shall I call the animal hospital too?"

"Yes, please," Antti said. "You'll take care of Iida? We can't take her to day care, since her presence could endanger the other children."

"Iida isn't a danger to anyone. Whoever did this is the dangerous one," I hissed, but Antti had already gone. As I dialed the number for the taxi service, I watched him stride across the tender grass with his long legs, completely ignoring the bomb squad. He had his back to me when he picked up the cat. Einstein lay limply in his arms, and at the sight of blood dripping on Antti's jeans, I gasped. Just then the taxi dispatcher answered.

Antti wrapped Einstein in a towel and carefully set the bundle in the carrier. Then he waved to Iida, who was standing at the window with me, and walked past the remnants of the mailbox to the street, where the patrol car was parked. Just then Agent Hakala from the NBI arrived. The way to the house was clear, and Muukkonen and Hakala came inside.

"That was good luck that it only hit the cat," Agent Hakala said and glanced at Iida. It wasn't until after Iida's birth that I had finally realized that my job description did not include endangering my own life. Prior to that I had a tendency to do thoughtless soloing, but in recent years I tried to avoid taking needless risks at work. And yet the job seemed to bring risks that I couldn't avoid and that could even extend to my family. Salo and his underlings couldn't have known that we had a cat. Had they watched us long enough to learn that I usually went out for the paper while Antti put on the porridge and coffee? Or did it not matter to Salo who in my family he hurt?

I told the NBI agents about waking up to the sound of the newspaper boy's scooter and then the car after it. I was furious: if I had gotten out of bed, I would have seen the bomb being placed, even though a professional would have masked his appearance. After taking down what information I could give, Muukkonen and Hakala disappeared, but the bomb squad continued their work. I would have liked to get to my computer at the station so that I could start compiling a list of suspects, but I didn't want to leave until the bomb squad was done. Taskinen had promised to assign a couple of patrol officers to watch our house for the time being. I thought about what Antti had said. Did Iida's day care need a guard? Salo was serving an eight-year prison term for drug trafficking and assault, and apparently additional charges didn't matter much to him. Revenge was worth a life sentence to him.

I played with Iida, but of course she could sense my worry and the tension of the bomb squad working in the yard, so she was having difficulty concentrating. Antti called just before noon and said that Einstein was in surgery. He had lost a lot of blood and one of his kidneys was damaged, but the veterinary surgeons were doing all they could to save him.

Antti said he would stay until he knew if Einstein had a chance of pulling through.

When word came that my car was clean, I decided to go to the station. First I fed Iida the rest of a macaroni casserole I'd found in the refrigerator. I still wasn't hungry.

"Now Iida gets to go to work with Mommy," I said.

"Iida go work!" she exclaimed. "Pekka play with Iida!" Koivu was Iida's godfather and her idol. He tried to conceal how much pleasure Iida's adoring gaze gave him, but I saw through him. I had watched in amazement at the way she pranced around him. Who had taught my two-year-old daughter how to flirt?

My gun was in the living room closet, on the top shelf, in a locked case. I took it out, loaded it, and grabbed an extra magazine. The shoulder holster disappeared under my jacket, but I was all too aware of its presence. A bulletproof vest and helmet would have been useful, but

I didn't have either at home. The bomb squad stayed to finish their investigation. I left for work on high alert, constantly scanning our surroundings as I drove. Those few miles felt like they would never end.

In the lobby at the police station, I could feel everyone's eyes on me. News spread fast. Iida wanted to stay downstairs and look at the department's giant stuffed-octopus mascot, but I dragged her past it to the elevator. There we were safe.

Koivu stood in the break room, and when he saw us he instantly rushed over to give me a hug.

"Hi, Iida. Are you our new recruit?" he said and gave my daughter one of the sticky oatmeal cookies that someone always bought, even though no one but Lähde liked them.

"Einstein has a boo-boo. Daddy took him to the hospital," Iida said, and Koivu cast me a questioning glance.

I shrugged. Antti had promised to call as soon as he knew more.

"The NBI guys are already grilling Salo. We'll have to see if he confesses."

"Was the bomb meant to kill?" Koivu asked.

"The bomb squad hasn't issued a statement yet." The explosion had been directed upward, so it probably would have mutilated the hands and face of whoever approached the mailbox. The bomb squad would probably be able to get a good idea of its construction and the skill of the bomb maker.

"I actually came in to look at my list of Salo's cronies. I know Jarkola has worked for him," I said as I poured myself a cup of coffee. It had been sitting for a long time and hit my empty stomach like a shot of whiskey.

"Could Seppälä's murder be tied to Salo after all?" Koivu asked. "What if he set the bomb to throw you off that trail?"

"I don't know. Let's think about that later. Guess where I was last night?" I told Koivu about my karaoke performance at Café Escale and was grateful when he laughed. I had brought a few picture books, and he promised to keep Iida entertained in the break room while I worked on the computer. Maybe it was misuse of police resources, but Koivu didn't seem to mind. Before going to my office, I went to the equipment room and checked out two bulletproof vests. Unfortunately they didn't have any in a child's size. After a second's thought, I also took a helmet.

We had plenty of information on Salo's gang, which I e-mailed to Agent Muukkonen. Staying out of the investigation was going to be difficult but necessary. Just as I was running through the criminal records of the torpedoes Salo used, Taskinen appeared in my office.

"I saw you and Iida through the window. I was in a meeting with the chief of police. You should have stayed home."

"I think it's safer here. Just think, Jyrki. I heard a car early this morning, but I didn't get up to look. I might have been able to get the license plate . . ."

"The chief and I will handle it. We're coordinating with the NBI."

"Good, but I want to see all the interview records as soon as possible. I have to know who to be on the lookout for."

"Have you thought about taking some time off? What if you and Iida went on a little trip for a while? Maybe to your parents' house or a spa or something," Taskinen said, but I didn't like his concerned expression. He wasn't worried about my safety or my family. There was something else.

I didn't get a chance to answer before the phone rang. It was Antti. Einstein had made it through the operation, but his condition was serious. He would probably survive, but he would have to be in the hospital for several days.

Tears of relief flooded my eyes. Antti said he was going to go in to work for a little while.

"This will be front-page news. Keep Iida away from any cameras," he said bitterly before hanging up. It felt so unfair that he was angry at me, but at the same time it increased my own feelings of self-loathing. How many times had I told a victim of a rape or domestic violence that the only person responsible for the crime was the perpetrator? It was hard to believe it when it happened to you.

Agents Muukkonen and Hakala would be turning the screws on Salo again. Law enforcement treated nothing so seriously as violence against their own. But even if they solved this case, it wouldn't guarantee that the threats or violence would stop.

"I don't have any intention of taking time off. I won't give Salo the satisfaction. Let's see what the NBI says," I told Taskinen calmly, though I felt uncomfortable. Maybe Antti and Iida should move somewhere else for a while. The thought that I might have to be separated from them was upsetting, but what choice did we have?

"Maria, come on. You don't have to play the tough guy just because you're a woman," Taskinen said seriously. "Just think about it."

I didn't promise anything. I took my laptop and a modem with me so I could work from home if I could get Iida to sleep. When I went back to the break room, I found Wang there with Koivu. Iida had no desire to leave, even though her eyelids were drooping. She fell asleep before the first stoplight, and I realized that I was ravenously hungry. The drop in blood sugar was making my hands shake so hard I could barely drive home, but hunger was a good sign. My body was starting to recover from the shock.

A forensic van was still parked in our yard next to the exploded mailbox. Men were taking pictures of tire tracks and collecting scraps of newspaper from under the trees. Iida mumbled in her sleep as I carried her inside, took off her shoes and coat, and tucked her into bed. Her cheeks were flushed from the warmth in the car and her breathing was steady. I wished I could protect her from all the evil in the world. How would I bear it if anything happened to her?

I had met women who had lost their children, even women who had killed their own children. Frequently I worried the next inconsolable mother would be me.

I ate a couple of sandwiches and drank a glass of buttermilk. Having a team of police officers combing the yard provided a false sense of security. I couldn't surround Iida or myself with guards forever. There would always be new Salos, new toes I had stepped on, new people who hated me for doing my job.

I plugged the computer in, attached the modem, and turned it on. The whole time I waited to hear racing footsteps, and a couple times I thought I saw a flash, but it was only a phantom image burned into the synapses of my brain.

When the phone rang, I practically attacked it. It was Agent Muukkonen asking for my e-mail address.

"You probably want to know what we talked about with Salo. I'll send the report as soon as I get back to the office."

"Thanks!" I said, not mentioning that Taskinen wanted to keep the investigation in his own hands. "Did Salo confess?"

"He didn't admit or deny anything. It'll make a fun read. We're going to keep at it. Take care of yourself, Kallio."

I went downstairs and put some coffee on. In the freezer I found the sweet cardamom rolls Iida had made on a recent rainy day. She loved to make smiley faces on the rolls with raisin mouths and eyes. I didn't like baked raisins, but of course I ate whatever my daughter made.

There were also cookies in the cupboard. Once I had everything prepared, I invited the forensics team in for coffee. Andersson from Patrol brought our mail, which the confused postal worker had only agreed to hand over once she saw that nothing but a concrete base remained of the mailbox. There wasn't much. A Green Party newsletter for Antti, a day-care bill for me, and a card for Iida from her grandparents in Tartu, Estonia.

"This thing was quite a contraption. A child could have slapped it together," the bomb expert said. "The cat was low enough to the ground that it didn't get completely torn to shreds, but for an adult human this bomb would have been really dangerous. It wouldn't necessarily have killed anyone, but it would have at least left you blind."

Andersson grimaced and sank his teeth into a pulla roll. Suddenly a completely unrelated thought popped into my mind: if we bought a security system for our yard, I would have a reason to contact Reijo Rahnasto. His company specialized in business security, but I could ask for consulting help based on our previous relationship. Would that be inappropriate? Or should we just find a new apartment and keep the address secret?

Iida came padding down the stairs, half asleep. At first she played shy around all the strange men. But after a pulla and a glass of milk, she turned on the charm and made the entire room forget their work. When the forensic team finally went back out, I sat Iida down to watch *Moomin* videos and went to check my e-mail. The interview record Agent Muukkonen promised had come.

Agent Hakala was a good clerk, and I could almost hear Salo's voice behind the words. Niko Salo was thirty and short, with a strong physique and expressionless eyes the color of April snow. He had the nose of a boxer and predatory lips, and his hair was usually short and dyed black. The last time I saw him he'd also had black sideburns and a goatee. He dressed fashionably and seemed to have gotten his mannerisms straight out of a Tarantino movie. Without the gold chain hanging around his neck he could have been a rock musician or a literature student. *Alibi* magazine had run an article about Salo's achievements a few years back, describing him as a man feared by criminals and police alike. Salo boasted of receiving an average of two marriage proposals per week in prison. If he became a cop killer, that number would only grow.

Agent Muukkonen had been obliged to reveal his reason for the interview: Salo was suspected of involvement in a bombing in Espoo.

"In Espoo? Hey, man, I was in prison all night. How would I have gotten to Espoo?"

Salo admitted threatening to kill me after his trial. When Muukkonen asked how he intended to carry out that threat, Salo clammed up.

"Hey, man, why would I tell? I want to keep that cop whore on her toes."

Salo didn't admit or deny anything. He threatened to sic his lawyer on Muukkonen when the agent announced he was requesting a warrant to access Salo's phone records from prison. That wouldn't necessarily help, though. Salo probably had several SIM cards he could interchange in his cell phone. He had only given the prison officials the number he used for his most innocent calls. SIM cards were so small they were easy to smuggle into prison. When the legal owner canceled the line, they would just steal another phone.

"So you're telling me that Kallio bitch got a bomb set off in her front yard? What does that have to do with me?"

As the interrogation progressed, Agent Muukkonen's questioning became increasingly unproductive. Sometimes Salo played completely ignorant. I knew he was a good actor and that he didn't want to serve more time. And Salo wasn't the type to rat on anyone. If his bomber was ever caught, that man would request a different prison or the secure section in Sörnäinen so Salo couldn't take revenge on him for his failure.

The interrogation yielded nothing of value, even though Muukkonen and Hakala had done their best to provoke Salo. It wasn't any use. Salo was too smart for that. Next the NBI would interview all of the explosives experts in the metro area who weren't currently in prison. The last line of the e-mail infuriated me.

Laine from your Organized Crime and Recidivism Unit called. He offered to help however he could. He seemed really concerned about your well-being.

Right, Laine wants to find the bomb maker so he can tell him to try again, I thought angrily. Just then the door opened, and although I knew it couldn't be anyone but Antti, I ran downstairs to make sure Iida was safe.

Antti's pants were still covered in dried blood. He had been walking around the city all day with those stinking stains on his jeans.

"How long are they going to be here?" he asked, motioning to the uniformed officers outside.

"At least until tomorrow night. We'll have to think about what to do after that. The cabin in Inkoo is empty until Monday. Maybe you and Iida should go there for the weekend."

Antti drained a glass of water and then started absentmindedly unzipping his jeans.

"Has the animal hospital called? They promised to as soon as there was any news."

"No. Here, let me help," I said quietly and started pulling Antti's pants off his legs. Iida was still engrossed in her video, and dinner could wait. Maybe we should celebrate that we were still alive.

"Come upstairs and we'll put these in the wash together," I suggested. I pulled Antti's arms around me, but when he felt my shoulder holster and the metal protruding from it, he kissed me on the cheek and said,

"Not now, Maria."

I realized I had forgotten to take my birth control pill that morning. Usually I had it with my coffee. Missing one wasn't going to make me instantly pregnant, but I should probably take it right now anyway. Because sex obviously wasn't on the menu, I started making dinner. I could hear Antti banging around upstairs as I made fish balls and grated horseradish for the sauce. Everything was so homey and peaceful, but it was strange not having a cat head-butting me to demand fish.

The animal hospital called and said that Einstein's condition was stable. He had a strong heart for his age, so the prognosis was cautiously optimistic.

"Agent Muukkonen also wants to interview you," I told Antti once I had the fish balls in the oven and the potatoes were boiling.

"Me? Why?"

"You're one of the victims."

"Have they found anything out?

When I shook my head, Antti cringed and suggested that we pack after eating. He said that going to Inkoo seemed like a good idea, but he wanted me to come too.

"I have to stay here to buy a new mailbox," I said jokingly, but of course I would be happy to go. I had removed my gun while I was cooking, but I put the shoulder holster back on after I was done. When I showed Antti the bulletproof vests, he sighed.

"I never would have thought I'd have to wear one of those."

I knew many men would have enjoyed this situation, men who would've stayed up all night clutching a gun and guarding their family from the bad guys of the world. Those were the men who kept outdoor-adventure services in business and played army out in the woods every weekend. In the fall they got their taste of danger during the moose hunt, and on Sundays they clutched the edges of their seats watching Formula 1 or screaming in the stands at the hockey arena. Those men needed exciting experiences, like the adult version of games of cowboys and Indians, but the kind where they could take a candy break whenever they wanted.

What would my grandfather, who had died in the war, have said to them?

I didn't wear the bulletproof vest to the grocery store, and no one followed us on our drive to Inkoo or on our walk down the narrow lane to Antti's parents' cabin. Only terns were waiting on the rocks along the shore. The open sea glinted in the setting sun, and even though the water was still frigid, it held the promise of outings on the sailboat and long, refreshing swims. Antti planned to help his father put the boat back in the water the next weekend. Next Sunday we could take a little boat trip, but on Saturday I would have to be at the Police Expo.

The weekend went by peacefully. We foraged for morels and young nettles, and we talked about our dream house on the water, with a new kitten to keep Einstein company. The birds kept up their racket from dawn until dusk, and Sunday brought the first swallows. Even though I slept with my pistol on the nightstand, I rested well. Our answering machine was full when we got home. One call was from my sister Helena, who wanted to make sure I was alright, and another was from the animal hospital. Einstein was conscious and had stood up. The danger had passed.

I was so overjoyed by that news I could barely stop to listen to the final message:

> *Hi, it's Eila Honkavuori. I'm sorry to bother you with work on a Sunday, but I've been making some inquiries and I think something is starting to take shape. Could you call me as soon as possible?*

18

The grass around the Helsinki University of Technology shone green, with tidy lines of tulips and daffodils dividing the lawns. A few rose hips from the previous year still hung on their bushes.

I sat in Eila Honkavuori's office. I had arranged the appointment immediately after our long Monday morning meeting. I hadn't told anyone I was continuing the Ilveskivi investigation on my own. The sunlight had started to feel like it was playing interrogation with me, so I kept my glasses on.

"It's always so hot in here during the summer, and of course the windows don't open. The engineers trusted the air conditioning. See how well that worked." Eila Honkavuori huffed as she closed the blinds. Thin rays of light shone through the cracks, casting stripes along the cream-colored wall and burnishing Eila's hair a shining ebony. With her flawless white skin and striking red lipstick, she reminded me of Snow White. However, the resemblance was marred by the flowing yellow dress the color of sunshine, which emphasized the ample curves of her body.

"I don't know if I'm right," Eila began as she poured us pineapple juice with ice, "but I've been poking around, and I get the feeling that Petri learned something about the planning for Laajalahti Bay that someone didn't want him to know about."

"Laajalahti? But isn't it a nature preserve?"

"Yes, for now. But there's pressure to change that, though no one is saying that out loud. At least not to people like me, who don't always succumb to the majority. The Keilaniemi shoreline is already full of construction, just like around here in Otaniemi. More land acquisitions would align perfectly with what the business community and the university want. Filling in the land between the islands isn't enough for them. Just think of office buildings stretching all along the bay up to Villa Elfvik. We all know that's what the city wants, and Rahnasto is leading the charge."

"But doesn't removing a nature preserve from protected status require permission from the Ministry of the Environment?"

"Of course. And the Ministry of the Interior. The strategy seems to be to gradually degrade the area, although they always call it 'development.' I agree that the improvements to the Ring I highway are necessary, but it is bringing more traffic closer to the sea and the protected areas. The wetlands will be the first to go. And then they'll work their way toward the Villa. You know how intense the demand for new land is all around the capitol. Why waste perfectly good waterfront property?"

I took a long sip of my juice. This all sounded a bit far-fetched. An issue as big as destroying a nature preserve couldn't be handled in secret. Besides, how could the elimination of Petri Ilveskivi be related to such a plan?

"I know Rahnasto and company have received campaign contributions from big corporations that are interested in expanding the technology parks into the Laajalahti nature preserve. And Petri's last job was those new couches for the Ministry of the Interior," Eila continued. "The week before he died, he visited their offices to see how the new pieces fit in with the decor. I called him that night. He was in a rush to get to some meeting and couldn't talk for long, but he said he ran into some familiar faces in the men's room at the ministry. It was the mayor and Reijo Rahnasto. When they realized he had overheard them, they got out of there real fast. The City Council chair, Aulikki Heinonen, was waiting in the hall, and she didn't seem happy to see Petri either. Petri promised to tell me more, but when I asked about it that weekend, he said we should wait until after our next Planning Commission meeting to talk about it. But in Petri's papers I found detailed information about all the property ownership in the area and a sketch, almost like a zoning map, with the entire shoreline full of new buildings. It looked like Petri's drawing. I didn't give it any more thought, but when you asked, everything started to add up."

"Have you seen Petri's papers?"

"I helped Tommi sort them. And I made copies of some of them. Sometimes it can be helpful to get a peek at other parties' memos," Eila said with a wicked grin.

"I know about Petri's turbulent relationship with Rahnasto. What about his relationship with the higher-ups at the city?"

"The same. Petri was a harsh critic of the current leadership style and for good reason. Heinonen and company aren't particularly interested in listening."

The City Council chair, Aulikki Heinonen, was an excellent example of how a female politician didn't need to be soft and compliant to succeed. She was a member of even more good-old-boy networks than the mayor or Rahnasto. She was always carefully groomed and stylishly dressed. Both her supporters and opponents called her the Margaret Thatcher of Espoo. And she was proud of that.

"I wonder if those three were at the ministry figuring out how to strip protections from that entire shoreline. That's how things work in Espoo. Just think about the amusement park or when they reclaimed all that land between Keilaniemi and Hanasaari. These decisions are made in secret, without any input from the public. Maybe they wanted to be able to present a final deal to the Planning Commission. The City Council is always complaining about how slow the zoning process is and asking for variances. Sometimes democracy is only a word in this city. The bigwigs decide, and there aren't very many of them, and speaking out against them can end your political career."

"I've heard."

"And it's the same at the national level. How much real power is there outside the Ministerial Committee for Economic Policy? It's too bad no one has ever done a study on workplace bullying in politics. Of course I'm an easy target because I'm big. Even people in my own party try to trip me up, but I won't let them. You wouldn't believe how many times I've been called a cow. We all know what's most important for a female politician is how she looks, not how competent she is. Which is why I didn't get to stand in the last parliamentary election. They told me no one would vote for a woman my size. I thought, fine, if the voters are only going to see how I look and not listen to my ideas, who needs them. I guess they can't take a fat woman who talks about poverty and welfare seriously. Their thinking is I should just eat less and give that money to the poor." Eila gave a crooked smile, and although her eyes twinkled, I could see the rage in them.

My work was the same. Coworkers, criminals, and victims all seemed to think it was their place to comment on my appearance. Meanwhile, men could look or dress however they wanted without it affecting their chances for promotion.

"This is all just a theory right now, but I'm trying to come up with something more concrete." Eila wiped a bead of sweat from her upper lip. My armpits were damp, so I removed my jacket. Could the city's entire top leadership be mixed up in this? If that were the case, who had given the order to halt the investigation into Ilveskivi's death?

"I haven't heard much about political murder in Finland."

"They probably just wanted to scare Petri. We were going to deal with the general plan for the area we've been talking about. Petri probably wanted to alert the Planning Commission to what was going on behind closed doors. There was a local reporter coming to the meeting who was interested in the progress of the big hotel project in Tapiola. Of course he would have loved to get a scoop on new plans for the bay."

"But why sit on the information until the Planning Commission meeting? Why not start making noise as soon as he learned about it?"

"The commission includes a wide range of experts on urban planning who don't always agree with the major party lines. A lot of us would have been extremely upset to hear about a proposal like this. So Rahnasto and his cronies couldn't let Petri talk."

I was still dubious. One mouthy city official couldn't be so dangerous that silencing him was necessary, could he? But the more I thought about it, the more plausible it seemed. Rahnasto had paid Marko Seppälä to rough up Petri Ilveskivi and then got scared when the whole thing spun out of control. So he shot Seppälä. Rahnasto knew the area around the landfill because the Planning Commission had recently handled a proposal to expand the dump. And elected officials often toured locations like the landfill.

Plus, Reijo Rahnasto had guns. How could I get the pistols in for testing? Would one of his guns match the bullet we found near Seppälä's motorbike?

"Aulikki Heinonen and I have a friend in common, one of the National Coalition Party delegates. I'm going to try to talk to her and everyone else who might have some inkling of these plans. Or should I just ask Rahnasto directly?"

"No! We already have two bodies. Be careful. I'm going to talk to my boss. Seppälä's murder investigation is still open."

Forensics had found a few unidentified fingerprints on Seppälä's belongings. Where could I get Rahnasto's prints? They weren't in any of our databases. Could Kim Kajanus help? I knew enough about fingerprinting that I could tell if two prints were possible matches by looking at them.

Eila Honkavuori frowned. "Did I remember to tell you about Rahnasto's cell phone? He had it next to him on the desk through the whole Planning Commission meeting and kept looking at it. He had the sound off but said he was waiting for a text message about work."

"Did a message come?"

"I don't remember. Rahnasto rushed through the end of the meeting, but that was just a relief at the time. I wanted to call Petri because I was worried."

Eila opened a desk drawer, pulled out a large lavender lace fan, and started waving it to cool herself off.

"This old invention is better than any of the gadgets the engineers have given us," she said with a smile, looking like a Rubens painting with her fan. I pulled my notebook out of my bag and started sketching an outline of Eila's theory.

"This city is playing quite a game. The economy is improving—you can't deny that—but at whose expense? City hall thinks that everyone should just to look out for themselves. I wouldn't be surprised if they came up with a rewards system for local taxes: if you earn enough, they lower your taxes because you're probably so rich that you don't use public health services anyway. They're only too happy to hunt down unemployment scammers and graffiti taggers, but who ends up in court if a child is injured in an understaffed day-care facility? The deputy mayor in charge of health and social services?"

Eila's cheeks were flushed, and suddenly she hid her face behind the fan.

"I'm sorry. I forgot this is a police interview, not a campaign event. God, I'm just so frustrated and angry. Petri was a good friend, and he could get my mind off these things when I felt like I was just beating my head against the wall. He was an optimist, sometimes to the point of naïveté, but he believed we could change things."

I collected my things. Listening to Eila Honkavuori's harangue would have been fun, but it wasn't going to solve any murders. She promised to call immediately if anything new came to light. As I was closing the door, she asked again, "The photographer, Kim Kajanus? He was at Petri's funeral. Why?"

"Ask him yourself," I replied and left. The parking area was unsecured but had enough traffic that someone would have noticed if anyone had tampered with my car, and it had an alarm. I took my keys out of my bag and opened the door. My prescription was still in there with all the other papers. I still hadn't remembered to stop by the pharmacy. And I didn't go now either. Back at the station I wrote up a memo about my conversation with Eila Honkavuori and all the other evidence that indicated Reijo Rahnasto might be behind both murders. Then I saved it on my hard drive behind two passwords and also put copies on two different disks. Then I called Taskinen.

"It's me, Maria. Have you had lunch?"

Taskinen's sigh was clearly one of disappointment. "Yes, and now I'm headed to a meeting with the county administrative board."

"Are you going to be gone all day?"

"I'll be lucky if I get to go home at all tonight. Do you have something urgent? Is it about taking some leave?"

Now his voice sounded hopeful.

"No. How is tomorrow, before our unit meeting?"

"Doctor at eight. I might have a stress fracture. Ten thirty would work. What about you?"

That fit with my schedule and would give me more time to develop my theory. I sent Eija Hirvonen online and to the library if necessary to look for a picture of Rahnasto's company's vans. Someone could go show it to the man who lived near the dump who had seen a strange van on his road the night of Seppälä's death.

The next day was still warm. I looked at the new mailbox Antti and I had installed the night before. The shiny red paint looked garish next to the aging house. On Sunday we had read through the real estate advertisements and stopped to look at a duplex in Masala on the way back from Inkoo. At the moment we had exactly one summer vacation plan: find a new home. The representative of the estate that owned our current house had deduced from the newspaper story that the police lieutenant whose house had been bombed was me and called to express his in concern. But he didn't care about us. He was just worried about damage to the property.

"The big ash tree got hit with some shrapnel. We'll have to see if it pulls through," Antti replied, and the lawyer's worrying had ended there.

I hadn't wanted to give a statement to the press, so I let the NBI investigators handle the media. We had agreed to draw as little attention to the incident as possible. Salo's threats were just intended to bolster his reputation in prison, and we didn't want to dance to his choreography.

Monday night we went to see Einstein. He seemed tired. A belt-like bandage wrapped around his belly, and a plastic collar was attached to his neck to prevent him from licking the wound. In his collar he looked like the court feline to Elizabeth I. If his recovery went as expected, he would be able to come home on Friday. Leaving him yowling with loneliness in his barren cage felt horrible. If it had been Iida, I never would have left the hospital for a second. I had asked Helvi to call me immediately if she saw anyone strange around the day care. I hated infecting other people with this fear, which was sure to spread from Helvi to the parents of the other children. Salo would have enjoyed this if he'd known.

Eija Hirvonen had found a picture of the model of van I wanted. I meant to give it to Mela, who was the least busy of all of us. He could practice interviewing the elderly, and he was sure to like the idea that a positive identification would be a huge step forward in a homicide investigation. But during our morning meeting, I changed my mind. I wanted to talk to Taskinen first. Seppälä's case was still moving slowly. Puustjärvi was looking for weapons that could match the bullet, but that wasn't likely to help much because the guns drug dealers used were usually illegal.

After the meeting, I motioned for Koivu and Wang to come to my office. Koivu was wearing blue-and-white-striped shorts with his strong thighs and yellow-fuzzed knees peeking out timidly.

"You two have time this afternoon, don't you? Go show Reijo Rahnasto's picture to Suvi Seppälä. Maybe she'll recognize him."

"Rahnasto? You mean the politician? We interviewed him right after the murder along with everyone on Ilveskivi's committee. He didn't know anything," Koivu said.

"I wouldn't be so sure."

"Why didn't you assign this during the meeting?"

"Because," I began, but only completed the sentence in my mind. Because I don't know who I can trust. Because gossip spreads at the shooting range and in the men's room.

"I just forgot to mention it. This is connected to Seppälä's shooting." Koivu nodded and exchanged a doubtful glance with Wang.

"OK, boss," Koivu said, emphasizing the final word in a funny way. I wish he would have told me directly what bothered him about the setup, but he stayed silent. Wang and Koivu left elbow to elbow, so apparently things were going well again. At least better than things were going for me.

Agent Muukkonen called and said that their second interrogation of Salo hadn't gone anywhere either.

"He has a secret, and something seems to be bothering him. Like he's irritated that no one died. We haven't come up with anything from our usual bomb makers either, but we'll keep at it. Your husband and I are going to talk this afternoon. I think we'll have this wrapped up before school gets out."

How would Antti do in his interview? A couple of times I had been questioned as part of an internal investigation. It wasn't pleasant, but it was educational, and sitting on the other side of the table had made me a better interrogator. Agent Muukkonen had a pleasant eastern Finnish accent that made me wish I was somewhere with forests, lakes, and silence. One summer I had served as the acting sheriff in my home town in North Karelia, and sometimes I threatened Antti with the prospect of my applying for the county police commissioner job there once the previous officeholder retired. We could buy an abandoned farm and get ten cats. Antti only nodded in amusement. He didn't think me and country living were a very likely combination.

I had prepared very carefully for my meeting with Taskinen. We met in his office because I didn't want to share my theories in the conference room, not to mention the cafeteria. Taskinen's office was in the northeast corner of the building, so the sun only reached it on summer mornings and left it alone the rest of the day. The desk and couch were the same as my own, but Taskinen had two armchairs. That had to be some sign of hierarchy.

We traded news before getting down to business. Only rest could heal the stress fracture in Jyrki's right leg. He would have to skip the Helsinki City Marathon, and he was worried about how he would cope with the forced lack of exercise. I suggested swimming. He had removed his suit jacket, and his shirt was a restrained red pencil stripe that matched his tie. On his chin he had a small scrape—maybe his razor had slipped that morning.

"I think I know why Marko Seppälä attacked Petri Ilveskivi and then who killed him to cover it up," I finally said and started laying out my story. As I worked through my argument, Taskinen's face became increasingly expressionless, and the fingers of his right hand rotated his wedding band, which was dulled by years of wear.

"How much do you really know and how much are you just guessing at?" he asked when I finished.

"I don't have any conclusive evidence yet. I'd like to get Rahnasto's fingerprints because we found two prints on Marko Seppälä's motorbike that we don't have matches for. Rahnasto works in the security industry, so he'll know all the tricks. His company also owns a small guard business. It doesn't handle security at the landfill, but Rahnasto has trained businesses to protect against break-ins. I found a brochure online about a seminar he gave last fall that demonstrated the easiest ways to defeat common locks. Of course the purpose was to show potential customers that locks aren't enough and that they need electronic security systems."

"You're right more often than you're wrong, but we all make mistakes sometimes. How reliable do you consider Eila Honkavuori? Are you sure she isn't harboring some sort of personal grudge?"

I was having almost the identical conversation I had had the day before with Eila Honkavuori, but the difference now was that I was the one presenting the theories that the other party didn't seem to believe.

"Decisions this big can't be made in secret," Taskinen said.

"No? Strange that you would say that, even though your wife is a city official. Hasn't she ever complained about the leadership walking all over the professional planners?"

"There isn't any need to bring Terttu into this," Taskinen said with sudden pique. "You haven't pitched this theory to your unit yet, have you?"

"No. I only asked Koivu and Wang to show Rahnasto's picture to Suvi Seppälä."

"You need to rescind that order," Taskinen said, looking out the window instead of at me. A patrol car sped off with lights flashing but no siren. When I didn't reply, Taskinen turned to me, his face as gray as yeast that had just come out of the freezer.

"Maria, did you hear what I said? I'll check with Koivu to make sure. You aren't going to make your subordinates lie for you, are you?"

"Of course not."

I would rescind the order, but no one was going to stop me from going to Suvi myself. I looked at Taskinen's carefully trimmed nails and the narrow arc of his jaw. I liked him very much. Why was he doing this to me when I most needed his support?

"Who gave the order to terminate the Ilveskivi investigation?"

"I'm not at liberty . . ." Taskinen cringed ever so slightly before continuing. "We decided together. The chief of police, the deputy chief, and I. It's good you came to me first with your theory about Rahnasto. This could have caused a lot of embarrassment in the top ranks. You don't have any evidence, so forget what Honkavuori said. Work with Narcotics and Organized Crime, and I'm sure you'll get to the bottom of the Seppälä shooting eventually. I understand that things have been hard on you, and you want to see results. Have you seen the department psychologist about the bomb attack?"

"I'm going this afternoon."

"Good." Taskinen stood up and clearly expected me to do the same. I stayed sitting for a few more seconds. I wanted to say something, but I didn't quite know what. Taskinen took a few cautious steps toward the window, his leg clearly hurting him. "I have to head over to the university. The police academy is sponsoring a seminar on immigration and refugee issues. Someone has to be there to represent a moderate perspective." Taskinen gave a forced laugh.

"So go to your seminar!" I shoved the chair out from under me, sending it sliding across the floor and into the coffee table. Taskinen walked over to me and set his right hand on my shoulder. He was nearly eight inches taller than me, so there was no way to avoid there being something patronizing in the gesture.

"Come on, Maria. We all make mistakes sometimes. Don't take this so hard."

I shook his hand off and headed for the hall. Bile rose in my throat, and my heart was beating like I'd just run up a hill. I had been such an idiot. Every boss had a boss, and the ones above Taskinen wanted to maintain a good relationship with city hall.

Koivu was in an interview, but I got him on his cell phone.

"So you don't want me to go play flash cards with Seppälä?" he asked.

"No. Where is the picture of Rahnasto now?"

"On my desk."

Koivu gave me permission to look for it; his door was unlocked. Because I thought the room was empty, I rushed in without knocking. To both our surprises, Puupponen was sitting at his computer and nearly jumped out of his seat when he saw me.

"I'm sorry. I didn't know you were here," I said and grabbed Rahnasto's picture. I felt like ripping it to shreds right there. I wanted to destroy something. If I hadn't had the appointment with the psychologist, I would have gone downstairs for some time on the punching bag.

"Are you working on Jarkola's interview report?" I asked in order to seem like a concerned boss, even though I didn't give a damn what Puupponen was working on.

"What? "No. I was just checking on something . . . do you spell 'recommend' with one *m* or two?"

"Two. And let me commend you on your newfound enthusiasm for proofreading reports," I said and then turned on my heels and returned to my office. A new raft of e-mails had collected in my inbox, and answering them seemed to take the edge off the worst of my rage. Shame crept into its place, and I had a hard time going downstairs to the cafeteria to eat, even though I was hungry. I felt as if I had the word "failure" scrawled across my forehead in red lipstick. The detective who didn't get up in the night to check on a suspicious car, even though she had received a death threat. The gullible idiot who swallowed any theory that came along if it fit her preconceptions. My mood was not improved by Detective Laine coming up to me in the line at the cash register and patting me on the shoulder.

"I'm glad to see you at work despite that bomb incident. Have they caught the perp?"

I missed my old enemy, Pertti Ström. He would have stabbed me in the back if he could, but at least he kept his weapons visible. Laine played by different rules, and I didn't have a clue why he wanted me in the ring with him.

Liisa Rasilainen was sitting at a table for two in the corner, so I joined her. She was shocked about the bombing and asked why I had disappeared from Café Escale.

"Those two guys said that's just how heteros are. Forget their friends and disappear after the first piece of tail they see," Liisa said teasingly.

"The redhead is part of a complicated case." I felt like unloading the whole sob story on Liisa, but instead I saved it for the psychologist. He believed I was suffering from posttraumatic stress, and he was probably right. His statement let me give myself permission to sit in my office for the rest of the day crying on and off. I decided to wait until tomorrow to call Suvi Seppälä if I still felt like it.

The weather had turned muggy as the day went on, and when I left work, the south wind was bringing tall black clouds. Thunderstorms in May. That wasn't normal. Rain whipped in front of me in a fast-moving silver-gray curtain I had no way of avoiding. It thrummed an angry tune on the roof of the car and then was past.

Helvi's yard was sunny. Iida wore rubber boots, and as we walked to the car she jumped in one large puddle after another. Mud splattered our clothing. I was sorry to be wearing my work shoes, because some splashing would have done me good too.

Instead I went out for a jog to vent my frustration. For a moment I stared at my service weapon but then locked it in its case. I didn't want to feel like a prisoner to guns, and I didn't want Iida to think it was normal that her mother didn't dare go outside without a revolver. I kept to busy streets, even though they weren't as nice as the roads through the fields. That was what women who were afraid of rapists did.

The rain had brought out the perfume of the birches and lilies of the valley, which even the stench of car exhaust couldn't ruin. Shame and rage washed out of me as sweat soaked my shirt, but the feeling that replaced them was worthlessness. I couldn't fail. I had to be at least twice as good as any man in the department. Quite a brutal attitude, the psychologist had said. I had a hard time allowing myself any mercy.

There were other people on the walking path, so I decided I was safe taking a shortcut. The path ended at a small but steep hill formed by an underpass for a busy road. At the top of the hill, I passed a woman leading two large dogs and a stroller. In the stroller sat a child about eighteen months old, who noticed a squirrel at the same time as the dogs and me. The dogs started pulling like mad, and the woman's hold on the stroller slipped.

The stroller started rolling diagonally down the hill, and I rushed after it. I managed to catch it a few feet before it got to the edge of the road, and I stood panting while the mother upbraided herself and the dogs.

"Thank you! Thank you so much!" the woman repeated, and I bounded off exultantly. It wasn't until half a mile later that I realized what was going on. I needed to be useful. That was the only way I could give myself mercy. That was what gave me the right to exist. This knowledge brought tears to my eyes.

I had just gotten out of the shower when the phone rang.

Antti was in the kitchen frying herring, so I rushed to answer, naked and dripping wet.

"Hi, it's Mikke Sjöberg."

"Hi. Wait just a minute."

I went to get my bathrobe and tried to quell the butterflies in my stomach. I couldn't talk to Mikke, not today of all days. Iida had climbed up and grabbed the phone, and she was babbling happily, even though she didn't have a clue whom she was talking with.

"Iida, give the phone to Mommy. Go help Daddy in the kitchen." After sending Iida on her way, I picked up the phone as if it were a poisonous snake. "What's up?"

"I know who put that bomb in your yard."

"What are you talking about?"

"I happened to overhear something in the weight room. Salo did a little asking around. He's in the same unit I am."

"You should tell the NBI. Agent Muukkonen is handling the investigation. I can give you his number."

"No! I don't want anyone thinking I'm a snitch. But I have a good excuse for talking to you."

"And what is that?"

"The investigation into my family's companies is still ongoing."

"Yes, it is, but I'm not handling it. So are you saying that Salo didn't order the bombing?"

"Exactly. Come here, and I'll tell you more. I can't talk long, and I can't give any names. But I know. Believe me."

Mikke's tone was anxious, as if he thought that someone was going to interrupt him at any moment or that I would hang up the phone. The sensible thing to do would be just that, and then send Agent Muukkonen to the prison.

"OK, I'll come. I'll try to be there tomorrow."

"You damn idiot," I said to myself after I hung up the phone.

I really didn't deserve any mercy.

I went to the kitchen and poured anise vodka down my throat, straight from the bottle.

19

I drove to Sörnäinen Prison at noon. Everyone thought I was going to the dentist, which was my excuse for not joining them for lunch. I wasn't hungry anyway. Actually, I felt a little sick. In the morning, as I explained to the prison officials why I needed to meet with Mikke Sjöberg as soon as possible, I felt as though I was listening to another person talk. When I merged onto the freeway, I realized I was like a junkie who knew she shouldn't take another hit but couldn't help herself. All at once I felt pleasure and shame, the moment of expectation like the euphoric effect of the drug overcoming the self-loathing. I tried to ignore the fact that Agent Muukkonen was only a phone call away, that he could go pick up Mikke and interrogate him, and I wouldn't have to see him at all.

I had slept fitfully the night before, dreaming of exploding boats and brains splattered on walls. Several times I got up to make sure Iida was still breathing and no one was outside. I tried not to wake Antti, who had taken a sleeping pill. He was afraid too, and was keeping it to himself just like me.

Laajalahti Bay glinted yellow and blue, and a pair of swans floated near the shore, oblivious to the traffic. Did executives really want to live between the noise of two highways, or would they build noise barriers, enclosing the cars in the vapors of their own tailpipes? In terms of the western Metro extension project, building up the bay area made sense.

Although I suspected that the only people on the Metro would be ideal-
ists, women, and the poor. The executives weren't going to give up their
company Mercedes. Even I was driving in my own car.

All of Helsinki seemed to have noticed summer was almost here.
Shorts, miniskirts, and sleeveless shirts exposed white skin that burned
under the brazen touch of the sun. Meanwhile, I was dressed as unsex-
ily as possible and only had on enough makeup to hide the dark bags
under my eyes.

I felt oppressed as soon as I entered the prison, as if the lack of
freedom hung in the air. I didn't pity the prisoners, since in Finland
you had to commit some pretty serious crimes to end up in a place
like this. I could always sense the feelings of a place, and there was no
way to avoid sensing the rage and despair contained within these walls.
Even the sparrows and crows fought over ownership of the yard like the
human leaders of rival gangs. There was always some prisoner who liked
feeding the birds and another who hunted them for his cat.

Getting into the prison was easy. Because I was a cop, the guards
didn't perform even a superficial body search. Right away they took me
to an interrogation room that reeked of sweat, with dented veneer furniture that could have been from the offices of any struggling business.
The thought that I was only a few hundred meters from Niko Salo was
dizzying. I hadn't brought anything beyond my old notebook to record
what happened.

If Mikke really knew something, I would have to turn him over to
Muukkonen.

The guard opened the door and let Mikke in. He wasn't wearing handcuffs. According to the assistant warden, Mikke Sjöberg had
a reputation for being an easy prisoner but suffered from occasional
depression. Mikke was even thinner than he had been the previous
fall, and his face now lacked its former sailor's tan. Instead of standing
up, I just shook his hand over the table, but I noticed everything: the
knuckles protruding through his skin, the light-brown hair darkened

by the winter and growing down over his ears. At first his blue-gray eyes avoided my own. But once the guard left, Mikke looked at me.

"Well, what do you know? Spill it," I said, looking back.

"Are you OK—and your family? The paper just said that no one had been injured in the explosion."

"Our cat set off the bomb and got hit by shrapnel. He'll recover."

"You look tired. Has work been hard?"

"Just the usual. And you?"

Mikke shrugged, and his mouth went crooked. "I'm trying to keep myself together by going to the gym. Once I get out on parole, I should be able to go out on day trips, right? Do you have your boat in the water yet?"

"Antti and my brother-in-law and his boys are going out next weekend to launch. Mikke, I'm in a bit of a hurry. What do you know about the bomb?"

Mikke leaned forward, and for a moment I thought he might grab me, but instead he put his elbows on the table and put his chin in his hands.

"Yes, OK. A couple of nights ago there was this guard in the gym who doesn't seem to care much about what goes on. I was doing bench presses when Salo stormed in and started throwing dumbbells on the floor. The guard turned and walked out. I thought he was going to get help, but no. Suddenly it was just me and Salo's main followers. I try to keep out of everybody's business, but I started to wonder whether I had stepped on Salo's toes by accident, and now I was going to get a beat-down. But they didn't even notice me. I continued my set and tried not to hear what they were saying. The less you see, hear, and say in here, the better."

Suddenly Mikke grinned, and laugh lines spread around his eyes. They were deeper than the last time I had seen him.

"Then I heard Salo mention your name. I didn't know you were on his hit list. The newspaper story about the bombing didn't mention it."

"That would only flatter Salo."

"I find him insufferable. He seemed to be mad that someone else got to you before he did. He talked about someone named Jani Väinölä. Do—"

"What? Väinölä?" I nearly bounced out of my chair.

"Just wait. Apparently this Väinölä guy already has a record and another conviction on the way. Salo said he could hardly wait for Väinölä to get back inside so he could teach him a lesson. At that point I decided to take a risk and ask if they were talking about you. I made it clear that you were the one who put me in here. Were your ears burning the night before last?"

"Not really. Or maybe a little."

I smiled involuntarily, but it was just from the excitement. Was Väinölä really behind the bombing? Was he really that angry I had stopped him from attacking the Somali boy at the bus stop?

"Väinölä had bragged to someone about making big money doing a torpedo job. He was hired to put the explosive in your yard."

"Hired? So it wasn't Väinölä's idea?" I felt the adrenaline level in my blood surge, and my ears started ringing as if I had a fever coming on. I swallowed, and the roof of my mouth was strangely dry.

"Not according to Salo. Väinölä was in a bar bragging to a buddy who's also one of Salo's men and said something about 'giving that bitch something to think about besides faggot murders.' Then the guard came back and Salo took off."

"Are you sure Salo mentioned the murder of a gay man?"

"Yes. But isn't that case already solved?"

"Only according to the papers."

Leaning back, I closed my eyes and ran my hands through my hair. I had been trying to piece together the wrong puzzle. Of course Väinölä's client was the same as Marko Seppälä's. How many murders was he willing to commit?

"Maria," Mikke said, and his voice was like a hand shaking me. "That isn't all. Yesterday morning I happened to be at a painting station next to Ónnepalu. He's another one of Salo's guys and a heavy addict. For a couple of Buprenex he was willing to tell me that Salo's source was named Jarkola. I remember him, since he just got out. He's supposed to be Väinölä's pal, but when Salo wants to know something, Jarkola talks. You should have seen Ónnepalu's expression. He's so damn proud to be under Salo's protection."

I opened my eyes and stared at Mikke across the table. There was no way he could've made this up. The puzzle kept falling on the floor and smashing, and I wished I could stop finding new pieces. Taking out my phone, I called Koivu.

"Hi, it's Maria. I'm still going to be here at the dentist for a minute, but there is one thing I need you to do. Send Patrol out to pick up Jani Väinölä right now. You have an arrest warrant. I want him as a witness for the bombing at my house. Yes, I'll let Agent Muukkonen know. Get a move on. I want this guy now! Don't call. I'm actually not supposed to be using my cell phone here."

Mikke leaned back in his chair with a curious expression on his face.

"At the dentist?" Mikke asked.

I grunted in irritation and hung up the phone.

"So you know Väinölä?"

"We've already questioned him a couple of times for cases we're working, and apparently he was telling the truth before. He really wasn't involved until he blew up my mailbox. My God, if this is all true! What a case . . ."

I stood up and walked to the window. It was so high that all I could see was a strip of aquamarine sky and an airplane gliding into the distance.

"On the phone you said you didn't want to get caught snitching. But you just may have become the key witness in the biggest case we've had all year."

I leaned against the wall, hoping it would hold me up.

"If we can get Väinölä to confess, we won't have to bother you any-more. I don't have to reveal my sources, not even to Agent Muukkonen and the NBI. But if not, would you be willing to testify? I can't promise you protection from Salo and his cronies yet."

"I'll just be happy if I can help somehow," Mikke said, sounding tired, and I remembered how he had looked on the deck of his boat right before he'd intended to blow it up, with him still on it. "There isn't anything noble about this for me. I'm just trying to buy forgiveness."

I tried to get my thoughts into some kind of order, but they bounded around wildly like sheep spooked by a bear. How could Rahnasto have known last week that I suspected him of being the instigator of all this? Who had leaked to him? Who did I dare trust now? I had to talk to someone, because alone I was never going to be able to put something together that would be coherent enough to nab anyone beyond Väinölä.

"Maria," Mikke said. "Are you alright?"

"Almost. And you? How are you holding up?" I asked, sitting back down at the table.

"These walls get to you eventually," Mikke said. "Drugs help for a while, but getting hooked isn't worth it. Kalle visits pretty often, and that keeps my head above water. I never could have survived the first few months without him. Maybe I'm starting to get used to prison, but every day I wish I would have gone to the police right after Harri died instead of taking the law into my own hands. Sometimes I play mind games with myself. If I killed Salo, he couldn't threaten you anymore . . ."

"That's childish," I said sharply.

"I know. Every day in here I see that violence just leads to more violence. No matter how you try to keep your ears shut, you can't help hearing it. I'm probably the only guy in our cell block who wasn't beaten or raped as a child. My mother had the sense to get a divorce and take me away, but my dad beat my half brother. I don't even have a history of violence as excuse for what I did."

Mikke's voice was hoarse, but there wasn't any self-pity in it. The grill on the window drew a crosshatch on the pale-green concrete wall, and the dull bang of a steel door echoed from somewhere in the building.

Mikke had rolled up his shirtsleeves, and his veins were clearly visible on his lean, muscular forearms. There were no needle marks on them.

"You asked me once if I've ever killed anyone. I said no, although what I should have said is that I've endangered my own life a few times and even the life of my unborn child. That was unforgivable. If Antti and Iida died because of my work, I don't know if I could go on . . ."

My voice failed. Continuing this conversation wasn't going to do anyone any good. All it was doing was ripping the scab off an old wound.

"I have to go question Väinölä. Thank you for calling me."

"Thank you for coming," Mikke replied.

I called the guard to take him.

"Hang in there," he said as he set off walking down the empty, echoing corridor. I should have been the one to say that to him. I would be fine. I was able to walk out the front gate, get in my car, and drive off into the lunchtime rush hour with all the other free people. On Aleksis Kivi Street I turned on the radio, and of course it was playing Ultra Bra's "You Went Away." Whoever was designing the soundtrack for my life had one hell of a sense of humor. I turned the radio up, even though my eyes were getting misty to the point that I could barely make out the license plate number of the car driving in front of me. When I stopped at the stoplight at Mannerheim Street, I took out my cell phone and activated the hands-free function. Then I called Agent Muukkonen. I said I had received an anonymous tip that Väinölä set the bomb at my house and that I had already issued an arrest warrant for him because it was well known that he had a grudge against me.

"I'm a little busy, so I wouldn't have time to question him today." Agent Muukkonen said, which worked out perfectly because as far as I knew Väinölä hadn't been arrested yet. Talking about the details of work like this helped calm me down. Muukkonen reported the explosive analysts' latest results. The bomb had been a simple device with a pressure trigger, and the builder couldn't have known in advance exactly how powerful it would be. Some of the gunpowder had failed to ignite, and the explosive analysts thought that whoever built it was either an amateur, an idiot, or someone who hadn't quite decided how much damage he wanted to inflict. According to his criminal record, Väinölä didn't have any experience with explosives.

"Let me know when you collar Väinölä," Muukkonen continued. "I'll be able to interrogate him tomorrow, first thing in the morning. I've been wondering why all of Salo's connections have been so quiet. We've been going after the wrong guy. I'll request a search warrant. If we find any explosives in Väinölä's apartment, so much the better."

I didn't say anything to Agent Muukkonen about Reijo Rahnasto, because all of that was still theoretical. At the station I marched over to Koivu's office with a half-eaten roll in my mouth and asked him and Wang to come see me. I had to trust them at least.

When I told them about my visit to the prison and what I had found out there, Koivu's face went white with rage. Wang listened more passively, although her eyebrows went up when I mentioned Jani Väinölä's name.

"So you believe Sjöberg's story?" Koivu asked once I was done.

"There isn't any reason not to believe him."

Koivu shrugged and started scribbling something on a piece of paper. It was a simple cause-and-effect diagram. He took off his glasses and rubbed his eyes. Then my desk phone rang and we learned that Jani Väinölä had been arrested and was on his way to the police station.

"Put him in a cell. The NBI will be here in the morning to question him. Please notify Agent Muukkonen."

"I imagine you'd like to be there for that interrogation," Wang said, a smile spreading on her face.

"Yes, I would, but I think I've played Lone Ranger enough for one day," I grumbled and then moved on to our other cases. Koivu continued to seem irritated, but Wang was surprisingly relaxed and happy. We talked about changing up partners again, and I tried without success to inquire about the progress of Koivu and Wang's potential new living arrangements. I imagined they would tell me when there was something to tell.

At two they left for an interrogation. I didn't really want to be alone, because solitude created space to think, and I didn't want to think, at least not about Mikke. Reijo Rahnasto's photograph still stared at me from my desk, and I grimaced at him. The newspaper clippings Eija Hirvonen had collected told about Rahnasto's habit of leaving proposals off the agenda when he disagreed with other members of the City Planning Commission. Of course a business leader would want to steer the city in way similar to how he might steer a company, but democracy didn't have much in common with that leadership style. But the city residents who identified with that sort of ruthless pursuit of success gave their blessing to Rahnasto's methods.

Rahnasto was a strangely faceless man. He was the son of a small businessman in Kokkola, the first in his family to go to college. He'd married his first wife while he was still a student. Based on the wedding date and Eriikka's birthday, it was obviously a shotgun affair. After graduation, he had worked in the arms industry and at a lock factory. In 1985 he founded Rahnasto Industrial Security Service. At first the company had been a small-time operation with only a few people importing security equipment. Now it had separate departments for personal and corporate security and handled accounts for nearly all of the major high-tech firms in Espoo. Even the city bought security services from Rahnasto's firm.

Rahnasto's political career had started in 1988. After landing a local council seat on his first try, the next election saw him move up to the City Council. Rahnasto's policy positions had a hard edge: dismantling social services, outsourcing city functions, privatization, building more big-box stores and highways. His slogan in the previous parliamentary elections had been "Passing on the Right." That hadn't propelled him to Parliament quite yet.

Not much personal information about Reijo Rahnasto the man was available. A profile in his alma mater's database mentioned hunting, gun collecting, snooker playing, and malt whiskey drinking as hobbies. I would have been an aficionado of that last one too, if I had the money.

When Lehtovuori came in to get advice on how to handle a domestic violence case, I put Rahnasto's file aside. Lehtovuori seemed astonishingly ill prepared, even though the whole time I had been unit commander I had encouraged my subordinates to step up their game in this area. I spent more than half an hour explaining the basics, trying not to show my impatience. Then Puustjärvi came in to talk about the possibility of his enrolling in a programming class. An e-mail reminded me that the department's third summer vacation coordination meeting would be on Friday morning.

Iida smiled from the bookshelf. The picture had been taken a few months ago, after getting out of the sauna. She was wearing a white nightshirt and a pink bathrobe, her wet hair curly and tangled, her cheeks red. Suddenly I needed to be with her, to hold her in my arms, to make sure nothing was wrong in her world. One of the other families at the day care was expecting a baby, and just the night before Iida had been grilling me about when she was getting a little sister or brother. I tried to change the subject, but it didn't work. Of course I was the one who had taught my daughter to be so headstrong. She demanded a bedtime story about how babies grow and are born, and once again I considered whether I wanted a baby, whether I would be able to give up work for even a couple of years. Would getting pregnant be a betrayal of the people who had chosen me to lead the Violent Crime Unit?

It was three o'clock. I took Rahnasto's picture and put it in my briefcase. If I was pushed out of my job because I was investigating a key figure in the city government, I would find another one. The prospect of changing jobs was feeling like a real possibility for the first time. On my way out, I stopped at a kiosk and bought a big bag of candy. A police officer was about to bribe the children of a witness.

Suvi Seppälä was at home and had already brought Diana back from day care. The smell of frying ground beef and boiled macaroni hung in the apartment, and Suvi was whipping eggs and milk to finish the casserole. Marko Seppälä would be buried on Saturday. On the kitchen table was a sewing machine next to a heap of black velvet and some white lace. Apparently Suvi was sewing funeral clothing for the children.

"Are you still investigating Marko's death?" Suvi asked bitterly as she shoved the macaroni casserole in the oven. "I thought you'd forgotten all about it. You think it's good that someone killed Marko so you can save money on trials and prison. So what do you want?"

I took out Rahnasto's picture and showed it to Suvi.

"Is there anything familiar about this man?"

"You could fit thirteen guys like that in a dozen. Why would I ever pay attention to someone like him? Who is he?"

"Think carefully."

"Mom, I need to poop!" three-year-old Diana shouted as she rushed into the kitchen. Suvi moved to undo the girl's overall shorts and went to help her onto the potty. Janita was helping Tony with his writing homework. School would be over soon. When Suvi returned, I asked her what she was going to do for childcare over the summer.

"My brother is watching the kids for a week, and then my class will be done. I'm just glad I have them. Otherwise I would have hung myself by now. But Marko talks to me every day, telling me to take care of our babies. He's promised to be their guardian angel," Suvi said and then started threading the sewing machine. The velvet dresses were almost ready. Suvi was attaching the final frills to the sleeve of the smaller dress when Diana called for her.

"I remembered one thing," she said after she returned. "About the cell phone. It rang a couple of nights before Marko . . . before everything. Marko was with Janita at the laundry, so I answered. It was this guy who seemed really grumpy. He didn't give his name. He told me to tell Marko to call and said he would know what it was about. Apparently he was pretty pissed that I answered and cussed Marko out when he called. Marko promised never to let anyone else answer the phone again."

"What kind of voice did he have?"

"Unpleasant, hoarse, rude. Used to giving orders."

"Would you be able to recognize his voice now?"

"Maybe. Sorry I didn't say anything before. I really didn't remember," Suvi said and started the sewing machine.

"I'm glad you're telling me now. Does the name Reijo Rahnasto mean anything to you?" I shouted over the noise of the machine.

"No. Who's he?"

"The man in this picture."

"Some rich guy?"

"I think so, yes."

"Did he kill Marko?"

Of course I couldn't answer. Suvi had finished the frill on one dress and was quickly working on the next. I hadn't sewn anything more complicated than a bath towel for Iida, since I never had time. Suvi could whip up whatever princess fantasy dresses she pleased. I wondered if she took custom orders.

"I need a smoke break," Suvi said and pulled a pack from her purse. She flicked her disposable lighter a couple times. It sparked but didn't produce a flame.

"Where the hell are all my matches? Janita, are there any matches in the bedroom?"

"Yeah, I'll bring them!" the girl yelled in reply. Janita bore a striking resemblance to her father, minus the police-lineup look of apathy in Marko Seppälä's eyes. Suvi lifted the box of matches to strike one, and then I saw the logo: RISS, white letters on a blue background.

"Suvi, where did you get that matchbox?" I asked, barely restraining my desire to grab her wrist.

"This? No clue. Marko was always picking up matches all over the place."

"Do you have more like this?"

"I don't know. Janita, will you see if we have any more of these?"

It turned out to be the only one. I told Suvi that it might be an important piece of evidence and went to the car to get a pair of gloves and a plastic bag out of my investigation kit. The matchbox probably only had the Seppäläs' fingerprints on it, but we always had to try. No one had thought to pay any attention to a common matchbox when they executed the search warrant.

The smell of the macaroni casserole was growing stronger. I was hungry too. I helped Suvi move the sewing off the dining table, and we continued chatting. I kept trying to come back to Rahnasto, but Suvi didn't know anything.

"I keep telling you I never got involved in Marko's business. I want to help you. I want to see whoever shot Marko rot in prison. Just tell me what I can do."

"We may need you to identify a voice."

"I'll do whatever. Not for me, but for the kids. Marko was what he was, but he loved his children. We would have had another three.

Children are better off when they learn to take care of themselves. You only have one, right?"

"Yes."

"How old are you? Thirty-five isn't too old yet. My aunt was forty-four when she had her eighth, and he was totally healthy. They aren't religious or anything; they just like kids. Like me and Marko."

"I actually need to go to pick up mine from day care. Call if anything new comes to mind or you just want to talk."

I stopped by the station to send the matchbox to the lab, then went for Iida. After dinner we visited the animal hospital to see Einstein, who was already perking up. After Iida fell asleep, Antti and I compared the loan offers we had from the various banks. Luckily I had a personal mathematician for whom interest rates were child's play.

"We can't really handle a mortgage and maternity leave," I said thoughtfully. "But interest rates won't stay this low forever."

"My grandma always said that a baby brings bread with it," Antti said with a laugh.

I laughed. "Huh, so did mine. Well then maybe we should practice a little if we're going to start thinking like our grandmothers . . ."

Sex was fun again, simultaneously intense and safe. With someone I knew so well it was easy to try new things, and even after so long there were still things to learn. I kept my eyes open the whole time, because I wanted to see who I was with, whose lips were nibbling my neck and breasts, who pushed me over the edge into the vortex of orgasm.

On Thursday I was decked out and in full makeup. Antti, who rode to work in his sweats, laughed and said that I could be on the cover of any business magazine. I practiced an appropriately deep tone for my voice, because apparently the higher pitch of women's voices wasn't as credible. Then I climbed the stairs to have coffee with the leadership.

I told my colleagues about the latest breaks in the Marko Seppälä murder case. The guys from Narcotics and Robbery listened with interest, and the deputy chief of police rubbed his eyes. The chief was currently in Stockholm at a Nordic policing conference. Taskinen looked elsewhere the whole time I was talking.

"So Väinölä hasn't been questioned yet?" Taskinen asked once I was through.

"Agents Muukkonen and Hakala from the NBI are coming at nine. Muukkonen got a search warrant yesterday for Väinölä's apartment, and they're probably already working there."

"Who is your nameless source? Why should we believe him?" Laine asked.

"He isn't nameless, but I'm protecting him for now."

"Does he even exist? I don't have anything against raking little shits like Väinölä over the coals, but are you sure you aren't wasting NBI resources?" Laine continued.

"Kallio, I'd like to hear who your source is too," Taskinen said seriously.

"All in good time."

"And what about Rahnasto? What evidence do you have? A matchbox and a gun that might fit a single bullet. Think before you go connecting one of the most powerful men in the city to a bunch of gangsters," Laine said. "Secret land deals, drugs, and murder! It isn't like we're in Italy. This is just about a drug deal, and Salo has his fingerprints all over it."

"Seppälä doesn't have any history with drugs," the detective from Narcotics said.

"Listen, Kallio, I know that your husband is an environmental activist. But that shouldn't influence your objectivity as a police detective," Deputy Chief of Police Kaartamo said coldly.

"What do you mean? What do Antti's opinions have to do with the destruction of Laajalahti Bay?"

"'Destruction' . . . just using that word shows you can't be objective about this case."

"So objectivity means accepting corruption in our government? Hell no!" I looked at Kaartamo, his graying, carefully groomed moustache, his 1930s-style three-piece suit, his round face, which was strangely unlined for a man nearing retirement. Kaartamo had been in the department for twenty years, and he was known as a man who could be counted on to oppose reform. The chief of police had had to force him to use a computer.

"When the Ilveskivi investigation began, the chairman of the City Council requested that we be discreet. Didn't Jyrki pass that on?"

The rage came in waves, making me sweat and bringing a flush to my cheeks. I stood up and took a step toward the deputy chief.

"Who paid you off? What did they promise you to get you to cover this up?"

The deputy chief of police looked coldly past me to Taskinen and Laine.

"I have five witnesses. I could sue you for slander, but I think we can handle this internally. How about we all just forget Kallio's little theory. And you can forget it too, Maria. I understand that you're upset since the bombing. A little rest might be in order. Why don't you move up your summer vacation a little? Jyrki can take over the Seppälä murder investigation."

I spun around so quickly that Laine jumped and coffee splashed out of his cup and onto his immaculate white shirt. Taskinen's disheartened voice stopped me on my way to the door.

"Maria, at least wait to see what the NBI can get out of Väinölä. Then we'll talk."

I didn't look back to show that I had heard.

All through our unit's morning meeting, I pretended nothing was wrong. Seppälä's murder was still on the shelf, and neither Koivu nor Wang commented on the investigation. But the previous nights had seen fists fly again in a couple of homes and at a park. We had a total of four assault reports, as well as a suspected violation of a restraining order. I divvied out the assignments as well as I could, but just as I thought I had everything arranged reasonably, we received word that someone had thrown himself in front of a train at a station on the west side. I sent Lähde and Mela there, leaving one of the assaults to wait.

I had a chat with the department press officer about some final details for our booth at the Police Expo. The event was being held at the old Helsinki Cable Factory, and I had promised to man the booth on Saturday afternoon. Iida was excited to get to see the police horses.

Agent Muukkonen knocked on my door around noon.

"Hakala is writing up the report downstairs, but there isn't much to be happy about. Väinölä doesn't have an alibi, but he won't admit to anything, not even that he hates you. You can read it between the lines, though. We'll continue tomorrow, although I doubt one more night in a cell is going to change anything for a guy like that. Isn't he on his way to Sörnäinen soon anyway?"

"Yes," I said tiredly.

Rahnasto had chosen his second torpedo well. Väinölä wasn't going to crack easily, and if he revealed his client, no one would believe him anyway. And if we did find some sort of evidence against Rahnasto, he would just hire a pack of high-powered lawyers to defend him. I imagined the trial with the defense witnesses including the mayor, the chair of the City Council, and a long list of other city officials, while the prosecution called on Suvi Seppälä, Eila Honkavuori, and Mikke Sjöberg. No prosecutor would ever take a case like that. Not without solid evidence.

Maybe I really should contact Rahnasto's company and arrange to meet with him about security for our house, I thought. Antti could come with me. We just wouldn't mention that we were only renting.

But Rahnasto would see that instantly from the real estate database, and I couldn't get Antti mixed up in my work. Best to forget that plan too.

I was just forcing myself to go downstairs for lunch when my phone rang.

"Agent Muukkonen here. Good news. We found traces of the same kind of explosives in Väinölä's apartment that were used to blow your mailbox to bits. And that's not all. There was also a diagram of your lot and a couple of pictures of your house. I'll be there at seven tomorrow, and we'll start turning the screws."

20

I found Taskinen in the cafeteria. His lunch was more meager than usual: pea soup, a piece of crisp bread, and an oven-baked crepe with only a small dollop of jam. He was obviously trying to avoid gaining weight during his forced break from running. At the table with him were a couple of guys from Narcotics I'd always gotten along well with. Which was why I felt comfortable telling my news about the explosives.

"Apparently your source knows what he's talking about," Taskinen said calmly. "Sit down."

"Let me get some food first." Hunger pounded in my gut. Luckily there was a vegetarian option for the pea soup. The Narcotics detectives disappeared while I was in line for my soup, and by the time I got back, Taskinen had moved on to his crepe.

"Now you and your family can sleep in peace," Taskinen said with false pleasure. "The NBI knows their stuff. Väinölä's going to be in prison for that much longer now. I'll talk to Agent Muukkonen. We'll be able to lock up Väinölä now, and he won't be getting out on bail before his trial."

After shoveling some soup into my mouth, I said, "You really want to believe that Väinölä acted alone, don't you?"

"It isn't a matter of what I believe. It's a matter of evidence. Be patient, Maria. Don't interfere with the NBI investigation, and make sure you don't ever let me hear you say something like what you did this morning. Kaartamo let you off easy."

I attacked my own crepe. The strawberry jam was sticky and thick like fresh blood. Licking my lips greedily, I realized I should have taken a double portion. Taskinen started asking about the progress of our house hunting, and I let the conversion shift. Talking to Jyrki was pointless. Was Mikke's information nothing but hearsay? Maybe I had shaved a difficult corner off the puzzle so it would look the way I wanted.

Over the course of the day, several people hinted at my exchange with the deputy chief. Apparently a rumor was circulating that I had finally blown it once and for all. I tried to act cheerful, like I didn't care, but that became difficult during my APC meeting at three o'clock. Accelerated Comprehensive Processing aimed at preventing young offenders from having to wait up to a year or more for trial, instead putting them before a judge within a few days if all went well. The goal was to interrupt the cycle of criminality before it could really develop. If the penalty for a previous caper wasn't overly severe, the likelihood of young offenders continuing to steal cars or break into houses would be lessened.

Laine said he was at the meeting to make sure his unit gradually became unnecessary. Plans were already underway to merge Organized Crime and Recidivism with the other units in the Criminal Division. Until the midnineties, the unit had been a part of Violent Crime, but because most repeat offenders had diverse rap sheets and were increasingly involved in drugs, Organized Crime and Recidivism had become its own entity.

Laine had come to take over the unit from the State Intelligence Service, but apparently his current position didn't live up to his expectations.

I was completely wiped out by the time I left for soccer practice. Wang and Rasilainen bummed a ride with me to the field. Rasilainen had been involved in Väinölä's arrest and repeated in detail all the curses and vituperation Väinölä had ladled out. According to Rasilainen, Väinölä had asked whether I would question him.

"Tell that to Agent Muukkonen," Wang suggested. "It shows that Väinölä knew he was suspected of a violent crime."

More women were on the field than last time, and we were able to put together two full teams. As we limbered up, I worked up a full sweat. My T-shirt and black tights were too heavy for the hot weather. The draw put me on opposite sides with Wang. Rasilainen volunteered to play goalie for my team, and I ended up sweeper. The game was more serious than the previous time, but we still had our heads about us enough to stop and whistle at a good-looking guy jogging by with his shirt off.

We played for about half an hour and then took a break. To my surprise, I realized we had an audience. A couple of male officers from Patrol were sitting on the grass with a six-pack. Rasilainen went over and bawled them out for disorderly drunkenness, which only made them yell louder. Officer Yliaho started playing sports commentator. When he began to describe each player's appearance in detail, I started to get peeved. Fortunately I only heard snatches of it because the game was so fast.

Near the end of the second half, Wang managed to fake out the rest of our defenders. Rasilainen yelled for me to help, so I sprinted for the goal, but instead of a clean tackle, I just managed to trip Wang, who fell against the goal post. She lay on the field holding her head, and blood trickled between her fingers. Rasilainen and I were by her instantly, and Liisa pulled off her headband to use as a dressing.

"I'm so sorry. I didn't mean to," I blubbered as blood ran down Anu's face. She'd hit her forehead on a rusty bolt protruding from the goal post. "Can you see OK? How many fingers am I holding up?"

"Don't worry," Anu groaned. "Heads always bleed a lot. It'll calm down soon."

"Are you sure? Should we take you to the hospital just in case?"

"No." Wang walked off the field, and I followed, still worried.

"Chicks are always like that, fussing over a little scratch," Yliaho said to Makkonen. "A guy would just keep playing. If you can't stand the heat, get out of the kitchen," he said and then took a long swig of beer.

I grabbed the first-aid kit from my car and cleaned up Anu's forehead as best I could. The cut didn't look like it would need stitches; a Band-Aid would suffice. Anu waited on the sidelines while the rest of us stretched. I noticed that she was sitting as far away from our male colleagues as possible.

"When do we get to play you?" Makkonen asked once we were done. "We could get up close and personal . . ."

"Don't hold your breath. We started a women's league exactly so we wouldn't have to listen your lame jokes during our free time."

"What does it matter if it's girls or men playing? Kallio did that illegal tackle because she was mad about getting slapped down by the boss this morning," Yliaho said.

"Oh, your simple, tiny brains," Rasilainen said with a sigh, but I wasn't laughing. Yliaho was right. I started walking back to the car with Wang following.

"Where should I take you two?

"I have my bike at the station," Rasilainen said. "You'll have to explain to everyone tomorrow morning that Pekka didn't hit you, Anu."

"As if. The Yliaho News Agency is sure to report to the entire department where Anu got her cut," I said. As I drove onto the highway, I unintentionally channeled all my anger into pressing on the gas pedal. Then I realized I was being an idiot and slowed down.

"Hey, Maria, you aren't fighting a one-woman war against the bosses," Wang said suddenly. "I think you're right about Rahnasto. Pekka was just tense yesterday because we were fighting again. He's worried about you. He didn't think seeing Sjöberg would be good for you."

"No, it wasn't," I said, "but it helped solve the case."

"Let's nail Rahnasto together," Liisa said. "I can try to come up with some reason to go to his office."

"There's one thing we could do right now," Anu said. "Liisa, let's go say hi to Jani Väinölä. Maria, can I borrow a picture of Iida? I want to make a color copy."

"What are you going to do?" I asked in confusion, but Anu only grinned and said she would explain in the morning. I went home to shower and eat Iida's favorite food, a cabbage casserole Antti had made.

The phone rang just as I was reading Iida her bedtime story.

"It's somebody named Kim Kajanus," Antti shouted from downstairs.

"Tell him I'll call back as soon as I get Iida down!" I yelled back and continued reading the animal book. Iida snuffled happily in the crook of my arm, and I thought of a languid mother cat nursing six kittens at a time.

"Who is Kim Kajanus?" Antti asked as we tucked Iida in together.

"Just someone from work. He might have a connection to the explosion."

Antti had asked surprisingly little about the progress of the investigation. Of course he was relieved when I told him about Väinölä's arrest, but he sensed the police still didn't know the whole truth. I told Antti as much as I would have told any victim of a crime. Which wasn't very much.

Kajanus answered on the first ring. He must have been sitting with the phone in his hand.

"I had a chance to look at Reijo's gun collection. Eriikka bought a painting in Brussels that we needed to hang, but neither of us had a masonry drill. Eriikka asked me to pick up a drill at her dad's company in Westend. I stayed to chat with Reijo, and suddenly thought to start talking about guns. I said I had thought about buying a pistol or a revolver, since I'm always carrying hundreds of thousands in camera equipment around with me. I asked if he could recommend something and what kind of gun would be most useful. You told me Seppälä was shot with a .22-caliber pistol and that Reijo has permits for a couple of those. His collection was missing a .22-caliber Hämmerli. I asked if that's the one he always carries with him, and he went quiet for a second."

I could hear Kim shifting position. He was pausing as if intentionally for effect.

"Reijo said it was stolen from his car a month ago. When I asked if he filed a police report, he said he didn't because it would be bad press for his security company. Then he slapped me on the back and suggested an air pistol. An inexperienced shooter couldn't kill anyone with that. Reijo promised to take me to the company shooting range to practice."

I listened intently. Kim had been too transparent. He tried to help, but his questions had probably only put Rahnasto on guard. Claiming a pistol like Seppälä's murder weapon was stolen was the obvious smart thing to do. Maybe he had sold it on the black market, or maybe it was resting at the bottom of the sea. The possibility that our ballistics experts would ever be able to test it was nonexistent.

That night I had troubled dreams in which I wandered through empty houses trying to find Iida before she stepped on a land mine. I woke up a little before six to full daylight outside. The yard looked peaceful, with a jolly hare bouncing toward the edge of the field while a blackbird pulled a worm out of the potato patch. The potato sprouts had started breaking ground, and soon we'd need to start weeding. I took Iida to day care and arranged with Antti to pick up Einstein. We were halfway through our morning meeting when my cell phone rang. Agent Muukkonen was calling from downstairs.

"Väinölä is significantly more talkative today, but he wants you here for the interrogation."

"I'm sure you told him that isn't possible, since I'm one of his victims?"

"Can you come anyway? Väinölä is seriously wound up. We need something to calm him down. The guard said he didn't sleep all night."

I thought about my schedule. The July personnel budget would have to wait. I promised to be down in half an hour, although that meant rushing through the rest of the meeting. Wang, whose forehead sported two Band-Aids, gave me a broad smile when I said we wouldn't talk about Seppälä yet because on Monday we might know a lot more than we did now.

Jani Väinölä really was upset. His fingers were twitching, and his legs seemed as if they were trying to move in different directions from each other and the chair. Withdrawal symptoms, but something more too: naked fear. His sparse stubble accentuated the anguish on his face, and the swastika on the back of his head was nearly covered by his hair.

In the closeness of Interrogation Room 2, four people felt like a crowd. Agent Muukkonen's aftershave smelled of vanilla and burnt rubber. Agent Hakala sat behind the computer looking tense. Muukkonen drank coffee at the table. I took up my place in the shadow next to him. The desk lamp was intentionally turned to shine in Väinölä's eyes.

"Detective Lieutenant Kallio arrived at nine fifteen. Shall we start at the beginning, Väinölä? You wanted to tell us what you were doing a week ago Friday, the night of May fourteenth."

Väinölä sat quietly for about a minute. When Agent Muukkonen repeated his question the third time, Väinölä finally answered.

"Yeah."

"What happened then?"

"I went to set a bomb at a house in Hentta."

"Can you give us the exact address?"

Väinölä repeated my address and then gave a slow, detailed account of setting the bomb.

"I was told the bomb wasn't supposed to kill. And it wouldn't have done much harm to an adult. The idea was just to mess up Kallio's arms. I was told that she always goes out to get the mail."

"Who told you this?" Agent Muukkonen asked just before I burst out:

"And what if a child had gotten the mail? What would have happened then? Would she have just been blinded, or would she have died?" I leaned forward in my chair, and Väinölä's dull-skinned face was only a foot from my own. "I'm sure you know how much guards and prisoners like child killers."

"He didn't tell me you have a kid."

"Who didn't tell you?"

"I don't know the dude's name," Väinölä said and glared at me defensively. Hairy hands ripped a piece of paper into quarter-inch shreds.

"Where did you meet him? Describe him," Muukkonen demanded. Several seconds passed before Väinölä spoke.

He had received a call the previous Tuesday. The call had come from a pay phone, which Väinölä knew because he heard coins being added.

"He knew I'd been interrogated for that fag's murder, even though I didn't do it, and that you've been messing with my business," Väinölä muttered. He had been speaking directly to me the whole time, even though Agent Muukkonen was asking most of the questions. "He suggested I do a gig that would be good for both of us. I would get revenge on you and make some cash, and he would get you to stop breathing down his neck."

"Is that what he said? What was his voice like?" I asked, and Agent Muukkonen glanced at me in confusion.

"His voice? Hoarse. Like he had a sore throat or something."

Väinölä wiped the sweat from his brow. There was no water in the room, but he clearly needed some. I went and filled a pitcher in the nearest bathroom and then poured a glass for Väinölä, who grabbed it greedily. Would we need to send him for detox after questioning?

Väinölä had arranged to meet his client last Wednesday night. The man had suggested meeting in the Suvela Elementary School parking lot. He had been waiting in the shadows when Väinölä came. The man already had a bomb constructed, pictures of the house, and a diagram of the lot, along with keys for a car rented for three days in Väinölä's name and a ten-thousand-mark down payment. He had promised to send Väinölä the remaining forty thousand by express mail once the job was done.

"What company was the rental from?"

"The Hertz at the airport. I took it back on Friday. Everything was paid for in advance. On Friday afternoon the rest of the money arrived at my house."

"Where is the money now?" I asked and thought of the bill Suvi Seppälä had given me. Would the serial numbers give us a clue this time?

"I've been having a lot of fun the last few days. I have old debts, and Jarkola has been breathing down my neck. Is he the one who snitched on me to you and Salo?"

"No," I answered quickly. So Väinölä had heard that Salo was looking for him. When Väinölä had been arrested on Wednesday, he had been at home asleep, still drunk from the night before. The search of his house had also turned up three Ecstasy tablets.

Agent Muukkonen tried to squeeze more information out of Väinölä, but he wasn't willing to say much more. He did say that his client was average height, in his fifties, and had been wearing a long, expensive-looking coat that was inappropriate for the weather. A dark, wide-brimmed hat covered his hair, and dark glasses concealed his eyes. He didn't have a beard or mustache, and a scarf had partially covered his jaw. The description fit Rahnasto, but I wondered if any judge would believe an identification made by Jani Väinölä. Rahnasto's picture was still in my office, but I didn't get it. Väinölä would have to pick him out of a lineup. After a positive ID, remanding Rahnasto for trial would be easy.

To my surprise, Muukkonen focused on asking where and with whom Väinölä had wasted his bounty money. Trying to remember anything from five straight days of drinking and drugs made Väinölä sweat. He was a patriotic guy: instead of taking a last-minute flight to the Canaries or Rhodes, he supported domestic bars and entrepreneurial local women. He bragged about being with three women at the same time, and as he thought about that, his expression brightened a little.

Agent Muukkonen motioned for me to follow him out into the hall. He wanted to talk.

"Apparently we're dealing with the famous Unidentified Man again. Who would have been prepared to pay to set off that bomb at your house?"

I told Agent Muukkonen about my suspicions and the reception I'd received in the department, and his expression darkened.

"We'll question Väinölä's drinking buddies. We have an APB out on Jarkola. Hopefully someone will be able to confirm that the money was payment for setting a bomb, not from selling drugs. We did find the express-mail envelope in Väinölä's apartment. The sender was listed as Jari Virtanen, and the return address was the same as Väinölä's. There were several sets of prints, but they were probably just from the postal workers. Guy's got to be pretty coolheaded to send forty thousand in the mail!" Muukkonen shook his head. "Of course we'll pay Hertz a visit too. They ask for ID. The person who bought the rental must have had a fake driver's license with Jani Väinölä's name."

"Getting that wouldn't be hard. I suggest putting Väinölä back in a cell and letting him spend the weekend squirming. I'll see what I can get out of the girls down on Aleksis Kivi Street. Probably not much."

I went back into the interrogation room, where Hakala was finishing up the interview record. Väinölä was lying half on the table with his face on his arms. His body twitched occasionally, and beads of sweat ran down the folds of his neck.

"Should we send a doctor to see you? You could get something for the shakes," I said to Väinölä, who lifted his head a little. A suspicious expression filled his bloodshot eyes.

"Are you shitting me?"

"No."

"What are you, some kind of Mother Teresa?"

"No, just a decent person," I replied. "You probably haven't met very many in your life. And you wouldn't now either if you had hit my daughter. But you aren't going to learn, even if you spend the rest of your life hung over, so it's just as well."

"I didn't know you have a kid!" Väinölä shouted and pounded his fists on the table so hard that Hakala jumped up from behind his computer, ready to intervene. "He only talked about your husband, some kind of fucking long-haired hippie draft-dodger type, but nothing about kids. Cute little chick, by the way. Thanks for the picture. I saw her dead in my dreams, last night I mean. I guess that's what your minions wanted!" Väinölä buried his face again in the dirty sleeves of his aviator's jacket and whimpered like a hungry greyhound.

"Then we had the same dream," I said quietly and left. I asked the duty officer to have the department physician drop in on Väinölä.

I ate lunch with Puustjärvi and Puupponen. The latter was practically bubbling over with bad jokes. A couple of nights ago, he was at a bar and a woman had said she was an energy healer, and that the next day she was going to have a colleague look at her astral body and diagnose the cause of her neck pain.

"So I said, 'If I told you you had a beautiful astral body, would you hold it against me?' But she didn't even smile. She just walked away!" Puupponen said with a grin. I tried not to choke on my chicken lasagna.

I ran into Wang and Koivu in our unit hallway.

"Hey, Anu, what on earth did you and Liisa say to Väinölä yesterday?"

Wang grinned slyly.

"We just threatened him a bit. We told him that Salo was furious and there would be a welcoming committee awaiting him at Sörnäinen. Apparently Salo's buddy Jarkola had told Väinölä the same thing. He went totally white. Exactly the color of the Finnish flag," Wang said with a laugh.

"Sounds like you enjoyed yourself," I said, still astonished.

"Guess how many times guys like that have called me a slant-eyed whore? I should get to have a little fun with them once in a while. Liisa told Väinölä that if he cooperated, the judge might agree to send him to Häme or Kakola instead of Sörnäinen. And Väinölä believed us."

"And the picture of Iida? What did you do with that?"

"We showed it to Väinölä and told him that she goes out to get the morning paper sometimes too. He doesn't have any bodies on his rap sheet yet. I didn't know what effect the picture would have, but apparently it worked."

"I owe both of you for this," I said, laughing. "Next Thursday, after soccer. Ice cream, beer, or both."

Wang, who never drank more than a glass, said she wanted both.

I still couldn't be completely happy about Väinölä's confession. It was a shame that making threats was the only method that worked on people like him, but we were just encouraging the cycle of violence by using it. Was there any other way?

"I'm tired of dealing with these types. Always the same story: no father, mother left for Sweden, shipped off to an orphanage, then a couple of foster homes, and then to a youth detention center. When they turn to crime, who are we supposed to blame? In this country we're supposed to have the freedom to choose. At least that's what the cell phone commercials claim."

"Some people do," Wang said, and then Koivu pulled her away.

Some expert in workplace psychology had decided that the department's summer vacation-coordination meeting should be held on Friday afternoon. I would have preferred to be anywhere but in another endless meeting. And, to top it off, some of the key players were gone. Robbery and Narcotics was at the Police Expo holding workshops about their specialties. When I arrived upstairs, Taskinen and Deputy Chief Kaartamo were already waiting. Kaartamo was responsible for department human resources and budgeting, so he was in charge.

"Well, Maria, what's new?" Taskinen asked, and stood to pull out the chair next to him. I sat down and told him that Väinölä confessed. I suggested that we pull Rahnasto in for a lineup. Kaartamo instantly turned salmon pink.

"We can't mix Rahnasto up in this just because some small-time crook is trying to save his own skin. And what were you doing at that interrogation?"

"Väinölä demanded that I be there. He said he would only talk if I was present."

Kaartamo shook his head, but he didn't say anything more, since the others were arriving. At the end of the meeting, Kaartamo brought up merging Organized Crime with Narcotics, and Laine looked flustered. The head of Narcotics was one of the country's leading experts, so there was no way he would leave the department. So Laine would end up in the number-two spot, which clearly irritated him. I verified that the staff-sharing system I had tentatively arranged with Narcotics would still work, so even during the summer our caseload wouldn't get too terribly backed up.

"The rape unit is going to be busy once miniskirt season starts," Laine said. "This morning I almost ran into a tree when I saw this chick at the bus stop in a belly shirt and a skirt about the width of my hand. And don't try to say she was just dressing for herself, Kallio."

Determined not to rise to Laine's bait, I just shrugged and let it go. After the meeting ended, Kaartamo looked at me with an expression that said he had something for me, but I escaped into the elevator with the head of Patrol. I picked up Iida, whose cheeks had started to show their first freckles. We met up with Antti and went to retrieve Einstein.

Over the past week he had lost at least three pounds, leaving the skin around his stomach hanging like an empty sack between his legs.

When I picked him up, he felt strangely light. I remembered how small Iida had felt right after she was born compared to this thirteen-pound cat. Einstein hated his Elizabethan collar, which he had to wear for another ten days. By then the stitches would dissolve.

Back at home, the poor cat ate a handful of shrimp but didn't have the energy to do more than wave a paw at the toy mouse on a string Iida tried to offer him. Soon he curled up on a chair warmed by the evening sun and fell asleep.

Inside I felt a familiar, dull pain: my period was starting. The pill made life easy—I could predict everything to within a couple of hours. My grandmother had frowned on people interfering with nature, although she had spared me her lecture about the will of God. "Now don't you start now," she had said to me during my first winter at the police academy, when I'd felt like maybe I wasn't going to be able to adjust to all the rules. "Don't you quit. You'll regret it later. No one regrets the things they do as much as the thing they leave undone. Believe me. I'm an old lady." I'd studied the network of wrinkles on my grandmother's face, her oxidized-copper-green eyes, which were almost blind without her glasses, and her best gray dress, which she wore when entertaining visitors. Would she have said, "Now don't you start now," if I had told her about my fear about pushing the investigation of Rahnasto? Or would she have told me to trust myself and keep going?

As if I had to ask. And I wasn't alone in my suspicions. I called my lawyer friend Leena and told her the whole story. She didn't think I was paranoid either.

On Saturday morning I went to the Police Expo. I would be working a booth where children could draw pictures of the police. For the first time in a long time I was wearing a uniform, which made me stand taller and keep me shoulders squared.

Iida thought I looked silly, almost like a man. She and Antti had promised to come to the fair around noon, when the police boats would be putting on a show.

The day passed quickly. Playing with the kids was fun, even though I'd never thought of myself as much of a babysitter. Iida tried every possible toy, from a police motorcycle to a snowmobile specially outfitted for use in Lapland. How she managed to turn on the siren I don't know. I had promised to stay to rip tickets for the concert in the evening, because I was interested in seeing how cops and punk rockers managed to share a stage. When the police choir and a rainbow-haired band named Kalle P. did the Clash's "Police and Thieves" together, I almost teared up.

"This never would have worked twenty years ago," I said to Koivu who was right there dancing next to me. "Neither side would have agreed to it. It's nice to see things getting better in some ways."

"Times they are a-changin', Maria," Koivu said solemnly. "I've been meaning to tell you . . . we're moving in two weeks. Will you help us?"

Koivu blushed, his expression like a little boy caught with his fingers in the cookie jar.

"Moving? Of course I'll be there," I replied. We'd have to handle the partner reassignment first thing Monday.

I admired the green of late spring covering the shore as I biked home. A flock of ducks took flight from the reeds on Laajalahti Bay and started to head out to sea but then decided to land near Hanasaari Island instead. On Karhusaari Island there were men in tuxedos smoking on a terrace and a wedding couple posing for pictures near the dock. Sailboats glided along the horizon, reminding me that Iida and Antti had gone out to Inkoo to launch our family's boat.

I would be at the expo tomorrow as well to speak to early-childhood educators about preventing violence in day cares. All I really had to say was that allowing violent games to be played or glamorizing hitting was not acceptable. That should go without saying, but the toy manufacturers were always pushing the opposite.

Silence awaited me at home, but Einstein was thrilled to see me. I thought I might indulge myself in one of the pearls from our video collection, but I didn't even manage to get *Priest* rewound before the phone rang.

"Is this Detective Kallio?" an agitated female voice asked.

"Speaking. Is that you, Suvi?"

"Yes. Listen, I called that Rahnasto guy. Marko was buried today, and I was feeling so bad . . . I wanted to show that bastard whose father he took away. I called him and said that I had found something of his in Marko's pocket, but I hadn't given it to the police, and that we could do a trade."

"What are you talking about?"

"I don't have anything, or actually I do, and he promised to come here. At first I thought it'd be OK because the children are here too, and so he wouldn't do anything crazy. But I'm starting to get scared. What if the same thing that happened to Marko happens to me?"

21

"Calm down, Suvi! You were smart to call me." I tried to sound composed. More worry wasn't going to help. "What did you arrange with Rahnasto?"

"He's coming here at ten thirty. I wanted the children to be asleep."

It was already ten past ten. Fortunately I hadn't opened my beer yet, so I could drive.

"I'll be right there, and I'm sending a patrol car. When the doorbell rings, call me again and leave the line open. Can you put the phone out of sight?"

"I can put it up on the hat shelf."

"Good. Don't let Rahnasto inside!"

"Why not? He wouldn't have agreed to meet me if he didn't have something to hide. He killed Marko, and now he's going to pay for it!"

"Do you have some kind of evidence you didn't give me?" I asked angrily, but Suvi didn't answer. "Don't let Rahnasto know that you think he shot Marko. Be careful. Let me inside. I'll ring the doorbell three times."

As I spoke I slipped my shoes on, pulled on my shoulder holster, and put on my jacket. Why the hell had I told Suvi Rahnasto's name?

I called Dispatch and asked them to send the nearest patrol car to Suvi's house, and to have the car contact me as soon as they got the call.

Didn't Rahnasto suspect a trap? Did Suvi think she could get Rahnasto to confess? That might work on TV, but reality was different. She didn't have a gun, did she? She could have hid it before we searched her house. Would Suvi fire shots in a house where her children were sleeping? Could I trust her?

As I passed through downtown Espoo, Liisa Rasilainen's voice came over the radio:

"Five-two-five calling Kallio. What's your ten-twenty?" Liisa and her partner were already at the library near the Seppälä home.

"Leave your car there and proceed by foot. It's better if Rahnasto doesn't see you."

"His car just drove by. Black Mercedes, license REI-100. Jukka checked with Dispatch."

"He's early. See you in a minute."

Just then my cell phone rang. Suvi didn't say anything but her name and then I heard a humming. I hadn't remembered to put on my hands-free, and the road was winding, so driving with one hand on the wheel was difficult.

"Hello," I heard Reijo Rahnasto say faintly on the other end of the line. "I haven't had the pleasure of meeting you before. My condolences on your husband's passing."

"We've spoken on the phone. I couldn't forget your voice."

Suvi sounded close. Apparently she had left Rahnasto standing in the entryway near the hat shelf. That was unwise. Rahnasto was only five foot nine, so his gaze wouldn't automatically land on the shelf, but he would probably notice the phone cord hanging down. Had Suvi had the sense to hide it behind the coats?

"I don't remember the call you're referring to," Rahnasto continued, his voice lower and hoarser than usual, as if he didn't want to be heard.

"You don't? You called Marko's cell phone, and I answered. Didn't he get that phone from you?"

"Is anyone else here?" Rahnasto asked, then his voice moved out of earshot. I accelerated past the train station and turned up the hill into the Seppäläs' neighborhood. Rahnasto had taken a risk driving his own car. He was unlikely to try to hurt Suvi, since the neighbors could testify that he was there. I left my car on the side of the road, grabbed my recorder and a tape out of my investigation kit, and shoved them into my jacket pocket. I spotted Liisa Rasilainen's slender silhouette near building H. The sun shining obliquely from the fields drew all color from the silhouette, so Liisa was only black. There was no sign of Jukka Airaksinen. I jogged over to Rasilainen with the cell phone still to my ear. The conversation was barely audible. While I couldn't make out the words, Suvi's voice sounded high pitched, and she was speaking rapidly.

"Jukka is behind the house, trying to see what's happening inside," Rasilainen said. She also had a phone to her ear. A baton and handcuffs hung at her waist.

"I'm going to ring the doorbell. We can't risk Suvi and the children's safety. You two stay outside, but be on your toes. We may end up needing witnesses. I don't know if Rahnasto is armed."

Two boys about ten years old skateboarded past, watching us curiously.

"Look, Tseba, two chick cops! Are you lookin' for the Seppälä kids' dad? You're a little late. His funeral was today." The boys laughed and skated around the corner.

"Did you set this trap for Rahnasto?" Liisa hissed as she followed me across the yard.

"Of course not. This is all Suvi. Wait here, and don't show yourself until I say so."

Liisa slipped behind the door, and I rang the bell three times as I'd promised. No one came to answer. I rang again, and to my relief I heard Suvi's shrill, agitated voice through the door.

"It's probably just the guy from next door. He always comes over when he's drunk. He seems to think I need male companionship now that Marko is gone. I'll tell him to beat it."

Suvi opened the door and whispered angrily, "Things are just getting going. He admitted he knew Marko." Pushing past Suvi's outstretched hands, I stepped into the entryway and motioned for Liisa to follow. Reijo Rahnasto sat in the living room, looking as if he owned not just the place but the whole block. When he saw us, his expression changed.

He stood but couldn't seem to speak.

"Good evening, Mr. Rahnasto," I said and extended my hand, which Rahnasto shook with an indifferent squeeze. "Officer Rasilainen and I were just dropping by to see how Suvi is holding up. I didn't realize you knew the Seppälä family."

Rahnasto sat back down on the sofa but then changed his mind and stood again.

"Shall I make coffee? We have pulla and sandwiches left over from the funeral," Suvi said, her tone full of false friendliness.

"I was just leaving," Rahnasto said quickly.

"Oh, don't, Reijo. You just got here. You were just saying how you knew Marko. I hadn't realized it before, but he talked about you several times."

A vein throbbed in Rahnasto's neck, and there was dandruff on the collar of his dark-gray suit. Eyeglasses would have suited him. They would have added character to his smooth face. No wonder Jani Väinölä hadn't been able to give a good description of the person who hired him to set the bomb in my yard. Rahnasto had no notable features.

"I didn't know him. We just met in passing. We ran in very different circles."

"Marko told a very different story. You arranged some work for him recently. And you gave him a phone," Suvi continued. Her dark eyes glittered, and the end of her nose was white like someone who had been out in the cold too long.

"Not true. I really do have to go now," Rahnasto said. He had his back to the living room window, behind which Officer Airaksinen stood, looking in curiously. How much could he hear?

"Why did you come to our house, then, if you didn't know Marko?" Suvi asked.

"I felt sorry for you when you said you were a widow with three small children. I came as a City Council member to see if there was anything I could do to help."

Rahnasto's voice was at once oily and hoarse, the voice of a person who was used to being in control of a situation.

"You promised we could make a deal—for this," Suvi said, and pulled a perfectly ordinary cell phone case out of her jeans pocket. On the black faux leather, the word "Nokia" appeared in gold letters with a smaller logo below: the blue-and-white Rahnasto Industrial Security Service symbol.

"Some of the stitching came undone. Marko asked me to fix it at my leatherworking class, but I forgot. It's been in my basket all these weeks. Why would Marko have a cell phone cover with your company's logo on it?"

"He could have stolen it. He was good at that, wasn't he?" Reijo Rahnasto snapped and moved toward the door. Suvi rushed after him, and I tried to hold her back. Suvi had already bungled enough, revealing almost everything to Rahnasto. He wouldn't need O. J. Simpson's lawyers to quash what little evidence we had.

Suvi grabbed Rahnasto's arm, causing his jacket to open and revealing the shoulder strap of a holster. Rahnasto broke her grip in a way that indicated regular self-defense training, but Suvi wasn't going to let him get away so easily. She grabbed onto his neck as if hugging a lover, and Rahnasto lost his temper and slammed Suvi against the wall before Rasilainen and I could intervene. Suvi slumped to the floor and started to cry.

"That was self-defense. You saw how she attacked me," Rahnasto said and wiped his face, where Suvi's ring had left a bloody scratch.

"Yes, we saw. We should probably go down to the station to sort this out," I said coldly.

"I'm not leaving my children!" Suvi spat. "I didn't do anything. Take him! He killed Marko!"

The doorbell rang, and Rasilainen let Airaksinen in.

"Jukka, you stay here for a while in case the kids wake up. The rest of us are going to the police station. We'll take my car. We'll bring you both back once you're done answering a few questions."

"Why do we need to go to the police station?" Rahnasto asked. "Isn't it clear what happened? I came to pay a courtesy call, and she attacked me."

"You appear to be armed. Let's have a look."

Rahnasto glared at me but then opened his jacket.

"This is completely legal. I always carry it with me."

"Especially since Petri Ilveskivi's death, is that right?" I asked, instantly regretting it. I couldn't make any more mistakes. "Let's go. This won't take long."

"I want to call my lawyer," Rahnasto announced.

"That's fine if you think it's necessary. Don't worry, Suvi. Officer Airaksinen will be here with the children. He has three of his own. How's your head? Are you hurt?"

"I have a headache," Suvi replied faintly. She grabbed some ibuprofen from the bathroom and took two tablets. Then she lit a cigarette.

"Let's take that cell phone case along too," I suggested. I asked Jukka to reserve an interrogation room and call in backup. I wanted to deal with Rahnasto myself, although at this point it was technically a case for Patrol.

Rahnasto demanded to drive to the station in his own car, but I refused, and he didn't put up much of a fight. Once we were in the car, he called his lawyer, who promised to come immediately. After that he sat quietly in the backseat next to Rasilainen. Suvi leaned her head against the front seat. She looked very tired and barely old enough to be faced with such adult problems. Liisa would have to take her fingerprints and get a statement for the sake of formality. Maybe she had been more help than hindrance after all.

I led Suvi and Rahnasto to the drab interrogation rooms downstairs in Holding. Rahnasto announced he wouldn't say anything until his lawyer arrived. In the meantime we fingerprinted him and sent the prints to the lab with the RISS cell phone case. The lawyer would probably protest the fingerprinting, and I would receive a reprimand, but I didn't have time to worry about that now.

"Liisa, get Suvi's information and then take her home. Make sure to ask her what Rahnasto said when she called him. Record everything. There's no point in waiting for backup to get here. This is just a formality with Suvi," I whispered in her ear. Liisa smiled and nodded, giving me a thumbs-up. I wasn't ready to celebrate quite yet.

"What's up with Väinölä?" I asked the officer on duty in Holding.

"The doc gave him some pills and he calmed down a bit. I doubt he's sleeping, though. Do you want to have a look?"

"I do."

At the door to the cell, I cracked the sliding window, which was so high I had to stand on my tiptoes in order to see inside. Väinölä lay on his bunk with his eyes open. I glanced appraisingly at the duty officer, a guy named Koskinen. I didn't know him very well and hadn't heard anything good or bad about him.

"Has Väinölä been outside at all today? Maybe a little stroll would do him good. Maybe that would help him sleep. Hey, Väinölä, want to go for a walk?" I called through the window. Väinölä climbed out of his bunk but apparently didn't realize I was the one who had spoken until I opened the door.

"What now? Don't you have to do interrogations before ten o'clock?"

"This isn't an interrogation. Are you going to behave yourself, or do we need to get the cuffs?"

Väinölä shrugged and then followed after the duty officer. The holding cell block corridor was bleak, and Väinölä's socks padded along slowly like a patient in a rest home. Hopefully he wasn't too doped up for what I needed.

I just happened to open Rahnasto's interrogation room door as Väinölä was walking past. The effect was as I'd hoped. Both men froze when they saw each other. Then Rahnasto snapped out of it and tried to pull the door closed, but I shoved my foot in the way. Väinölä started to shout, "That's him! That's the man who paid me to put the bomb in your yard!"

Rahnasto tried to jerk the door closed again, but I wouldn't let him. Officer Koskinen stared in confusion at the three of us. Liisa Rasilainen had rushed into the hall when she heard the shouting, and Suvi peeked out behind her.

"Jani, are you sure?" I asked.

"Yes! Tell her, you bastard! You didn't tell me the whole truth! Were you the one who ratted me out?" Väinölä screamed, and Koskinen had to restrain him from attacking Rahnasto. Eventually I had to step in and help.

"I've never seen that man before in my life." Rahnasto's voice trembled with rage. "I demand to be released immediately! What kind of a game is this?"

I sent Väinölä back to his cell with the promise that we would talk again soon. Despite it all, Suvi looked triumphant. Apparently she believed Rahnasto would never be getting out. She and Rasilainen left to take her back home.

I knew that wasn't how it would go, and that was confirmed once Rahnasto's lawyer, Joel Sammalkorpi, arrived at the police station. It was two o'clock in the morning before we reached any compromise in our juridical debate. Rasilainen was called back to the station to report what had happened at the Seppälä house. We couldn't deny the facts.

Suvi had attacked Rahnasto, and Sammalkorpi knew which laws to appeal to.

Rahnasto denied ever having seen Jani Väinölä before, and Sammalkorpi attempted to invalidate the identification, which he claimed was staged. We had to let Rahnasto go. Agent Muukkonen would interview him the next week, and I would return to the Marko Seppälä case if my superiors allowed it. Removing me from the case would be easy, since one of the suspects for Seppälä's murder was also now suspected of a crime against me.

I got home a little before three. My presentation at the Police Expo was at noon, so I would have to try to sleep before then. But I couldn't. I watched the sunlight as it felt its way into the bedroom, illuminating the dressers and the print of Van Gogh's *Wheatfield with Crows* that hung on the wall. The yard was silent other than the calls of a blackbird and a robin. I missed Iida and Antti. Luckily Einstein hopped onto Antti's pillow. His plastic collar banged against the edge of the nightstand as he tried to find a comfortable position behind my head. I scratched his back for a while, and finally I fell asleep to his steady purring.

I woke up a little before eight. Even though I told myself to go back to sleep for another couple of hours, I couldn't. Flashbacks of the events of the previous night wouldn't leave me, not Suvi's hysterical voice or Rahnasto's defiant, self-satisfied smile as he left Holding. Today I would have to answer for everything I'd done.

I got up, drank a glass of juice, and put on my jogging clothes. The neighborhood was still asleep, and during the first two miles I only met a tabby cat returning from its nocturnal adventures and one dog walker. I tried to concentrate on my upcoming presentation, but my mind kept going back, trying to scrape together some real evidence against Rahnasto. We still didn't have enough for a trial, but there was plenty enough to ruin his reputation. I wished I had an option besides resorting to dirty tricks.

I managed to collect myself for the presentation by reminding myself that its purpose was to prevent the development of more Jani Väinöläs. I felt daunted by the prospect of these day-care professionals listening to me as though I were some great authority, since I felt like such an inadequate caregiver myself. How could I lecture anyone about how to raise children so that they would never use violence to solve disagreements, when my own child had become the target of a bombing because of my job?

After my presentation, I called Agent Muukkonen. He was fishing in the islands off Porvoo, but got excited when I told him about Väinölä identifying Rahnasto and promised to pick up the questioning first thing Monday morning. I didn't bother to tell him all the details, since there was still a crowd around me, and Muukkonen deserved his days off. Then I returned to my previous day's post at the children's drawing station, which couldn't help but cheer me up. As I was hanging a picture one eight-year-old boy had drawn of me arresting Napoleon, I spotted Eila Honkavuori sashaying toward me.

"Hi, Maria. I hoped I'd find you here! I have some good news!"

I pulled her aside and told the other officer at the booth that I would be back in a minute.

"Yes?" I asked, and my whisper echoed like a shout in the hallway we had retreated into.

"I was having coffee with Jaana Tuhkamo-Karvonen on Friday. She's a mutual friend of mine and City Council Chairwoman Aulikki Heinonen. Jaana said that Aulikki had been unusually tense lately. She couldn't stand hearing any mention of Petri Ilveskivi's death, as if she felt guilty about it. I went on talking about other things and then said that I had heard rumors about zoning changes for Laajalahti Bay. Jaana immediately got embarrassed and asked who had been saying that. So I just let it go. Then yesterday she called and asked again where I had heard the rumors. I'm sure Aulikki Heinonen made her do it."

"Thank you for the information," I said. "Reijo Rahnasto was arrested last night for attempted assault, but we had to let him go. There isn't enough evidence against him."

"What?" Eila shouted. "So he can just murder Petri without any consequences?" Eila's face flushed, making her look like a ripe strawberry.

"Who do you think knows about the Laajalahti Bay plan?"

"The South Espoo General Plan is still wide open because no decision has been made about the Metro. The government owns the land around the EU Natura preserve, but once the changes in the Land Use and Building Act come into effect, zoning authority will go to the municipality, and approval from the Ministry of the Environment won't be needed anymore. For the past few years the state has seemed eager to sell off its property. Why wouldn't it sell its land to Espoo so they can rezone it for commercial use and luxury apartments and then sell it? Everyone gets a cut. Who cares if they're building on the edge of a nature preserve? They just have to wait a few years and there won't be any animals or plants left to protect. Then they can remove the protected designation and build more. That's how they want it to go."

"Why didn't Petri go public immediately?"

"Who of us is always sensible?" Eila said sadly. "Even if it destroys my political career, I'm not going to wait to go public. And I won't be alone. There are people in all the parties who are sick of how small the circles are that decide things in this city. I'm going to call the city beat reporter at the paper. I owe Petri at least that much."

My turn at the coloring booth ended at three. Afterward I went for coffee at the café in the event center and saw Laine and Deputy Chief Kaartamo sitting at table together. The latter waved a hand for me to come over, but instead I went outside with the K9 dog handlers who had gathered to smoke.

That evening I drove to Inkoo to pick up my family. The sailboat, the *Marjatta*, rocked proudly on the waves, and Iida bragged about learning a sailor's knot from her cousins. Matti and Mikko were already thirteen, and Matti's voice was changing. Iida worshipped both of them. The rest of her cousins were all the way in Joensuu, so she rarely saw them. Antti's sister and her husband were worried about the boys moving up to junior high since—according to them—there were drugs even in the best schools. Suddenly I felt like I had never left the expo.

Iida fell asleep in the car, so I told Antti about what had happened the previous night. He listened with a serious expression and then sat silently for a long time after I was done.

"Listen, Maria," he finally said. "When I decided to spend the rest of my life with you, I also decided to accept the risks that came along with your job. But is any job worth you killing yourself—not physically, but emotionally?"

"What do you mean?"

"I mean, how are you going to cope if Rahnasto never has to answer for what he did?"

I didn't know how to reply.

The next morning was like riding a hurricane in a dinghy. Our unit meeting was lighthearted because of the Police Expo, but as I was just starting to discuss the partner reassignment with Koivu, Wang, Puupponen, and Puustjärvi, our unit administrative assistant barged in.

"Maria! Deputy Chief Kaartamo wants to see you immediately."

"Oh shit," I said.

"Buck up," Puupponen said and slapped me on the shoulder. Suddenly the others joined in with pats and hugs, and everyone wished me good luck, even taciturn old Puustjärvi.

Taskinen was also in Kaartamo's office, along with Agents Muukkonen and Hakala. In addition to coffee, carefully constructed cold-smoked salmon sandwiches were laid out, but I didn't feel like eating.

"First, Kallio, a complaint has been filed against you. Over the weekend you made an unnecessary arrest and conducted yourself in an unprofessional manner. Tell us your version of events," Deputy Chief Kaartamo demanded.

As I did, I saw Taskinen's lips twitch in a couple times, but when he worked up the courage to look at me, his expression was sad. The sun shone directly in my eyes, so I moved my chair a little.

"And then Jani Väinölä's identification of Rahnasto: Did it come spontaneously, or was he given prompting?" Kaartamo asked.

"Officer Koskinen was present. Ask him. I haven't seen Väinölä since Thursday, and during that time there were always witnesses present and complete records were kept of everything that happened."

"Väinölä stands by his testimony," Agent Muukkonen said, interrupting. "In my opinion, we need to question Reijo Rahnasto as soon as possible. Agent Hakala interviewed a few of Väinölä's drinking buddies last night, and they were all ready to swear that the drinks Väinölä bought them were from money for a bombing. We're currently looking into who rented the car in Väinölä's name. It might help to show Rahnasto's picture around the rental office."

"But why would someone in his position do something so insane?" Kaartamo asked and stood up. He paced the floor, his gray mustache wagging worriedly.

Then he stopped in front of my chair. "Who is your anonymous source? Who told you about Väinölä?" he asked.

"It was a phone call. I didn't have time to put a trace on it, since it was over so quickly."

"And you took this anonymous tip seriously?"

"He seemed to know what he was talking about."

"Goddamn it!" A fist slammed down on the desk, too close for comfort. "Isn't it enough that we have the bomber? Väinölä is a thug. What reason do we have to believe his accusations?" Kaartamo turned to Agent Muukkonen.

"I don't answer to you. My orders are to investigate the explosion in Kallio's yard, and I'm going to do that to the best of my ability as long as that order stands," Muukkonen said sternly. "The explosives we found in Väinölä's apartment appear to be from a robbery of a construction site in March. At the time there were some indications that it was an inside job, and one of the guards was fired. Now he works for Rahnasto Industrial Security Service."

I looked at Muukkonen in surprise. He had learned much more than I had imagined. Kaartamo dried the sweat from his forehead and sat back down.

"Fine," he said. "Everyone is equal before the law. But be tactful. And Kallio, you're off the Seppälä case. Jyrki will handle it."

I managed to restrain myself.

"I'll make sure you get all of our interview notes," I said to Taskinen. "Koivu and Wang know the most about the case." Taskinen returned my gaze, but all I saw in his expressionless eyes was a reflection of my own disappointment.

I took the same elevator down with Muukkonen and Hakala.

"Smile, Kallio!" Agent Muukkonen said and tipped my chin up. It felt nice. "Now you're going to tell us everything, including what you didn't want Kaartamo and company to know. We aren't going to get anywhere in this case otherwise."

I started with Ilveskivi's death. Muukkonen listened and Hakala took notes, and I gained even more respect for my colleagues' powers of deduction. At noon I received an e-mail from the crime lab. Apparently they didn't know I had been moved off the case.

Rahnasto's fingerprints matched some found on Marko Seppälä's motorcycle saddlebags. I jumped out of my chair and must have shouted for joy for half a minute.

"Slow down!" Muukkonen shouted when I called him. "Did you ask if they also match any of the prints on the envelope Väinölä got with the cash for the bombing?"

"I don't have that authority. I'm not on the case anymore."

"But I am," Muukkonen said, and I heard him start typing at his computer. The answer came back within a few minutes. One of the prints on the envelope unquestionably came from Reijo Rahnasto's left little finger.

22

Fingerprints alone weren't enough to solve the case. Agent Muukkonen didn't get to question Rahnasto until Wednesday. Rahnasto's lawyer had already demanded that his client's fingerprints be thrown out because he hadn't been told why they were being taken. The NBI had assigned more resources to the bombing investigation, and Taskinen and Muukkonen led the group working the connection between Seppälä's murder and the explosion of our mailbox.

Outside, summer had come, and inside I spent fifteen minutes with a coffee cup and a sheet of paper hunting a wasp that had strayed through the window of my office. Lähde was surprised by my antics when he came in to request an arrest warrant.

"Well aren't we tenderhearted," he said, munching a donut. Sugar fell on the floor and Lähde's shirt, but he didn't seem to notice. His shirt had pictures of flowers and bees on it, and the hot pink and bright blue reminded me of tropical beaches. Lähde would start his summer vacation soon, and given the shirt, he was obviously counting down the days.

Taskinen called me into his office on Tuesday afternoon. He was reviewing the Marko Seppälä preliminary investigation files and asked me to clarify a few points.

"The van spotted near the dump," he said. "Did you ever get a more specific description of it?"

I remembered that I had intended to send Mela to interview the eyewitnesses but had later rescinded the order.

"Probably too late for that now," I said bitterly. "The old man isn't likely to remember anything from a month ago at this point."

"Don't underestimate people, Maria. Instead of Mela, I think I'll send Puupponen. Mela can sort through Rahnasto's gun collection. He appears to have one that uses the same kind of bullet that killed Seppälä."

"That probably won't be much use either," I said and told him everything about Kim Kajanus, including how Rahnasto had claimed to have lost his Hämmerli. As I talked, Taskinen stared at me even more pointedly, shaking his head.

"What else isn't in these reports?" he asked, tiredly massaging his face. He had his injured leg up on a chair. Between his dark-blue trousers and socks of the same color, I could see a strip of ankle covered in blond hair. In the past I might have felt an urge to touch it, but not anymore. That made me sad. Taskinen leaned over the desk, then hesitated and suddenly drew back.

"I have something I haven't told you too. Someone told my wife that she would lose her job if the Ilveskivi investigation wasn't closed after Seppälä was found to be the guilty party."

"What the hell? Who made that threat?"

"The day-care administration office is making cutbacks, and Terttu's position is one of the ones in danger. The Social Services Committee opposes the cuts, but the City Council is bulldozing them. No one said anything directly. We were just made to understand. Finding a new job wouldn't be easy for a fifty-year-old social worker, and we can't afford for Terttu to go on unemployment. You know how expensive Silja's skating is."

"Was it someone in the department who threatened you . . . was it Kaartamo?"

Taskinen's face was red, and he had a hard time looking me in the eye.

"No. Kaartamo just encouraged me to be generally careful. He belongs to the same Freemason lodge as the mayor. Terttu was the one who was threatened. They asked her to tell me to stand behind my superiors' decisions. You know how it feels when your job puts the people you love in danger, don't you?"

"Of course I do! But that still doesn't . . ." I stood up, barely able to breathe. "Why the hell did you let them pressure you?"

"You're so dogmatic. Things aren't that black and white. What would you have done in that situation?"

"I would have continued my investigation. Giving in to intimidation makes you complicit in it!"

Taskinen swallowed.

"The situation has changed now. I'm going to question Rahnasto myself. I want you there with me, but that isn't possible. I can use Koivu and Wang, though, right?"

"Better Koivu and Puustjärvi. We switched their partners because Wang and Koivu are moving in together," I answered coldly. "Is there anything else?"

"No," Taskinen said, but when I reached the door, he cautiously said my name. Instead of turning back, I marched right out of the building, sped home, and vented my rage by beating all the rugs. Even after that I still hadn't come to terms with what Taskinen had done.

Being sidelined from the investigation wasn't easy, but I gave myself permission to work a couple of shorter days. Iida and I washed the windows and baked cookies together for the spring party at her day care. Einstein finally worked up the courage to go outside on Tuesday night and seemed frustrated when the plastic collar got in the way of his hunting.

Eila Honkavuori called me at work on Wednesday morning. Her excitement was loud and clear over the phone.

"Have you seen today's paper?"

"Not yet. What's in it?"

A big story about Laajalahti Bay and Rahnasto. If something doesn't happen now, it never will. Rahnasto admitted that there have been secret negotiations about the area around the bay. I can hear the mayor's teeth grinding all the way across town! My phone has been ringing off the hook all morning."

"Does the article give any hints about Rahnasto's part in Ilveskivi's murder?"

"It doesn't hint, it says right out that Rahnasto has been questioned for both Petri Ilveskivi's and Marko Seppälä's murders and the bomb that went off in your yard. This is going to be interesting."

I asked our unit administrative assistant to get the paper, and when I had it, I sat down, opened a new bag of salmiakki, and put my feet up on the desk to read. Apparently Rahnasto wasn't afraid of publicity anymore and was openly voicing his opinions about development in the city.

It doesn't make sense to reserve the most valuable land for the birds. An advanced technological society requires high-density construction. The Otaniemi-Laajalahti area could be Finland's Wisconsin, a trendsetting model for all of Europe. If we build up these unused shorelines, we might not have to reclaim the land between Hanasaari Island and Koivusaari Island. Which option will the residents of the city prefer?

When the reporter asked about the secret negotiations, Rahnasto admitted that there had been some low-profile conversations, but only for the common good.

We've been trying to avoid sparking unnecessary upset and the never-ending cycle of litigation surrounding municipal decision making that slow down every major initiative. For the present situation we need quick decisions. I want to emphasize that we aren't damaging the natural area, even though I personally believe that the city is the city and the country is the country. Don't we have enough untouched nature in Kainuu and Lapland for everyone from Espoo to enjoy? Nowadays you can get a flight across the country that take about as much time as driving across town to the bay.

In the color photo of him standing in his company's data management center, Rahnasto wore a self-confident smile. According to the reporter, he flatly denied any connection to the crimes he had been questioned about. He said it was nothing but a political witch hunt. Neither the mayor nor the chair of the City Council had agreed to an interview, but plenty of other local politicians, including members of Rahnasto's own party, harshly criticized the way the Laajalahti Bay matter had been handled. Some said that because of the suspicions surrounding Rahnasto, he should immediately relinquish all of his positions of trust.

My phone was no less popular than Eila Honkavuori's. The next caller was Suvi Seppälä. She asked eagerly how much compensation she could demand from Rahnasto. Should she hire a lawyer?

Kim Kajanus didn't call. Instead he came to the station. When I went down to get him from the lobby, I accidentally ended up in the middle of a media circus. Reijo Rahnasto was coming in for another interview, and a gaggle of press photographers was hot on his heels. A television camera was trying to get a close-up of him as he smiled calmly. His lawyer clutched his briefcase, looking dour. Could he possibly believe his client was innocent? Agent Muukkonen, Taskinen, and Assistant Chief Kaartamo waited for Rahnasto in the hall, and Kim Kajanus, who had been hanging out by the reception desk, jumped behind the giant stuffed octopus like a character in a comic opera. Uniformed officers attempted to shoo the photographers out of the building. A crime reporter asked for a comment, but I didn't give one.

Kim Kajanus looked so guilty climbing out of his hiding place that I started to laugh.

"I probably should have whistled the all clear," I joked.

"Is it all clear? Are you sure Reijo had Petri killed?"

"We're investigating that," I said and opened the door to our hallway. Puupponen and Wang were engaged in a heated discussion in the break room, but otherwise it was quiet. It was as if the whole building had paused to listen to the conversation occurring on the upper floor. Reijo Rahnasto was such a big shot that they didn't take him to the normal interrogation rooms.

"I told Eriikka everything yesterday," Kajanus said and slumped into a half-supine position on my couch. "I really do love her, and I don't want to lie anymore. I still don't know what I am, gay, hetero, or bi."

"Does it really matter that much? Does everything have to have a definition?"

"No, but I don't know what's going to happen. Of course Eriikka is totally messed up because of her dad. Her beautiful, simple world is in pieces now. I think she'll break up with me. She was really hurt that she wasn't told the real reason for the police interviews."

Kajanus sat on my couch as if he were at a friend's house, and I got the feeling he had come to me because he couldn't get an appointment with his therapist. I could have told Kajanus that I didn't have time to talk to him, but I wanted to hear what he had to say. And besides, I didn't mind resting my eyes on such a beautiful young man. I offered him some salmiakki. Together we finished off the bag while talking about relationships and Reijo Rahnasto. Kajanus didn't know anything that could help the investigation, but that didn't matter. Having a conversation instead of conducting an interrogation was nice for a change.

"Do you believe there are different kinds of love? That there isn't just one right person for everyone?" Kajanus asked.

"Hard to say," I replied, thinking of Mikke Sjöberg. What I felt toward him I couldn't call love. It was something, though—something big and painful.

After Kajanus left, Agent Muukkonen and Koivu came to my office to report on their progress. Both looked exhausted. Taskinen was currently in a meeting with the police leadership and the county prosecutor. Koivu had grabbed a pilsner and two donuts from downstairs.

"Ugh, what a snake," he moaned and collapsed on the couch in the same position Kim Kajanus had. Poor Muukkonen had to be content with the armchair.

"He has an explanation for everything, as can be expected from a politician. Guess how he explains his fingerprints on Seppälä's motorcycle saddlebag."

Supposedly Rahnasto had spent the whole night sitting up thinking and finally remembered that sometime in late April a motorcyclist in black leathers had pulled up next to him in the parking lot at the city-planning center while he was walking to his car. The man had asked him for a light, and Rahnasto remembered patting the motorcycle in admiration. He had asked the man to keep the matchbox. Rahnasto didn't know whether anyone had witnessed it. Rahnasto's lawyer demanded a review of the analysis of the other fingerprint, the one on the envelope addressed to Väinölä. It was true the print was a partial, and there might be some hope for the defense there. And Rahnasto explained that his visit to Suvi Seppälä's house was motivated by his social conscience and his natural needs as a man.

"According to him, the poor girl sounded out of her mind with grief. He considered it his duty to go and see that she was alright, and he was also flattered that a young woman like her would call him, even though he is old enough to be her father," Muukkonen said with a snort. "But let him go ahead and lie. Our team of investigators is making quick progress. Rahnasto isn't just a good shot, he's also an experienced lock pick. Kallio, you're probably too young to remember Skeleton Key Salminen, the legendary lock pick? Nowadays he's an upstanding citizen, a Christian even, and he trains security professionals on robbery prevention. This winter he was training at RISS and personally walked Rahnasto through all the tricks of the trade. With that background, opening the lock on the gate at the landfill would've been child's play. Rahnasto claims the gun in question was stolen, but he never filed a police report because it would have been bad press for a company like his. He managed to look genuinely embarrassed when he talked about it."

"Slippery as a bar of soap," Koivu said with a sigh. "Anu and Puupponen went to talk to the old man who lives behind the dump, and he was pretty sure that it was a van with the RISS logo he saw speeding by on the night of April twenty-second. But we didn't have any luck with the Hertz at the airport. The worker who rented the car in Jani Väinölä's name didn't recognize Rahnasto's picture and couldn't remember how old or what the man who rented the car looked like. The social security number was fake, and according to it, our bogus Väinölä was born in 1970. We've sent the signature for analysis."

"Could the renter be one of Rahnasto's employees, for example the guard who was fired after the explosives theft from that construction site?"

"That crossed my mind too," Muukkonen said. "We're going to question him. And Väinölä is sticking to his identification. This morning he was transferred to Katajanokka to await trial. Rahnasto, on the other hand, got to sleep in his own bed at home in Westend, but we confiscated his passport. This is going to work out," Muukkonen said reassuringly.

I listened to my colleagues' reports without joy or excitement. I felt strangely numb, as if it didn't really matter whether Rahnasto answered for his crimes or whether the revelation of the Laajalahti Bay plan had any practical political consequences. What felt much more important was that Iida had just learned to roll her *r*'s with confidence, which she'd

spent all Wednesday proudly demonstrating. Antti had set an appointment with our realtor to go look at a fixer-upper near a lake northwest
of the city on Saturday. It even had a playhouse in the front yard. The
rest of the weekend we would spend on the boat, since the weather was
supposed to be warm.

"Do you remember when Iida was so small that we had to put her in
a bouncer on the boat deck?" Antti asked wistfully. The TV news was
showing the latest turn of events in the Chechen conflict, and I muted
the sound. "We'll have to see how she likes being on the boat this year.
We'll probably have to tie her to the mast."

"And we'll have to be prepared to read out loud to her 24/7."

"Why? Isn't that what books on tape are for? And if we have to, we
can get a portable TV for the boat," Antti said with a grin, and I threw
a pillow at him.

"Hey, look!" he said as the screen changed to show the lobby of
the Espoo Police Station and a reporter began explaining the scandal
around Rahnasto. I caught a glimpse of myself with my arms akimbo
and a withdrawn look on my face. Rahnasto smiled at the camera as if
he was on his way to his wedding.

The reporter ended on an ominous note: "If the charges involving a
leading city politician's role in two murders and a bombing are proven
true, we're sure to see more political bombs dropping in Espoo. The
city government has admitted to participating in negotiations about
the purchase of the land surrounding the Laajalahti Bay nature preserve
and rezoning the area but flatly denies any involvement in the attack on
City Planning Commissioner Petri Ilveskivi. It also remains to be seen
how airtight the evidence against Rahnasto is and what pawn might be
sacrificed in this game of political chess. Does this mean that political
murder has come to Finland? These are the questions we will consider
tonight on *Studio A.*"

I stared at the news, my mind blank. I felt as if I needed to prepare myself for anything and everything, including the possibility that I would be branded a bad cop who, as a woman, had been driven by hysteria. And I didn't want to get Mikke mixed up in any of this. But it was looking like he would have to come to court. And eventually I would have to explain why I had wanted to protect him.

I snuggled closer into Antti's arms and turned off the television. We sat in the summer evening light for another half hour, neither of us saying a word the whole time. We didn't get up until we needed to let Einstein inside to stop his meowing at the back door.

Rahnasto's interrogation continued on Thursday, but I didn't have time to think about it, since Lehtovuori had broken his wrist and was out for two weeks, and the unit had to be reorganized to cover for his absence. At noon I heard that a RISS employee had admitted to renting the car in Jani Väinölä's name. He hadn't known he was doing anything wrong because Rahnasto had told him the car was a gift for a special client. Why a special client needed a car rented with forged documents the man hadn't bothered to wonder.

After lunch my computer went on the fritz. The screen started to flicker, and to my horror, smoke began to rise from the power cable connector. I pulled the cable out, but the smoke alarm still went off, and Puupponen rushed to my office to see what was wrong.

"You burnt out on the Rahnasto case?" he asked, but I didn't have it in me to laugh. After spending a couple of hours watching a guy from IT fight with the machine, I finally decided to call it a day. Iida was thrilled when I showed up at three thirty again. I hate shopping, but we both needed new summer clothes. Iida wanted flowers and frills, and who was I to deny her such adornments?

I bought myself a slim-fitting flowery dress too, the kind I never could have imagined wearing just a few years before. We both ended up choosing the same kind of wide-brimmed straw hats. Antti's expression was dumbfounded as we showed off our purchases at home in the yard.

"Your daughter is turning you into a shopaholic," he said, and I just laughed.

Taskinen called later that evening and said he had spent the past few hours with the county prosecutor. Rahnasto still hadn't admitted anything, but the prosecutor thought the evidence was sufficient to file charges anyway. The janitor at the Suvela Elementary School had come forward and reported seeing Rahnasto and Väinölä in the parking lot together two weeks before.

"The City Council chairwoman told me on the phone that she had always been afraid that Rahnasto would go too far someday. She intends to see to it personally that Rahnasto is pushed aside—either he'll resign or be impeached."

"Never leave an injured man—unless it's a political emergency," I said. I still hadn't forgiven Jyrki for what he'd done.

"Come upstairs for coffee tomorrow morning. You have good reason to gloat after being right about everything," he said. "Agent Muukkonen and I are embarrassed about getting all the glory for solving the case when it was really you who did it."

I didn't want to gloat. Puustjärvi had caught Marko Seppälä's trail, and thanks should also go to Suvi Seppälä, Eila Honkavuori, Kim Kajanus, and Mikke Sjöberg. Wang and Rasilainen had driven Väinölä to confess. I hadn't actually done anything. And something still bothered me. As if I had forgotten something essential to the investigation.

By Friday morning I was feeling better. The sun had been shining for days, and its warmth was starting to sink down into the earth. Antti's coworkers at the Meteorological Institute predicted that the seawater would warm quickly. I turned off the last of the radiators in our house.

The papers were still full of the Rahnasto incident. I was grateful for every article that didn't mention my name. My car was nearly one hundred degrees inside, so I decided to bike to work. I was there faster than if I had gone by car. I saw three different butterflies and a lesser spotted woodpecker and got to smell the freshly blooming clover.

It was summer.

I was in a cheerful mood as I locked my bike to the rack and walked to my office to fix my helmet hair and exchange my shorts for a skirt. Would it be completely improper to appear without pantyhose on a hot day like this? I decided it wouldn't be. The sun blazed through the break room windows as fans tried to drive out the excess heat.

Taskinen and the head of Narcotics were already digging into the sandwiches. I took one, even though I had just had porridge with Iida. Laine came for coffee too. He wasn't wearing any socks with his boating shoes. The courtesy everyone else paid me was amusing. Once again I was a "good guy" and "our girl," even though a few days ago everyone would have preferred to see me on an extended sick leave or gone for good.

"Have you issued an arrest warrant for Rahnasto yet?" I asked Taskinen quietly.

"Yes. No one but the leadership knows yet, though. We'll see how things develop. You seemed to have caused a real political firestorm."

Deputy Chief Kaartamo had a new light-blue summer suit, and he gave me an unctuous smile.

"You may not have heard yet, Maria, but you don't have to worry about Salo for a while now," he said and placed his hand protectively on my shoulder. "Salo gave one of his fellow prisoners a serious beating. The man suffered a traumatic brain injury and isn't likely to recover. Salo will be in solitary until the trial. The prison staff intends to demand that he be kept in isolation indefinitely, and I think they'll get what they want."

The world went momentarily black. All I could hear was my heart trying to beat its way out of my chest. Not him. Don't let it be him. Not Mikke.

"Maria?" Taskinen's voice came from somewhere far away.

"Did they tell you the victim's name?" I asked. My voice sounded muffled and distant in my ears.

"Some Estonian guy. One of Salo's underlings."

"Õnnepalu? Oh thank God!" I slumped against the table and buried my face in my hands. Fortunately everyone misinterpreted my relief and began to reassure me that everything was over now. I wished I could cry. Bodies, funerals, beatings. What I wanted were weddings and christenings.

After that we avoided talking about work. The detective lieutenant from Narcotics was going fishing for a week, and Kaartamo and I compared our experiences at the guest marinas at Hanko and Barösund. Taskinen smiled at me inquisitively now and then, but I didn't say much.

When Deputy Chief's Kaartamo's phone went off, no one paid it any attention. I was probably the first one to notice his voice rising and his free hand loosening his tie. Gradually the others fell silent too, waiting for the call to end. Kaartamo wiped his brow a couple of times before he managed to say, "Reijo Rahnasto was just apprehended at the West Harbor. He was on his way to Estonia with a fake passport. The border guard recognized him from the news. He was carrying nearly half a million US dollars."

The others were completely silent, but something inside my brain clicked into place.

I realized what had been bothering me the night before.

"Goddamn it!" I shouted and threw my half-eaten sandwich on the floor, sending a sprig of dill flying right onto Taskinen's plate. "Which one of you warned Rahnasto?"

I gazed around, and everyone looked completely thunderstruck. Except Laine. The color had gone out of his face, and he couldn't keep us from seeing the trembling of his hands.

23

Laine is a common name. When Agent Muukkonen and I had studied the list of Rahnasto Industrial Security Service investors together, neither of us paid any attention to the name Maritta Laine. But she was my coworker's wife.

Laine didn't admit anything, even though the phone LUDs showed that he had called Rahnasto from his cell phone on Thursday night. He claimed they only talked about hunting-club business. Why did Laine want to hinder the investigation? Did he think he would be able to take over my position in the VCU when Organized Crime and Narcotics merged, or was there something else behind it? I didn't get a chance to ask him, since he went on sick leave the same day that Rahnasto was arrested at the West Harbor terminal.

There was also general consternation that Rahnasto had resorted to a gambit like traveling on a false passport. What had driven him so far? Had the mayor signaled that he wasn't going to receive any sympathy, or had the City Council chair made Rahnasto believe that she and her supporters were going to wash their hands of the whole business? Maybe Rahnasto had acted alone in the Ilveskivi case. Maybe the others had known the truth but thought it best to keep quiet.

The City Council chair swore up and down that the Laajalahti Bay plan would have been presented according to standard procedure to the appropriate democratic bodies once the time was right.

"'Standard procedure' means they make the decision and then ignore the rest of us," Eila Honkavuori said. We were eating ice cream on the patio at the Tapiola Stockmann department store. It was my treat.

"I can't see it going quite like that now that the plan was leaked so early on," I said.

"Two lives is too high a price to pay for this," Eila said and closed her eyes in pleasure as the cherry from the top of her ice cream disappeared into her mouth. "But I don't think this incident changes anything. Petri and Marko Seppälä are still dead and Rahnasto is in prison, but everyone else got away practically unscathed. You heard the mayor's statement. You never know, even with reliable members of your own party. Everyone has their weaknesses."

Under interrogation Rahnasto still denied everything besides the Laajalahti Bay plan, which he tried to pin on the mayor's office. He maintained that he had never even met Marko Seppälä or Jani Väinölä. However, his attempt to flee the country was considered an aggravating factor, and the prosecutor was preparing to charge him with two counts of conspiracy to commit murder and murder in the first degree.

Detective Lieutenant Laine, however, wasn't going to be charged with anything. Ultimately he admitted to leaking information to Rahnasto about the Ilveskivi attack and later about the progress of the investigation of Seppälä's shooting. He claimed he was acting in good faith, simply trying to maintain good relations with a local politician who was also a hunting buddy. Maybe Laine didn't know that Rahnasto was a murderer. Or he had just wanted to make my job more difficult. His sick leave continued until August, and by midsummer I heard a rumor that Laine was taking over as the new head of the guard-security division of Rahnasto Industrial Security Service.

The City Council removed Rahnasto from his position during their last meeting before the summer break. The reshuffling resulted in Eila Honkavuori becoming the deputy chair of the City Planning Commission.

"I'm still worried about Tommi," Eila said. "He just sits at home alone, surrounded by pictures of Petri."

I had visited Tommi Laitinen to tell him everything that had happened in the case of Petri Ilveskivi's death. Outside it had been eighty-five degrees, but in Tommi's house November was still in full swing. Everything was neat and dark, the shades pulled down to keep the sun at bay. There were dozens of candles and pictures of Petri everywhere. Maybe Tommi felt that all the life blossoming outside was an affront to his sorrow.

"Tommi largely lived through Petri. He didn't have his own friends, other than his coworkers. I've invited him over for dinner or to go to a concert, but he won't," Eila told me.

The Jensen men had said the same thing, and Eva had ordered them to keep trying. I remembered my deceased colleague Pertti Ström and my school friend Sanna, and thought about how easy it was to leave a person alone with their sorrow. They weren't grateful for the attention, driving friends and family away so they could go back to their brooding. Then the day came when it was too late. I said that to Eila, even though she already knew it all too well. She promised that she wouldn't leave Tommi alone.

"Turo and I are still thinking about children," Eila said. "We've decided to try adoption again. No one's going to give us a baby, but we're ready to take an older child. To give a home to someone who doesn't have one. Maybe that's meant to be our lot in life."

"That's not a bad lot at all."

"We aren't going to set any conditions. Race, sex, or health status don't matter. I couldn't put any conditions on a child I was going to give birth to. And the crazy thing is that I feel like somewhere out there a child is waiting just for us. Hopefully we won't have to wait for him or her for very long."

Eila and I were quickly becoming good friends. I had promised I would attend a belly dancing class with her in the fall. She had been doing it for years. I needed variety, some sort of soft and feminine movement to offset the soccer tackles and weight lifting.

Suvi Seppälä exuded vindictiveness. Death had turned Marko into a saint for her. Suvi told herself that Marko had only intended to rough up Ilveskivi. The fact that the situation had gotten out of hand was just bad luck. Suvi intended to demand half a million marks from Rahnasto in compensation for Marko's death. *Seven* magazine sent the family on a vacation to Majorca in exchange for exclusive rights to Suvi's life story.

The media debated about what had driven a man like Rahnasto to such a desperate act as murder. I wondered that myself as I watched a tape of his interrogation about Seppälä's slaying. He insisted that he had only met Seppälä in passing, and the expression on his pleasant, anonymous face never wavered. His attempt to travel to Tallinn on a false passport he tried to explain away, claiming that he had essential business to conduct in the city.

In their interviews, his ex-wives spoke of his violent nature, but his subordinates praised his efficiency and boundless ambition. In army reserve officer school Rahnasto had been seen as a natural-born leader. Nothing seemed to be able to penetrate his Teflon exterior. In cynical moments I wondered if Rahnasto would manage to wriggle out of the charges against him.

We still hadn't found a new home, but my vacation would start at midsummer. Gradually the idea of moving was starting to sound exciting. We had lived in our current house for almost five years, longer than I had ever stayed in one place in my adult life.

Koivu and Wang had found a new home, and their move went quickly because Anu's brothers and cousins all showed up to help. The cops handled the beer. The apartment was a medium-size, one-bedroom affair, which at least gave them a door to close if life together ever got rough.

The housewarming party was the day before the Midsummer Eve national holiday. Antti's parents picked up Iida in the afternoon to take her to the cabin with them. We would join them on Friday and set sail. The forecast was for continued heat.

Antti had baked bread, and Iida and I had painted an old olive jar to make a decorative salt container. A bottle of Koivu's favorite liquor rounded out the classic Finnish housewarming gift. The couple waited in the entryway, looking important.

"Look closely," Koivu said, tilting his chin toward Wang. I looked. Five seconds later I realized what I was supposed to be noticing. Koivu and Wang were engaged.

Rasilainen and I immediately set about planning the bachelorette party, and Antti suggested that he and Koivu found a Lady Cops' Gentlemen's Club. Puustjärvi's small, shy wife drank two glasses of punch and announced she wanted to dance. Koivu managed to clear some space in the living room. So many people dancing in such a small space reminded me of the clubs of my youth. I spent some time bouncing to ABBA tunes and then went outside on the balcony to cool off. Between the neighboring buildings, I could see all the way to the sports park, and the sounds of traffic were muffled. A breeze made the fir trees below sway, and I wiped the sweat from my face.

I didn't know how to thank Mikke. The thought of visiting the prison was too much, but a card or a phone call were too little. I had started several letters but had ripped them all up. The previous day I had received a long letter from him. Mostly it was serious, but there was the occasional irony. An eternal outsider like Mikke could see the humorous side of prison life. That was what made me cry the most.

> *I don't expect you to write to me, but of course I'd be*
> *happy if you did. But don't do it out of pity. I like you,*
> *but I'm not nursing any hope. I'm finally getting myself*
> *together and starting to think about the world outside*

*these walls. You were right. The sea isn't going anywhere.
I've already started planning my next trip, even though
a parolee can't leave the country. There are still plenty
of places in the archipelago I haven't explored yet. Fair
winds to you and your family.*

Maybe I would write. Apparently time and distance weren't enough; you only got rid of painful feelings by living through them. Trying to bury Mikke in the back of my mind was pointless. The pain would stop festering eventually. I didn't have to talk to anyone else about it. Knowing what I felt and what I didn't was enough.

Taskinen snapped me out of my reverie. Relations were still cool between us, although he had made some attempts to mend fences. I could see from his eyes that he was a little drunk. That was rare.

"It's warm inside," he said cautiously.

"Not too bad out here," I replied.

"I'm really embarrassed about giving in to those threats. I always thought that would never happen to me, that no one could ever blackmail me. I thought I was better than most of my colleagues. It isn't easy admitting that you're just like everyone else."

Taskinen's eyes were misty, and he was still favoring one leg. His summer vacation was starting at the Midsummer holiday too. Earlier in the spring we had planned to go sailing together, but there hadn't been any more talk of that.

"I haven't told anyone about the blackmail except you. Everyone else is a colleague, not a friend. We are still friends, aren't we?"

I believe everyone deserves a second chance. I've even been able to hold to that when thinking about murderers, like Mikke. Finding the right words wasn't easy, so I just hugged Taskinen. I didn't trust him like I had before, but that was alright for now. Maybe we had both been trying too hard to go it alone, and that had led to mistakes.

"Oh, so we're hugging my wife out here, are we?" Antti said from the balcony door. He knew about the rift between Taskinen and me, and was visibly relieved that things seemed to be returning to normal. I extracted myself from Jyrki's embrace and went to the bathroom. On the way I gave Antti a kiss on the cheek.

Puupponen was waiting for me in the entryway.

"I have a reason to celebrate too," he said, looking proud of himself. "I finished this yesterday." With that, Puupponen took a thick stack of paper bound between plastic covers out of his briefcase.

"*The Blond in the Red Shoes*," I read from the cover. "A mystery. Written by Ville Puupponen. Wow! So this is what you've been up to all spring?"

Pride mixed with panic on Puupponen's face.

"Yes, but not during work time! Or just a little. It's really fast paced and fun, and the main character is a cop from Savo. I'd like to ask you a favor, since you know something about books. Would you mind reading this and telling me if it's any good?"

"It would be an honor," I responded in surprise.

"Don't tell the others," Puupponen whispered, and I hid the plastic binder in the bag Antti and I had brought our presents in. Hopefully Puupponen's story wasn't too gory. I got enough of that at work. I didn't want death to become commonplace, to see beaten corpses day after day and eventually become so numb that I thought violence was normal. I was tired of it. I needed something else to balance out all the death.

I went to browse Koivu and Wang's music shelf. Anu's nineteen-year-old brother smiled at me shyly. He had just aced his college-entrance exams and been automatically admitted to the Helsinki University of Technology to study physics. Anu thought her brother would have his PhD in four years flat.

Tucked in among the Van Halen and Bon Jovi I found some classical music, but what I chose to put on the turntable was Luonteri Surf, a Finnish cross between the Ramones and California beach music.

Although the first track was about fall, it was also a perfect fit for a summer evening. It spoke of the cold autumn sun setting beyond a lake and oat stubble underfoot in a field, of the strength that comes from familiar things, of the bedrock that's so close to the surface everywhere in our land.

"So if 'Kallio' means bedrock, is this song about you?" Puupponen grinned. Antti wrapped his arms around me, and we swayed with the music. The last record was hardcore punk, and I managed to get everyone else bouncing with me. We danced in a circle with our arms around one another's shoulders until the downstairs neighbor came to the door to tell us that she would call the police if we didn't quiet down. We turned off the record player and managed not to burst out laughing until she had gone.

Koivu had lit a few lanterns on the balcony. The summer night illuminated itself, but the shadows cast by the candles made the concrete walls and floor feel homier. Warmth still radiated from the walls, and violets bloomed in the flower boxes.

"Antti, come here for a minute," I said and drew him out on the balcony. Based on his expression, he was expecting either a kiss or a cigar. Instead I pulled the crumpled birth-control prescription out of my purse. I felt strong because I knew what I wanted.

"I'm supposed to start my pills again today, but I don't want to. What do you think? Do we need this?"

"No," Antti said and pulled me into his arms. After a long kiss, I ripped the prescription into pieces and burned them ceremoniously in the flame of a candle.

One month later I was pregnant.

ABOUT THE AUTHOR

Leena Lehtolainen was born in Vesanto, Finland, to parents who taught language and literature. A keen reader, she made up stories in her head before she could even write. At the age of ten, she began her first book— a young adult novel—and published it two years later. She released her second book at the age of seventeen. She has received numerous awards for her writing, including the 1997 Vuoden Johtolanka (Clue) Award (for the best Finnish crime novel) for *Luminainen* (*The Snow Woman*) and the Great Finnish Book Club prize in 2000. Her work has been published in twenty-nine languages.

Besides writing, Leena enjoys classical singing, her beloved cats, and—her greatest passion—figure skating. Her nonfiction book about the sport, *Taitoluistelun lumo* (*The Enchantment of Figure Skating*), was chosen as the Sport Book of the Year 2011 in Finland. Leena lives in Finland with her husband and two sons.

ABOUT THE TRANSLATOR

Photo © 2015 Aaron Turley

Owen F. Witesman is a professional literary translator with a master's in Finnish and Estonian-area studies from Indiana University. He has translated more than thirty Finnish books into English, including novels, children's books, poetry, plays, graphic novels, and nonfiction. His recent translations include the first three novels in the Maria Kallio series, the satire *The Human Part* by Kari Hotakainen, the thriller *Cold Courage* by Pekka Hiltunen, and the 1884 classic *The Railroad* by Juhani Aho. He currently resides in Springville, Utah, with his wife, three daughters, one son, two dogs, a cat, seven chickens, and twenty-nine fruit trees.